BECAUSE
OF
YOU

Dianne Venetta

BECAUSE OF YOU
Book #2

Silver Creek Series:
Romantic Mystery/Adventure
NOT WITHOUT YOU ~ #1
BECAUSE OF YOU ~ #2
ALL ABOUT YOU ~ #3
ONLY WITH YOU ~ #4

Other novels by Dianne Venetta

Ladd Springs Series:
Cozy Mystery/Romance
LADD SPRINGS ~ #1
LADD FORTUNE ~ #2
HOTEL LADD ~ #3
LADD HAVEN ~ #4
LOSING LADD ~ #5
LADD CHRISTMAS ~ #6

The Gables Trilogy:
Romantic Women's Fiction
JENNIFER'S GARDEN
LUST ON THE ROCKS
WHISPER PRIVILEGES

Women's Fiction
CONDEMN ME NOT

Copyright 2015 by Dianne Venetta

All rights reserved

ISBN 9780991118267

Because of You
Copyright 2015 by Dianne Venetta
ISBN: 978-0-9911182-6-7
Publisher: BloominThyme Press
Editor: Best Foot Forward
Cover Design: Seductive Designs

Acknowledgements

When I first imagined this book, I fell in love with the idea of creating a heroine who was feverishly devoted to animals and the environment, a woman who would "talk the talk" and "walk the walk." She would be spirited, independent, and genuine to her core. She would live her passion, make no excuses for her lifestyle or her choices but instead, wear them like a badge of honor.

Meet Kinsley Fairchild. She's intense, driven, and while she has her flaws, I think that once you get to know her heart you'll love her as much as I do. From our shared love of animals to a sincere desire to harmoniously coexist with wildlife, Kinsley and I are kindred spirits. I'll admit I'm not a vegan—but I could be, and with very little effort. One only has to visit my garden blog BloominThyme to realize how easily I could live on vegetables! Oh, and all things sweet—which *are* derived from plants, mind you. Cacao, sugar cane, stevia...need I go on?

But I digress. Food choice aside, Kinsley and I would be friends. And while this particular heroine of mine might prove controversial, I hope that in the end you'll ultimately come to understand her and appreciate her for who she is.

Dedication

This novel is dedicated to animal lovers everywhere.

Chapter One

Satiny fur brushed against Kinsley Fairchild's cheek, stirring anger deep in her gut. It felt like the supple coat of a kitten, a helpless baby. Baby mink, to be exact. Spitting strands of fur from her mouth, she focused on her target. Tucked between fur coats, Kinsley watched as the shop owner closed up for the evening. *Say goodbye to your vile livelihood. It will look a lot different the next time you see it.*

Draped in gold and ruby jewelry, and dressed in a cashmere turtleneck, long black wool skirt and expensive leather boots, the owner moved with the grace of good breeding and wealth. Kinsley knew hundreds of people just like her, well-heeled friends of her parents who strode around with an air of expectation and conceit as if they owned everything and everyone. Tonight was the big gala reception for the resort partnership for which they were all in town, a party this woman would likely be attending. Most of the Silver Creek business owners were in support of the resort expansion and would no doubt suck down the free champagne and fancy hors d'oeuvres as the developers presented their latest plan. None of them cared about the wildlife that would be displaced as they lined their pockets. None. Not even her own parents who would also be in attendance.

People ignored the facts. Kinsley had done the research, understood the impact, the consequences, and for the last six weeks had posted argument after argument, fact after fact on her blog, *Wildlife Neutral*. Except these people—the business owners, the ones with the power to prevent the expansion—refused to listen to reason.

There was only one way to get their attention. Hit them where it hurt. Displace *them* so they'd know how it felt.

As the fur shop owner turned out the lights and let herself out, Kinsley heard the jangle of keys clang against the front door. Satisfied the woman was long gone, she emerged from her hiding place, and mindful of the security surveillance camera, scouted for the best spot, the one sure to wreak the most havoc. Kinsley glanced around the dimly lit boutique where round hanging displays were crammed with deep brown and black fur coats. The walls held more of the same, a few lighter colors pressed between the dark. Several shelves were home to a line of matching hats and ear muffs, and fancy leather gloves trimmed with fur. The woman even sold fur key chains.

Resentment surged warm and hot through Kinsley's breast. Zeroing in on the front display window, she decided it would be the spot to place her ink bomb, ruining the most coats and leaving her organization's telltale signature for all to see. *Fur coats ruined and not for sale.*

Carefully pulling the bulky device from her parka pocket, she dialed the timer to twenty minutes, giving her ample time to make her getaway. The plan was simple. Once detonated, the explosion would spray the interior with red ink while she was sitting at Adele's for a quiet dinner with her close friend and associate, Sebastian Wu. He was her right hand man and resident master bomb-maker. This was his creation she held in her gloved hands, his genius.

With one last look around, Kinsley placed the device in the window and murmured, "This one's for the innocent." Hurrying to the door, she unlocked the deadbolt and let herself out. Pulling the collar of her parka up against the growing flurry of snow, she angled her head slightly down and away from potential witnesses. There were cameras posted on corners throughout the village but none that would capture her image with any clarity. Not with a slew of ragged snowflakes falling heavy and fast.

A quarter the distance across the cobblestone street intersection, Kinsley slowed her long-legged strides, reminding herself to walk leisurely. *Take your time. Don't call attention to yourself.*

Pretend you are your mother. Visions of the wealthy socialite from San Francisco swarmed in Kinsley's mind, her similarly lithe figure, her identical cascade of shiny black hair that fell in waves down her back. Kinsley had been told countless times how the two of them were near mirror images, save the thirty years that separated them in age. It was a comparison Kinsley shunned and simultaneously coveted. Her mother walked with the fluidity of a runway model, had the poise of refined education and training...and was exquisitely beautiful.

Pushing her shoulders back, Kinsley mimicked the gait she'd envied her entire life, almost able to see the flash in her mother's dark eyes. *Slow, graceful. Walk without hurry, darling.*

Kinsley's mother never moved fast. Not only ethereal in her movement, she was fashionably late wherever she went. Victoria Fairchild never worried that people would start without her. They wanted her money and for that they would wait.

Pretend, Kinsley told herself. *Pretend you are her.* Sebastian will wait. He always does.

Pulling her creamy wool Fedora snugly over her brow, Kinsley sauntered across the wide swath of street and around the corner then headed for the rendezvous where her partner would be waiting. Together, they would walk down the narrow pass between buildings and into a restaurant on the next block where they would order Morel Risotto and Roasted Red Pepper Crostini, along with a side of her favorite sourdough bread and pesto. Ten minutes later, she would raise her glass and toast their victory as thousands of dollars of fur were destroyed several blocks away. Should anyone ask as to her whereabouts at seven-thirty on Friday night, Sebastian would honestly reveal them. They'd been dining at Adele's.

As she turned the corner, a thrill raced through her at the sight of him. Sebastian was leaning against the brick façade of an art gallery, deft fingers working his smart phone. He was dressed in a black overcoat and slim white jeans, pants that tapered neatly over his black shoes, the pointed ends of which stood out against the fresh fall of snow. Sebastian was total urban tech and style, his presence commanding, leading most within the organization to carry out his every bidding. Few had a passion for activism that rivaled hers, but Sebastian Wu was certainly among them.

As she neared, he looked up and the two shared a wicked smile.

"It's done," she told him, adrenaline firing through her limbs, accompanied by a rapid-fire pulse. No matter how many times she'd struck, each blow felt as exciting as the first.

"Wonderful news." Slipping his phone into an interior pocket of his coat, he offered her an elbow. "Shall we?"

Kinsley smiled. "We shall."

Snowflakes pelted their path as they walked the planned route. She leaned close, giving them the appearance no different from any young couple taking an evening stroll. The rich spice of Sebastian's cologne enveloped her, infusing her with comfort and familiarity. "It feels good, doesn't it?" she whispered. "Knowing we're making a difference?"

"Most definitely. This one will cost the shop owner thousands and send a message to every store in the town. Support for expansion will carry a steep price."

"Maybe she'll get the hint and move on to selling something less endangering."

Sebastian chuckled at her double entendre. "Let's hope, though we both know some people learn quicker than others."

True, she mused. They'd planted three ink bombs in one store on Rodeo Drive, but each and every time the store owner reopened, even had the nerve to post a sign in the window: *Proud sellers of farmed mink.* The move had irked Kinsley. If they thought cute signs in their window would dissuade her, they were wrong. She wouldn't give up. She would never give up. She was determined to close the sales channels that harmed animals, and direct the world onto a more humane path. It was a cause she had devoted her life to. Her every thought, her every move. Kinsley would pursue the cause until she changed the trajectory, changed the course of history.

It was her destiny. She knew it from the first day she had spotted a starving deer on the side of the road during a trip to Napa Valley. She'd been thirteen at the time and insisted her parents stop the car. Her mother had leaned back from the front seat and off-handedly replied, "Darling, we can't save every lost animal wandering the side of the road." Then Kinsley's father chimed in, "It's probably been displaced by the new Grande Seasons Resort and Spa. They just opened one in the valley."

Kinsley had freaked. "You mean there are starving animals wandering around because of a new hotel? We have to stop!" Her mother had frowned, then blew Kinsley's mind when she said, "We can't. It will most likely reproduce and aggravate the problem." Unable to fathom her mother's complete disregard for the well-being of the animal, Kinsley had whirled in her seat and stared at the poor thing as they left it behind. There was no mistaking the pain and fear in its eyes. None.

The incident never left Kinsley. The minute she had arrived at their ranch in Napa, she went to the computer and searched for the truth. Had the new resort hotel displaced the animals as her father had indicated?

The words she read next forever broke her heart. *While we understand some animals will be displaced in the process, we cannot stand in the way of economic progress that lies at the very heart of our survival*. Were they kidding? Economic survival? Animals were dying—starving to death because a hotel company decided it deserved the land more than the animals!

Unbelievable. Reading those words had marked the beginning of Kinsley's journey into activism. Someone had to give voice to the helpless. Someone had to give a damn that animals were being pushed out of their natural habitat for no other reason than the comfort and enjoyment of humans. That someone was her.

Two buildings down a single lamp spotlighted a name scrolled in semi-cursive lettering etched across a creamy beige sign; Adele's. It was named for chef and owner, Adele Simms. The woman had relocated from New York almost five years ago and already her restaurant was the gem of Silver Creek. Sleek lines of glass and wood defined the exterior, drawing one's eye into the butter hues of the interior where formally-clad servers wove in and around tables in an orchestra of precision movement.

Moments 33later, Sebastian opened the door and held it for Kinsley as she breezed inside, swallowed whole by the toasty warm interior. Decadent aromas of rosemary, garlic and fresh-baked wheat bread imbued her with pleasure. As expected, the restaurant was busy, with only two open tables.

"Two this evening?" a female attendant asked, automatically reaching to take the jacket from Kinsley's shoulders.

Sebastian nodded and handed over his coat as a young man came up behind the hostess and exchanged two tickets for the coats.

"It's nice to see you again, Mr. Wu, Ms. Fairchild."

Sebastian and Kinsley shared a glance as the hostess checked off their names from her printed list. Gathering two menus, she replied, "This way, please."

Kinsley followed, taking stock of the predominantly middle-aged crowd seated around white-clothed tables. There were a variety of ethnicities, many of whom were regulars, but the bulk of faces she saw were new. Silver Creek was attracting visitors from all over the world, precisely what the resort developers wanted and the antithesis of everything she wanted. Pulling her gaze away, Kinsley took the seat Sebastian had pulled out for her. Unimpeded growth was a trend that needed to end. Enough was enough.

Dropping a white napkin into her lap, a seamless match to her turtleneck, she thought about their meeting tomorrow.

She and Sebastian were scheduled to meet regarding the up-coming vote on the resort's expansion plans. The town council had the power to reject Palmer International's request, had even publicized some grumblings over the massive scope of the project, indicating via regional news outlets that it would harm the natural habitat of the area—an extreme negative in the eyes of most of the locals—yet Kinsley suspected the council would approve it. A bigger resort equated to a bigger tax purse, and that's all anyone cared about. Money. The commissioners, the developers, the whole world it seemed, revolved around money. She ground her jaw. But not her world. Hers revolved around justice, and she would exhaust every option available in her efforts to stop Palmer International from spoiling the pristine mountain terrain.

A young male waiter appeared tableside. "Good evening and welcome to Adele's." He cast a pleasant glance between them and asked, "May I start you off with a cocktail, a glass of wine, champagne?"

Knowing full well what Kinsley wanted, Sebastian took the liberty of ordering. "How about a champagne toast this evening?" he asked her. "Followed by a Malbec with our meal?"

"Sounds perfect," she replied.

"My pleasure."

Kinsley settled in as the waiter went to retrieve their bottle and thought, Malbec, Cabernet, Zinfandel—she loved them all. Born and raised in California, Kinsley had learned everything there was to know about fine wine and champagne before she was able to take the first sip. The first legal sip. Her parents were connoisseurs who saw no reason to deny a young woman of eighteen the option to indulge in the glorious experience. For as long as she could remember, wine had been a standard dinner beverage in her home. Kinsley's grandparents owned a winery in Napa and the supply seemed endless. Over the years, she spent countless hours absorbing the winemaking process. From planting to harvest, from discerning the subtle nuances between Cabernets to the technicality that champagne from California wasn't champagne at all—the name was an honor reserved solely for vintages created in a small region in France, northeast of Paris—Kinsley had thoroughly enjoyed the art of winemaking.

And the consumption. As did Sebastian. Settling in across from her, he glanced around the restaurant and said, "We need to finalize our strategy. Our uniques this month are soaring as a result of our battle against the resort and we need to capitalize on it."

He was referring to the unique number of visitors who visited her blog each day. With the very public and widely publicized fight they'd picked with the popular resort, the number of hits on *Wildlife Neutral* had received a distinct bump. Normally she boasted half a million followers but lately that number was closer to seven hundred thousand.

"Good," she replied, mindful to keep her voice quiet. "It means people are paying attention. The more minds we can change, the better chance we'll have at stopping this latest expansion. It's a complete overreach by Palmer International and people are outraged."

"Agreed, and it's an outrage that translates into bigger ad revenue."

"Yes." Money was an integral part, enabling her and Sebastian to effect the change they sought, but Kinsley preferred to focus on the heart of the matter. The animals. "It's money that will be put to good use in the event we lose our campaign on the ground. We'll need to launch an aggressive ad campaign if we expect to turn public sentiment against the resort."

"We won't lose," Sebastian said.

Kinsley arched a brow. His response was a bit overconfident. "You have a crystal ball I don't know about?"

He smiled. "I have faith in the organization and its people."

Kinsley stilled, locking onto him. Sebastian's black eyes melted into his face with an easy sensuality, accentuated by his high, flat cheekbones and elegant brows. His nose was sharper than most, not flat or small, making for a distinctive combination. Memorable.

Soaking in the ambiance of Adele's, Kinsley knew lighting was everything. Her father owned the largest chain of lighting stores on the West Coast. It was crazy what lighting could do. From models to artwork to business interiors, it was all about the lighting. And this lighting was perfect for Sebastian's looks. Not that he needed any help in that department, the guy was drop-dead gorgeous.

The waiter arrived with their champagne, setting two crystal flutes filled with pale gold bubbly on the table with all the precision and flair of a grand vintner. "Would you care to order dinner?"

"Not at the moment," Sebastian replied.

"Very well." With a slight nod, the young man excused himself.

Sebastian raised his glass and Kinsley did likewise. "To the cause."

"To the cause," she repeated and clinked crystal rim to crystal rim, the shimmer of liquid dancing in the candlelight. Kinsley brought the sparkling wine to her lips—

An explosion rocked the quiet. Wine spilled over the edge of her glass, dousing her hand. Heart pounding, Kinsley whipped a glance around the dining room. Concern and confusion wrenched the expressions of fellow diners as they glanced around in search of answers. *Does anyone know what just happened?*

A man stood and stared out the window. He was looking in the direction of the fur store.

"What was that?" Kinsley asked without thinking, plunking her glass to the table.

"Sounded like an explosion to me," Sebastian replied coolly.

Kinsley froze, an inkling of suspicion raising the fine hairs at her neck. "But that couldn't be ours. Ink bombs don't make that kind of noise."

Lowering his glass, he merely shrugged.

Whispers commenced, filling the dining room with an odd tension. Two men hurried out of the restaurant. Several others were standing now, collecting in a group near the corner of the restaurant. Kinsley couldn't see beyond them, but something told her she didn't have to. She knew exactly where they were looking. Instantly she wondered if the police had been called.

Surely they had. The police station was located only three blocks over. Images of flames burst into her mind's eye, playing out like a movie on the big screen. They would be called and respond in minutes. Was there fire? Were there flames? Frightened murmurs punctured the sedate ambiance. People looked around, silently checked from one to the next as though registering all were safe, all were accounted for. Yet with every passing second, Kinsley felt as though eyes were turning to her. Lingering, pausing, she could feel the curiosity burning behind the elegant expressions. But Kinsley had no reason to fear their accusations. She hadn't set a bomb—not a real one.

A chill raced down her spine. Glued to her seat, somehow the knowledge didn't prevent a mild panic from taking hold. She latched onto Sebastian. The man was jarringly calm.

Sebastian angled his head, his tone slightly mocking as he posed, "Would you be sad to know a fur store blew up, Kinsley?"

"No, of course not," she snapped, careful to keep her demeanor calm, her focus squarely upon him.

"Didn't think so."

Suddenly, she had a bad feeling, like Sebastian had switched the ink bomb for a real one. Glancing around, she touched upon the myriad shocked expressions. She looked through the pane-glass windows but detected no smoke, no fire. Didn't mean there wasn't any. She couldn't see the fur store from this vantage point.

But still... Kinsley evaded Sebastian's direct gaze. She was an activist not an arsonist. She wasn't like those people who set the resort buildings on fire several years back. That was criminal. Those people went to jail. Her tactics amounted to simple property destruction, a dozen or so ruined furs no one should be allowed to wear in the first place. She didn't incite the kind of destruction that could threaten the very wildlife she was trying to protect.

Adele walked through the double doors leading out from the kitchen, her big, brown eyes filled with alarm. She spoke to the staff in hushed tones, clearly aware she was garnering stares from her customers. People would want to know what happened. They would want to know if they should stay or go, evacuate. Kinsley could only imagine the accusations that would follow. *There's been an explosion. Someone said it's the fur store.*

The activists.

Adele knew Kinsley's background, knew her feelings about the resort's expansion, yet it was a conversation they avoided. Adele was dating Kinsley's best friend's father, and no one wanted to engage in uncomfortable dialogue. Kinsley was fine with it. No sense in causing trouble for those she counted as allies, supporters. And Lisa Richardson was definitely that, a supporter of the cause. A grad student dedicated to saving the boreal toad from extinction, she understood the need to protect wildlife. Adele understood, too. Both women were dedicated vegans, both women encouraged Kinsley's blog activities, but neither would support violence. Ink bombs, maybe. Real bombs, no way.

But with each passing moment, Kinsley's instincts hummed louder, harder. Clenching the stem of her champagne glass, she tried to read the lips of the front hostess. *Explosion. Was anyone hurt*? Nodding, the woman hung up the phone, relayed a message to the coat attendant. Shock washed over his features as he stared blankly at his coworker.

Kinsley resisted the urge to get up from the table and march down the street to see if the awful sound had actually come from the fur store. Maybe something else had caused the explosion. Maybe it had been coincidence.

"What's the matter?" Sebastian asked.

"I want to know what happened." Resisting the urge to look around, she muttered under her breath, "That loud noise didn't come from Giovanna's, did it?"

Sebastian leaned back in his chair. He held the flute of champagne before him, gently swirling the effervescent liquid in his glass. The lustrous color and gentle sparkle reminded Kinsley of diamonds. Privilege. Champagne was her mother's drink of choice. Diamonds, her jewelry of choice. If her mother found out she'd been involved with violence, she'd cut her from the family, something her father had practically done already.

"Sit, Kinsley. You're acting as though you'd be upset to learn of the fur store's demise."

Hovering inches above her seat, she glared at him. "I don't want to go to jail for an explosion."

"Who said anything about jail?"

Plopping down, Kinsley kicked him under the table and hissed, "*Hush*. Do you want someone to hear you?"

He glanced around, and a complete and total look of loathing took up residence in his black eyes. "These people are too self-absorbed to pay any attention to us."

On the one hand, Kinsley couldn't disagree. She understood these people and knew Sebastian's words held truth. No stranger when it came to family money, he understood them, though his parents were of a different mindset, a different culture. They didn't flaunt their wealth. On the contrary, they hoarded it. They spent money on things like Sebastian's Ivy League education, used the remainder to support family back home in China. However, their response would prove no different than her parents'. If the Wus learned the real nature of their son's activities, they'd disown him. His shame would stain the family name.

Feeling trapped as diners around her continued to speculate on the massive sound, Kinsley asked, "What did you do, Sebastian? What did you do to my ink bomb?"

"I added a little fireworks."

"What?" Despite her suspicions, his confession rattled her. It had not been part of their plan. Not hers, anyway.

"Relax," he said. "You wore gloves, didn't you?"

"Yes," she replied, reflexively glancing around the restaurant.

"Then we have nothing to worry about." Sebastian set his glass down and picked up his menu. "Now what are you having for dinner, Kinsley?" He smiled, his perfectly straight, white teeth as flawless as his olive-hued complexion. "Tonight's on me."

Lingering on his face, his eyes were slits of black, his jet-black hair glimmered in the supple lighting, Kinsley wavered. No one in here would have seen her anywhere near the fur shop. Even the security cameras in town would have trouble picking up on her identity. It was snowing outside, fat flakes continuing to drench the black of night outside their window. People were calming, releasing their concern.

Indulging in another sip of wine, Sebastian appeared right at home. It was no wonder he dated only the most affluent and beautiful women. Who wouldn't want to be escorted by Sebastian Wu?

A need to visit the scene continued to gnaw at Kinsley. "I want to go see."

Sebastian cocked a brow. "Are you serious?"

"Yes," she replied, a certainty spreading within her. "I want to go see and make sure everything is..." Sebastian frowned and she pretended amenability. "Mission accomplished."

His smile returned and he asked, "Since when have you become impatient? That's not like you."

It wasn't like her. At all. Since the day they met during a protest outside a commercial aquarium in southern California, Sebastian had praised Kinsley's sense of cool. Protesters had been arrested around them, insults hurled into their faces, yet Kinsley hadn't blinked. She'd stood her ground, knew her rights inside and out, and practically dared the authorities to violate her person.

Sebastian had been duly impressed, claimed she was different from the other activists. So many tended to lose their temper when the confrontation heated, shouting, pushing, shoving—but not Kinsley. She never lost her poise, and instead drilled forward with her plan of action.

Tapping a red-polished fingernail on the wet tablecloth, Kinsley considered the circumstance. Maybe all was not lost. They had a plan—destroy the merchandise and influence the store owner to think twice about selling it. Unbeknownst to her, Sebastian went "off plan," a fact that grated on her, but the end result might yield the same. Unless they were caught.

Sharpening her gaze on him, she dropped her voice to a sliver and said, "I never agreed to explosives. It's too much and not necessary to forward the cause." Maintaining a hard line on him, Kinsley didn't look away or back down. Sebastian had to know this wasn't okay. If he wanted to remain involved with her, he could not change the rules without her consent. *Wildlife Neutral* was her business, not his. It was her name behind the organization, her face in front of it. She was still the leader of the organization, no matter how much he coveted her position. "I'm going," Kinsley announced. "Are you coming?"

"Are you serious? And lose my table at Adele's?"

Kinsley savored his startled reply. Though he tried to make light, it was clear he understood. She wasn't kidding. Rising to a stand, she offered one last time. "Are you coming?"

Glaring at her, he downed his champagne and expelled a sigh. "It won't make a difference. The damage is done."

Exactly what she was afraid of.

Collecting her purse, Kinsley walked to the entrance, a jumble of emotions swirling through her belly. "May I have my coat, please?"

Recognizing her as a recent arrival, the man quickly overcame his surprise and replied, "Of course."

As he went to retrieve it, Kinsley felt the nausea build-ing. It wasn't drinking on an empty stomach that was respon-sible. It was stress over the prospect of damage-control.

Chapter Two

Grant Powell jumped at the explosion. Clutching at a tightening in his chest, he whipped a glance toward the store next door. Smoke billowed into the air, a sickening mass of orange-gray mixing with the flurry of snowfall. Struggling to register what happened, thoughts of Giovanna pummeled his brain. Was she okay?

Sucking in a breath, Grant slammed a display case closed and sprinted out the front door of his jewelry store. Giovanna DeFiori owned the boutique next door. Coats, hats, and accessories made from the finest furs, imported from all over the world—the store was her entire life.

He had to get to her, had to make sure she was okay. Battling a rancid cloud of smoke and frigid air, he stopped short. What the—?

The front window had been completely blown out of her store. He coughed, yanked the front door open and charged inside. "Giovanna! Giovanna!"

Burying his nose in the crux of his elbow, Grant squinted through the smoke. Flames curled up the wood exterior of the window frame, licked at the furs inside. Coats lined the walls of the salon, more hung from circular displays down the center. The manikin that had occupied the front window was broken into pieces, its coat haphazardly flung over the checkout counter several feet away. There was no sign of Giovanna. "Giovanna!" Grant shouted. "Are you here?"

Silence.

It was closing time, but Giovanna usually stayed late to close out the sales. Grant bolted toward the back office. "Giovanna?" When he received no answer, he tried the office door. Unlocked. He pushed inside. But the place was dark, empty. Breathing a sigh of relief, Grant sucked in a gulp of clean air and turned back. Jogging several steps toward the main showroom, he saw that the flames and smoke were building. The entire store would be consumed in minutes.

Fire extinguisher. He had to get a fire extinguisher. Making a quick dash back into the office, Grant flicked on a light. Desk, chair, computer, shelves, cabinets. No extinguisher. Maybe she kept it by the register. He whirled and started for the front but froze at the distant sound of sirens. Better to let the professionals handle the fire. With the fire station located at the edge of the village, they'd be here momentarily.

Grant exited out the back door of Giovanna's store and darted into the crowded street. Located on the corner, her store's dual access allowed him to escape without confronting the flames. Heart pounding, he worked to catch his breath, organize his thoughts. Around him, people gathered, their dazed expressions reflecting the shock he felt thrashing through his gut. Giovanna's storefront had exploded. The inventory would be a total loss. More than smoke, it smelled like a skunk had sprayed the interior of her store.

Grant stormed back around to the front of the building, remnants of the foul-smelling odor lingering in his nostrils. Her place was ruined. Even if Giovanna could salvage some furs and clean them, it would be cost-prohibitive. After a slow start to the season, her profit margin would be flattened. Pulling a cell phone from his waistband, Grant dialed her number. Giovanna needed to know what happened.

Pressing the phone against his ear, he paced and waited through several rings, wondering himself what happened. Why had the front window of her store been blown out? Could there have been a gas leak? And what was that smell? More than wood, it smelled rotten. Unnatural. Was it the fur skin? Puzzled, Grant absently rubbed the stench from his nose. Whatever it was, it was nasty.

Mingling with the growing collection of tourists, Grant neared his store and hovered outside. The air was biting cold, snow coming down heavier and heavier with the impending storm. A few passing skiers were schlepping their stuff from the slopes but slowed at the grisly sight. Others were dressed and on their way to dinner, sidetracked from their travels as they stopped and stared. Seven o'clock marked the end of après-ski and the beginning of resort nightlife. It was a cycle that continued without fail, December through March.

Only a blown out storefront was not part of that cycle.

Hello. You've reached Giovanna's cell phone. I'm unavailable to take your call at the moment, but please leave a message. Thank you for calling.

"Giovanna, Grant. There's been a...a..."—he wasn't sure quite how to describe it—"an emergency at the store. Please call me."

Pulling the phone from his ear, Grant glimpsed a couple standing beneath the eaves of a clothing store across the street. Pausing, he re-clipped his phone, mesmerized by the woman. She was drop-dead gorgeous, with sultry dark eyes, elegant brows and full lips. Dark brown hair fell in waves over her white parka and from beneath a matching hat, her face framed to perfection and appearing almost photo-shoot ready. Leaning into her companion, the woman's stance seemed practiced, posed, her dark gaze oddly dialed into the chaos. It was more intent than he'd expect from a curious bystander.

The young Asian man with her was equal in height, equal in looks, his body nearly as slender as hers and outfitted in black and white. Grant tried to turn from her, but a niggle of curiosity had hooked his attention. Returning to the woman's face, he couldn't help but wonder at her expression. Unlike her partner, her face held an intensity that went beyond shock and curiosity. If he didn't know better, he would have thought it was her store going up in smoke.

But it wasn't. It was Giovanna's. His phone rang. At the caller ID, Grant felt a quick stab to his heart. "Giovanna."

"Grant, what is it? What's happened?"

"There was an explosion." Turning from the fire and smoke, the growing squawk of sirens, he cupped a hand over the mouthpiece and said, "It happened in your shop."

"My shop is on fire?" she shrieked.

"The front window was blown out."

"My furs!"

Opening the door to his store, Grant slipped inside to better hear. "Help is on the way, but I think you should come down."

"Yes, yes. I'll be there in ten minutes."

Ending the call, Grant imagined she must have just made it home, only to turn around and come back to the destruction of her business. As he raked a hand through his hair, his thoughts went to the cause. With the initial shock fading, his mind honed in on the likely culprit. While gas could have been the cause, these buildings were extremely well-built and barely a decade old. Deliberate sabotage was more likely the cause. With the expansion of the resort, there had been threats against the local business community. The usual rank and file protesters were on hand, shouting their anti-capitalism, pro-animal sentiments as they railed into anyone trying to earn an honest living in ways they didn't approve, but this went too far.

Glimpsing the fire department arriving on scene, Grant returned to the jewelry case where he'd been working at the time of the explosion. He made sure the lid was closed properly and locked it. Closing up shop, he readied himself for the police. They would need a statement, something he'd be happy to provide. While he hadn't seen anything firsthand, hopefully someone else had, and they'd find the guy who did this. Disgust rolled through Grant's midsection. Why couldn't people leave the resort community alone? Since when was it a crime to make money?

Wildlife. Animals. Recalling yesterday's protest on the square, the myriad signs and shouts to save the animals, Grant wanted to hit something. There were hundreds of thousands of acres of land out there, yet these zealots cried foul because Palmer International wanted to expand operations. *It's not fair! Animals have rights, too!*

Why couldn't man and beast coexist peacefully? That's what he wanted to know. Since when was it a mutually exclusive concept? If the resort expanded, some animals would stay, some would relocate themselves to quieter terrain. Palmer International wasn't harming anything by growing its business. On the contrary, Grant knew for a fact that the resort owners had donated a hefty sum of money to land preservation, not to mention instituting one of the most extensive recycling programs this side of California. He'd challenge any company, any group or organization where thousands of people gathered together to do a better job when it came to dispensing of waste, conserving water and electricity. The company went so far as to recycle old ski equipment! They were a topnotch outfit when it came to environmentally-minded business operations and didn't deserve the treatment they were getting. Glaring at the congregation of people outside, he fumed inwardly. Neither did the town business owners.

Intimidation was the business of thugs, a reality Grant was all too familiar with and the reason he left New York City. His store had been hit five times because he refused to play along with the local syndicate of organized crime. His jewelry business had been enormously successful, and the thugs decided they wanted a piece of the action—a request he heartily denied. Images of a fiery storefront detonated in his mind. They had decided to torch his place in retaliation. Gold and platinum melted, rare gemstones cracked. His inventory had been a total loss. Months later, Grant left the city. It had been the last thing he wanted to do, because it meant letting the criminals win. But in the end he was a businessman and he couldn't do business with a mark on his back and a bull-seye on his front door.

It had been a sad day for him. As he cleared the inventory from his shelves and cases, Grant had felt overwhelmed by a sense of failure. His brother owned a café in the city and was the only family Grant had left. He hated to leave him but knew that if he stayed, his health would have suffered. That's when Grant packed up and headed west, relocating to the fresh air and slow pace of Silver Creek. While he missed the food, entertainment and constant motion of New York, the resort clientele here proved a perfect fit for his jewelry business and the food was outstanding. Particularly Adele's.

Grant walked to his front window and cast a glance outside, skimming the crowd of bystanders looking on as firefighters doused the flames. Watching the action unfold, Grant realized he hadn't escaped the brutal hand of intimidation by force when he left the city. Unfortunately, people everywhere resorted to violence when they didn't get their way.

Giovanna raced into his store. "Grant! My store—it's ruined!"

Grant went to her quickly, enfolding her in an embrace. Pure-blooded Italian and in her mid-sixties, she remained a beautiful woman. Giovanna and he were not intimate, but the gesture felt natural, warranted under the circumstances. "I'm so sorry," he murmured into her hair. "It's horrible what's happened."

"Who would do such a thing?" she cried into his shoulder. "I don't understand."

Grant did. He understood all too well who was likely behind the incident. The realization had been grating on him since the explosion, digging in with more and more certainty. "Don't worry, Giovanna. We'll find who did this and put them behind bars."

Pulling away, her heavily-mascaraed eyes blinked. She looked more than distraught. With her eyes rimmed in watery red, Giovanna look tired, worn. Sales hadn't been good this season, and with only two months to go before the slopes closed, this would likely end her prospects for the year.

"I have a video," she said. "A camera in my shop. It will tell us who did this to me, no?"

Her fighting spirit tugged at his heart and he smiled. "You bet it will. It will give the police a solid lead to go on so they can arrest this thug."

"But my furs..." She dropped her gaze. "It won't fix them."

"No. But you have insurance, don't you?" When she nodded, he said, "Well, then, your losses should be covered."

"Only my cost, no profit." Raising her face, she looked at him directly. "I can't make it on cost alone. I'll have to close my shop."

"Giovanna..." he protested, but his words fell away. Grant understood business. It was a simple equation of mathematics. With the insurance money, Giovanna would end up with a net zero on her inventory and in the red on her rent, utilities, time and effort. Grant felt a tightening in his chest. The whole thing made him angry enough to explode. He'd handle the culprit with his bare hands if he could. "If there's anything I can do to help," he said, "anything at all. You let me know."

Tears swamped her lids. "Thank you, Grant. You've been a good friend." Glancing toward the entrance door of his store, she murmured, "First, I must clean up."

"But what about the gala tonight? You're going, aren't you?"

She shrugged. "I was, but now? I don't think it's wise."

"Giovanna. There's nothing you can do here tonight other than give the police a statement and let them do their work. The gala is a one-time event."

"I don't know..."

Taking her lightly by the arm, he led her toward the door. Imploring her with a steady gaze, he said, "Please, don't let them win. Don't let whoever did this have the satisfaction of knowing they've interrupted your business." Pausing, he held her arms and said, "That's what they're after, you know. They want to drive you out of business. I feel sure it's one of those protesters who's responsible."

Her brow lifted in surprise. "You do?"

"Yes, and we can't let them win. Go to the event and hold your head high. Show them they cannot win with these methods."

A faint smile crossed her dark red lips. Giovanna might have lost her merchandise, but she still had her pride. "You are right, you know. They should not think this is okay. It isn't."

Understatement of the year, Grant mused but kept it to himself. "I'll walk you next door. We'll survey the damage together and give statements to the police."

Giovanna's smile broadened. Lightly patting his cheek in maternal fashion, she said, "You are a good man, Grant Powell. Someday a woman is going to 'lasso' you for her own."

Grant laughed. "You've been living in the mountains of the Wild West for too long, Giovanna. I think the altitude is getting to you!"

She winked. "Don't be too sure."

Grant was more than sure. He'd survived two marriages and one bitter divorce fight. There was no way he was trotting down that road again. Women were fine to be admired and enjoyed, but being tied down by one was a completely different story, one for which he already knew the ending. Women were alluring and stimulating in the beginning of a relationship, but once you slipped a ring on their finger, the dragon awoke and swallowed you whole.

Involuntarily, his gaze darted across the street. The woman he'd noticed earlier summoned her partner for an abrupt departure. *Good luck, buddy. Bet she can turn into a fire-breathing dragon, if the situation warrants.*

Chapter Three

Unsettled by the growing presence of police, Kinsley turned from the scene and strode down the brick-paved street. She wasn't exactly a stranger to the authorities, having several run-ins over the years during protests, but she had no intention of involving herself with them now. Her blog, *Wildlife Neutral*, was well-known for its passionate defense of animals, its staunch advocacy for change, which gave her a reputation for rhetoric stronger than a steel trap. But she advocated due process. Protest vocally, appeal to the masses, and pull their heartstrings by showing them the evidence in full-blown color. Fully blown-out windows were something else.

Pulling the collar snug around her face, Kinsley searched for a place to stop and talk. Spotting a space between buildings, she darted into the dark recess. Palmer International was overreaching with this latest expansion, jeopardizing animals of all sizes and an ecosystem that couldn't sustain it. Animals that required hundreds of acres to roam would be relegated to a mere hundred which wasn't right. It was wrong. Dead wrong.

But she wasn't a fanatic. She was an activist, a catalyst for change. With a little nudge, she made people change their behavior for the long-term. What Sebastian had done tonight simply crossed the line. It demeaned her credibility. And it angered her deeply, particularly because he'd made the decision without her knowledge.

Satisfied they were alone, she said, "I want to talk to you."

"Here?" Sebastian emitted a soft chuckle as he took in their surroundings. Walled off from passersby, they were completely hidden from view. "I mean, if you wanted some privacy with me all you had to do was ask. My hotel is only around the corner."

His cavalier tone grated on her. Kinsley had no interest in him romantically, nor would she ever mix business with pleasure. "What did you think you were doing switching the bomb on me?"

In the dim light, Sebastian sharpened his focus. "What's going on, Kinsley?"

Kinsley jammed her hands into her pockets. "What's going on? What do you think is going on? You switched my ink bomb for a real bomb!"

Sebastian smirked. "Since when did the method become the issue?"

"Since it wasn't in the plan. Since I never agreed to it."

"But the end result is no different. Why so concerned?"

She balled her fists as she hardened her gaze. "A simple ink bomb would have damaged the fur, nothing else. Yours was considerably more destructive, don't you think?"

"It's not as though it blew up the store."

"You blew out the front window!"

"Must have been a malfunction."

"Malfunction, my ass."

"And…your point is?"

"My point is, we had an agreement."

"An agreement to stop the resort expansion by sending a message to the local businesses that it wasn't in their best interest to stick around," Sebastian rattled off. He shifted his weight and crossed his arms over his chest. "I think we accomplished that, don't you?"

Kinsley hesitated. Yes and no. She agreed with the goal but not the method. But Sebastian didn't officially work for her. He wasn't an employee she could threaten with the loss of his job. He was a fellow activist, a member of the movement. Granted he had made himself invaluable over the last couple of years, securing the position as her second in command, but this was outrageous. If he wanted to dictate the methods of operation, he should start his own organization.

However, saying as much would alienate him. One of the reasons they were more powerful together was because each had built an impressive network of supporters. Sebastian had his friends, those loyal to him and not to her. She had hers. Now that they were working together, any dissension among the ranks would weaken the cause. And that's what they shared in common. The cause. Her blog was rooted in the cause. It grew from the cause. It blossomed because of the cause. A cause in which Sebastian was extremely influential.

Exhaling, Kinsley calmed her voice, "You know how I am, Sebastian. I'm a planner. I like details and I don't like them to change midstream."

Sebastian smiled. "Maybe this is your sign to lighten up. Relax, stay flexible."

She didn't want to relax or stay flexible. She wanted to achieve the goal.

She wanted to win.

Taking a step toward her, Sebastian cooed, his breath puffs of steam, "I don't know what you're so worried about. No one saw you, right?"

Kinsley shook her head.

"You're in the clear."

The fur store had surveillance cameras but she'd been careful to keep her identity concealed beneath hat and coat. Sebastian was right. She was in the clear. Except for the gnawing guilt of knowing she was the one who planted the bomb—the real bomb—Kinsley could not be connected to the explosion.

Sebastian rolled his eyes. "Tsk, tsk, Kinsley. You're not losing your edge, are you?"

She stiffened. "Not at all. I'm merely pointing out the lack of foresight. Our mission here is to stop the expansion of the resort, not get ourselves arrested for criminal activity. It would only taint the cause," she said, thrusting the disdain she felt into her voice. Sebastian needed to understand that she had her limits—limits that she dictated, not him. "From now on, how about you let me make the decision on what type of bomb I place." Walking past him, Kinsley added, "Otherwise, find someone else to work with."

"Maybe I will," he murmured under his breath, but not far enough that she couldn't hear him.

Heading for her hotel, Kinsley ran through the ramifications of the evening's blast. If Sebastian was looking for a showdown, then a showdown he would get. She'd be damned if he was going to call the shots—shots he neglected to inform her of in advance—and decide a course of action for her. She'd been at this for a long time and was very clear on her objectives. Animals had rights. They should not be eaten, worn, experimented on, used for entertainment or pushed from their natural habitat. Smoking those coats would have sent a message. Tomorrow's protest would send another.

But hers were messages focused on a problem, not chaotic examples of mass property damage and destruction. Someone could have gotten hurt. Innocent people could have been affected. What the heck had Sebastian been thinking?

As Kinsley forged ahead through the increasing snowfall, ragged flakes stung her face. She tapped her gaze to passing faces—couples, families—they were wealthy tourists from all over the world. And they were part of the problem. They gave a market to retailers like the fur store, the leather stores, the handbags, belts and boots made from the hides of animals. Those were the true innocents. They were the ones that mattered.

Preventing herself from making eye contact with anyone, Kinsley concentrated on the ground ahead of her. She had to rethink her plans with Sebastian, perhaps write him completely out of future endeavors. Unpredictability did not sit well with her when it came to her partners in business and Sebastian had proven himself unpredictable tonight. He was a liability. A risk. Sadness pricked her heart. Which was a shame. He had shown tremendous promise with his sharp mind, steely-edged conviction and ability to strategize two steps ahead of their opponents. Kinsley would miss his brilliance, but it couldn't be avoided. Anyone willing to override her decisions in favor of their own was no friend.

They were the enemy.

The cell phone in her pocket rang. Shaking the tinge of gloom from her thoughts, Kinsley pulled it free and slid it under her hat. "Hello?"

"Hello, darling."

"Hello, mother."

"What are you doing?"

"Walking to my hotel." She owned a townhome outside of Silver Creek, but preferred to be in the epicenter when working an active protest scene. The convenience and proximity helped her stay on top of the action.

"Have you changed your mind about tonight?"

Kinsley spewed a sigh and envisioned her mother's knowing smile. "You know I haven't."

"Just checking." After a weighty pause, her mother rolled out, "Your father and I have discussed it, and we would like to request that you keep a low profile this week. These events are important to Lee, and we don't want to infringe upon his accomplishment in any way."

Lee Palmer, of Palmer International. Kinsley's stomach tightened. "You're asking too much."

"Are we? The 'cause' can't survive without you for one week?"

More like she couldn't survive without the cause, but to reveal as much would only draw mockery from her mother. Victoria Fairchild wasn't a believer. While she touted herself as an animal lover and appreciated her daughter's compassion for the same, her mother didn't like the title of activist. She said it made Kinsley sound like one of those vagabonds who camped out during protests, brandishing signs and shouting obscenities. It wasn't becoming of a Fairchild. Kinsley had responsibilities, a legacy to uphold. Running around with a bunch of crazies was not good for her reputation or the family's image.

Image. That's what it all boiled down to with her mother. Image, propriety, being seen with the correct Who's Who in town. Her father was more direct. *You're wasting your time. People are going to buy what they want, eat what they want, and your spouting off on a website isn't going to change their minds.*

Old resentment bubbled to the surface. Action would change their minds. Media coverage would change their minds. She and her people had already made significant strides, and she wasn't about to quit now. "No, mother. The cause cannot survive without me." Especially not now. Not when they were so close. Public opinion was turning against the resort. People were learning about the real impact this expansion would have on the surrounding wildlife, and they were not happy. This community cared about its natural treasures. More than most, people who lived in this part of the country were sensitive to the issue of preservation and cared enough to do something about it.

Not bothering to hide the disappointment in her voice, her mother replied, "I'll pass it along to your father. He won't be pleased."

Never is, Kinsley mused bitterly. Not when it came to his daughter and her chosen line of work, anyway. "Have a nice time with your friends, mother. I'll talk to you tomorrow." Ending the call before her mother could respond, Kinsley fought a rising irritation. She loved her parents, but they were so polar opposite from herself that she wondered how they shared the same blood!

As Kinsley replaced the phone to her pocket, her stomach growled. No longer in the mood for Adele's, Kinsley decided to head over to Sweet Marjoram for a bite to eat. She knew the maître d' and could easily be seated, though she could just as well sit at the bar. Suddenly, she wondered if Kyle was working. He made for good company, not to mention a pretty face to look at. Not that she was interested in anything more. Kyle Willis was gay. Very gay and very taken. She would get nothing but smiles and sweet talk from him. Two things she could use right about now.

Chapter Four

Located front and center to Silver Creek's main entrance, the police station was a beautiful brick and wood building, the exterior more resembling a residential estate home than a police department. Sidewalks were heated, same as the cobblestone streets in town, and lined by piles of snow. Overnight, a blizzard had dumped four feet, leaving today beautiful, crisp and sunny. Brown-tinted windows lined the building and kept the stiff Colorado sun from piercing the interior, while allowing for unencumbered views of the ski mountain. Chief Wade Davis had a prime spot of real estate to conduct his business, one any business owner would covet.

Grant opened the door, instantly consumed by warmth, and walked up to the receptionist, an attractive blonde in her forties sitting in what looked more like the lobby for an upscale lodge than police headquarters. "I'm here to see Chief Wade Davis."

He was here because the police chief had called. He'd reviewed the video from Giovanna's store and captured images of the person responsible. It was a woman.

A woman. Part of Grant had been surprised to hear a woman had been the one to set the bomb. Pretty ballsy, if you asked him, but females were changing. They weren't the mild-mannered women of his parents' generation but instead, uncompromising go-getters with ambition and drive equal to men. If damage and destruction were the goals, why shouldn't a woman be the one to place the bomb? She'd blend in better at a fur store than any man, that's for sure.

"Please sign in," the receptionist instructed as he wrote his name. Grant knew the drill. Next would be photo identification. Setting the pen down, he pulled the wallet from the back pocket of his jeans, retrieved his license and handed it over.

"Thank you."

Dutifully transcribing his information, she made a copy of his driver's license before returning it to him with a smile. Grant absently took in the décor as she scribbled out a temporary name badge for him. Photographs on the walls were scenes from all over the state, from animals in their natural habitat to meadows littered with colorful wildflowers. They reminded him of the photos hanging in his jewelry store, images captured from his favorite grad student and part-time nature photographer, Lisa Richardson. Her father was a close friend of Grant's and one of the first real friendships he'd formed after moving to Silver Creek. Wade Davis was a close second.

The receptionist handed the name tag to Grant and pointed. "Right through that door, then down the hall on your left."

"Thanks." Slapping the sticky tag onto the right side of his chest, Grant headed for Wade's office. Walking down the spacious corridor, Grant admired the wood floors. Black walnut with moderate variation, they blended nicely with the amber tone of the walls. The doors lining the hall were also dark wood, the craftsmanship evident in the raised panels and solid hardware. Wade's office was night and day from those Grant had visited in New York. Dingy and impersonal described the city's finest, while Wade's digs embodied the elegance and style of Silver Creek.

As he turned into the last doorway, Grant's heart skipped a beat at the sight of Giovanna. While beautifully dressed, the black of her silk turtleneck underscored the heaviness in her eyes, eyes that appeared defeated. Did that mean bad news?

"Grant," Wade addressed him as he entered.

"Wade." Taking up position next to Giovanna, he looked to the seasoned veteran for answers. Despite the fancy adornments of his office, a continuation of the elegant interior from the lobby, there was nothing soft about Wade Davis.

Dressed in a navy blue suit—almost black—he was tall, his build strong and solid, his dark brown hair thick and trimmed short. Full brows and mustache gave him a western air, though Grant felt he was every bit New York cop. Tough, gritty, the lines around his aging brown eyes said it all. Wade was no stranger to criminals. "What have we got?" Grant asked.

"Not much." Pointing to his computer screen, Wade gestured for Grant to take a look for himself. "We have a female on camera clearly placing the bomb in the front window before exiting the store, but as you can see, we have no positive ID."

Grant peered at the screen. No ID, because she was wearing a white hat and coat which served to completely conceal her face. "That's it?" he asked, knowing it was, yet unable to restrain the impulse spurred by disappointment.

"Afraid so. We've run it time and time again, trying to determine if maybe this woman had been in the store earlier in the day giving us a better view, but it appears this was a one-time visit. She came in just before closing and didn't leave until after Ms. DeFiori left."

Grant looked to Giovanna. "Do you remember her?"

"No," she said, disappointment filling her eyes. Cupping a hand to her head, she confessed, "I don't remember her at all. I was so busy getting ready for the ball that I missed her entirely."

Placing a hand to Giovanna's narrow shoulder, Grant gently squeezed. "This isn't your fault, Giovanna. This woman probably knew you were headed out and intentionally came in at the last minute to hide between the coats."

"Remind me to deputize you, will you?" Wade asked with more than a hint of tease. "Your assessment is spot on." Pointing to the monitor, he said, "She came in five minutes before close and went straight for the furs. At the sound of the door, Giovanna came out to look for a customer but when she saw no one in the store, she assumed she'd mistakenly heard the front door chime and went back to her office."

With a sheepish smile, she held her hands up. "I'm an old woman. I accept that my hearing isn't as good as it used to be."

"Your hearing is fine, Giovanna. What you couldn't have expected was someone to ditch themselves in your fur." Leaning in for another look, Grant was bothered by something. It was as if he'd seen the woman before, like he knew her.

Did he? Was she a customer at his jewelry store?

The video replayed and Grant scrutinized her figure, her movements, as she exited through the front door. A sense of familiarity gnawed at him. Straightening, he asked, "Is it possible she was caught on one of the town videos?"

"I've already called over to city hall and put in my request," Wade responded. "We should have the footage by this afternoon."

Expelling a sigh, Grant combed a hand through his hair. He'd been hoping for better news. Giovanna lost the bulk of her inventory because of this explosion and deserved to know who was responsible. "Appreciate your time, Wade. Keep in touch, will you?"

"You know I will."

Giovanna collected her leather purse from a nearby chair and said to Wade, "Thank you."

"No problem. It's what we do. And don't worry, we'll get to the bottom of this. It's only a matter of time."

"Do you think it was one of those protesters?" Giovanna asked.

Wade pursed his lips. "Could be. We've had trouble with them before but nothing this serious."

"It's possible they've amped up their game," Grant said.

Wade acknowledged him with a nod of his head. "It's possible. If it is one of them, they're going to learn pretty quickly I don't take kindly to their brand of activism."

"This goes beyond activism," Grant said, a crisp wave of anger capping his thoughts.

"Yes," Giovanna put in, "It's not right what they did. If they don't like my furs, don't wear them, no?"

"I'm with you," Wade said. "Next, they'll be going after my leather boots." He dropped his gaze to the pair of shiny black ostrich boots. "No one touches my boots."

Grant followed his gaze. Wade was a good cop, a first-class police officer, yet he had an odd penchant for boots. In the few years Grant had known him, he'd counted at least six different pair, including a red, white and blue pair Wade reserved for July Fourth celebrations. Last year he strutted around town like a proud peacock, boasting a patriotic streak a mile wide and a unique knack for fashion.

Shaking his head, Grant pulled his thoughts back to the issue at hand. Fashion aside, destroying private property carried a felony charge. As far as he was concerned, whoever did this deserved jail time. Lightly grasping Giovanna by the arm, Grant said, "Let us know if there's anything more you need from us."

"Will do. And you'll be the first to know what I find on the town's video stream."

"Appreciate it."

Grant followed Giovanna back to town, partly because she seemed so distraught, partly because he felt a shared connection to the crime. His store was attached to Giovanna's, separated by only a wall. Watching her unlock the door to her store, anger welled hot and fast as images of the fiery storefront inundated him. That fire yesterday could have easily spread to his place, destroying yet another one of his jewelry stores. "People who think they can control others through force make me mad as hell. They're criminals, thugs, that's what they are, hiding behind the guise of activism."

Giovanna sighed, pushing inside. "It's not only activists. This sort of thing used to happen back home in Italy. If a store owner didn't pay a 'protection tax,' they woke up one morning to find their business ruined. My brother, Fabio, still battles them with his *ristorante*. They want their '*pizzo*' but he and others are not willing to pay."

"You're right. Organized crime is alive and well here in The States, too. It's the reason I left New York City. Between the mafia and the gangs, my jewelry store was hit five times."

Giovanna gasped. "Five times?"

Pausing with her just inside the doorway, he nodded. "The last time they hit me they used fire. At rush hour. There I was, standing outside my store waiting for the fire department to make its way between a sea of yellow cabs at a dead stop, horns honking, sirens blaring in the distance, and all I could think was *never again*. Never again would I be held hostage by someone who thought they could bully me into submission." Looking into her dark eyes, Grant found an empathy he wished she couldn't give. "You work your whole life to achieve, to produce, only to be undercut by someone who wants to use your success for their own means."

"But why your store?"

"They wanted to use my business to launder their dirty money, as if I would partner with filth like them." The memory of three men entering his store, strolling about his place as if they owned it, flicking their cigar ashes on his gleaming glass counters made Grant recoil. Even today, five years later, the memory cut raw. Nobody pushed him around. Nobody told Grant Powell what to do and how to do it—ever.

When he'd refused the first time, one the bodyguards snickered, as though Grant was a child who had no clue what he was doing. He'd been wrong. Grant knew exactly what he was doing. The men who had paid him a visit were too comfortable, too at ease to be anything but seasoned veterans in the game of corruption. He informed the authorities immediately and was not surprised to learn that officials from both local and federal agencies had been watching the crime family for years. With his help, they were able to take down one of the junior members, a rising star within the criminal family.

Unfortunately, standing up to the thugs included a price greater than the loss of his business. To this day, Grant looked over his shoulder. It had been constant in the months after he relocated to Colorado, days when he half-expected a bullet to fly through a window, headed straight for his chest. The feeling persisted, though waning with every passing year. In the back of his mind, however, Grant knew the possibility of retribution existed. It was unlikely, the police had told him, but a reality he had to accept. "We can't give in to threat and intimidation, Giovanna. If we do, they win."

Glancing around the charred ruins of her store, the rank scent of burned fur and wood heavy in the air, she sighed. "They've already won."

"Don't say that. You can rebuild. You have insurance. You can rebuild and come out stronger than before and put whoever did this behind bars where they belong."

She shook her head. Soulful brown eyes clung to him as she said, "I am finished, here. It's time for me to return home."

"But *this* is your home. You've been here for over ten years." Giovanna loved the mountains, the small town atmosphere, the quiet sophistication of the village, said it reminded her of the Old Country. During the summer months, the two frequented the farmers' markets and she commented often how the bounty of fresh flowers and vegetables reminded her of Italy, only better. Here, she enjoyed independence and freedom. For two months in July and August, she'd close her store and travel the states. She had relatives in California, Texas, and Florida, and she'd visit them all, taking side trips and excursions that she'd share with Grant upon her return. She'd even taken the test to become an American citizen. If anyone deserved success and prosperity it was Giovanna. "You can't go back, now."

Tears swamped her lower lids as she smiled. "I do not have enough money to continue. Sales have been slow, people are changing..." As she glanced away, a tear spilled onto her cheek. Wiping it free, she added, "Perhaps this was meant to be."

"This was not meant to be," Grant growled, overcome by a flash of anger. "This was a crime that needs punishment."

"Yes," she replied wistfully, "but it doesn't change the facts. I'm tired. I don't have the energy to rebuild."

The finality in her voice sliced him in two. Giovanna was giving up. She was letting them win because they had managed to catch her in a vulnerable stage of life, destroying her livelihood at a time when she couldn't afford to fight back. Sweeping his gaze over the scorched remains of beautiful fur coats and hats, a white manikin streaked by black soot, the stench caught in his nostrils like bile in his throat. This would not go unanswered. Grant Powell would make sure of it.

Grant stayed as Giovanna picked her way through the debris, saving what she could, cataloging the rest for insurance purposes. Grant knew from experience the insurance would take time to kick in and offered to loan Giovanna money for the interim, an offer she declined. She had enough for living expenses. Replacing the inventory and renovating the shop is what would have proven costly and time consuming, neither of which she was inclined to do. She was cutting her losses, calling it quits, despite Grant's every effort to the contrary.

Handing her the last of the salvaged designer key chains, he asked, "Hungry? I'm heading over to the square for food."

"No, thank you. I have plenty to eat in the office."

Giovanna had a small refrigerator behind her desk, the contents of which usually consisted of an assortment of salads, cheese, paté and sparkling water. Grant knew her to keep a bottle of wine on hand, as well. On more than one occasion the two had relaxed over red wine, mostly Chianti and Amarone, chatting about the day's business. A Cabernet drinker himself, he had developed an affinity for the Italian reds during his time spent with Giovanna.

Grant smiled. "Text me if you change your mind."

Giovanna walked over and pecked his cheek. "You're such a dear. I don't know what I would do without you." With a wave, she headed back to her office, her stride unhurried and proud. She was a woman of grace. Strong and dignified, she had a solid core. If such things were possible, Giovanna's heart would be made from pure gold.

She reminded him of his mother.

Turning, Grant pushed out through her front door, immediately heading into his store. "How's it going in here?"

"Sold a diamond bear pendant this morning, three pairs of earrings, and two rings—one being the last turquoise from the David Bentley collection."

Grant released a soft whistle. "All that before lunch?"

Beau James smiled. "It's been a good start to the day."

One of four employees hired to help carry the workload of manning the store, Beau had been with Grant the longest. Tall and lean, he dressed in nothing but suit and tie when he worked, despite Grant's insistence that it was unnecessary. In a ski resort, "casual was king" and business casual attire would suffice while on duty. But Beau wouldn't hear of it. He was selling high-end gold, silver, platinum, precious gems and stones, and he needed to look the part. Said customers preferred dealing with someone who mirrored the quality of the merchandise they were selling.

Grant couldn't disagree. He received more compliments when Beau worked the counter than any of his other employees. Probably because the ladies loved him. With his All-American good looks, blue eyes, thick head of brunette hair and a complexion most women would mortgage their home for, Beau was a natural when it came to sales. Not only had his good looks put him through college on a modeling income, his easy smile made sealing the deal a breeze. The man was worth his weight in gold. "I'll call the rep this afternoon.

Right now, I'm going to grab something to eat. Can I get you anything?"

"A hoagie from Dexter's?"

"You got it. Your usual?"

Beau nodded. "A Coke and chips would be great."

Grant laughed. To look at Beau, one would never know he consumed food like a football player, but then again, the man was blessed when it came to good genes. "Consider it done."

Grabbing a jacket from the coat rack by the door on his way out, Grant pulled it on and zipped the front as he walked. The square was a good three blocks away and the air cooler than normal. Some talked about another blizzard on the way, but Grant had learned to ignore them. Mountain weather was as unpredictable as the female mind. One minute you had sunny and shine, next you had rainy and blue. Dodging skiers as he traveled against the flow of traffic, Grant headed for the center of action. Two o'clock was a bit late for lunch and somewhat early for après-ski, and instead that hour of the day when skiers trickled off the mountain. By three o'clock most bars and restaurants would begin to fill and by four, getting a seat would be nearly impossible.

Shoving hands into his pockets, Grant maintained a brisk pace and mulled over the videotape he'd seen in Wade's office. A lone woman had entered the store, concealed herself between the furs, then strategically planted the bomb near the front of the store, exiting immediately afterward. The bomb had been remotely detonated, undoubtedly to give the woman time for an alibi elsewhere in town. It was a clever plan, but not foolproof. No plan was foolproof.

Nearing the central square, he noticed a crowd of people had collected, most hovering around the center fountain. Situated between restaurants and retail stores, the fountain had been designed as a focal point, complete with a sitting ledge border, providing a perfect gathering place for visitors. Not your basic fountain, the water spray for this one was a choreographed dance of streams, synced with music and a show of

LED lights that came to life every afternoon about this time. The display delighted kids and adults alike as they set down skis and poles, boots and bags, and watched. It was a recent addition to the village as part of the resort's planned expansion. Palmer International was beginning with a complete renovation of the central shopping and dining district, followed by new lifts and mountaintop lodge facilities—once they received approval, that is.

Circling the fountain, Grant could smell the café before he could see it. Located around the corner, it was adjacent to the ticket windows and gondola, and specialized in smoked meat and barbecue, the scent of which permeated the square. Imagining the smoked turkey club already in his mouth, Grant slowed, his gaze drawn to a woman on a raised platform. The pseudo stage was used for summer open-air concerts, but at the moment it had been overrun by a group of protesters. Marching around, they pumped signs high into the air. Parading between him and the café, they shouted "Stop the growth, before it's too late!"

"Nature, not annihilation!"

Their calls drifted over the clatter of ski boots plodding over cobblestone. Most protesters were men and women of varying ethnicity, dressed casually in ski jackets and jeans. In the center of the activity on stage was a beautiful woman. She had long brown hair and sultry dark eyes. Homing in on her, Grant realized he'd seen her before.

His brain rapidly processed the information—her face, her features—and at once he realized where it had been. Last night, across the street from Giovanna's store. She had been standing with an Asian man.

Pausing, Grant stared at her as intuition hummed. *There was something about her, something familiar.* Grant locked his spine. Suddenly, everything clicked.

The white coat. The white hat. She was the woman from the video!

Chapter Five

"Grizzlies, not greed!" Kinsley shouted. "Deer not dollars!"

The crowd around her consisted mostly of her supporters, a mix of young men and women in their mid-twenties thoroughly devoted to the cause, along with a spattering of Sebastian's. He wasn't on scene which meant the bulk of his people wouldn't be. Tourists walked by and around the protesters as they descended from the mountain in droves, most curious as to the commotion but none interested in stopping for further dialogue. It was the beginning of après-ski and Kinsley had strategically chosen this location because it placed her group smack in the middle of the stream of foot traffic. They might not want to stop and talk, but they couldn't fail to see them.

"Stop the expansion while you can!" Gabby Olsen called out. "The wildlife depends on you!"

A man broke from the crowd, storming toward Kinsley with anger churning in his eyes. Graying at the temples, his expensive haircut and clothing marked him as a wealthy tourist, one of many that descended upon Silver Creek every year. But this one wasn't oblivious like the others. This one jogged up the steps and came to within feet of her.

He pointed a finger in her face. "I saw you the night of the explosion. You were *there*."

"What are you talking about?" she asked, a batter of heartbeats erupting in her chest. Who was he? How did he know?

"The fur store. There was a bomb set." His voice dropped dangerously as he accused, "You were the one caught on the store video setting the bomb."

Kinsley stepped away from him. Darting a glance to some of the male members in her group, she replied, "I don't have any idea what you're talking about."

"I think you do. You know exactly what I'm talking about. I can see it in your eyes."

One of Sebastian's men moved between them. Six-foot-two, about two-hundred-fifty pounds, Norell Williams tossed the dreadlocks from his face and said, "You heard the woman. She doesn't know what you're talking about."

The stranger turned to him, and Kinsley felt the instant assessment between fighters, who could take who. Norell looked like a street fighter and had the scars to prove it. Sebastian's right-hand man, he was used to intimidating people and getting his way. Surprisingly, the older gentleman didn't back down an inch. Instead, he leaned toward Norell and snarled, "I'm talking to *her*, not you."

"She's with me." Norell thumped his chest, then extended a hand to include the other members of their group. "With us."

Two dozen men, about twenty women, Kinsley's group would band together against any outsider. Looking between opposing sides, she thought, this guy didn't understand what he was dealing with. Especially when it came to Norell. The man had a hair trigger temper when it came to opposing voices.

"I'm warning you to back off," the stranger said, then stuck a rigid finger between them. "Once."

Norell shoved the man's shoulder. The guy grabbed Norell's meaty hand, yanked it forward and down, then twisted it behind him in a tight lock between his shoulder blades. Norell dropped to his knees and cried out in pain. The older guy repeated, "I said, *back off.*"

"Stop!" Kinsley cried out, shock pouring through her disbelief. No one had ever challenged Norell that way. No one without a badge, anyway.

"Back to my point," the stranger said, homing in on Kinsley. "I saw you at the scene. You were wearing a white hat and a white parka."

Gabby stepped forward. "You mean like this one?"

He stared, confusion discharging in his gaze as he recognized the coat as the one he saw the night of the bombing. But Gabby was short and blonde and clearly not the woman from the video. Kinsley's gut zipped closed.

She was.

Tuning into the stranger's hesitation, Norell jerked against his grip and grunted, "Let me go."

Loosening his hold of Norell, the man released him.

Norell turned on him. Nostrils flaring, he said, "Stop causing trouble, mister. You won't get lucky next time."

Another male protester approached and warned, "Stop trying to pin stuff on us, man. It ain't cool."

Kinsley kept her mouth shut. She and Sebastian purposely did not share their plan with the others for this very reason. The less people who knew, the better to keep it quiet. Score one for Sebastian, she mused sourly. That was his idea, too.

Catching a glimpse of a blond man, Kinsley's heart lurched. Dressed in a black and red ski coat and matching pants, Hal Richardson, Lisa's father, carried his skis on one shoulder, poles in his opposite hand, while his ski boots pounded heavily over the brick-red cobblestone as he walked over. Slowing to stop next to the stranger, he stood in the slightly knee-bent position common to skiers, a concerned gaze moving from Kinsley to the stranger. Was he here to defend her?

"Grant, what's going on here?"

"There was a bomb set off at Giovanna's fur store yesterday," he told Hal. "I saw the video and she was there."

"Kinsley?"

Kinsley gave a small wave. "Hi, Dr. Richardson."

Confused, Grant looked between them. "You know her?"

"Yes, she's a friend of Lisa's. But you said she was in a video?"

"Yes," Grant replied, the fire gone from his temper.

Kinsley took the lead. Offense was always better than defense, and this was her opening. "He claims there was a woman captured in a video at the scene of the bombing," she explained. "A woman with a white hat and jacket."

"Like mine," Gabby asserted. Copping an attitude, she retorted, "So now I'm a criminal 'cause I wear white? Dream on, mister. White coats are common. You can't prosecute based on that."

Kinsley silently mocked Gabby's impassioned performance. She was taking advantage of the situation to taunt the men because she could. It was easy to thumb your nose at someone when you knew you were nowhere near the scene of the crime. It was a whole different story when you were guilty and one of your best friend's father was staring you in the eye over the matter.

Kinsley controlled her breathing, careful not to give anything away as she said, "It's a case of mistaken identity, Dr. Richardson. No big deal."

Grant drilled her with a glance that said otherwise, but didn't say a word.

"I see." Turning to Grant, Hal said, "Have you talked to the police about it?"

Grant nodded. "Saw Wade this morning."

"What does he say?"

In a guarded voice, he replied, "He's still reviewing the evidence."

Raking a wary glance over Norell, Hal said, "Maybe we should discuss this elsewhere."

No surprise, Kinsley mused. Dr. Richardson wasn't a fan of her activist friends, despite the fact that his daughter was of like mind and like spirit. But Lisa didn't follow the activist route. She was too busy tracking her precious toads, leaving her no time to save the other animals. But Kinsley cut her slack. Lisa's heart was in the right place. It was her schedule

that posed the problem. Working on her PhD took every wak-
ing hour. She went to class, went to the lab, hiked the mountain, went to sleep and started the whole cycle over again. She
barely had time for a social life, and up until this past summer, that included no time for a boyfriend. That was before
she met mountain man.

Make that military man. They met while Lisa was chasing her toads in high country. He was up there, living on the
mountain like some weird recluse and the two crossed paths.
McIntyre Walsh was a Marine first, second and third, and the
reason Lisa had made it home safely from that hiking trip.
Seems a murderer had been on the loose, killing women, and
Walsh was credited for putting an end to the murderous spree.
Walsh was edgy, stern and stiff. He and Kinsley didn't get
along. At all.

Watching Hal and the man named Grant walk away,
Kinsley returned to the business at hand. She could discuss
the new development regarding a video with Sebastian later
this afternoon. At the moment, their voices must be heard in
protest against the resort's plans.

Pulling him away from the group, Hal said, "Grant, you
need to be more careful. Some of those kids are pretty radical.
They have no qualms about going to jail for assault."

"I'm not worried about them. They don't scare me."

Considering the scent of marijuana in the air with the tattered clothing and unkempt hair, Grant decided this group
was nothing but a bunch of pot-smoking hippies who'd rather
spend their days shouting down society than getting a real
job. Sure, some looked capable of violence, but he wasn't
concerned. He could handle himself physically and was prepared for whatever came his way. If they wanted a fight, a
fight he would give them.

Involuntarily, as he mulled over Hal's revelation,
Grant's attention was drawn to Kinsley, to the slender curves
of her legs outlined in black leggings, her narrow build and
shiny dark brown hair. Marching around like a soldier on pa-

trol, she was clearly the leader of the group, surrounded by a mindless band of followers ready and willing to step in on her behalf. Disturbed by the connection to Hal, Grant tried to assimilate the information as he continued to stare at her. "You said that's a friend of Lisa's?"

"Yes. They met when Kinsley moved here from San Francisco during high school. In fact, Kinsley's parents are friends with Lee Palmer. You might have crossed paths. Gregory and Victoria Fairchild?"

"Doesn't ring a bell," Grant replied, captivated by Kinsley's looks. She was stunning. Up close, her skin was flawless, her lips supple. Her eyes were dark and rebellious, sparked by a fierce intelligence and spirit. She didn't shrink back when he accused her. Not an inch. She had been calm and composed, yet he sensed a churning beneath her cool exterior. She knew something. The minute he'd made the accusation, something in her gaze flinched, he was sure of it.

"Kinsley is a good girl," Hal said. "I'm sure she had nothing to do with the bombing. I heard about it at the hospital. No one was hurt, thank God."

"No, but they could have been." He could have been. Hell, the sound alone had almost given him a heart attack!

"Listen," Hal continued, "she's passionate, but not criminal. Her parents are nice people. In fact, her father is one of the investors in the resort development."

"He is?"

Hal nodded.

"How does he feel about a daughter who's trying to oppose him at every turn?"

"Gregory doesn't care for it at all, but his wife does. Victoria protects Kinsley and defends her right to protest while soothing the tension between father and daughter."

"Sounds like a tough job."

"Not really. Gregory has a soft spot for Kinsley and lets her get away with murder."

Grant grunted. "I think we just found the problem."

Hal waved him off like a nuisance fly. "The man's got more money than the state of Colorado. I doubt Kinsley's efforts will make a dent in his plans."

"An insolent child with an open checkbook is a dangerous combination."

Hal chuckled. "Agree with you there, but actually, Kinsley makes her own living."

"How?"

"She runs a successful blog called *Wildlife Neutral* and makes a nice living from it. She has over half a million followers which translates into some pretty significant advertising dollars."

Grant let out a low whistle. "A blog? What does she write about—how to destroy capitalist development so no animal ever dies but people starve?"

Hal grinned. "Something like that. She's an advocate for the vegan lifestyle, including everything from diet to wardrobe."

"I see the connection to Lisa."

Hal laughed. "And half the community around here! Adele loves reading the blog and says Kinsley's arguments are solid."

"Do they include vandalism?"

Hal grew serious. "Are you sure it's her?" Scratching at thinning blond hair, he glanced askance. "I'd be really surprised. Kinsley is smart. She's going places. I don't think she'd risk getting involved in something criminal. Mischievous, yes. Criminal, no."

"I can't say with one hundred percent certainty," Grant admitted, "but my gut tells me she's the one."

"Give her a second look. I think you'll find you might be mistaken."

Doing exactly that, Grant turned and focused in on Kinsley. Continuing to parade around the stage, she was directing her comments to a group of women who had stopped to listen.

"Someone in their crowd is responsible," he muttered. "It's no coincidence that those activists are massing at the very time the resort is announcing its expansion plans, that businesses are getting hit."

Hal followed Grant's gaze. "I can't argue with you there. They're not happy about the environmental impact the resort is having, but progress is progress. They'll have their say and move on, same as they always do."

"Giovanna can't move on. Her store is ruined." Anger welled in Grant's gut. "I have no intention of letting them have their say and move on, not on that count. Not without criminal prosecution, I won't."

"I understand," Hal said. Placing a hand on Grant's shoulder, he added, "You do what you have to do. I'm just asking you reconsider your conviction of Kinsley Fairchild. She might be innocent."

Maybe. Zeroing in on her, Grant admired the packaging but suspected the package. She might be innocent, she might be guilty. It was his job to find out the truth.

Chapter Six

Grant clicked the window closed on his computer screen and slid the mouse across his desk. He eased back into his office chair as images and assertions swam through his brain. *Wildlife Neutral* had been more than he anticipated. Not the fanatical rant he expected, Kinsley's blog was a rational, incredibly well-thought-out argument for the protection and rights of animals. Article after article advocated alternatives to fur and leather, meat and dairy products, each complete with footnotes citing research that supported her position. It was clear Kinsley had done her homework on the issues, complete with links to documents and videos for anyone who doubted the veracity of her statements—her very passionate statements that cut to the heart of each and every issue.

Grant crossed his fingers and brought them to his lips as he stared at the blue screen with a list of icons lined in vertical rows. Kinsley asserted that animals were here before humans, or at least inferred that was the case when it came to the subject of commercial land development. They had first possession which gave them dibs. They should be allowed to coexist with humans on mutually beneficial terms. Further, they shouldn't be eaten, beaten, worn, experimented on, used for entertainment or pushed from their natural habitat—because animals had rights.

While Grant couldn't entirely disagree with her position—maintaining that animals should be treated humanely and considered in any land development proposition—he thought Kinsley a bit extreme. After all, "survival of the fittest" was a key concept to the idea of natural selection and evolution. If one wanted to espouse the virtues of animals and their right to exist in their natural habitat, one also had to remain true to their principles and accept that humans were at the top of the food chain.

Didn't they?

Thinking back to Kinsley's opinion piece on a recent case involving bear attacks in a suburban neighborhood, a residential development surrounded by a state preserve, he recalled how she advocated that people should be forced to sell their homes and move, versus the alternative—the control of the bear population by wildlife officials which could entail relocation or the killing of those deemed a threat to humans. Such a stand might suggest she would disagree with his assessment that humans dominated the animal world.

Grant shook his head. He'd grown up in a neighborhood that bordered a conservation area, and there had been no issues between man and beast. Back then, people were able to live together without issue. Bears, snakes, lynx, moose—they all worked around one another as they went about their business. But as each increased in number, Grant understood choices had to be made. In his book, humans should prevail. They should be good custodians of their animal neighbors, but in the end, when push came to shove, humans should win. Kinsley seemed to disagree.

Pushing up from his desk, he turned out the office light and headed for the front door of his jewelry store. Gold and jewels gleamed from glass cases, many pendants actually shaped in the form of animals. People loved animals, some even revered them. Maybe it made him a bad person to put humans first, but Grant didn't think so, nor should he be made to feel guilty about his position. It was the law of nature. None of these activists seemed to mind animals killing animals out in the wild. Why did they have issue when a human entered the equation? Humans were mammals, same as bears. They marked their territory, defended their young.

Letting himself out, Grant locked the door, the metal jangle of his key ring clanging against the brass door handle as he double-checked it. With the onslaught of protesters in town, he couldn't take any chances, especially when they were willing to use explosives. Not that he was worried the protesters would care about his jewelry store, but who knew?

Maybe mining for precious metals was a sin in their culture.

Slipping the keys into his coat pocket, he cast a glance toward Giovanna's dark storefront and his heart pinched. Such a waste. She didn't deserve to have her livelihood ruined because someone disagreed with her choice of merchandise. If Kinsley and her kind wanted to put an end to the fur trade, then they should do it the legitimate way—change the law. That was another point about humans. While they shared with animals a common instinctual desire to defend their territory against trespassers, humans worked by the rule of law, not force.

Lucky for the protesters. If Giovanna were an animal, she'd be perfectly within her rights to kill the activist responsible for destroying her business. It's how things worked out in the wild. Don't enter the lion's den if you can't handle the consequences.

Grant walked the four blocks to the restaurant, marveling at the amount of snow this year. Rooftops were buried by what looked like puffy marshmallow coating—buildings encased by mounds of snow, untouched and pristine. Lights twinkled from bushes in a colorful extension of the Christmas décor that had drenched the village during the holidays and now remained through the entire season, giving the town a magical appeal. Up on the mountain, Grant could see the headlamps of snow cats busy at work as they groomed the slopes for another day of skiing, their lights eerily cat-like as they moved from side to side. The moon was nearly full tonight, softening the landscape with silvery-gray hues. There was just enough illumination for him to make out the faint contour of mountains and trees high above.

The snowfall from this afternoon had subsided, but the forecast called for another round later tonight. If only he had time for a ski run tomorrow. He'd love to hit the slopes, take the edge off his pent-up stress, but he'd promised Giovanna he would go to the police station with her. Wade said he had more video to look at and since Grant had been the one on scene and not Giovanna, it made sense he should go and take a look with her.

Rounding the corner to Adele's, Grant slowed. Up ahead, walking toward him from the opposite distance was none other than Kinsley. He made eye contact and his pulse stirred. Dressed in a fancy pale gray coat and matching hat, her brown hair meticulously draped over her lapels as though once again on display, she walked like a runway model. Her long lean legs were covered in patterned leggings and tucked into sleek black boots. Unlike the bulky snow boots she wore earlier, these lent an air of chic sophistication to her appearance. Kicking up his pace, Grant maintained eye contact as he neared.

Deciding there was no time like the present to begin his own investigation, he met her outside the entrance to Adele's and introduced himself. "Hello," he said tentatively, "it's Kinsley, right?"

The use of her name stopped her cold. "It is. And you're Grant."

"I am. Grant Powell." Extending a hand, he added, "I'm sorry about this afternoon." When she didn't reciprocate the gesture, he continued, "Unfortunately my emotion was running a little high when I saw you, and I got carried away." Dipping his chin, he smiled. He was a decent guy. He wasn't interested in convicting an innocent person. Only the guilty. "It won't happen again."

She placed her hand in his, albeit a bit reluctantly and said, "Kinsley Fairchild."

As they shook, Grant was amazed by the fragile strength of her grip. Her hand was half the size of his, yet she managed to match his vigor. "May I buy you dinner?"

"Excuse me?"

She was almost as startled by the invitation as he, but now that it was out there, why not? "Dinner, to make up for

my rude behavior this afternoon. Hal said you're a friend of
Lisa, and they're good friends of mine. After the way I treated you and your friends today, it's the least I can do. Trust
me, I don't make a habit of insulting people." He paused as
the obvious occurred. "Unless, of course, you're meeting
someone."

"No," she said, glancing toward the glass-inlaid door of
Adele's. "I'm not, actually."

"Great. So what do you say, dinner's on me?"

Hovering in place, she seemed to think twice about accepting his offer. After all, she didn't know him personally,
and what she did know of him had been confrontational.
Standing beneath the front lantern, Grant waited, taken by the
glow of lamplight in her eyes as she looked at him. Up close,
he marveled at the creamy quality to her fair skin, the flawless delicacy of her features. Her makeup was heavily applied, creating dark, smoky accents around her eyes while her
lips were colored a deep red. It made for a very sultry combination. Grant swallowed back a rise of desire. She appeared
almost vixen-like. "Hal would never forgive me if I didn't
make it up to you," he said, hoping to capitalize on their mutual acquaintance.

As though she understood Grant was harmless, Kinsley
acquiesced. "Dinner will be fine, thank you."

Opening the door, he waved her ahead of him. "After
you."

As he followed her inside, the stark heat of the interior
flushed through him, mingling with the hot shards of want
coursing through his veins. He stood beside her as they waited for the host and the scent of her perfume practically swallowed him whole. Exotic and entirely feminine, it smelled
expensive, nearly as expensive as her clothes. Grant knew a
thousand-dollar coat when he saw one, and Kinsley's was at
least that, maybe more. Did she pay for it herself, or did her
father's money afford her the luxury?

"Good evening, Ms. Fairchild," the host greeted.

Grant raised his brow. Was she a regular here? As a frequent diner of Adele's himself, he was surprised he didn't remember seeing her.

"Good evening, Luke." Glancing over her shoulder, she took the initiative and requested a table for two.

"Certainly. May I take your coat?" he asked, proceeding to remove it from her shoulders without waiting for a response, then looked to Grant. "And yours?"

Handing over his jacket, Grant took the coat ticket for the two items.

Gathering a couple of menus, he said with an easy smile, "Right this way."

Grant noted the man's obvious pleasure. Without her coat, Kinsley's silken black sweater outlined the contour of her body, revealing ample breasts and narrow waist. About the same age as Kinsley and equally good-looking with his chiseled features and sandy blond hair, their host made Grant feel like an old man as he followed them through the restaurant. As usual, Adele's was packed. Normally he opted for a seat at the bar but not tonight. Seems Kinsley had connections. Either that or a standing reservation.

Pulling out a chair for Kinsley, the young man saw to her first and then Grant, handing each their napkin and a menu. "Your server will be right with you," he informed them.

Kinsley smiled. "Thanks, Luke."

Watching the kid go, he asked, "You come here often?"

She nodded. "It's one of my favorites."

"I'm surprised I haven't seen you before."

She shrugged a shoulder. "It's a busy restaurant. Lots of people coming and going."

"Yes," he said, unable to stray from her face. Kinsley was an incredibly beautiful young woman. Smart, passionate, she was a bit young for him, but in another time and place, he wouldn't mind a quiet candlelight dinner with her. Adele's would certainly suffice for the occasion with a dimly lit interior that screamed romance. But, Grant reminded himself, he was here on a mission. He wanted to find out what Kinsley knew about the bombing.

Taking the short menu in hand, Grant scanned the half dozen specials and decided on the chicken. He'd prefer a juicy steak, but it was against doctor's orders. Fish and chicken and lots of vegetables were the new mainstays of his diet, despite how badly he could taste chargrilled red meat on his lips. Or venison. The game meat served in Colorado was second to none, not to mention the staple of his diet when he first moved here, but a few trips to the hospital had convinced his taste buds otherwise. "So," Grant began, setting the menu aside, "Hal says you're a friend of Lisa's."

Gazing at him over her menu, Kinsley nodded.

"Nice girl."

Kinsley didn't reply but instead continued to peruse the menu at leisure. Grant looked around the restaurant, checking for familiar faces, not exactly sure why. Many tables were occupied by couples, most others were four tops with one large party of eight seated in the center of the restaurant. The noise level was at barely constrained polite levels. Adele's wasn't a large establishment, but a popular one, with bar conversations overflowing into the dining area.

Recognizing no one, Grant returned to Kinsley and mulled over how to begin. Diving right into the meat of his investigation was probably inadvisable. No sense in sending her antennae up too soon. "You have some passionate supporters," he said. Since the confrontation from earlier wasn't a secret, it seemed like a good place to start.

A hint of smirk touched her lips. "That was an interesting move you performed on Norell."

"Norell?"

"The friend of mine you twisted into an arm lock."

"He should have listened to my warning," Grant replied coolly, walking on fragile ground. The man was her friend, possibly his bombing suspect. "People mean what they say."

"He was in the right to defend me."

"I wasn't there to assault you."

Kinsley arched a brow. "You weren't? Funny, but I seem to remember it differently."

"I was there for answers."

"In the future, you should be more careful how you go about seeking those answers."

Holding onto her gaze, Grant was struck by the strange sensation that *he* was the target of investigation and not the other way around, as though she were tempting him to reveal himself.

A waitress breezed up to their table. "Good evening and welcome to Adele's"

Absorbed in his own thoughts, Grant didn't acknowledge her.

"May I offer you something to drink?"

Grant watched as Kinsley ordered, "I'll have a glass of Caymus."

"Make that two," Grant said, admiring her taste in wine. The Cabernet was abundant in textural tannins yet soft as velvet.

The young woman wrote nothing and instead, folded hands behind her back, smiling modestly. "Have you had a chance to look over the menu? Any questions?"

"I'll have the Zucchini and Heirloom Tomato Lasagna," Kinsley replied.

Grant followed. "I'll have the chicken."

"Excellent selections. I'll be back with your wine and some spring water."

As the woman walked off, Grant turned to Kinsley. She was staring at him, hard, and he realized at once that his order placed him in enemy camp. "I hope you don't mind, but I'm not a vegan."

"I didn't expect that you would be."

Grant felt the jab of insult, but merely smiled. "I read your blog today." The revelation seemed to surprise her. "You've done a nice job with it."

"As in, it looks pretty?" she asked, her tone mocking.

"As in, the content is impressive. You make some good points."

After a moment's hesitation, she replied, "Thank you."

"I don't agree with them all, but you've articulated your position well. You should encourage your friends to follow your lead. Use words, not bombs."

Kinsley snapped off a smile. "Are we back to that again? I certainly hope you didn't invite me to dinner to accuse me and my fellow activists of a crime. If you have, I assure you, I have better things to do."

"No." He shook his head. "Though it seems odd, doesn't it? That an explosion is set in a fur shop around the same time as a group of animal activists known for such activities are in town?"

Kinsley stiffened.

Chapter Seven

Kinsley shook the sudden chill from her shoulders and considered her words carefully. This man was no fool. He had clearly seen her on the surveillance video from the fur store, a consequence she had prepared for yet nonetheless found unsettling. An ink bomb carried totally different consequences than a fire bomb. Thank God, Gabby had coincidentally decided to wear her white jacket this morning. It had offered the perfect on-the-spot defense for Kinsley. If not a complete defense, it had given her plausible deniability during the heat of the moment.

But this man didn't appear to be placated. Instead, it felt to her as if he were probing for answers. Setting her hand on the table, she outstretched her fingers and replied, "The activists are in town to protest the unconscionable expansion of this ski resort, an expansion that is being executed without regard for the animal habitat it will destroy. We are here to protect innocent lives, not set fire to the town."

Grant smiled. "Are all your fellow activists of like mind?"

"Yes," she lied, angered by the fact that Sebastian had compromised her integrity. "If you read my blog, you should understand my stance on the subject, better than most."

"Some of your pictures are pretty disturbing."

"What's *disturbing* is the abuse suffered by animals at the hands of people."

Grant nodded, but said nothing. The waitress appeared with their wine, and a small pitcher of water. As the two faced off across the table, the young woman filled their glasses with water and silently made her departure.

Encircling a hand around the base of her wineglass, Kinsley drew the half-filled glass near the center of her place setting. She didn't drink. She wanted answers first. "You said you went to my website. Did you watch the videos?"

"I did."

"And you can still order chicken?" Kinsley asked with unmasked disgust.

"I'm sure Adele uses only free-range chicken."

It was true. Adele took great care with the food she served, the animals she used to create her menu. But still. Giving a market to the industry only lead to more demand, more commercial food sales—sales generated from an industry completely indifferent to the animals it butchered.

"Not all of us are vegan," he said, stating the obvious. "Some of us enjoy our protein. Native Americans used to live on this land, eat the wildlife. It's the way nature works. Bears eat animals. Lions eat gazelle. Fish eat other fish. Is it the meat you object to, or the method? Because I see no reason why a man can't hunt and fish and enjoy the meat of his labor."

As she brought the wine to her lips, the intense bouquet of dark chocolate, sweet tobacco and vanilla soured in her nostrils. Her appetite for a nice meal had dwindled, just as it usually did when thinking of slaughtered animals. It riled her to no end that people had no regard for the well-being of the animals they ate. Dogs and cats they cherished. Cows and pigs they butchered.

Vegan was the only compassionate choice. "I understand people hunt and eat their wild game," she replied evenly. "Some even go to great lengths to use the hide and other parts of the animal, as opposed to wasting them, but that's not what we're talking about here. I'm talking factory farms, barbaric slaughter, inhumane conditions... You said you went to my website. You should know precisely what I'm referring to. You cannot justify these conditions, under any circumstances, during any time in our history. Frankly, I'm surprised you can put a piece of meat in your mouth after watching just one of the videos posted on my website."

"I'm sorry." As if he understood how pathetic she found his apology, Grant looked her straight in the eye and said, "I'm not here to criticize your stance on animal rights or your choice in lifestyle."

"What are you here for?" she asked, shocked by the quick edge to her tone. Kinsley was not a rude person, but something about this man bothered her. He had an ability to irk her which was unusual. With most people she could simply flip a switch and turn off her emotional reaction but not with him.

"I'm here," he responded calmly, "because a good friend of mine has lost her business. Her fur store was destroyed, her inventory ruined, and I'd like to help her find out who's responsible."

Nerves zipped Kinsley's stomach taut. "And you expect me to give you that answer?"

Pausing, he wedged his gaze squarely into hers. "I believe you're in a position to know."

"Because I'm against the use of fur as a wardrobe choice?"

"Because you associate yourself with people who might be blinded by ideology and think their position justifies the means, including the demolition of a fur store. You clearly seek to establish change through the proper channels. Others do not."

Kinsley brought her glass to her lips and sipped. This man was like a pit bull. If he had his way, there was no doubt in her mind she'd be sitting in a jail cell for what she did. *What Sebastian did*, she mused bitterly. *This was Sebastian's fault*, not hers. "I'll keep that in mind," she replied, unsettled by his piercing stare. *And I'll keep an eye out for you*, she added silently.

Lifting his glass, Grant shifted gears and proposed, "How about we try to enjoy dinner." He raised his wine above the table. "To friends with opposing opinions."

Friends. Is that what he considered her now?

Staring into his dark brown eyes, eyes that simmered in the evening light, Kinsley felt a surge of ambivalence. While he clearly posed a threat to her, she couldn't help but be drawn to his looks. He had to be over forty, yet it was clear he hadn't lost his virility. The way he had handled Norell this afternoon had been impressive. And he wasn't bad-looking. On the contrary, the gray at his temples combined with his broad shoulders and lean build set off by the black mock turtleneck gave him an air of strength and sophistication. It was a combination she found quite attractive. But friends?

That might be pushing it.

"What do you say?" Grant's gaze relaxed into pleasure and he winked. "Humor me?"

Startled by the swift change, Kinsley thought perhaps an evening of benign conversation wouldn't hurt. Maybe it would even dissuade him from making the connection between the bombing and her, if she could charm him with banal conversation about her travels, her friend Lisa, her father, Hal. The danger had passed. As she had intended, her face had not been revealed on the surveillance video. If it had, he would have nailed her butt to the wall. But he hadn't. She'd used gloves, successfully managed to conceal her identity, leaving him no way to assign her the blame for the bomb. The bomb Sebastian switched on her. Kinsley was still mad at him, but should she let it ruin her evening?

Shaking the hair from her face, she summoned her best smile and said, "Friends." Until this dinner was over and they went about their separate lives, she mused and spiced her grin with a dash of flirtation. Grant Powell would enjoy a lovely evening with the very woman he was looking for while she savored the private victory of elusion.

But as dinner was served, Kinsley found herself captivated by him in very real ways. Grant was unlike most successful businessmen she'd met. Despite his age advantage over her, he wasn't controlling or assuming, patronizing of her work or belief system. Unlike her father and his associates, Grant seemed genuinely interested in what she had to say. Even when he disagreed. It was unusual, and refreshing. Titillating, if she allowed herself to go there. But she wouldn't, no matter how comfortable she felt around him, she had to remember that he could mean serious trouble for her.

Grant finished a bite of risotto and chased it down with a swallow of water. "Do you find many businesses around here that cater to a vegan lifestyle?"

"With regard to food, most definitely. Adele's is the perfect example. She uses only fresh, local ingredients and creates incredible gourmet meals with them. Like this lasagna," Kinsley remarked, cutting into it with the edge of her fork. "The pasta is made from spinach, while the sauce is completely vegetarian. And when you think about it, with delicious food like this, there's really no reason why people should eat anything other than vegan."

"How about protein?"

"That's a misnomer. It's always the first thing out of a meat-eater's mouth in defense of their choices, yet entirely inaccurate."

"How so?" he asked, slipping another bite of chicken into his mouth.

Kinsley inwardly cringed, but steeled herself to the reality that not everyone had jumped on board with an animal-free lifestyle. That would take time, and she was a woman with patience. Persistence would win this race. "Legumes, soy, tofu, nuts and seeds...even mushrooms and broccoli. They're all great sources of protein and all your body needs for an adequate supply. They are rich in the essential amino acids your body requires and are much easier to digest. Much better than red meat and chicken. Even fish. If you knew the amount of poison in their flesh, you'd never eat another one."

"Why don't you tell me," he goaded, and Kinsley didn't know whether he was ridiculing her or sincerely interested. Thus far he'd seemed the latter. Had the tide turned?

"The levels of mercury in fish have been well-documented. It's not a secret that consumption of fish carries a risk. And when you think about it, the idea of fish swimming around in pools of their own feces is disgusting."

"What about wild? I saw one of Adele's specials included trout."

"Research has shown that elevated mercury levels in Colorado's fishing waters impact a trout's olfactory response, which in turn can harm its ability to feed, navigate, and reproduce."

"Not enough mercury to kill me."

"So you're content with depleting the natural resources of the Colorado River? Harming the delicate ecosystem?" Kinsley shook her head and took another bite of food.

Across the table, Grant chuckled.

The sound grated on her. Swallowing, she asked, "Something funny?"

"No." He shook his head. "Nothing at all. I just think someone like you should funnel their energy into something more productive."

"Someone like me?" Exactly who did he think she was? And was he calling her blog unproductive?

"You're obviously a smart woman. Why not take your smarts and use them to create a line of clothing, one that is sustainable and non-animal?"

Kinsley gaped at him.

"You obviously enjoy nice things," he said. An unexpected flash of desire entered his gaze as he raked it over her person. Admiring, sharp, Grant was suddenly looking at her with the telltale mark of lust.

Kinsley's heart kicked. It felt like a bolt of lightning had struck between them.

"Why not create a fashion empire any vegan would be proud to wear?"

"What?" Kinsley asked, aware of a slight flush of warmth at her neck and chest beneath her sweater. She reached for her glass of wine. She hated to feel clueless, but where was this coming from?

"Beautiful women should have beautiful cruelty-free clothing, shouldn't they? Why not give it to them?"

Swept off balance by the spark in his eyes, the stunning suggestion—coming from him—she replied, "There are plenty of clothes out there suitable for a vegan lifestyle. Cotton, linen, nylon, polyester…"

"How about your shoes?" Grant briefly touched his gaze to the table to imply a glance at her boots. "Faux leather, I presume?"

"Of course," she snapped. Kinsley didn't need animals for food or clothing.

"Do they hold up like real leather?"

"They hold up fine."

"Have you ever considered inventing a material that would?"

"Excuse me?"

"Have you ever considered creating a decent pair of boots, the type that would hold up like the real thing yet make vegans proud to wear? You know what they say—need is the mother of all invention." With a small smile, he added, "That's gotta be tough—to be a well-dressed woman and not be allowed to wear leather?"

He had a point. Most synthetic materials used to mimic leather and suede were of poor quality and design. It had always been one of her pet peeves. Where did a woman find strappy high heels without resorting to leather? Or winter boots. Shifting her feet beneath the table, Kinsley hated the pair she had on, the fit and craftsmanship so far beneath her standards it almost embarrassed her to wear them. She loved the refined look of Salvatore Ferragamo or Hermès. They were the perfect fit for her narrow feet with the most elegant lines and refined stitching, but they were leather. Exquisite, but wholly inappropriate.

Recalling the last pair of boots she'd owned, the cells in Kinsley's brain began to spark. It would be nice to have a pair of boots that looked like leather, and wore like leather, but were not actually leather. The ones currently on the market lacked not only the luster and supple quality of leather but the durability. It was definitely a hole in the market. Fixing on the concept, she dialed into Grant. Maybe he was on to something.

"Have you ever seen any on the market?" he asked.

"Yes and no." Shifting in her seat, Kinsley leaned forward. She was intrigued by the direction their conversation had taken. He wasn't trying to tell her she was silly for refusing to wear leather. Instead, he was taking a subject she cared about and putting a new spin on it. Kinsley couldn't remember the last time someone did that. "There are synthetics on the market," she admitted, "but most look plastic and wear the same. I've seen a few good designs in Europe but nothing here."

He grinned. "Do you make it a habit to shop in Europe?"

Kinsley paused. She didn't want to come across as some kind of jet-setter with nothing better to do than shop, but the truth was, her mother and she did make an annual excursion to Paris and London for clothes. "My parents travel abroad twice a year. Occasionally, I join them."

"Next time you should consider it a research trip. Take a look at your favorite products and create a line of your own to sell here, in the States."

It wasn't a bad idea. Not a half bad idea at all, she thought pleasantly, absently swirling the wine in her glass.

"You might even set up shop here in Silver Creek. Seems to me you have a built-in customer base."

"True. There are a lot of eco-minded people in this area."

"So long as you have the capital to stick it out for a season or two of low sales, you should be set."

"I've seen very few slow seasons in Silver Creek. Visitors are growing in number, not declining." Hence the resort expansion, she thought wryly.

"My friend who owns the fur shop might disagree. This explosion couldn't have come at a worse time for her. After the slow economy, she doesn't have enough cash reserves on hand to stay afloat. Insurance won't cover the retail value of her inventory, so it looks like she's going to pack up and move back home to Italy."

Kinsley's spirits slumped. Setting her glass down on the table, she mumbled, "That's too bad."

"Yes. Imagine someone hacking into your blog, compromising subscriber information, members' identities, scaring off your advertisers and all without your knowledge." Grant frowned and Kinsley felt the brunt of his sadness like a sledgehammer to the back. "You'd be pressed pretty hard to pick up where you left off, not without a huge investment of time and money." Cradling the crystal bowl of his wineglass, Grant's previous pleasure drained from his voice. "It's not fair."

Kinsley didn't know the first thing about this woman Grant spoke of, but if someone hacked her blog and destroyed her revenue stream—forget fair, she'd be furious! Sharing a moment of sympathy with him, she uttered, "You must care a lot about her."

"I do."

"Is she your girlfriend?" Kinsley asked, despite herself.

"No. Just someone who matters to me."

For a second, Kinsley almost wished Grant was talking about her.

In the wake of his spiel about starting her own line of fashionable vegan shoes and clothing, Kinsley had almost begun to believe that the two of them were becoming friends. Two friends brainstorming an amazing business venture. Gazing into intelligent brown eyes, windows to a sharp mind and generous heart, Kinsley felt a bit deprived. Grant seemed like a good man to have in your corner. A man who stood by his friends with a fierce loyalty, strong enough to propel him to challenge a stranger and nearly wind up in a physical confrontation because of it. Was he sure this woman was only a friend?

"Giovanna is a good person," Grant said quietly. "She worked hard to come to the United States and start her own business. She deserves better than a trip home with her tail between her legs because some fanatic decided she shouldn't be selling fur coats to women who want them and are willing to pay good money for them. This is still a free country. Capitalism is the engine of our economy. If people want to buy and wear fur, leather, they should be allowed. If activists want the practice to stop, they should appeal to their congressmen and women, not blow up the businesses of law-abiding citizens."

Exhaling a tight sigh, Kinsley realized they were back to square one. Grant was a businessman who put money before conscience. And his friend. If this Giovanna had enough money to open a store in Silver Creek, enough money to move back to Italy when the going got tough, then she wasn't hurting that badly. She made a choice. People made choices.

Tapping her gaze to Grant's empty plate, Kinsley realized he would never understand the need for a vegan diet, a vegan lifestyle. Because he chose otherwise. He would never understand why a woman like her did what she did. Because his was a different mindset. For a moment, Kinsley had allowed herself to be lured in by his talk of making a difference on a commercial level, on a very personal level, and maybe she still would.

On her own terms. As she did everything. Sebastian was on notice. Next time he thought it would be cute to switch her device, he'd better think twice. Kinsley Fairchild was not a woman to double-cross.

Chapter Eight

Whipping the plush blankets from her body, Kinsley rolled out of bed, her feet sinking into thick carpeting of her hotel room as she stood. Running fingers through her hair, she pulled it from her face, securing it behind her head with a cotton tie from her nightstand. She couldn't stay in bed another minute. Between dreams of explosions and images of runways in New York crowded with lithe women modeling her new clothing line, Kinsley was restless, eager to get to her computer. For her, blogging sometimes took the form of venting, relaxing her when she was wound up over an issue, only this time the issues were about her.

Could she really begin her own clothing line for vegans? Her own shoe line?

Why not, right? Wasn't that her standard reply when someone questioned her ability to get things done? Why not? *If you can dream it, you can do it.*

For as long as she could remember, Kinsley loved that saying by Walt Disney. It spoke to her about the incredible potential life had to offer, that *she* had to offer. Disney created a theme park from nothing but the thin air of his imagination. Since then, the attraction had gone global, enduring time through movies and stage and music, and it all began with a mouse.

Need is the mother of all invention.

Smacking tongue against her teeth, Kinsley was struck by a sense of morning dry mouth and detoured for the bathroom. Jarred by the cold marble flooring beneath her feet, she cursed herself for not remembering to set the floor heaters. Moving quickly to a bath rug, Kinsley tapped the light on, grabbed a glass of water and filled it from the faucet. Staring into the mirror, she groaned. Her eyes were slightly reddened with the faintest of dark circles forming beneath them.

"Ugh," she muttered. No sleep. It would kill a girl's complexion.

At the moment, she didn't care. No one had to look at her and she had more important things to do than scrutinize her appearance. Like work through the ideas ricocheting through her brain.

Need is the mother of all invention. Kinsley had heard the quote before. She didn't recall where or when. Hadn't much mattered at the time. She hadn't been in a place to mentally receive the information. But when Grant uttered the words last night, they made complete and total sense. Women shouldn't have to suffer through poor or limited fashion choices simply because they opted for a vegan lifestyle. They should be able drape themselves in the most luxuriant of materials, soft and supple, durable, and of top-quality.

Growing up in San Francisco with a mother toting an unlimited expense account, Kinsley had become accustomed to expensive clothing and jewelry from a very young age. She'd worn only designer labels, carried only designer handbags. It wasn't until high school that she decided the shirt on her back had to go, the shoes from her feet—fancy designer labels or not.

Unfortunately, her options now consisted mostly of cotton and canvas and rubber. Not exactly the sexiest of choices, and Kinsley wanted to feel sexy, attractive. She wanted to feel beautiful, as all women did. But she'd made a choice to take the high road and spare the lives of animals in her quest for fashion. From her diet to her makeup and everything in between, Kinsley swore off the products made directly or indirectly from animals. She refused to give a market to companies that would exploit the innocents. If she didn't fight for those without a voice, no one would.

Kinsley didn't choose to be an activist—or the ridicule that sometimes accompanied the nametag, the odd stares, the naysayers. Activism chose her. It wasn't an easy path, but it was a worthy one. Flicking off the light, she went to her computer and flipped open her laptop. Within seconds, she found her fingers typing in the words "vegan designer clothing" into the task bar search engine then hitting enter. Pages popped onto her computer screen, ranging from the standard mega sites trying to capitalize on her key words to smaller sites offering images to lure visitors into choosing their link.

Kinsley clicked on a photo, a pair of what looked to be leather boots and was instantly transported to a website predominantly covered in pop-up ads. She clicked back and searched through several other sites on the list until finally a professional-looking webpage displayed on her screen.

Kinsley frowned. It was basically a T-shirt site with a few accessories made from cotton and faux leather. There were others—Herbivore Boutique, Eco-couture, Vegan Design—but nothing that rose to the level of quality she desired. Sitting back in her chair, Kinsley pondered the possibilities. Could she do it? Could she fill the niche and design her own line?

She had a savvy sense of fashion. Her mother had always said she had great taste. But to design a line of her own? It was one thing to pick from a selection of other designers' creations. It was entirely another to design one herself. Where would she begin? Did one sketch the clothes, and then hire someone else to create them? Did she have to draw specifics, first, or could she work with a team of designers to make them? And where would she produce them? The States, China?

Question after question fired through her brain, the list growing until Kinsley became overwhelmed. There were so many options, so many considerations, it was almost paralyzing to think through them all. Who could she call to get answers? Advice?

Help. Kinsley cupped a hand to her forehead. Because the more she thought about it, the more the idea found its home. Grant was right. She should design a line of clothing for vegans, but one any non-vegan would be proud to wear. It would create the change she sought—real change—from the inside out. The key ingredients were choice, quality, availability.

Restaurants like Adele's and The Oasis were already doing it with regard to food. Supermarkets and specialty stores were offering more and more animal-free selections. It made sense the next frontier should be clothing. What we eat, what we wear, how we live... Who knew? Maybe home furnishings could be next. Once she found solid leather alternatives, the possibilities were endless!

Maybe she could ask her father. He knew a lot of people. He was bound to know someone who could help give her direction. Resentment scraped at her heart. At least it would be something he would approve of, a nice, good old-fashioned capitalistic business venture instead of her activism. Kinsley hated that her parents disapproved of her job, but they did. Her mother not so much as her father, but even she didn't understand the importance of her daughter's blog. Referred to it as a hobby and not a career. Thankfully enough high-paying advertisers thought otherwise, and appreciated her six hundred thousand "uniques" every month. It was like customers walking through her cyber doors, their eyes valuable when it came to strategically-placed advertising.

Her cell phone erupted with music. Kinsley leapt from her desk, wondering who would be calling her at eight in the morning. Plucking it from the nightstand, she answered, "Hello?"

"Hey, Kinsley."

"Sebastian."

"Did I wake you up? You sound grumpy."

"No. Actually I've been up for hours."

"Get lucky last night?"

Irritated by the snicker in his voice, and the fact that the man she had dinner with last night posed a direct threat—a threat caused by Sebastian—she was in no mood for jokes. "What do you want?"

"Ex-*cuse* me..." he replied.

"It's early and I have a busy day." She walked over to the window of her hotel room and pushed aside the heavy curtains. It was snowing again, the streets crowded with bulk-ily-dressed skiers heading for the slopes, their outerwear a rainbow of varying colors and styles. "Was there a reason for your call?"

"Yes," he clipped. "Are you still meeting me at the commissioner's office this afternoon?"

"I planned to, why?"

"No reason. Just confirming."

For the third time? He'd asked her twice yesterday. Did he think she'd forgotten? "I'll be there," she replied, but her instincts began to hum. There was something Sebastian wasn't telling her, as though he had another agenda. "Has there been a change in plans?" she asked.

"No, not at all. You know me, I'm obsessive when it comes to details."

Controlling was more the word she'd use, but let it go. "I'll be there. Four o'clock."

"Four o'clock," he replied, an uptick in his tone. "Oh, and do try and catch up on your beauty sleep, Kinsley. We want to put our best face forward for the commissioners to-day."

"Goodbye," she snapped, and ended the call.

Sebastian could be a real moron when he wanted to be. Just because he was obsessed with his appearance and the appearance of those around him didn't mean everyone else was. Marching back to her computer, she shook the pessi-mism from her mind. On second thought, the fact that people cared how they looked worked to her advantage. Depositing herself into her chair, Kinsley slid the mouse across the desk and typed into the search engine. *Clothing manufacturing.* Her blog post for today could wait.

Three hours later, Kinsley had amassed ten pages of notes, a compilation of thoughts, concepts and themes for what she wanted to do, how she wanted to do it, including where she could ultimately take her business. As she glimpsed the time in the lower corner of her computer monitor, impatience swelled. She needed to get her daily *Wildlife Neutral* post written. She needed to meet with her group for a protest outside the main resort hotel where several of the investors were staying. She needed to formulate her thoughts for the meeting this afternoon. But all Kinsley wanted to do was research this new venture.

The hotel phone rang, but she ignored it. Anyone who really needed to speak with her knew her cell number. Scrolling through the screens of photos, her mind latched onto one in particular. Pausing, she scrutinized a woman wearing a gorgeous black coat and boots, the material sleek, elegant in its simplicity. Beneath the coat, the model wore a black camisole over jeans. Admiring the ensemble, particularly the boots, Kinsley pondered whether or not she could find engineers or scientists to help her develop the new material she had in mind. They could send a man to the moon, create a phone the size of a credit card, surely they could devise a faux-leather product.

Her mind buzzed with possibilities and she made some more notes. Her cell phone rang and glancing at it, she groaned aloud. It was her mother. Now what?

Grabbing the phone, Kinsley answered, "What's up, Mom? I'm kinda busy at the moment."

"Good morning, sweetheart. I was calling to check in. What are you doing?"

"Research." Purposefully vague, Kinsley didn't want to give her mother any material for conversation. She had no time to entertain familial chit-chat.

"You're so dedicated, darling. I really admire that about you."

Kinsley grunted under her breath. Clicking on a thumbnail photo on her computer screen, she peered at the hot pink strappy sandals, the cork wedge heels. Those were cute. Zooming in on the image, she checked out the sole, the imperceptible stitching on the narrow straps. Nice. Who was the designer? Scrolling down, she read the name. Never heard of him.

"Kinsley. Are you listening to me?"

"What? Yes, of course, mother." Saving the webpage to her favorites, Kinsley glanced up from the screen. "But like I said, I'm kinda busy right now."

"I want to know if you'll respect your father's and my feelings and not take part in the protest today."

"Why?" Other than the fact her mother disapproved of a public display of discord in general, what did she have against Kinsley standing around with a group of protesters? It wasn't like it was the first time, and it certainly wouldn't be the last. "What gives?"

"Your father and I will be with some very important clients. It wouldn't be appropriate for them to see you with the others."

Appropriate for whom? Kinsley almost asked, but she didn't need to. She already knew the answer. Her parents. It wouldn't be appropriate for them to have to explain why their daughter was vocally protesting against their investment.

But it was old news. Kinsley was an adult, her parents were adults. Both sides were entitled to their own opinions. "I'm sorry, but I can't *not* show up." These were her people, her supporters. And Sebastian's. They'd worked tirelessly to get here, put a lot of effort into planning, paid money to travel here... Kinsley couldn't abandon them now because her mother felt uncomfortable. Kinsley Fairchild was head of the organization, and it was her job to lead them in protest. "I won't make eye contact, I promise."

"You know it's more than that, Kinsley. We have a reputation. *You* have a reputation."

One you're ashamed of, she thought bitterly. *One you don't want your business associates to know about.* Tamping back old resentment, she replied, "I'm proud of my reputation, mother. I'm sorry this expansion has put us on opposite sides of the same issue, but I can't back down simply because you and Dad will be uncomfortable."

Get over it, she wanted to add, but wouldn't. Her mother wasn't anti-activism. On some points she even agreed with Kinsley. A vegetarian convert after watching some of the videos Kinsley had posted on her blog, her mother was horrified to think people would treat animals so cruelly. And she understood how the market worked. Without demand, commercial poultry farms and cattle ranches would go out of business and the abuse would stop. It was the goal, anyway. The more people who turned away from eating meat, the less meat would be raised and slaughtered. Her mother was on board with that ideology. She just couldn't stomach the protests.

"I'm asking as a favor to me, Kinsley. Your father has worked very hard on this project. I don't want anything to ruin it for him. And you know he's made every effort to respect the wildlife in the process."

The wildlife he was pushing back by the mere expansion of the property? How many ski runs did one resort need? How much money did one corporation need? Certainly Kinsley could admit that Palmer International did a fantastic job when it came to recycling and clean-up. They even offered an educational "nature hut" for tourists to learn about the habitat around them. However, their mere "footprint" in an area where people didn't belong was over the line. People and animals had to coexist and share the same planet, but people didn't have to get greedy about it.

Though tempted to search more photos on her computer, she closed out the screen. Her mother's phone call reminded Kinsley that she was behind schedule. She had yet to update her blog, and she was expected at the square after lunch. "I'll keep a low profile, okay? No shouts, no signs, I'll be a silent partner in this afternoon's protest." Besides, she and Sebastian had a meeting, which meant she couldn't stay long, anyway.

"Thank you, sweetheart. I know your father will appreciate it."

Kinsley blew a fallen strand of hair from her face. *I'm sure he will.*

Mid-morning, Grant hung up the phone with his friend in New York. Yes, he knew of a quality bag manufacturer located in the city, but no, most of the clothing manufacturing was done overseas. No surprise there. In order to compete these days, price points reigned king. If you couldn't make a garment for pennies on the dollar, you couldn't sell it to the retailer giants. Kinsley would be working with upscale buyers giving her more wiggle room on price and cost, but the fact remained, cheap labor was a key component to the equation, and in New York City, labor didn't come cheap.

But it was a start. Walking into his office, he dialed Hal's number. A vegan fashion line was a perfect fit for Kinsley; the ideal pairing of intellect, passion and personality. Passionate about the vegan lifestyle, possessing the experience and taste to know what wealthy women wanted, gorgeous enough to model her own line, and probably the access to enough money to back any venture she chose to pursue, Kinsley could take his idea and make it her own. As her blog suggested, she was smart. Sharp.

Grant hoped she'd be excited to hear what he'd learned. Waiting through rings, he indulged in a private smile. Who was he kidding? He wanted to see her again for purely personal reasons and this was his in.

"Hello?"

"Hal, its Grant."

"Hello, Grant. How are you?"

"Great. Listen, I was calling to get the number for Lisa's friend, Kinsley." Met with silence, he continued, "I had dinner with her last night, and we discussed some potential business opportunities for her. I spoke with some of my contacts in New York this morning and wanted to relay the information."

"What kind of business opportunity?"

"Manufacturing." *Keep it simple. Don't elaborate. More doesn't need said.*

As though he understood, Hal replied, "Sure. I'll text Lisa and get it for you."

"Thanks."

"So I can assume you're satisfied she's not mixed up with that explosion next door to you?"

No, but that was beside the point. Grant still believed she could uncover the name of the culprit, if she had a mind to, but they weren't there yet. Maybe a few more dinners and they would be. Either way, he wanted to see her again. "I don't think she planted the bomb," he confessed bluntly. "I jumped to conclusions, that's all."

"Good. I'll get back to you in a few."

"Appreciate it."

Ending the call, Grant walked back into his store and, taking a deep breath, released the tension he hadn't realized had been building in his chest. Was he tense or nervous?

But that was silly. Nerves—at his age? Shaking the sensation from his mind, he laughed at himself. It might have been a while since he dated a woman like Kinsley Fairchild, but that didn't mean he couldn't jump back into the saddle if he wanted to. His first wife had been gorgeous. His second one too, though she'd been a money-grubbing gold-digger bound and determined to drive a stake through his heart and snatch the gold from his possession. She nearly managed to do both, draining his bank account while stressing him to the point of a heart attack.

But that was eight years ago. He was over it and his heart had survived, thanks to the help of his cardiologist and outstanding medical facilities. His wallet survived, thanks to a savvy attorney. *Make her go away*, Grant had told him. *Make it all go away*. Ever since, he stuck to shallow relationships and friendships. They were much easier to manage.

Expelling a sigh, he thought about Kinsley. She wasn't exactly money-grubbing material. Her blog was packed with advertisers, some surprisingly big names, and her parents were loaded. But they were on opposite sides of the social spectrum when it came to this activism of hers, not to mention almost half his age. Would a woman like her be interested in a man like him? And if so, Kinsley struck him as the type who went all in, not the kind that dabbled in superficial sex.

Grant's cell phone bleeped, signaling he had a text message from Hal. Glancing at the screen broadcasting Kinsley's cell phone number, his heart squeezed. *Guess we'll see soon enough.* With no one in the store, a flurry of snow falling outside, Grant stowed himself away in his office and dialed her number. If anyone entered, he'd hear the door chime.

She answered. "Hello?"

"Kinsley. It's Grant Powell."

"Hello..."

He didn't like the trepidation in her voice, but it was to be expected. She didn't know him. He wasn't one of her activist friends. It was understandable she'd be wary. "I've been thinking about our conversation last night and decided to call a few friends of mine in New York. After making some inquiries, I have a couple of names of manufacturers you might like to contact to help get the ball rolling. That is, if you're interested in pursuing the idea."

"I don't know what to say..."

"Nothing, really." Grant realized it might have been a bit presumptive of him to call, but thought she seemed genuinely intrigued by the idea last night. Could have been the wine talking. They'd had three glasses apiece. "I thought you might like to have the information."

"I would. Very much."

Her softened tone sent ripples of pleasure through him. "Good." Relaying the information he'd learned, the names and numbers, he asked, "Let me know if there's anything else I can do to help."

"I will, and thank you." She paused, before adding, "It's funny, but I was thinking about this very thing when you called."

"Really?"

"I have to admit, your idea has captured my attention."

"I'm glad." Seizing the moment, he asked, "Would you like to have drinks this evening? Maybe we could do a little brainstorming and hash out some ideas."

Grant tensed when she didn't respond. Had he overstepped?

"How about Adele's...at six?"

Releasing his tension in a stream of breath, he smiled into the phone. "See you there."

Grant ended the call feeling more excited than he had in months. He tapped a glance to a photograph on his wall, a beautiful landscape of mountain wildflowers with a backdrop of the bluest sky in the world. It was a photo taken by Hal's daughter, Lisa. The girl was talented, which is why he had several more like it posted throughout his store, framed images he sold on her behalf. Visions of the fresh-faced brunette inundated Grant's mind and for a moment, he felt weird about the prospect of getting together with Kinsley. She was Lisa's age, a young woman Grant had come to think of as his own daughter.

He didn't kid himself. While he wanted to help Kinsley with her new venture, a larger part of him wanted to get close to her. Hal was probably right. Kinsley didn't have anything to do with the bombing at Giovanna's and shouldn't be counted as guilty because one of her activist friends had. He shouldn't hold the actions of her associates against her.

Pushing up from his desk, Grant filed away the rationalization. Kinsley liked his idea. She'd been thinking about it when he called. Did those thoughts include him, personally?

Chapter Nine

"Moose not money!"

"Animals need space too!"

As she promised, Kinsley hovered in the background, allowing the others in her group to take their enthusiasm to the crowd, shouting above the rhythmic plodding and scratching of heavy ski boots over cobblestone streets. They'd started during the peak lunch hour and continued until the skiers made their way down the mountain. In an hour, the meet and greet for resort investors would begin, putting the protesters front and center, equating to prime "stage time."

Kinsley mingled quietly in the rear. Rubbing gloved hands together, she tried to warm the chill permeating her fingers. February was cold, the coldest time of the year when even the best sportswear was tested to keep every inch of her body warm and comfortable. But at least the sun had come out. Colorado weather was an odd creature. Forecast to snow all day, the front had hit the range and changed direction, or broke apart. Something. Because instead of a whiteout, there was nothing but blue skies overhead. Being a meteorologist must be a pretty cush job. Didn't matter whether your forecast was on the money or not, you could blame it on Mother Nature and call it a day.

"Deer not dollars!"

A shudder gripped Kinsley's shoulders and she began to pace. Skies might be blue but the air was cold as ice. *Keep the blood flowing*, she mused. *Warm. Stay warm*. As she changed direction, she spotted her parents walking down the street. Her mother was elegant in a full-length cream-colored parka and matching hat, long dark waves of hair cascading past her shoulders, gold bangles at her wrist shining in the midday sun, her lips glistened deep red. Kinsley's father opted for his standard black wool overcoat and jeans, his thick head of black hair combed back, his face slightly round, the signature appearance of a wealthy man accustomed to fine dining and high living. Together they looked every bit the part of cosmopolitan world travelers, here for a two-week ski vacation before jetting back home to Paris or the Alps, or somewhere equally luxurious. They didn't appear to have a care in the world, other than how much money they would make on this investment, how much could be allotted to her mother's favorite charities.

Beside them walked a couple equally well-dressed, slightly older in age. The man appeared similar to her father but with thinning hair, while the woman posed stark contrast to Kinsley's mother, boasting platinum blonde hair coiffed behind her head, and tucked neatly into a hat. A brown fur hat—Kinsley noted unhappily—that matched her ankle-length fur coat. Fiery images from the other night flashed in Kinsley's mind as she stared at the woman. Women like her were the antithesis to the cause. They were everything Kinsley detested because they wore the hide of an animal as a luxury, as though no suffering had occurred during the taking of its fur. And for what? So they could wrap it around their body and strut through town like some imperial queen?

Kinsley turned away, anger tying a knot in her stomach. She needed to keep a low profile. She had promised her mother that she would not stand out, and she would honor her word, no matter how much effort it took to keep her mouth shut when the woman passed.

As her parents and associates neared, Kinsley took a step into her crowd of protesters, using Norell's massive body to block her from view. The blonde woman swiped the group with a disapproving look. Smug, conceited, she walked with an air of superiority swirling around her head like a crown. Kinsley wanted to spit. She wanted to throw ink on that woman's coat and spit in her face.

"Kinsley!'

At the sound of her name, she looked up the street to see Lisa Richardson waving wildly. Her friend was dressed in a bright red Patagonia and jeans, her shiny brown hair straight and loose around her shoulders. Heartened to see a friendly face, Kinsley waved back. Lisa was a kindred spirit. Though she didn't take an active role in any of the protests, she understood the cause, believed in what Kinsley was doing. Spirits lifting, Kinsley thought maybe she could talk Lisa into hanging out for a while. It had been a few weeks since the two last sat down and chatted.

The thought was short-lived. Walking alongside her, McIntyre Walsh came into view, a group of skiers detouring around them as he slowed. Lisa and Walsh were officially dating now, and while Kinsley wanted to like Lisa's boyfriend, she couldn't. Not because he wasn't a decent person, but because he was a hard-nosed Marine type. A judgmental, hard-nosed Marine type who made no secret of his feelings with regard to her career choice. But what did she expect from a man who'd made a life in the mountains surviving off the kill-of-the-day?

Kinsley shook the animosity from her mind. It was unproductive. She'd focus on Lisa. Her friend. "Hey, Lisa," she said gaily as the two strolled up. Ignoring Walsh, Kinsley asked, "What brings you out today?"

"My dad. He invited Walsh and me to the meet and greet." Lisa cast a glance beyond Kinsley, her gaze quickly retreating as she made the connection between protest and event. "Um, he's inside. Your dad invited him to come and mingle."

The guilt in Lisa's voice bothered Kinsley. It was as though she thought Kinsley would be upset with her for crossing enemy lines. "Your father isn't investing in the expansion, is he?"

"Oh no, nothing like that. Just a show of support for a friend," she said, breathing easier as though the revelation plucked her off the hook. By her side, Walsh was a statue. A very good-looking statue—with his deeply-tanned skin and pale green eyes—but a statue nonetheless. His muscular build was accentuated by a snug-fitting chocolate-brown turtleneck, and his jeans fit like they were tailor-made, underscoring some of his better features. Kinsley had to admit Lisa had found herself a stud. Between his eyes and his body, his was a stunning combination. So what if he was as unfriendly to Kinsley as an incoming missile. He adored Lisa and that's what mattered.

Hesitating, Lisa gnawed on her lower lip. "You're not mad that I'm going in, are you?"

"Of course not." Lisa wasn't a part of the resort, nor would she give them money if she had the money to give. She was going because her father invited her. She was a nice person that way, her motives pure and uncorrupted. It was one of the things Kinsley liked best about her pal. Lisa was a good person, through and through. "Probably some great food and wine inside," Kinsley offered lightly.

Lisa brightened at the "out" she had given her. "Probably."

Walsh remained silent, his penetrating gaze reminding Kinsley of a hungry snake. He would have no words for her, not unless she challenged him in some way, as she'd been known to do in the past, and then he'd let loose. But then again, Walsh was a man of few words in general. He was a Marine. A meat-eating, animal-hunting Marine who disregarded the feelings of anyone but himself and those he cared about, which made for a very short list. If you were part of his team, he'd defend you to the death. If you weren't, he'd just as soon step over your dead body.

Placing a hand to the small of Lisa's back, Walsh nudged her toward the direction of the restaurant. "Wanna have dinner later?" Lisa asked, pausing to wait for a reply. "Walsh has a business meeting and I'm running solo."

"Can't." Slanting an eye toward Walsh, Kinsley wondered what kind of business he could have. As far as she knew, he was a part-time associate with the police department. Since when did they meet at night? Shaking the supposition from her thoughts, she replied, "I have a meeting myself." Staring into Lisa's brown eyes, it occurred to her that Grant Powell was a friend of her father's. How would Lisa feel if she knew Kinsley was meeting with him for drinks? A tingle of excitement skirted through her pulse. Ostensibly it was for business, but Kinsley knew full well things could easily take a turn toward the personal. All she had to do was say *yes*.

"Maybe another time," Lisa replied easily.

Kinsley smiled. "Definitely."

As she watched Lisa and Walsh make their way inside, Kinsley's thoughts were divided between them and her upcoming date. *Date.* The more she thought about it, the more the idea intrigued her. She'd never dated a much older man before. She didn't imagine it would be much different than dating men her own age, other than the physical aspect, of course.

Nerves fired and popped. Would she get physical with Grant Powell? And if she did, what would it be like? Would he have the smooth hand of experience, or the tired moves of age? Would it be good? Kinsley suppressed a grin. Something told her she might find out, and soon.

Reeling her thoughts in, she tamped back a swell of desire and refocused her attention on the protest at hand. There would be time enough later for thoughts of Grant Powell. Right now, she had a protest in process. "Moose not money!" she shouted, breaking out into the open.

An hour later, Kinsley and Sebastian were directed to the commissioner's office by a secretary. Through the slice of open doorway, Kinsley glimpsed a middle-aged man wearing shirt and tie sitting behind a desk covered with white papers. As the secretary opened the door, Kinsley's gaze involuntarily went from desk to man, his chin and neck enormous in size, and protruding over his collar in pinched fashion.

"Mr. Bowling, your appointment is here."

The man didn't bother to stand. "Great. Have a seat," he said, his gaze landing squarely on Kinsley. "What can I do for you?"

She exchanged a knowing glance with Sebastian. The man probably hadn't done the first ounce of homework with regard to their meeting. Did he even know who they were? Why they were here? Rejecting the seat offered, she realized this meeting would be short and to the point. "We're here about the Silver Creek ski resort expansion."

The man nodded. "Yes, yes, great project. The council is leaning toward expediting the approval process."

Ice streamed through her veins. "We're here against the expansion."

"Against it?" he returned, confused.

"We feel the public should have a say in the matter."

"We held the third of four public hearings last month. I don't recall any objections to the proposed expansion from any members of the public," he said, pudgy lines forming across his brow. "I believe everyone is in agreement with the project going forward."

"That's because they weren't given all of the pertinent facts," Kinsley countered.

Mr. Bowling straightened in his chair. "What pertinent facts are you referring to?"

"The facts with regard to the displacement of wildlife."

"We're not displacing any wildlife," he defended, a slight blush rising to his cheeks. His gaze darted between the two of them. "In fact, the developer has assured us that every consideration is being made to minimize the environmental impact."

"Have they submitted a proposal in writing?" Kinsley demanded.

"Er, no, not yet." The man slid a pen from one side of his desk to the other. "But I assure you it will be included with the final paperwork. Here in the state of Colorado, we take our conservation seriously. Maintaining our pristine environment is of the utmost importance, and we will not allow our mountains to be injured in any way."

Kinsley crossed her arms over her chest and stared down at him. "So you have no such commitment."

"Now listen here, young lady. This is an important decision for our town, and we will take every measure to ensure the developers are doing their part." Abruptly, his gaze narrowed, as though it suddenly occurred to him who they were. And it didn't please him. "I remember you now. It was you and your bunch that tried to disrupt the meeting."

"We tried to shed light on the reality."

The bulge of skin at his collar flushed bright red. "By shouting down the town council?"

There were always a few in the crowd who felt the need to yell. They weren't her people, but rather some students who had apparently driven in from Boulder for the meeting. Where they overflowed in passion, they lacked in restraint. No matter how well-versed one was with the issues, sometimes it was better to fly under the radar than paste a target on your back.

However, staring at the man across the desk, Kinsley understood that cool heads didn't always prevail—on either side. This man seemed as though his decision had already been made and was offended they would question his position.

Glancing to her side, Sebastian goaded her with a mocking smile. *Told you it was a waste of time.* Irritated, Kinsley turned to the commissioner. "Has the town made any allowance for conservation easements? Any effort to mitigate the construction impact on nesting birds and mammals? Legacy and old-growth tree cutting? Have you considered the adverse effect this will have on the watershed? Are you requiring *any* concessions by the developer?"

"Yes, yes, all good points that will be sorted through in good time," he answered, as though placated by an opening where he could provide positive answers. He shuffled papers around on his desk but offered no more.

"So you have nothing at the moment."

"It's in committee."

Ignoring the obvious lie, she asked, "When does the council make its final vote?"

Folding his arms over his desk, the commissioner replied, "Not for another few weeks. Until then, we'll have plenty of time to fine-tune the final plans to a mutually beneficial arrangement. I assure you, Miss, Miss..."

"Ms. Fairchild."

He smiled. "Ms. Fairchild, I assure you we've worked and re-worked this proposal to ensure we're not only making sound business decisions, but most importantly, environmentally responsible ones. We take our stewardship of the land seriously and applaud your enthusiasm in this matter."

Kinsley heard a spiel rattled off by a man already counting the influx of tax revenue. Sebastian might be right. The only way to stop the development would be to stop the developer from pursuing it, or the business community from supporting it. Releasing a tight breath, she grew uncomfortably warm in the stifling dry heat of the office. "It is our understanding that the Lynx habitat study has not been fully evaluated at this time. How do you expect to move forward with a vote when the Forest Service has specifically requested you hold off on any such decisions until it determines its findings?"

The commissioner choked out, "That study is not an enforceable part of the process."

"Why not?" Kinsley knew for a fact the Forest Service had written a letter to the council regarding the expansion, even claimed two members of the council were on their side in the matter. How could this man sit here and dismiss it as a non-entity in the debate? An animal's survival might depend upon it!

"Look here, Ms. Fairchild. All interested parties have had their chance to be heard, and now it's in the council's hands to make a decision. We don't need anyone stirring up trouble or trying to derail this project." He scowled. "This expansion means a lot of jobs and economic growth for this community. Why are you willing to jeopardize that for an animal that will simply move on to greener pastures when the development comes to pass?"

Kinsley didn't hear a word he said and instead wondered how much of the money would end up in his pocket. Probably a hefty chunk, she mused bitterly. After all, money greased palms and melted principles. Even if this man did care about the animals or the environment, people caved when presented with large sums of money. It was the American way. "I think the Forest Service will disagree," Kinsley stated, covering the defeat she felt inside. It was clear he had made his decision, but hopefully the United States Forest Service had not. They, too, had a say in this matter and Kinsley planned to do everything within her power to see that their say was "no."

Turning abruptly, she stalked out of the office without another word. Sebastian trailed her as she strode down the hall and out the front door, the cool air biting against her cheeks. She cursed under her breath and stopped in place. *Friggin' bureaucrats.*

"Told you it wouldn't work," Sebastian crowed close to her ear. "They don't give a damn about the environment. They couldn't care less about your precious animals. Did you see the look in his eyes when you mentioned the Lynx study?" Sebastian scoffed, steam mushrooming from his breath as hatred inked his black eyes. "The guy is a joke. Like I told you, the only thing his kind understand is money."

Kinsley couldn't disagree with his assessment, only hated that he was right. Blood ran hot, coursed through her body despite the cold gripping her face. She nailed her gaze to Sebastian's and said, "And it will be his greed that takes him down."

Chapter Ten

Savoring a sip of the Châteauneuf-du-Pape Cuvée Réservée, Kinsley decided Grant definitely knew his wine. Eighty percent Grenache with mostly Syrah and Mourvèdre making up the balance, this particular vintage had earned a place in her parents' wine cellar—a cellar that didn't house anything less than collectible status. And this vintage made it in for good reason. The wine was intense, she mused, indulging in the flavors bursting across her tongue. It had a rich core of crushed plum, blackberry paste and braised fig and an excellent choice that would pair wonderfully with her Portobello Mushroom Risotto.

After pouring two glasses, the waiter had replaced the decanted wine to the table and left Grant and Kinsley alone. Dinner would be out shortly. Handling the glass by the stem, Grant brought it to beneath his nose and inhaled deeply. Emitting a groan, he said, "Nothing like the French when it comes to wine." Swirling the burgundy-colored liquid in his glass, he remarked, "Southern Rhone is one of my favorite regions."

"Agreed." Lifting her glass to savor the aroma, Kinsley said, "My parents and I toured several wineries in the area one summer, and I absolutely fell in love with the wine."

"It's beautiful country."

A smile formed on Kinsley's lips as fond memories swam through her heart. "It is, and so unlike California with the ancient castles scattered about the landscape."

Grant grinned. "I know what you mean. During my last visit, a friend of mine and I took a bottle of wine and picnic lunch and hiked up to one of those castles. We scaled a wall, set out our lunch and enjoyed a bird's eye view of the countryside with some of the best bread and cheese on the planet.

And of course, wine." Tipping his glass toward Kinsley, he winked. "It made for a fantastic afternoon."

She bet it did. Climbing up to an old castle, spreading out a picnic lunch...it sounded spontaneous, adventurous, fabulous by its sheer excess. Wondering if the "friend" had been a female, Kinsley imagined Grant would be fun to travel with. The two of them shared similar tastes, traveled in similar circles. It wasn't a stretch to imagine they would make perfect travel companions.

"So tell me about your conversation with Gianni," Grant said, easing back into the business of conversation. "Was he able to help?"

A rush of excitement flushed through her as she recalled the conversation. Gianni had more than helped, setting her up with enough names to get an entire manufacturing business up and running in no time! "He was *amazing*. The man has more contacts at his fingertips than the entire phone book of Silver Creek!"

Grant chuckled. "I thought he might be a good place to start."

"Start? The man has me producing shoes, handbags, accessories and a complete clothing line—and that's before I've penciled the first design." She shook her head. "Gianni is sheer energy."

Grant nodded. "He's a bulldozer, no question. He'll get you faced in the right direction and with the right people in no time. People you can trust." Pausing, he added, "And that's a pretty tall order in the manufacturing business. Any business, for that matter."

Kinsley felt the stab. She was certain Grant hadn't intended to plunge the knife of accusation, but unwittingly, he had. Trust. Something she had managed to side-step with his accusation regarding the fur store bombing. Though her dodge didn't change the facts. She was guilty. Nerves scattered across her chest. If not guilty by intent, she was guilty by association. Sebastian was the real culprit. He had intended to blow out the window. "I don't even know where to begin," she said vaguely, her mind divided between thoughts of the past and thoughts of the future. "It's all so overwhelming."

"How about beginning where every savvy entrepreneur does? Fill a need. Make products women will want to wear, while at the same time, feel good about their purchase. There has to be a lot of women who would support a cause like yours. Make it easy for them by allowing them to show their support with the clothing on their backs. Make it attractive, stylish." Grant smiled, the gesture more pleasure than encouragement. "I'm sure you'll have no problem in that department. Just look at you, you're style in motion."

Enjoying his flattery, she replied, "Yes, well, I'm not sure exactly how many people that will amount to. I mean, I don't want to spin my wheels catering to a sliver of the population. Where's the profit in that?" she asked.

Producing clothes was a great idea in theory, but once she got to thinking in more detail, the numbers didn't add up. Vegans were few and far between. It was a lifestyle that had yet to go mainstream, and Kinsley didn't want to be holed into a small niche market. She wanted to go big, go "global," as Grant had so aptly suggested. How could she do that with a minority market share?

"You create the need in the market, and then you build the desire."

"That simple, huh?"

Grant beamed. "For you, yes, I'll bet it'll be that simple. With every product you sell, you tell your story. Print a summary of your story on every label that's attached to your products. Let people know the importance of buying non-leather, non-animal. People want to feel good about themselves, their decisions. And those decisions include buying decisions. Like you, the current void in the market could simply boil down to a *lack* of selection. There's nothing on the market they can buy or would wear, so they don't. That's where you come in. Give women what you believe to be ethically conscientious choices and make them look good. I'm telling you," he insisted, raising his glass, "you will be an overnight success."

"How can you be so sure?" Grant didn't know her. He didn't know what she was capable of, or incapable of. How could he stand so adamantly behind her and insist she would be successful?

"I told you. I've read your blog. You could convince an Eskimo that ice was toxic for him, if you wanted to, and he'd mortgage his igloo for a plane ticket to Florida. And I can tell by looking at you that you have good taste in clothing."

Grant's gaze lingered, and Kinsley flushed beneath his appraising gaze. Hot and fluid, he was now a man seeing her as a woman. She took another sip of wine, swallowing the healthy gulp over a flutter of pulse.

"With you at the helm, women all over the world will choose vegan fashion because it makes them look good, and feel good." Setting his glass on the table, Grant formed his hands as though looking through a lens as he peered at her. "I can see it now...they'll be proud to wear a Kinsley original."

Grant went on to describe a friend's business, a luggage dealer out of New Jersey who swore by Gianni and his staff. A stickler for details and an absolute genius when it came to production design requests, the man vowed Gianni could make anything happen. Trick handles, secret pockets—if a customer could think it, Gianni could create it and mass produce it like no one else. Lifting the decanter from the table, Grant filled his glass halfway and said, "He will love working with you."

Kinsley didn't know about that, but she was feeling pretty good in the spotlight of Grant's attention. He treated her like the competent businesswoman she was, asserting this venture was totally within her realm of possibility. Listening to him go on, Kinsley liked thinking of herself in his terms. Currently the CEO of *Wildlife Neutral*, there was no reason she couldn't parlay her talents into the field of fashion. With regard to the cause, it would be a lateral move. Her goals would remain the same, her actions instrumental in inciting change. Real change—the kind the average person could wrap their head around and actually support. Clothing was a tangible way to connect people with the animals. By reducing a person's reliance on leather and animals for their clothing, Kinsley could reduce the demand for animal farming and subsequent slaughter. Think of the lives she'd be saving, the suffering she'd be eliminating... Emitting a nervous laugh, she said, "You're a pretty ambitious guy."

"Aren't you a pretty ambitious woman?"

Staring at him, she replied automatically, "I am."

Ambition was her middle name. It described her core. At twenty-six, Kinsley Fairchild had skyrocketed to the top of her chosen profession after only five years on the job. It was an impressive feat, one she felt no compunction about touting. She was ambitious, competent. Smart. There was no reason she couldn't do anything she set her mind to do.

"I think you can do it."

Holding him in her gaze, Kinsley felt a tumultuous shift in emotion, as though she were swimming through the waves of the Pacific Ocean. The possibilities were endless. Tides could change, people could change, and *she* could be the reason why. Sure, Grant made it sound easy, but she understood the realities of starting a new business, the challenges, the risks, and she knew how to write a business plan. It would be an uphill battle. Competition would be cutthroat. She didn't kid herself. Nobody but she and Grant would want to see a new player enter the field. It would only detract from the existing base of customers. But Kinsley liked that Grant believed in her. It was like having both a coach and a cheerleading squad tucked away in her back pocket. If she never drew the first sketch, manufactured the first stitch, or sold the first purse or pair of shoes, she was glad to know he thought she could do that and then some.

After almost two hours spent eating, drinking and talking, dinner ended much too soon for Kinsley. After brainstorming ideas for her new venture, Grant entertained her with stories of his adventures. Skydiving, heli-skiing, auto racing, the man was a veritable daredevil willing to try anything to quench his need for thrill. The closest she had managed to thrill-seeking was a hot air balloon ride over Napa Valley. It had seemed daring at the time. Floating in a basket over a thousand feet in the air had scared her half to death! She couldn't imagine doing half the things Grant had done, yet part of her suddenly hungered to do so, to feel the excitement of pushing the limits, to thumb her nose at death. But could she actually drive at speeds of two-hundred miles an hour? Could she jump out of a plane?

The mere thought gave her goosebumps.

Rising from his seat, Grant extended his arm to her, asking in the softest of tones, "Shall we?"

Kinsley nodded. Pushing up from her chair, she slipped her hand through his bent arm and allowed him to escort her from the table. Gliding through the restaurant, it felt like they were a couple, as though she'd known Grant far longer than the two days they been acquainted and had simply shared another wonderful evening together. It was odd how their paths hadn't crossed before. With both fans of Adele's, and Grant being a friend of Lisa's father, it seemed they should have run into each other at some point. As they paused for their coats, she caught a fresh drift of his cologne. Was it possible she had seen him but overlooked him?

Turning as Grant slid her coat onto her shoulders, Kinsley pulled the collar snug and laughed in the quiet of her mind. Probably because older men had never been on her radar. Until now. Kinsley stepped out into the night, her facial skin zipped taut by the brisk temperature. "I swear the temperature must have dropped twenty degrees since we went inside."

Grant chuckled. "We were in there for quite a while. I think Adele was concerned we wouldn't ever free up her table."

Kinsley gazed into Grant's face, his dark eyes dancing with tease. He knew full well Adele would hold any table for

Kinsley. She was like family to Lisa and Hal. And Hal, well he and Adele were practically married. "You don't think she'd want us to go anywhere else, do you?"

"Didn't matter if she did. Adele's is the only place worth eating at around here."

"And vegan friendly."

Grant winked. "My pesto was delicious."

Kinsley smiled. She wondered if Grant had ordered the vegetarian dish for her sake, or had he really wanted pasta for dinner. Either way, she appreciated his choice. It made the dining experience all the more pleasurable. "Adele has her own greenhouse herb garden and probably made it fresh this afternoon."

"It was phenomenal."

"Healthy, too."

Pulling her arm through his, he tucked it snug against his body. A mischievous grin lit up his face. "Why, Ms. Fairchild, are you implying I need to watch my diet?"

"We should all watch our diet, don't you think?"

"Actually, I should." Patting his chest, he said, "My ticker isn't what it used to be."

Caught off guard by the comment, she asked, "Are you okay?"

Grant smiled. "Would it matter to you if I wasn't?"

Kinsley stammered, "Of course it would. I mean, sure, I don't want anyone to be ill." Was he? Did he have a heart condition? But he seemed so full of life, of vigor, his naturally-tanned skin flushed with healthy red tones. He couldn't have any health problems, could he?

"I'm fine, but I like your concern." And in that moment, Kinsley felt a current move between them. Charged with a desire built up through the course of an intimate dinner, she knew their feelings were mutual. Grant was feeling the attraction she was feeling. "May I walk you to your car?"

"I don't have one. I mean..." She brushed the hair from her eyes and clarified, "I'm staying here in the village."

Grant lifted a brow in surprise. "You have a place here?"

"I'm leasing one of the hotel residences here in town. It makes better sense to be close during the protests."

"I suppose so." After the mildest awkward pause, he asked, "May I walk you to your place?"

Nerves bubbled up in her breast. "Sure. That would be nice."

The two fell into a slow, easy rhythm, Grant keeping close by Kinsley's side as they walked through the town. Wide cobblestone streets were black-red, heated from underground and always clear, snow or shine. They passed boutiques and restaurants, open areas for gathering, including the occasional children's play area. Most businesses were adorned with colorful lights and bows. Massive evergreens were drenched in twinkling lights of green, red and white. Christmas was over, yet the appeal was enchanting and thus continued. Tonight was crisp and clear and alive with tourists, men and women walking without hurry. Casual was the dress code, with most men in jeans and ski jackets, some of the older men sporting overcoats. Women were dressed to the hilt with fur-trimmed jackets, emblazoned gold insignias, ornate gold and diamond jewelry dangling from their ears. It occurred to Kinsley that she and Grant blended in seamlessly with the tempo and flavor of the village nightlife. To passersby, they probably looked like a couple on vacation, one more in a town of many.

If only they knew. She smiled inwardly. She was more like the enemy, the covert operative cavorting out in the open. If she had her way, the ski resort would be shut down entirely and these people left with no place to go.

"Where do you normally live?" Grant asked casually.

"My parents have a place a half-hour from here. I have a condo in the valley, but I usually stay with them when I'm not traveling."

"You travel often?"

"Yes. I like to keep my finger on the pulse of the organization."

"How about a trip to New York City? Do you see that in your schedule anytime soon?"

Kinsley smiled. She liked his persistence. "I think it's worth a visit, sort of like a scouting trip."

"I lived there for almost twenty years and would consider it an honor to show you around. If you wouldn't mind the company, that is."

A blast of excitement splintered through her veins. She'd love it. "Sounds like a good idea, but can you get away? This has to be high season for you."

"It is, but I've hired the best assistant manager in town. He can hold things together while I shoot out of town for a few days."

As she glanced askance, the short black curls of hair against his smooth-shaven skin sent ripples of desire through her. A quick trip to New York City with Grant sounded enticing. Very. And if this new venture worked out as well as he envisioned there would be more trips—to New York, L.A., Chicago—she'd want to hit all the major retailer hubs in the country, maybe slip in a few side trips with him. Who knew what adventures they could discover?

When they arrived at her hotel, Kinsley felt a pinch of longing. The evening was coming to an end and while she didn't want him to go, she wasn't quite ready to invite him up to her room. It was too complicated, too dangerous. She wanted to be certain she was in the clear on the fur store bombing before she allowed herself to imagine spending more time with Grant. Serious time, meaningful time. Grant, lingering beneath an ornate lantern on the side of her building, seemed to be waiting for her to take the lead.

"Thank you for dinner," she said, her voice low and deliberate. "I really had a lovely time."

"Me, too."

"Will I see you tomorrow?"

"I hope so. What's your schedule?"

"I have a protest scheduled for the afternoon." But after the dismal results of her and Sebastian's meeting with the

commissioner, the two of them needed to regroup and strategize going forward. "As for now, the rest is up in the air."

His gaze darted back and forth across hers. "Can I call
you?"

She nodded, her breath steaming between them in visible
release. She'd hate him if he didn't.

A smile tipped the corner of his mouth. "Maybe I can
steal you away for lunch."

"Sounds good to me."

Grant took her in his arms and without warning, his
mouth covered hers in a kiss, soft and seeking, as though im-
mersing himself in the taste of her. Swept off balance, she felt
a quick ache wind low in her belly. Grant smelled good, felt
good. Perfect. Pressing into him, she surrendered to the warm
flood of desire surging between them. It was piercing cold
outside but not where their bodies touched. Where they
touched, it was warm, like they were fused together as one
body.

Pulling back, Grant murmured huskily, "That was nice."

Kinsley's brain was a jumble and she hummed softly. It
was more than nice—*it was amazing.*

Grant reached down and threaded her gloved fingers
through his. "I'll call you," he whispered.

Consumed with the touch of him, the connection, she uttered, "Yes."

Gazing at her as though he knew he had her right where
he wanted her, Grant winked. Without another word, he
turned to go and Kinsley reluctantly released him, trailing his
figure down the bustling lane as her hand fell to her side.
Lingering, she placed a hand to the heavy metal bar of the
entrance to her building. Grant paused at the corner. With his
face caught in the soft glow of lamplight, the two shared a
smile that hung buoyant in the air between them, before he
disappeared from sight with a small wave.

Kinsley sighed. Cold clung to her exterior but couldn't
touch the heat stirring inside her. Heady feelings swirled
through her like a drug as her mind swung like a pendulum

between the present and the future. Visualizing Grant's face, recalling the supple feel of his mouth on hers, Kinsley felt like tomorrow couldn't come soon enough.

Chapter Eleven

Sitting at a corner table in an over-heated café, Kinsley sipped her coffee. Hot liquid fired through her senses, stimulating her brain to action, despite its lack of focus. It had been another restless night, but this time, images of her and Grant had intermingled with visions of models and runways. The scent of fried eggs and bacon saturated the air, the restaurant near empty as most skiers were making their way up the mountain by now. A few women lingered by the hostess, dressed for a day of shopping or sightseeing in an assortment of sweaters, jeans and boots.

Across from Kinsley sat Sebastian, buttering a croissant in meticulous fashion with a slim silver knife. He wore a silk black turtleneck that fit his body like a glove, his red jacket slung over the chair-back behind him. More concerned with his "standing" in the world than anything else, Sebastian didn't ski, didn't partake in any sports as far as she knew. On the verge of failing to block the expansion, Sebastian seemed more determined than ever to win.

"So what's our next step?" Kinsley posed absently. They were here to strategize, to plan, but her mind was elsewhere.

"Action." Setting the knife on the rim of his plate, he said, "We give them a sense of urgency."

"How do you propose we do that?"

"By getting their attention."

Kinsley exhaled heavily, disappointed with his response. Falling back on the protest tactic felt like failure. She had hoped the mention of the Forest Service study during their meeting yesterday afternoon would have thrown the commissioner off his game, but it hadn't even fazed him. It was as if he knew what she knew—the Forest Service would allow the project to move forward despite its likely adverse impact on the habitat of the lynx and other animals because they were splitting hairs. The Forest Service was splitting environmental categories into "high-quality" habitat and "low-quality" habitat. Kinsley had it on good authority that the decision to approve the expansion had already been made by the Forest Service, citing it was possible for the animals to coexist with the ski resort. The animals had other areas to roam, and the benefits of expansion far outweighed the harm to the environment.

It was crap. The Forest Service was caving, pure and simple. They were capitulating to the power of money. Kinsley suspected their approval had been sweetened with an influx of money to their pet projects, but she had no proof. Her investigation had only turned up inferences, distant linkages between a recent large donation to some of the more costly Forest projects and the decision to approve the expansion. Drawing a sip from her mug, she cringed as the coffee singed the tip of her tongue. Wait until one of the wild cats attacks a tourist, she mused. Then we'll see how well the government thinks the two groups coexist.

"The whole system is corrupt," Kinsley spat.

Sebastian raised his croissant to his lips. "Exactly why they deserve what they get."

She assumed he was referring to the miscellany of vandalism they had perpetrated, but ink spray and the like were tired campaigns against an institutionalized apathy. Protests did nothing but make the protesters feel like they were doing something. They didn't change anyone's mind. They didn't stop projects from moving forward. The developers would get their way and expand operations halfway across the mountain, displacing who knows how many animals, destroying hundreds of acres of sensitive ecosystems in the process because they would pay for the right to do so.

At least Lisa's toads would be spared, the majority of which existed higher than most lift chairs ascended. Some lived at lower elevations, emerging from their marshy habitat predominantly during summer, but it was doubtful any bulldozers would be blowing through water. Allowing her gaze to drift outdoors, Kinsley settled on the fall of snow. It seemed to mellow the landscape, casting the village in peaceful hues. Skiers schlepped past, hauling an inordinate amount of ski equipment to the slopes. Boots, skis and poles, every day it was the same. In the morning, a sea of people plodded up the mountain, and in the afternoon, a sea of people plowed down the mountain.

Skiers passed, dressed in brightly-colored jackets and pants, goggles strapped around their helmets, the skin around their eyes was stark white against a wind-burned tan. Kinsley thought they looked like an army of raccoon-eyed resort soldiers. Wealthy soldiers. Ski gear didn't come cheap. Lift tickets didn't come cheap. Add food and drink and lodging and it made for an expensive vacation, filling the resort owners' coffers with cash. Enough cash that they were nearly doubling their mountain presence within a dozen years of doing business.

Catching the gaze of a passing woman, her legs coated in black stretch pants, her body swathed in a waist-length matching jacket lined with fur, Kinsley didn't think the woman gave the first thought to the displaced wildlife the resort was causing. Animals were nothing more than a fashion statement to her, a material to keep her warm and looking good. With a scowl, Kinsley broke eye contact. There had to be a better way. She had to think bigger, broader. She had to seriously consider this idea of starting her own clothing line. It would equate to the kind of change she sought. Real change, tangible change.

Kinsley cupped the warm coffee mug within her hands and peered over the rim at Sebastian. Partner. Right hand man. What would he think about a change in tactic? "I'm considering a new venture," she said. The muscles in Sebastian's jaw jumped while he chewed, his eyes dark and hot and intent upon her own as he waited for her to elaborate. "I'm thinking about starting a vegan clothing line."

Taking a drink of orange juice, he stared wordlessly.

Kinsley stared back. Did he not like the idea? Did he think it foolish? "Well, what do you think?"

"Why?"

"Why what?"

"Why would you want to divide your attention by starting a clothing line?"

"Because I think it would be a great way to elicit real change for the movement."

"By getting women to dress up in non-animal clothing?"

Sebastian was mocking her. Grinding her jaw, Kinsley slapped back, "By inspiring women to choose clothing that spares the lives of animals."

"Don't waste your time."

Anger fired through her heart as she set her mug to the table with an unexpected thwack. "How is that wasting my time?"

"You're dividing your time, losing sight of the goal."

"The goal is to spare the lives and suffering of animals."

"The goal is to stop people from capitalizing on the hides of animals and eliminate the industry altogether."

"And how is my idea inconsistent with that mission? The way I see it, offering vegan clothing choices will eliminate the industry by giving consumers something else to fill their closets."

Sebastian's eyes became black slits in his creamy gold complexion. "You are losing focus by thinking that the clothing market is the only way in which animals suffer. *Wildlife Neutral* is working on a broader scale. We go after food, clothing, the entertainment industry. Why would you limit yourself to one facet of the whole?"

"I'm channeling my focus into one area where I can exact tangible change. Taking vegan clothing mainstream would eliminate countless slaughterhouses, furriers, farms. How is that not a positive?"

"You're thinking small. You need to remember the cause and fight across industry lines. You need to get serious."

"I am serious," she snapped. And she didn't care for his insinuations to the contrary. "If I can offer a viable alternative to the wool industry, countless sheep will be spared a cruel and gruesome existence. Cattle won't be raised only to be killed. Mink won't be skinned alive for their hides." Disgust rolled through her. "Rabbits, goats, leopards—the list goes on. Millions of animals would be spared, if one industry was transformed. The clothing industry. How does that not make total and perfect sense to you?"

"Capitalism is not the answer. It is the problem."

"You think I want to do it for the money?"

"Are you planning on giving the clothing away for free?"

"There is nothing wrong with the concept of earning a living. If I recall," she reminded, "you haven't had the first problem using the money I earn from my blog to fight for the rights of animals."

Sebastian glanced away. Kinsley knew he didn't like to see himself as dependent, but he was, financially speaking. *Wildlife Neutral* was her blog, her income stream. She was in charge, and he'd never shown the first qualm about using her money to travel around the country in high style as he fought animal abuse. Why should he care about the source? Blog or clothing line, both ventures shared the common goal.

"Using capitalism to our advantage is not the issue," she said. "It's a means to an end."

Sebastian took another bite of food, moving his gaze between her and the resort town outside their window. Snowfall was mounting in intensity, peppering the tourists with white flecks as they marched past. Kinsley could feel the wheels spinning in Sebastian's brain, the switches flipping, the wires tightening. He didn't approve of her desire to move beyond the blogosphere and into the brick and mortar of business. In his mind it would amount to taking refuge with the enemy.

Well, Kinsley wasn't the enemy. She was a leading voice in the movement, cutting-edge in her thinking and purpose. She didn't have to follow the tired old ways of doing business. She recognized the need to stay nimble, flexible. Her generation was more sensitive to the rights of animals. They were getting the message. They understood there must be an end to the abuse and suffering. Perceptions were changing, momentum shifting. The mood was turning in her favor.

Animal rights organizations were making progress, getting laws enacted. If they could minimize the radical wing of their movement and guide the mission down mainstream avenues, Kinsley believed they would draw more support—support they needed to effect change on a grand scale.

Behind his dark eyes, she could see Sebastian's mind was closed. He wanted nothing to do with her new venture. A radical at heart, he believed his way was the right way, the only way. It wasn't. It was an emotional appeal that incited passion, but made very little progress. If the general public dismissed animal rights activists as a bunch of nut jobs, Kinsley knew they would never reach their goal of zero animal abuse. *Animals should not be eaten, beaten, worn, experimented on, used for entertainment or pushed from their natural habitat. They should be allowed to coexist with humans on mutually beneficial terms.*

The more people Kinsley could convince of the same, the less likely that developers like Palmer International would be able to buy their way into ruining the natural habitat, driving animals toward starvation and ultimately, extinction. Local communities would rise up and say *No, enough. You may not endanger or hurt another animal in the name of business.*

Expelling her breath in a rush of futility, Kinsley stood. "Enough" was right. She'd had about all she could take of Sebastian at the moment. The man was pompous. "I'll see you this afternoon."

They were holding another rally, this time outside the ritziest hotel in the village, the one home to Lee Palmer and his investment guests. Hopefully her parents wouldn't be around, though it was a distinct possibility. A possibility that was neither here nor there. Until the rally, Kinsley had other important matters to deal with. She was scheduled to call

Gianni in thirty minutes. Excitement zipped up her spine. It was a call she wouldn't miss. She couldn't wait to hear what he had to say about her latest idea.

Seated before the desk in her hotel room, Kinsley answered the call from the New York area code on the second ring. Nerves sputtered in her breast as she said, "Kinsley Fairchild."

"Ms. Fairchild, Gianni Marche."

"Gianni, thank you so much for calling."

"It is my pleasure," he replied, his Italian accent rich and sultry, much too personal for a professional association. She'd since learned Gianni didn't draw boundaries between the professional and non-professional, rather spoke to people as if they were close, personal friends. "How can I be of service?"

"I have some ideas I wanted to run by you."

"Please, darling. Tell me your thoughts."

"I've been doing a bit of research and came across the possibility of using coconut shells and their husks to make clothing fibers. It's based on a technology that incorporates activated carbon derived from recycled coconut shells. According to what I read, over twenty billion coconuts are produced to support the food and cosmetic industry and their husks are tossed out as waste. If we could get our hands on some of that raw material, it would make for a great source of material for my vegan line of thermal wear. Have you ever heard of the technique?" Met by silence, she wondered if Gianni thought she was a crackpot. "The pore structure on the surface of the activated carbon creates a wicking effect for perspiration, removing it quickly from the skin while absorbing odor at the same time. I think it would be an excellent choice for winter wear."

Chuckling softly, he replied, "Grant has found an extremely rare gem, hasn't he?"

Kinsley hesitated. Gianni was talking about Grant? Was he not listening to her?

"I have not heard of this technology, but I have no doubt it exists. I know of one company that is using recycled plastic bottles and turning them into fleece coats. Why should coconuts be any different?"

"Really?" Kinsley was intrigued. Plastic bottles? Did they know what a huge service they were providing the earth? "How are they doing it?"

"They chop, grind and melt the bottles, then extrude them into polymer filaments which can then be turned into yarn. They use a machine to process the material to give it texture which in turn gives it the essential properties of stretch, softness, comfort."

Kinsley was stunned. How did he know so much about the textile industry? The man made luggage, not clothing. "Wow. It seems there are a lot of people out there with an eye for doing what I'm trying to do."

"I disagree! You are high fashion. Most of the products on the market currently are geared toward the sport industry. You will go for the *haute couture* woman, no?"

"Yes." Yes, that is exactly who she wanted to go after, though Kinsley wanted to include a mass-market line of affordable clothing as well.

"I would also take a look at spider webs."

Scribbling notes on a pad of hotel-embossed paper, Kinsley's hand froze mid-motion. "Huh?"

"Oh, yes. I've captured your attention, now, haven't I? A scientist has been working with spider webs, utilizing the most advanced technologies in the field to craft a material that is strong and pliable and soft as silk."

"Spider webs?" Images of the creepy animal crawled through Kinsley's mind.

Hearing the skepticism in her voice, Gianni replied, "I assure you the final product is elastic and very desirable. I can put you in touch with him, if you wish."

Once again, Gianni amazed her with not only the depth of his knowledge, but the extent of his contacts. Next, he was going to tell her he could get her a meeting with the President. A shudder raced through her. How awesome would that be? To have the ear of the one person who could carry her message out to the world like no one's business?

It would be incredible. Amazing. A dream come true!

Shaking the silly reverie from her mind, she centered on the task ahead. "Thanks, Gianni. For everything. If you could give me those numbers, I'd appreciate it."

"Not a problem. Can I hope to see you in New York some day?"

At the tease in his voice, Kinsley replied, "Absolutely. And maybe I can convince Grant to join me."

"He is putty in your hands, darling." Gianni made two quick kissing sounds and said, "Hold the line and I will put my secretary on. She will provide you with whatever you need."

"Thank you, Gianni." Holding the phone tightly in hand, Kinsley was more stoked than she had been in years. This clothing line was going to be a reality. She could feel it in her bones.

Chapter Twelve

"I'm doing it," Kinsley told Grant, toying with a chopped leaf on her salad, her appetite nonexistent. Silverware and glassware clinked in the back of the restaurant as waiters moved briskly between tables carrying plates laden with gorgeous food, every bit of it fresh, organic and vegan friendly. Kinsley had suggested The Oasis, one of her favorite restaurants in town, but food wasn't on her mind. Business was. "I'm convinced it's the way to go."

Dabbing the corner of his mouth with a white napkin, he agreed. "I think you're going to be a great success. What did I tell you? You're made for the clothing industry."

She wasn't so sure. "I'm already behind the curve." Staring at her plate of greens, she stabbed a cherry tomato with her fork, nerves pushing into her stomach. "There are a ton of companies in the business of using sustainable materials to make clothing, so I might be cast off into anonymity before I ever start."

"Nonsense. No one can ignore you. Gianni can't wait to meet you."

At his change in tone, Kinsley looked up. "What? You talked to him?"

"He called me this morning after he'd spoken with you. Said you were a winner, a real firebrand."

"There was no way he could have determined all that by a ten minute phone call."

"The man is sharp. He knows quality when he hears it." Grant's gaze softened. "Same as I know it when I see it."

While she enjoyed his compliments, Kinsley didn't want to be patronized. She wanted to be valued for her competence, not her looks. "We'll see. In the meantime, I have to admit, I'm excited about the prospects."

"It shows."

Holding Grant in her gaze, Kinsley felt a tug at her heart. It was nice to share her plans with someone who believed in her, someone who shared her enthusiasm. Sebastian's reception during breakfast had been cold, like an ice-bath to her spirits. She hadn't expected him to jump up and down like a cheerleader, but he could have at least seen the value in what she was doing and encouraged her. Acknowledged the impact it would have on the cause.

But it would have been beyond his capability. Sebastian was jealous. Insecure. He wanted the spotlight, but he didn't want to do the work it took to get there. He'd been riding her success for years now, and she had let him. "Why" she had let him, she couldn't answer. But she had. After their conversation this morning, it hit her. Her future was bright, but it was changing, a change that didn't include him.

But it did include Grant.

Warm feelings stirred the nerves in her belly. Deep and low, Kinsley had been thinking more and more about Grant. Had he been serious about wanting to join her on a trip to New York? She'd already scheduled two meetings with potential manufacturers, one in Massachusetts, one in New York. Would he come with her? Would they cross the line into the more intimate realm? "I'd like to meet Gianni," she said, a burst of nerves skating through her pulse. "Are you still interested in joining me on a trip to New York?"

"Absolutely," Grant replied, but something in his gaze shifted, as though she were asking him an entirely different question. "When were you thinking of going?"

"Next week."

Grant smiled, a swift pleasure registering in his expression. "I'll clear my schedule."

Her fork clanged loudly against the ceramic plate. "That quickly? Can you do that?"

A subtle challenge rose up between them as he posed, "Do you want me to go?"

"Yes," she stumbled, heartbeats firing in her chest, "I'm just surprised you can get away so easily."

"Where there's a will there's a way," he said quietly, dark eyes simmering.

Kinsley swallowed, realizing she'd just upped their relationship to the next level. She dropped her gaze but returned it quickly. The current of emotion flowing between them was unmistakable. A short trip to New York would mean more than a lunch or dinner date. It would mean intimacy, miles from prying eyes. Grant took a sip from his water, his gaze locked upon hers. He knew it. She knew it.

Grant reached over and touched a finger to the top of her hand and caressed her skin. Soft and delicate, the sensation electrified her senses. "It will be fun."

Fun. Kinsley smiled inwardly. She imagined it would be that and more.

"I'll show you New York's best side."

She'd been to New York a hundred times, shopping, dining, attending the theater. It always proved to be a good time, an enjoyable time, but with him, the city would take on a whole new light. She doubted Grant could show her a side of New York she hadn't seen, though she was looking forward to him trying. Seeing it from his arm, their hands entwined, their lips...

Kinsley laughed.

"Something funny?"

"No." Yes! Her ridiculous overthinking of their first romantic getaway was inane, yet she couldn't help herself. There was something about this man that made her want to get close to him. Very close. Withdrawing her hand from his touch, Kinsley forced her thoughts in a different direction. A more sane direction. Entertaining fantasies of Grant Powell would not serve any purpose. Not until she was prepared to do something about them, anyway. "What's on tap for the rest of your afternoon?" she asked.

"Oh, I don't know. I'm open to suggestion. How about you?"

Peering at him, she wondered if the man was reading her mind. Was he thinking the same thing she was? Reaching for her glass of water, Kinsley thought, probably. Most definitely. She was no neophyte when it came to men. She understood what consumed their thoughts. The fact that it was consuming hers was the new twist. But Grant was a good-looking man. Smart, sophisticated. She liked him in black, too, the turtleneck he wore fitted, flattering next to his salt and pepper temples. Any woman in her right mind would want to be with him.

Taking a healthy swallow of ice-cold water, she doused her distraction and stated, "I have a rally later today."

"A rally. Guess that doesn't include me."

She laughed at the sudden pout. "It can if you want it to!"

He grinned. "That would be funny, wouldn't it? A prominent businessman in town hooked up with the protesters?" Then, as though the full impact of what he'd just said hit home, she noted a distinct retreat in his gaze. The protesters had blown out the front window of a neighboring store. His friend's store.

Kinsley felt the blow. And while he didn't know she was responsible for the explosion, Grant had rightfully attributed the culprit to be one from her group. *One of her kind*. Stabs of regret punctured her heart. If Grant ever discovered it had been her, she wouldn't have to worry about becoming distracted by silly thoughts of romance and trips to New York.

Their relationship would be over.

In that moment, the realization buried her like an avalanche. One act stood between them. One moment, one rebellious show of defiance stood between her and the man she was beginning to have feelings for. Serious feelings. Tears pushed behind her eyes, but she forced them back. Kinsley could not reveal herself for who she was. She could not let on that she had picked up on his retreat. It would only draw attention to her and the protestors once again. And Sebastian, her resident bomb-maker.

Grant's gaze reached out to her. "You know, I'm not against your cause. I understand the debate over habitat and environment."

"On a theoretical basis."

"On a real basis. I could give up eating meat if it meant saving an animal from suffering."

"You could?" Kinsley asked, not fully convinced but intrigued just the same. It meant he was working to close the gap, the philosophical divide that would ultimately rise up like a wall between them, should they ever seriously entertain a relationship. Kinsley couldn't live with someone who wasn't a vegan. Tapping her gaze to his plate, an identical salad to hers, she asked, "Is that why you ordered a salad? Are you testing the vegan waters?"

"You want to say something about it?" he dared light-heartedly.

"No. Nothing except that it's a better choice."

"You're not kidding." Pausing, he waggled his brow like a mischievous kid. "Does it impress you that I could live without meat?"

"It does," she replied, meaning it more deeply than she had planned. "It's the first step to your recovery," she teased. "The next step is dairy."

"Oh, that's a tough one. I do like milk with my cookies."

"You eat cookies?"

"Doesn't everyone?"

Kinsley drew back in her chair. Actually, she couldn't remember the last time she had a cookie.

Picking up on her hesitation, Grant joked, "Please, tell me you don't have anything against cookies."

"I don't. Not really." Except they were made with butter and butter was dairy. But launching into a lecture was the last thing she wanted to do at the moment and instead replied, "Too fattening."

"You're probably right, there." Patting his stomach, he grinned. "I could stand to lose a few pounds."

"Where?" Her gaze went straight to his stomach. Black was slimming, but his shirt revealed the outline of a man with minimal pudge. "You're in great shape." Realizing how quickly she'd responded, she walked it back—a hair. Clearing her throat, she added, "For a man your age, that is."

Expelling a sigh, he replied, "I'm old, aren't I?"

"Not in my book." Heartened by the smile entering his eyes, Kinsley wanted Grant to feel her attraction for him, wanted him to know she considered him sexy and was totally interested, despite the fifteen or twenty years between them.

Very interested. "I think you're mature and accomplished."

"Mature," he said dryly. "Just what every man wants to hear."

"Nothing more attractive than a man who knows who he is and what he wants out of life. It makes for more interesting conversation."

"Glad to know I'm not boring you."

"On the contrary," she replied guardedly. "You have my complete attention."

Outside The Oasis, Grant pulled Kinsley into his arms. Parka-to-parka, they were like opposites, he dressed in all black, she in all cream, yet their padded bodies became one very quickly, a unit of warmth compared to the icy twenty degree air around them. And cozy. Kinsley felt cozy and comfortable within Grant's arms, as though she'd been there for years, would be for years to come. Snowflakes caught in his dark hair, his cheeks pink from the cold. Squeezing her close, he said, "I miss you already."

Kinsley smiled. Funny, but she felt the same way.

"Maybe I will join you for that rally. What time is it?"

"Three o'clock."

"Three o'clock," he repeated. Hesitating, his dark eyes danced with challenge. "Would you be shocked if I showed?"

"Yes," she said flatly, liking that he would consider it but not entirely sure she wanted him there. It wasn't his thing.

Grant would be out of his element. He would be in hers, where he didn't belong. Seeing him standing alongside the likes of Norell and Gabby, Sebastian and the others would undermine the attraction. Kinsley liked Grant for who he was—a businessman with a heart. He wasn't leading the charge against the expansion but was sympathetic to her cause. Their worlds were different, yet converging. Oddly, Kinsley didn't want Grant assimilating into her world. She wanted to assimilate into his.

Grant chuckled. "Don't worry. I won't embarrass you by attending."

"You don't embarrass me, Grant."

"After my behavior the other day, I think some would disagree. You might get some pushback if the capitalist pig showed up."

The observation had merit. As though he sensed he'd scored, Grant's smile faded. "Hey, it's okay. So long as you continue to see me on the sly, I'll survive."

He made what they were doing sound dirty and wrong. It wasn't. Grant believed in her. He believed in her ability, encouraged her to dream big. How could that be wrong?

"They wouldn't know a pig from a hog," Kinsley said wryly. "I see who I want, when I want. Nobody tells me otherwise."

"Good." Leaning in for a kiss, Grant placed his lips on hers and feathered them across. Moist steam built between them as the sensation of his mouth on hers knocked any and all thoughts from her brain. Through hooded eyes, he looked at her with a hot fluid desire he made no effort to conceal. "Hey, you don't protest in the nude, do you?"

Startled, she stammered, "What?"

"Because that would change the equation entirely. I think I'd have to become a full-fledged convert then," he breathed into her mouth, plunging forward and preventing her reply.

Kinsley's knees buckled. Her insides dissolved as Grant kissed her. Warm wisps of breath commingled with the scent of his cologne. Solid, masculine, Grant felt good. Right. Gently, he continued to probe, the gesture seeking, wanting, mirroring the emotion swimming inside her. She slipped her arms inside his coat where the thin fabric of his sweater revealed a firm physique. Stiff desire slipped low in her belly. What she wouldn't give to lock herself in a room with him right now and shut out the world. If only for a moment, a break in time, where there were no protests, no explosions, nothing that could jeopardize the connection building between them.

Only them. This. That's what Kinsley wanted, and she wanted it now.

Grant pulled away, leaving her warm and dizzy, like she'd had wine for lunch when she hadn't. "You have to stop kissing me like that," he murmured.

"Me?" She laughed. "I can't even see straight!"

Squeezing her to him gently, he said, "I won't go far."

"Don't."

Her swift reply wasn't lost on him. Hungry want rose sharp in his gaze. Nuzzling his nose against hers, he whispered, "Can I take you to dinner?"

"Dinner." She nodded. "Dinner would be good."

Chuckling as though he knew he completely owned her, Grant said, "I'll pick you up at seven-fifteen."

"Seven-fifteen."

With that, he broke the spell with his release. Kinsley brought a hand to her lips and watched him go, her heart hanging from his back. She was going to have to be careful. Very careful. Grant Powell was about to take over her world.

Chapter Thirteen

Jogging down the front steps of her hotel, Kinsley pulled her gloves on and strode the three blocks to the rally site. Where her mind should be immersed in the expected confrontation with Palmer, it was instead immersed in thoughts of her new venture. And Grant's post-lunch kiss. Their relationship was moving at warp speed. Between him, Gianni, Palmer and her shift in career focus, Kinsley had been barely able to focus on her blog post for the day titled, "You Can't Take It Back." In an unprecedented move, she decided to openly excoriate the Forest Service for its hypocrisy, accusing them of corruption in the ranks while they masqueraded as a defender of wildlife. Donations accepted from organizations that destroy wildlife habitat should be seen for the bribes that they were and refused. Period.

Kinsley didn't like to alienate allies but felt no compunction over revealing the connection between the Forest Service's acceptance of Palmer International money and their subsequent decision regarding the expansion. Let the public decide. Let them know exactly how their money was being spent. It was *their* government at work. If they were okay with it, then so be it. Kinsley was tired of fighting a losing battle. If taxpayers didn't care that their tax dollars were complicit in this matter, what could she do to stop it?

With each passing day it was beginning to sink in. Massive government corruption fell upon deaf ears because people couldn't understand it. It was too big, too anonymous. It was out of their control, out of their reach. But vegan apparel wasn't. It was something people could hold and handle, feel good about wearing. Sebastian was young, immature. He didn't understand the larger picture at work. Like any young male, he understood what felt good at the moment and that's where he buried his focus. Not her. Not Grant. Warm feelings washed through her as she hurried down the street toward Palmer's hotel near the base of the gondola. She and Grant understood the need to broaden her horizons and affect the masses.

Turning the corner, Kinsley spotted the early formation of a protest line, her crew gathering around the gondola station. Sebastian's black head of hair stood out in the crowd. Coupled with his firecracker red jacket and pale gray jeans, she couldn't miss him. That, and he was surrounded by several protesters in what appeared to be one of their usual pre-protest huddles. Everyone was given an assignment, a target. Everyone had a role to play.

Gabby clung to Sebastian's arm like the starry-eyed eighteen-year-old girl that she was. Leaning toward the more radical wing of their organization, she looked up to Sebastian with a mix of awe and lust, making her easily manipulated. It was a combination Sebastian preyed upon.

Kinsley's snow boots absorbed the impact as she kicked up her pace and hurried over. Gabby was asking for trouble, sucking up to Sebastian that way, but it was a lesson she was going to have to learn the hard way. Kinsley had.

"Sebastian," she called out.

Both he and Gabby turned. When he saw her, Sebastian pulled a veil over his expression. Motioning for Gabby to give them some space, he maintained eye contact with Kinsley as she approached. Suspicion snaked through her as she closed the distance. What conversations could not be shared with her, head of the organization?

"Kinsley," he said politely but in measured tones, "I enjoyed your post today."

Coming face-to-face with him, she wondered if it were true or fluff to keep her favor.

"And? Your thoughts?" she asked, only remotely interested in what he thought but knew it was the expected reply.

"Interesting." A smile slipped onto his lips, more smirk than pleasure. "I'm surprised you had it in you to publish such a scathing rebuke. You don't normally go after those on our side."

"In this case, they aren't, are they?" Sebastian was at the meeting. He knew as well as she did that the fix was in. "Their decision clearly reveals them for who they are and where they stand. I just thought it was time that people heard the truth."

"I've been telling you that for months. Glad to see you've finally come around."

Irritated by the condescension in his voice, Kinsley replied, "I work on my own terms, Sebastian. You of all people should know that."

"Oh, I do." Pushing his shoulders back, he turned and held up a hand. "As does everyone here. We all know who's in charge around here."

Kinsley honed in on him, sliding a quick glance toward the protestors. It felt as though Sebastian were trying to start something, insert a divide between her and the group. Several protesters were taking note of their interaction, while others took up arms and began to shout their message to passersby.

"Animals are dying! Animals are starving!"

Gabby smiled and Kinsley swore there was something more sitting behind those awe-filled eyes of hers than attraction, but this wasn't the time or the place to question. "Great afternoon for a protest, isn't it?" Gabby chirped.

Kinsley rolled an eye toward the sky. Mountain weather was fickle. One minute you couldn't see the ground through the snow, the next it was blue skies and sunshine. "Yes," she replied stiffly, uninterested in banal conversation. Moving her gaze over faces in the crowd around her, skiers and non-skiers alike, Kinsley logged in a group of children paying no attention to anything but themselves as they played in the snow, their bright orange ski vests identifying them as ski school participants awaiting pick-up. Several forty-somethings stood nearby, the women in leggings and knee-high leather boots, their jackets thigh-length and ornately embroidered. Each woman lugged an oversized designer purse, and Kinsley's imagination instantly switched their bags out with some designs of her own. Earlier, she'd sketched a few logo designs using her initials, KF. She hadn't settled on anything yet, but had a couple she really liked.

"Are you here to protest or people-watch?" Sebastian asked.

Turning to him, Kinsley returned, "Have you seen Palmer?"

"Not yet." Sebastian flicked a glance toward the hotel behind her. It was an eight-story building boasting a façade of heavy wood timbers and flagstone. Spacious balconies were perched from every room, a few currently populated by guests. Below, a wide berth of steps fanned out from the front entrance. A few guests lingered outside with coffee to-go cups in their hands. "He and his entourage haven't arrived."

"They have a meeting scheduled though, right? You double-checked?"

"I did."

"Good."

"Where have you been all day?"

"Working."

"It took you all day to write one post? We could have used you outside of city hall."

Kinsley iced him with an annoyed glance. "My presence is not needed at every protest." She was the brains of this operation, not the brawn. Her blog was the vessel to get the word out, keep the general public informed and supporters up-to-date. Sebastian's job was that of supervision. "We all have our roles, remember?"

"Of course. How could I forget?"

Kinsley did not like his tone. Sebastian was baiting her, hovering just shy of starting a fight. About to ask why, she was distracted by angry shouts.

Lee Palmer and several men jogged down the front steps of the hotel then headed toward her, their stride brisk and determined.

Fire ripped through her belly. Time for confrontation. Ditching Sebastian, Kinsley took up residence on the front line of protest, flanked by Norell and Gabby, and nailed her gaze to Lee Palmer. Late fifties, a slight paunch beneath his ski jacket, his black hair colored to conceal his gray, he met her gaze directly. Kinsley could feel Palmer's instant assessment as he catalogued the presence of protesters. It appeared he considered them one more hurdle to jump in the business of resort development.

A hurdle that didn't seem to concern him. In fact, his arrogance coarsened the closer he came. The men with him mirrored his lead. They weren't alarmed by the group of protesters, merely alert to their presence.

"Guess your payoff to the Forest Service worked," Kinsley cracked.

Palmer zeroed in on her, a mix of amusement and condescension mingling in his sharp-eyed gaze. "Kinsley Fairchild."

Pressure pushed into her midsection. So he remembered her. Fine. It changed nothing, other than she'd get an ear-full from her parents. "Correct."

With a fleeting glance to the protesters around her, he said, "Your father should be here shortly. Perhaps you would like to join him for the meeting, considering it is *your* inheritance that is benefiting from the expansion."

Kinsley ground her jaw. The man was making an obvious ploy to incite dissension among the members of her group, but he was wasting his time. Her reputation was stellar when it came to the cause. "I don't accept dirty money— unlike the Forest Service."

Palmer returned a thin smile. "Speaking of reputations, Palmer International is the gold standard when it comes to environmentally-friendly development. We, alone, are responsible for more recycling than the entire town of Silver Creek."

"Turning waste into wealth is about your wallet, not the environment," Gabby charged.

"It's about money, same as it always is," Norell threw in.

Palmer's expression drained of cheer, the lines around his eyes hardening. "If you people had your way, we'd be living like a third world country. You're against anything even remotely threatening to animals, rendering every modern convenience of the twenty-first century off-limits—except those that suit you, of course."

"We live our values!" a female protester shouted from behind them.

Palmer snickered. "I'll remind you that you didn't arrive to protest on the back of a bicycle. Your connection to the internet from your smart phone doesn't appear out of thin air. The clothes on your back, the glasses on your face...someone like *me* created them." With a smug smile, he added, "You're welcome."

Norell took a step forward. "I oughta cram—"

Palmer iced him with a warning, "If you prefer to sit in jail, we can make those arrangements."

Grabbing Norell by the arm, Kinsley cursed under her breath. His temper was inexcusable. He was making them look like a bunch of hot-heads instead of a rational group of individuals who wanted a humane coexistence with animals and nature. "That won't be necessary," she replied. "While we appreciate your ingenuity, we don't appreciate your lack of concern with regard to habitat. Animals will suffer because of your expansion. They will be displaced, many will die. All we're asking is for some consideration, some degree of moderation when it comes to the extent of your expansion."

Turning his attention to Kinsley, Palmer replied, "You know as well as I do that there will always be some degree of discomfort with coexistence. People suffer, too. They are attacked, mauled, made ill because of animals. It happens. Animals suffer without human intervention. People suffer without animal intervention. It's called life. We live, we risk, and we survive."

Kinsley stared at him. Palmer was dodging the issue. He was trying to paint a philosophical picture with regard to injustice and removing himself from the details. It wasn't going to work. Not with her. "We make choices, Mr. Palmer. You, me, even the animals. But theirs are rooted in instinct. We, on the other hand, benefit from the ability to rise above instinct. We are the custodians of this planet. We have a responsibility to do our best to take care of it, including all of the living creatures around us—human, animal, plant—everything. Is that too much to ask from an accomplished man like yourself?"

Lee Palmer eased into a plastic smile. "Not at all," he replied, his breath curling between them. "In fact, we are meeting here today to discuss that very issue. Now, if you'll excuse us, we have work to do."

Without waiting for her reply, Palmer walked around her and into the line for the gondola, followed by his colleagues. Each and every man avoided eye contact with her, undoubtedly logging the episode as a win for their side. Cold stung her cheeks as she watched the last backside disappear into the gondola station. Kinsley vowed she would not be minimized. Their position was valid, obtainable. Persistence would win this battle.

Behind her, Norell muttered, "I can't wait to see that pompous smile burned off his face."

Kinsley's pulse bolted through her skin. Was Norell suggesting violence? She turned in time to see the guy next to him nod and chortle in agreement. When he saw Kinsley staring at him, he quickly turned a shoulder to her and walked off. Her pulse ticked up. The last thing Kinsley needed was for a rogue activist to take matters into his own hands. Minor demonstrations of rebellion were one thing. Major acts of violence were another.

As the group dispersed, manning their signs and marching in unison, Kinsley searched for Sebastian. Was he in on it?

"Ms. Fairchild?"

Whirling at the sound of a deep male voice, Kinsley turned to see Wade Davis, Chief of Police and friend of Lisa's father. He smiled cordially, deep lines forming around his mouth. The two had met on several occasions at the Richardson home, though they were far from close acquaintances. "Hello," she replied, instantly wondering if he was here to hassle the protesters. "Can I help you?"

He cast a wary gaze at the protesters and said in a hushed tone, "Do you mind if I have a word with you?"

"We aren't breaking any laws." It was her patent response when approached by the authorities. Invariably, police departments around the country felt entitled to throw their presence around, intimidating activists with the "threat" of legal trouble. But she was well-versed in the law. They weren't doing anything wrong by being here.

"Didn't say you were," he replied quietly.

Most protesters she knew didn't bat an eye when the police came around. Though in Chief Davis' regard, they might bat an eye for other reasons. The man had to be in his sixties, though you couldn't tell by looking at him. Over six feet tall, Chief Davis' solid build was evident beneath the lines of his black three-piece suit and overcoat, his head of hair full, thick and neatly trimmed, including a bushy mustache. Add his sexy brown eyes, and he was tall, dark and handsome, defined. Kinsley found it odd that he insisted on dressing so formally in a town known for casual resort attire, but perhaps it was his way of making himself stand out.

Kinsley released a soft sigh. It worked.

But Chief Davis struck her as a fair man. No reason not to entertain a conversation with him. Slipping her hair behind an ear she asked, "What can I help you with?"

"Do you mind if we have this conversation in private?"

Alarm bells clanged in the back of her mind. "Sure. No problem." Walking several feet from the group, Kinsley stopped near a massive pine tree, its branches laden with green lights barely visible in the afternoon light.

"I wanted to discuss the bombing at the fur store."

Kinsley's heart thumped in her chest. Stay calm, she warned herself. There was no evidence to connect her as the bomber. Notwithstanding, her legs felt like jelly sticks. "What about it?"

"I reviewed some video that seems to show you had some involvement."

She angled her head, reached a hand up and rubbed a spot behind her ear. Was he talking about the video Grant saw? The one he used to accuse her of the bombing? If so, there was nothing definitive to connect her with the bombing—other than a white hat and coat—clothing anyone could own. "Are you talking about the store video?"

He arched a brow. "You know about that?"

Kinsley nodded, brushed the hair at her ear, a nagging concern nipping at her calm. "Yes, but a lot of women have white hats and coats."

Deep lines carved the space between his brows. "Yes, they do. However, not all women look like you."

A lump rose hard and fast to her throat. "What do you mean, look like me?"

"In addition to the store video, I've reviewed some of the town's video. One angle in particular captures your face pretty well. It's not a hundred percent, but I'm willing to bet a jury will tag it as you." Sucking something from his teeth, he looked at her and asked, "So, is there something you wanted to tell me?"

Fear exploded in her chest. Not a hundred percent? Did that mean he was guessing?

Chief Davis waited. Apparently he expected Kinsley to give herself up.

Not without a fight, she wouldn't. "Chief Davis, it's possible you might have captured me on video. I was in town that night having dinner with a friend."

"Can he or she vouch for you?"

"Of course," she lied smoothly, amazed by the calm tenor of her voice, despite the thundering in her chest. "I was with my associate, Sebastian Wu."

"Before or after you placed the bomb?"

Heartbeats battered, but he couldn't see them, and so long as she held fast to her story, she was safe—for the time being. However, answering any more questions was not in her best interest. Not without a lawyer present.

Protesters shouted behind her, tourists milled about. Looking about the vicinity, Chief Davis visibly mulled over his options. It was clear he didn't believe her. It was equally clear he didn't have enough proof to convict her. Wade Davis pushed his tongue over his teeth, as though removing a remnant from his lunch, then said, "So you're telling me you didn't walk into that fur store, conceal yourself between the furs, and place the bomb just after closing?"

Kinsley said nothing.

With a quick glance askance, he softened his tone. "Listen, I don't like to see animals put out of their habitat any more than you do, but there are ways to go about helping them and property destruction isn't one of them. Trust me, a criminal felony arrest is the last thing you want on your record."

Exactly. It should be on Sebastian's!

Clicking back into official police officer mode, Chief Davis said, "I'm giving you some leeway on this, because you're a friend of Lisa's. But I'm warning you, I will not tolerate this brand of radical activism. You want change, go about the legal channels or find yourself in jail. It's that simple."

Kinsley swallowed, the lump in her throat painfully tight. She didn't want Lisa and her father brought into this—it would only cause them embarrassment. It would strain their relationship, a relationship Kinsley valued as family. The first fingers of chill crept beneath her coat.

"Do we understand each other?"

Staring into the hardened gaze of the seasoned police officer, Kinsley nodded. She had no doubt the man meant what he said. Her "free pass" had just expired. Next time, he'd take her straight to jail. Resentment gurgled in her gut. Because

Sebastian had taken it upon himself to plant an explosive bomb.

Reflexively, she searched for sight of him in the assembly of protesters and wondered, where was he?

Chapter Fourteen

Chief Davis had left Kinsley slightly unraveled. While he hadn't arrested her, he'd made no secret of his intent—and his conviction that she was indeed the person responsible for the bombing, despite her lies to the contrary. Circling the group, Kinsley stewed over the mess and hunted for Sebastian. Where could he be? He was here ten minutes ago. Looking between heads, she searched for his thick black hair and red jacket, but there were nothing but blues and grays. Tourists were mixing with the protesters as they made their way off the mountain, the number of skiers multiplying quickly as they made their mass exodus. With the ski day ending, Palmer and his investors would be left in relative peace as they conducted their meeting on the mountaintop. A guy on a bicycle weaved his way through the crowd, nearly hitting an elderly couple.

Pulling her focus from the crowd, Kinsley shook her head. Sebastian should be here. This was his place, his role in the group. Organize and lead the protests. He thrived on it, relished the center stage. Why wasn't he here, and where could he have gone?

"...fireworks they won't soon forget."

"Fourth of July, man."

Kinsley jerked her head. Several people away, she overheard snippets of conversation. Fireworks? Her pulse ricocheted off her ribcage. *I can't wait to see that pompous smile burned off his face.* Norell's earlier words chilled her spine. Instinctively, she pushed her way through bodies in search of him.

"Wildcats need the wild!"

"Plant trees not poles!"

Kinsley didn't see Norell but confronted the two men she'd overheard. "What are you talking about? Fireworks?" Her gaze leapt between the two. "What fireworks?"

A smile crawled onto a young blond man's face. Kinsley recognized him as one of Norell's roommates. "Relax, babe," he said in the gritty voice of a smoker, his long hair pulled back into a tangled ponytail. "We're just making conversation."

The dark-haired guy with him chuckled, chopped layers of hair falling across his eyes from beneath his khaki-green ski hat. "Dude, she's *uptight*."

Kinsley glared at him. The second man was one of Sebastian's people who had flown in from California. From what she'd observed, both of these guys were diehard for the cause. "Is Norell planning something?" she demanded. Whipping her glance around, she searched for sight of him. "And where is he?"

"Norell's cool," the blond replied. Swiping his buddy with a warning glance, he nodded. "He's working for the cause."

"Where?" Kinsley asked, unable to shake a growing sense of doom. "Where is he?"

Reaching for a sign from a fellow protester, the guy handed it to her. "C'mon. Raise the message." He chortled as though stoned. "It'll make you feel better."

"Yeah," the other chimed in. "Those capitalist pigs were downers, man. They laughed in your face, but don't worry, they're gonna get what's coming to them."

Kinsley didn't like the cagey underpinnings in his gaze. The guy knew something—something she didn't know—and he was purposefully keeping it from her. Flashing a glance up the mountain, she followed one of the rising gondola cars. Lee Palmer and his men were in one of those cars floating beneath the heavy cable that would carry them to the top. She couldn't see the gondola station or the restaurant housed above, but she could see them in her mind. Three levels of restaurants, gift shops and meeting space, an outdoor patio deck replete with bungee jump and wall-climbing attraction, Kinsley knew the area like her own backyard. There was a snowmobile rental place behind the ground floor of the building, a ski patrol hut adjacent to the second level. Upstairs was housed a fine dining facility and banquet room—the location where Lee Palmer would host his meeting. She could visualize people milling about the entrance to the gondola as they made their way down, others on their way up seeking the last few hours of daylight. Was Norell up there? Was Sebastian?

Kinsley's reverie popped. Something was wrong. Very wrong. Suddenly her gaze was drawn to a dark-haired woman entering the gondola building. Shiny waves of brown caught the afternoon sun as she disappeared inside. Kinsley's heart caught. *It was her mother*.

In the space of an instant, Kinsley understood. Fireworks. Sebastian. Fur store. Burn. Norell. She hitched her gaze to the rising gondola cars. Something bad was about to happen. Very bad. She didn't know what or when, but she knew with every ounce of her being something "off plan" was about to transpire.

"You look tense, man."

The other laughed and elbowed his buddy. "She does, doesn't she?"

Kinsley wanted to rip the heads from their shoulders but there wasn't time. She had to warn her parents, Palmer and his investors. *Everyone*. She didn't know exactly what she had to warn them of, but she knew there was something.

The certainty of it streamed hot through her veins.

Kinsley yanked the cell phone from her jacket and dialed her mother's number. It went instantly to voicemail. She tried her father's, but ended the call. If her mother's cell didn't have reception, it was likely his wouldn't either. Kinsley whipped her glance around the area. Could she call the ski patrol? The restaurant on the mountaintop?

Bolting from the swarm of protesters, she raced toward the gondola building. Shouts of protest punctured the air as she dodged skiers, skis and poles, handily crossing the terrain in seconds. She had to get up there. She had to get up there and warn them. Her boots crunched loudly over crusted snow as she ran. Grabbing hold of a metal stairwell railing, Kinsley swung herself around and down the steps where a gondola attendant waved a handheld electronic ticket reader over her jacket. He held up a hand. "Sorry, but you need a ticket."

"Isn't it free?" she chanced, checking her watch as he shook his head.

"Not for another hour." Tossing a gloved hand over his shoulder, he said, "You can purchase a half-day gondola ticket over at the window."

Kinsley's stomach pitched. She didn't have time for a ticket—her parents were aboard a car as they spoke! But this guy didn't know that, nor did he care. A man walked around Kinsley and the attendant waved his wand over the front of him as he passed. The device beeped. "Have a great afternoon!"

Expelling a disgruntled sigh, Kinsley turned on her heel and ran to the ticket window. A few guests were in line ahead of her, including a young mother with two small children hovering around her legs. Kinsley bit back a curse. This would take forever! She had an annual pass, but with no intention to ride the gondola, had left it in her hotel room. At this point, it would be quicker to simply buy a new ticket.

Kinsley stared at the phone still clenched in her fist. She could call someone up top, an employee, a station attendant, but what would she say? I have a funny feeling something is going to happen? One of my protesters might have placed a bomb in your building?

It was lunacy. They'd arrest her on the spot for the mere implication.

As one man departed the window with ticket in hand, she listened as the woman behind the window greeted the young mother and her children, then proceed to ramble on about all the wonderful activities awaiting them at the top of the mountain. Kinsley groaned, struggling to keep her impatience in check. She didn't want to be rude, but she couldn't wait while this woman planned their entire vacation!

Heartbeats hammered in her chest as she slung her gaze back toward the gondola. If anything happened to her parents because a couple of radicals thought it would be a good idea to blow up the gondola, she'd never forgive herself. She brought these people here. She invited Sebastian to the front lines of the battle and welcomed as many activists as he could rally.

But mobilizing an army of protesters was one thing. Enabling a group of radicals with a hidden agenda was quite another. If they acted beyond her control, she would still be held responsible. Turning back to the window, Kinsley forced herself to remain calm. Breathe, think. Where would they likely attack? Would they actually use an explosive device where people were in the midst of a crowd?

Sebastian had set a real bomb in the fur store—a vacant store. He wouldn't risk a bomb where people could get injured, would he? He understood the ramifications as well as she. Eco-terrorism was a federal crime. He'd go to jail for life. Kinsley whipped her gaze back toward the gondola. The uneventful movement of cars along the cable line scraped over her nerves. Cold seeped into her bones. Everything looked normal. Sebastian wouldn't hurt people. He wasn't a murderer. The fur store had been empty. No one had been in harm's way. He wouldn't risk something as stupid as taking out the gondola lift, the building above.

He knew her parents would be there. He wouldn't harm them. She was making mountains out of molehills. He'd go for visual impact. Kinsley had chosen the front window of the fur store for the same reason. It was about making a statement, not creating mass casualties. Kinsley's thoughts went to the phone in her hand. She was already under suspicion for the fur store bombing. If she called, they would think it a scare tactic or arrest her on the spot. Neither of which would help her cause.

Calling to mind the layout of the gondola building at the top of the mountain, Kinsley pressed her mind to think. If Sebastian were out to create chaos, where would he do it? The entrance to the building? The top dining room where Palmer intended to have his meeting?

It made sense. This was about Palmer, and that's where Palmer would be. Unfortunately, there could be collateral damage. Pulling her gaze from the mountain and back to the window, Kinsley watched as the woman and her children walked away. Her heart squeezed. At this hour of the day, there would be a host of kids at the top of the mountain—jumping, climbing and playing in the snow.

"May I help you?"

Kinsley stepped forward with a renewed sense of urgency. "One gondola lift ticket, please."

"For this afternoon?"

"Yes." Of course, she wanted to snap. Today. *Now.*

"Twenty dollars."

Kinsley already had the money sliding under the window partition.

"Thank you." Taking the twenty dollar bill, the woman pressed a button on her cash register. The door clanged open. "Do you need a lanyard?"

"No." She needed to get out of here and on her way!

"Okay." The woman slid the square ticket under the window and said, "You can place it in your pocket, or use one of the plastic zip ties to secure it to your jacket."

"Thanks." Kinsley snatched the ticket and took off for the gondola.

Jogging back to the entrance for the line, the same guy waved his digital wand over her person and scanned for her ticket, then smiled and waved her through. With no line to speak of, Kinsley entered a moving gondola car and was seated in less than a minute's time. The ride up was a different story. Minutes ticked by like hours as she floated up the mountain. Glancing out the window-encased gondola car, she saw skiers zig-zagging across the main ski run. A few of the more advanced skiers flew over moguls, cruising over the huge bumps in snow like they were bouncing on a trampoline. Kinsley had never been that good of a skier, more content to hang around at the bottom than to take the time to learn and practice the sport. Grant mentioned he went heliskiing on occasion. Peering down at the bump skiers, she couldn't imagine flying in a helicopter at high altitude, let alone jumping out onto the mountain and skiing down.

A shudder raced through her. Grant. They were supposed to have dinner tonight. Would they? Or would he learn of the town video first, the one apparently showing her walking out of the fur store. There was no way to deny her identity if it had caught her face the way Chief Davis had indicated. Kinsley could only hope they didn't have enough evidence to go forward with a public release of the video. She knew the system. The police could have all sorts of evidence that placed someone at the scene, gave them motive, indicted them based on someone else's testimony, but if they didn't have it all wrapped up like a pretty present, they had nothing. And divulging a half-cocked accusation could invite lawsuits against the department. Kinsley had seen people walk, despite a mountain of evidence against them, because it hadn't been enough. There was a missing piece, or the suspect had a component of deniability—something. It might come down to that *something* in Kinsley's case. Her heart suddenly began to pound, and she pulled her gaze from the skiers. But her "something" would be "someone."

Sebastian.

Behind her the village was shrinking in size. In less than ten minutes, she'd be at the top. Moving her gaze upward, Kinsley latched onto the first visible signs of the gondola building, the third story roof line a dull gray against the brilliant blue sky, and images of another explosion formed in her mind. Another group, another radical, another mountaintop lodge gone up in flames in the name of activism. Could Sebastian be doing likewise? Could he be involved in a copycat bombing that he hoped to pin on the ancillary group?

It was possible. He was cunning, smart. She wouldn't put it past him.

Dread filled her. If Sebastian blew up the gondola building, she'd denounce him publicly. If he harmed her parents—any of those people up there—she'd sever all ties and never look back. She'd give him up to the police on the spot. Other than the fur store bombing, he had no leverage over her. None. She had worn gloves. She had concealed her face while in the store. Other than a video showing her leaving, there was no proof that she had placed that bomb. Sebastian could have done it—did, in a way. He was the one responsible for the damage by explosion, not her.

What she couldn't give up, was the growing sense of guilt she felt over her role in the matter. Kinsley *had* meant to destroy the furs. She *had* meant to intimidate the woman out of business. For that alone, Grant would never forgive her.

As gondola cars swept into the station, each catching invisible hooks in the cable line and slowing one at a time, she scooted to the edge of her seat. When her car entered the building, Kinsley battled a swell of anxiety and mentally mapped out her search. She had no idea what was about to transpire or where it would occur, or even if something was going to occur, but she couldn't stand idle. If nothing else, she could head upstairs to the meeting rooms and reassure herself that all was well. At the moment, she was working off instinct, running blind on a hunch and a hastily-contrived response.

As the gondola car swung around, its cable line caught with a jerk. Kinsley stood, grabbed hold of an overhead bar, and waited while the doors slid open. She hopped out and crossed the loading area with long determined strides, avoiding eye contact with several people waiting for downward traveling cars. If Sebastian was here, she'd find him.

Emerging from the station, Kinsley took in her surroundings. As she feared, kids were everywhere, most in street clothing which meant they were here for the mountaintop attractions. For the next several hours, activity areas would be open and crowded. There would be a ton of people scattered about and potentially harmed if Sebastian set off an explosive.

Kinsley ejected the thoughts from her mind. She couldn't panic over things that hadn't happened—weren't certain to happen. Turning on her heel, she strode into the building and scaled the stairs two at a time. The third floor restaurant was an upscale version of a hunting cabin, semi-gourmet dining in the main room with a private wing off to one side. Adele catered many of the events up here until the resort decided to hire its own staff. Now Lee Palmer utilized the private room like a "members only" club. His meeting would be there.

Reaching the top step, chest pounding, Kinsley felt a headache coming on. She paused and sucked in a few deep breaths to calm the throbbing in her skull. Exertion, stress, high altitude—it could be due to any number of things, though she'd put her money on the stress and lots of it. With one last breath, Kinsley entered the wood-paneled room. Several gentlemen were gathered beneath a massive antler chandelier, its golden glow glazing the room with warm hues. The space was substantial, accentuated by twenty foot ceilings with massive exposed beams. A large stone hearth took center stage, home to flames spitting and crackling as a number of fat timber logs burned. Kinsley glanced about the people seated near wood tables and on deep-cushioned leather chairs but recognized no one. Walking toward the private room where double doors stood slightly ajar, Kinsley heard voices coming from the interior before she saw anyone. She slowed and peeked inside. She didn't need to go in. She was only here to scout the area for signs of trouble. It occurred to her how unlikely it was that she was going to detect a hidden bomb, and a little finger of panic curled around her heart. It could be hidden anywhere. And if her suspicions about Sebastian were right, she could be caught in the middle of an explosion. It didn't need to be large to create chaos or injury-causing damage.

"I hope you're not here to cause trouble."

Kinsley jumped. Heartbeats nearly burst from her chest as she whirled. "Dad!"

A stern distrust filled his dark gaze. "Why are you here?"

"I'm—*nothing*, no reason," she sputtered, struck by the chill in his voice. The men behind him watched the exchange.

Her father's eyes turned black as coal. "Don't lie to me. Are you here to disrupt the meeting? Because if you are, it will be the last time. I'm warning you, Kinsley—"

"Dad—" she held up a shaky hand then yanked it down by her side. No reason to let on that she was nervous. It would invite questions—questions she didn't want to answer. "I'm not here to disrupt anything, I promise." Well, technically, that was a lie. She was, only not the way he thought. "I just wanted to stop by and say hi to Mom."

"I'll tell her you said hello."

Just wanted to say hi. Could she have come up with anything more inane?

Seriously. Her father was going to think her more of a nut job than he already did. But she wasn't crazy. She'd only lost her bearings, though one thing was clear. He wasn't allowing her anywhere near that room. Blowing out her breath, she tried to smile. And there wasn't a thing she was going to do to change his mind. "Okay. Thanks."

Her father remained entrenched in place, waiting to witness her exit.

Grateful he couldn't see the pound of her heart, the wedge in her throat, Kinsley made a quick departure. She would not stand up to his interrogation, not in this condition, not under these circumstances. Her nerves were fried!

Descending the stairs to the second level, her gloved hand sliding down the wide wooden railing, she decided against going down to the basement level. There would be more activity up here than below and that would be Sebastian's goal—activity, people, witnesses.

Fear. Panic. Chaos.

Automatic doors opened as she neared and she sailed outside. The icy shock of air felt good to her cheeks—refreshing, like it could knock some sense back into her. Kinsley paused and breathed in as much as she could. She had to snap out of her "freak" and get a grip, get tuned-in to Sebastian's whereabouts. On impulse, she pulled the cell phone from her jacket pocket and called his number. Maybe she could gain a clue as to his location, or talk some *sense* into him.

"Kinsley."

"Sebastian, where are you?"

He laughed softly. "Why, do you miss me?"

Pressing the phone to her ear she began to walk, dipping her chin as she spoke to conceal her voice. "Where are you? What are you doing?"

"Whoa, back up. Did someone appoint you my mother and not tell me? What's with the interrogation?"

Kinsley cupped a hand over her cellphone and demanded, "I want to know what you're planning. I know you're up to something, and I want to know what it is."

"Same thing I'm always up to—protest."

"I didn't see you at the base. Where did you go?"

"Is there a problem, Kinsley? You sound upset."

Turning from a passing couple she snarled, "You're damn right I am. I heard some of the guys talking about fireworks. That wouldn't happen to mean an explosion, would it?"

Sebastian laughed. "What gives you that idea?"

"Your little fireworks display in the fur shop." Kinsley stalked off the outdoor deck and out into the snow to evade eavesdroppers. "It was an *explosion*. A real one. Are you planning another?"

"And not tell you? Of course not," he denied flatly. "Didn't we already have this discussion? As I recall, you chewed off my left butt cheek for it."

But did he listen?

That was the question. Calmer, Kinsley walked along the perimeter of activity, a cushion of relief growing with every step. Maybe she'd been wrong. Maybe she'd jumped to conclusions. And if she had, who could blame her?

She'd been walking a tightrope lately, entertaining a relationship with Grant, a man whose friend's shop she destroyed. Add Chief Davis' unexpected visit and it was amazing Kinsley didn't have blood shooting out her ears. Inhaling deep and full, she hovered off the corner of the patio. People were coming and going as usual, an equal mix of those arriving for the afternoon activities and those finishing up their ski day. All was as it should be.

Allowing herself a moment of calm, Kinsley said, "I'm sorry, Sebastian. I've been on edge lately, what with the Forest Service caving to Palmer. It's really crushed my mood." As did his bomb switch. The only thing lifting her spirits of late had been toying with the idea of this clothing line. That and her growing affinity for one Grant Powell. Kinsley knew how to skirt danger but playing with the devil's neighbor was not smart. If Grant caught wind of Chief Davis' video find, they'd be done. Heartbeats peppered her chest. *So* done.

"Are we through here?" Sebastian snipped.

"We are." Kinsley glanced toward the gondola station and said, "I'll catch you later."

"Dinner?"

"Can't. I have plans."

"With your new friend, the jeweler?"

Kinsley sucked in her surprise. So he knew. Had she expected he wouldn't? Sebastian seemed to have eyes and ears throughout their entire network. Any one of them could have seen Kinsley and Grant together. And if they had, they would have immediately reported the fact to Sebastian.

"You two hooking up?"

"Now who's doing the interrogating?"

"Touché. Perhaps you'll share your personal life with me at another time."

Maybe. Probably not. Ending the call, Kinsley fell against a post. The icy metal seared through her jacket within seconds. Lifting away, she stopped suddenly. Headed into the gondola station was a black-headed man in a red jacket. Her heart kicked in her chest. Was that Sebastian?

Kinsley's body automatically moved several steps toward him, watching helplessly as he blended into a group of departing skiers, disappearing from view. Panic dissolved her bones. Staring after him, she thought, it couldn't be him. Could it?

Fastened in place, Kinsley couldn't move. She couldn't think, couldn't speak. Her gaze shot upward. The windows of the third floor glowed with light. Inside, her mother and father were meeting with Palmer and his people. Kinsley's pulse grew sketchy. Uncertain. If she'd miscalculated, people could be hurt, lives could be lost.

A man stalked out from the gondola doorway below, snapping her attention like a lightning bolt. Fear cut her in two. The imposing figure belonged to Chief Wade Davis. A second man appeared, and Kinsley's heart stopped. McIntyre Walsh. He worked part-time special operations for the police department and his presence could only mean one thing. A knot lodged hard and fast in her throat. *They must know something.*

Kinsley's vision tunneled into a dark hole. They must know something or they wouldn't be here. Her instinct was to warn them—run over and tell them what she suspected. Her legs moved several steps and nearly buckled when her mind registered the connection. Kinsley froze.

She was their lead suspect in the fur store bombing. They wouldn't listen to her. Hell, they were probably looking for her!

Wavering, Kinsley's gaze darted from ground to third floor. Chief Davis and Walsh assimilated into the crowd around the patio. People congregated outside the building. They posed for pictures, shot videos, grappled with skis and boots. A chill slithered down her spine. Time stood still, yet life continued around her. She felt trapped in a time capsule. But she couldn't stand by and do *nothing*. She couldn't stand mute while potential catastrophe hit.

But how could she tell them what she knew? She didn't *know* anything! Kinsley's heart stopped as Chief Davis recognized her. He pointed, gesturing for Walsh to look. Their eyes met like a knife to the gut. Even from this distance, Walsh's green-eyed gaze skewered her like the guilty rat he believed her to be. They started toward her. Kinsley gasped.

Chapter Fifteen

An explosion rocked the air. Screams broke out, flames leapt into the sky in a torrent of smoke. Black smoke, ugly smoke. People scattered. Women and children ran for the gondola entrance. Wade and Walsh took off toward the explosion.

It had come from the ski patrol hut.

Kinsley stood dumbfounded. She tried to digest what happened—an explosion—not in the main building but in the ski patrol hut. *The ski patrol hut?*

In an instant, she was moving, racing in the opposite direction from the panicked tourists. Bodies bumped and shoved but need drove her forward. Stopping short of the deck leading to the patrol hut, Kinsley processed the scene. The mob of frightened people had cleared. Horrific reality came into view. The hut was on fire, flames shooting out from the rear, leaping into the sky in a sway of orange and yellow and black.

Chief Davis and Walsh pulled people from the small building. Staff staggered across white snow—snow littered with black sooty debris—and ran clear of danger. Two patrol staff members worked quickly to drag a heavyset man from the building, his seemingly lifeless body carving a wide trail in the snow. A medic placed a hand to his chest, then dipped down and listened for his breathing and quickly began performing CPR.

The sight ripped Kinsley in two. *Oh no...*

Beyond, men manned bright red fire extinguishers, feverishly spraying the fire. Shouting, they directed one another toward the back to the largest area of flame. But the spew of white spray was no match for the now raging fire. Flames crawled up and over the building's roof, licked the edges as they leapt high into the sky. The building was consumed.

Kinsley's heart sank. Unable to move, she simply stared as though in a stupor. This couldn't be happening. This couldn't be real. A woman shrieked and waved frantically for someone to come. Kinsley's gaze leapt to her as Walsh ran to help. In seconds, he emerged with an enormous Golden Retriever in his arms. It was one of the patrol dogs used to help with avalanche search and rescue.

Kinsley fell to her knees, arms limp by her sides. Tears swamped her lids as she watched Walsh set the dog gently to the ground. Resort staff swarmed around to attend to the animal. Medics, ski instructors, even a few bystanders stood ready to assist. The woman who originally called for help sat hunched over the animal. She nestled her face close to the dog's, and Kinsley's heart gushed open. The woman was attending to the animal's spirit while the others attended to his injuries. Tears blurred Kinsley's vision, streamed down her face. A guttural moan ripped from her core. "*Please let the dog be okay...*"

Guilt gutted her, crushing, wrenching. She could feel the woman's anguish as if it were her own. An animal was hurt. Her focus flashed to the man lying on the ground. Innocents had been caught in the line of fire. This couldn't be happening!

Walsh left the animal to address the fire. With people safely out of the building, priority one was to put out the flames, contain the damage. Kinsley couldn't bear it. She couldn't accept that an animal had been hurt in the name of saving the wildlife. Yet she had to face reality. People had been harmed, vacations ruined, lives altered. A building had been destroyed. By a single act, the entire trajectory had changed.

Sebastian's words trickled into her mind. *Same thing I'm always up to—protest.*

This was no simple protest. This was an act of violence. Gazing about at the shocked faces, it felt like an act of war.

Kinsley's thoughts went quickly to her parents, the lights on the third floor. She hadn't seen her parents exit the building. Looking for them now, she realized no one from the meeting had ventured outside. There was no one around but the resort staff and a spattering of guests, guests the staff had pushed back to keep out of harm's way.

No one stopped to comfort Kinsley or check on her well-being. Rescue operations went on around her but no one seemed to notice she was even alive. It was as if the world was happy to move on without her. It wasn't until Chief Davis came over to her that she was even acknowledged. Towering above her, he was a jagged spear of stone, a looming threat of consequence and punishment. Crossing arms over his chest, he stared at her, his expression grim. There was no sign of the man who earlier had tried to empathize with her cause—her mission, but not her methods.

Methods that included bombs. Methods that included harming others.

"Why am I not surprised to see you here?" he asked.

Slumped on the ground, Kinsley had no words for him. She had no words, no clever excuses, nor any desire to run. She had nothing.

"Disappointed," he added, "but not surprised." With a grunt of disgust, he commanded, "Get up."

Kinsley did as she was told, her mind numb, her body weak. A shiver wracked her shoulders. She wanted to crawl into a hole and die.

Two ski patrol hut staff members carried the heavyset man by on a stretcher, pulling her gaze to him until they carried him out of sight. Kinsley wondered as to his condition, how badly he'd been hurt, if he'd survive. She had never wanted to hurt anyone. She'd never meant for anyone to be in danger. Stealing a peek at the animal lying on the ground, fur marred with burn marks, she felt dead inside. She'd only wanted to change hearts, change behavior.

Walsh abruptly left the patrol member he'd been speaking with and stormed over to her and Chief Davis. Daggers shot from his eyes and he jabbed a finger into her face. "This was you, wasn't it?"

Fresh tears pushed into her eyes.

"This was you. You did this."

She shook her head and hot tears fell onto her cheeks. Warm and wet, they instantly froze into an icy film on her skin. "It wasn't me. I had nothing to do with it, I swear."

"I don't believe you." His eyes flashed. "This has your fingerprints all over it."

"He saw the video," Chief Davis informed her. Deadpan tone, the man sounded oddly defeated. Then he grasped her by the arm and said, "You're under arrest. You have the right to remain silent. Anything you say can and will be used against you in a court of law."

A paramedic ran out of the gondola station. Tall and blond, a red bandana tied at his neck, the guy had to be six feet in height, maybe more. Spotting the dog on the ground, he charged toward the animal and dropped to his knees. He placed his face near the dog's and stroked his head, comforting it as though it were his own. Then he lifted up and checked the bandages on the hind end of the dog's body. He said a few words to the staff attending the animal and they moved back, allowing him to sweep the animal from the ground as if it were made of paper. He carried the dog to the gondola and exchanged a hot angry glance with Walsh as the animal hung limp in his arms.

Kinsley clapped a hand over her mouth. *Please, let the dog be alive*, she uttered silently.

Next to her, the Chief of Police continued rattling off the Miranda warning. "If you cannot afford a lawyer, one will be appointed for you."

He could stop at any time. Kinsley knew her rights. She'd been arrested many times during protests and knew the drill. "I understand," she mumbled. "We can go."

She wasn't going to fight him. It would only earn her a handcuffed trip down the mountain, and she was humiliated

enough with Walsh breathing down her neck. She didn't need
the added pressure of metal cuffs biting into her wrists.

Walsh leaned close to her face and said in his gruff
voice, "Go ahead and lawyer-up, Kinsley. It won't do you
any good. This was terrorism, straight up, and you're going
down for it."

She flinched. His anger was palpable, scathing. She imagined Walsh would deliver his own brand of justice and be
done with it. Lisa had said he'd wanted to do as much to the
man who shot her on the mountain. And though Lisa had ex-
pressed some doubt as to whether or not he would have gone
through with it, Kinsley didn't. Not for a second. Staring into
cold green eyes pulsing with hatred, she understood the dark
side of a person's soul far better than Lisa. It was totally within Walsh's personality to kill a man. He was ex-Marine.
Steely, from his soul to his spit.

"I didn't do it," she told him, not exactly sure why since
he certainly wouldn't believe her. But she felt compelled to
try. "I wouldn't knowingly put people's lives in danger." Especially not an animal's." Casting a weary glance toward the
ski patrol hut, the channel carved in the snow where the man
had been dragged, the flattened bloody space where the animal had lain, her heart split in two. It was her fault they'd
been hurt. Her cause, her associates. The blood of innocents
was on her hands. Not her deed, but certainly her fault as
Captain of the ship.

Handing a bracelet over the glass counter, Grant paused.
He looked to the woman across from him, wondering if she'd
heard it. It sounded like a distant boom. Gripped by an eerie
sensation, he moved his gaze out through the front window of
his store and visions of another sound swept through him. A
sudden crack of noise. Giovanna's bombing had been unmistakable, but this sound was different. Muted. Distant.

Returning his attention back to the business at hand,
Grant said, "Let me help you with that." Gingerly, he encircled the woman's narrow wrist with the silver chain and

when she turned her hand palm up, he clipped the silver clasp secure. The bracelet was layered in diamonds and turquoise.

"It's beautiful," she murmured, turning her hand to and fro.

"It's an Alani original. We're the only authorized dealer in the state of Colorado."

Middle-aged blue eyes lit up at the mention. "It's an amazing design." Tracing the delicate stones with professionally manicured fingertips, she raised her hand for a closer inspection.

"The diamonds are colorless and the turquoise is practically infused into the silver," Grant explained. "It's a special technique Alani uses to make the stones appear as if they've melted into the metal."

"The lines are seamless," she admired. "You can tell it's of very high quality."

"We don't carry anything less," he replied, bothered by the expressions on the faces of passersby outside his store. As if mesmerized by the sky, they moved in unison toward the main square. Alarm tickled the hairs at his neck. They looked like they'd seen an alien or something.

Extending her arm, Grant's customer studied the fall of the bracelet at her wrist. Slightly large for her petite frame, it hung low on her hand. "May I see the one next to it?"

"Of course," he replied. Slipping a hand under the glass countertop, Grant pulled out a second bracelet and helped her remove the first. Unable to resist the impulse, he commented, "Looks like aliens have landed."

"What?"

He motioned for her to look outside. Her gaze sharpened on the people standing outside his store. "I wonder what they're looking at."

Best way to find out was to go take a look for ourselves, he mused, but wasn't about to suggest the same. His job was to service his clientele. Hers was to determine where that service began and ended. As if on cue, she wandered toward the door. "There's definitely something going on..." Pushing out through the front door, she walked outside, Grant close at her heel. The two followed the direction of the gazes. Grant's heart stopped. Black smoke billowed from over the ridge near the gondola station. Acid churned in his stomach as he realized the likely cause.

An explosion.

"Oh, my!" The woman gasped and pointed. "Something's on fire—the mountain's on fire!"

Grant flashed a glance back to Giovanna's store, the sight of her boarded window sending a slice of panic through him. Kinsley. Where was Kinsley? Was she okay?

With a hand to her mouth, the woman stood shocked, staring up the mountain. Grant's bracelet dangled from her wrist, the other was clenched in his palm. He had to call Kinsley. He had to make sure she was okay.

"Did you still want to see the other bracelet?" Grant asked curtly. He hated to sound pushy in the wake of what was obviously a crisis, but he wanted to get back into his store and get on the phone, find out what happened up there.

Startled, she turned to him. "Uh, no, thank you." Casting her glance back up the mountain, she fumbled for the bracelet on her wrist, sputtering, "I'm sorry, but—"

"I understand," Grant told her, reaching for the bracelet. "We can do this another time."

She smiled awkwardly. "Yes, I'm sorry. It really is quite lovely."

Grant hurried back into his store. He set the bracelets on the display counter, grabbed his cell phone and punched in Kinsley's number. Waiting through rings, it went to voicemail. Should he leave a message? The tone beeped for him to speak. "Kinsley, Grant. Just checking in for our dinner this evening. Hope we're still on for seven-thirty." Ending the call, he felt stupid. Surely, she was okay. She was holding a protest at the base, not the top of the mountain. Now she'd probably think him some kind of lovesick fool for calling to confirm their dinner date.

His gaze moved out the front windows of his store to the growing spectacle of people. Kinsley couldn't have missed the sound. He'd heard it and he was indoors. A strange sensation overcame him. An explosion. Accidental? Deliberate?

Questions deluged him. Was she up there? Had one of her people planted another bomb? Tingles raced up his neck, curling around his face like prickly fingers. He glanced in the direction of the mountain, envisioning it in his mind. No. She was holding a protest this afternoon—at the base of the mountain. Her group would be demonstrating outside Lee Palmer's hotel—not the mountaintop gondola station. Checking his watch, Grant decided to go see her. He'd see her with his own two eyes and know that she was okay, that her group wasn't part of whatever happened up there.

Could have been an accident. With three restaurants up there, it could have been a kitchen explosion. Quickly replacing the bracelets to their respective slots, Grant closed and locked the display case, strode to the front door and flipped his "Open" sign to "Closed." Ten minutes away from the store wouldn't kill him. Ten minutes, he'd be to Kinsley and back and his mind would be at ease. She wouldn't even have to see him. So long as he saw her, all would be well. He grabbed his jacket. Struck by a stab of guilt, followed by a tinge of embarrassment—he was a grown man going to spy on the woman in his life. Stupid, but somehow he felt it necessary. Warranted. Grant locked the door behind him and prayed she was there and he was being foolish. The alternative was unthinkable.

But it was something he had to know, one way or the other.

Kinsley had chosen the site of Palmer's hotel for her protest to ensure Lee Palmer would see them and hear them. Apparently, confrontation was part of the formula. *Be heard, be seen, take your grievance to the source.*

Grant didn't know about Palmer, but at this hour, when skiers were pouring off the mountain, Kinsley would definitely get an audience. Add those arriving for après-ski, the draw of smoke billowing from the top of the mountain, and it would amount to a virtual glut between the gondola and the village. Grant neared the hotel, but with so many people milling about, couldn't get a fix on her. At least he knew what to look for. During their lunch she'd been dressed head-to-toe in cream, which should make her stand out. But with bodies coming and going, one giant throng of humans, Grant couldn't get a hit. Angling his body, he made his way to the center of the protest. As leader, Kinsley would most likely take up position there, if not the front line.

"Save the land!"

"Palmer International is raping the environment!"

Weaving through the protesters, Grant looked from jacket-to-jacket, face-to-face. Blues, grays, blacks but no cream. Men, women, but no Kinsley. Had she changed clothes? Was she protesting from a different location? Spotting the blonde girl from the other day, the one who stepped forward wearing the white parka Grant had seen in the video from Giovanna's store, Grant went to her.

As he neared, she eyed him warily, as though he were about to inflict harm. Grant couldn't care less if she thought he was Genghis Khan, he had questions and she likely had the answers. "Hey," he called out. She turned from him and he walked up next to her. He pulled her by the arm to face him. The woman looked ready to attack and he instantly released her. He wasn't here for trouble. He was here for information. "Have you seen Kinsley?"

"If I had, I wouldn't tell you."

Grant ignored the hateful glare in her otherwise pretty green eyes and said, "I just want to know if she's here."

The young woman's gaze darted upward. "I don't know where she is."

Grant noted the girl's dodge. In an afterthought of reaction, he followed her gaze to see a column of smoke climbing high into the sky. Everyone on the ground around them was aware something awful had happened, although this young woman didn't seem to be particularly concerned. "She's supposed to be here for the protest," Grant continued. "Have you seen her?"

Tipping her face up at him, she visibly tightened her mouth, sealing it closed. With a shrug of her shoulders, she shook her head, though her gaze practically dared him to push.

Grant stared at her. This was lunacy. The girl was playing games—games he had no time for! Taking a step backward, he moved clear of the protesters. Several looked at him, and their expressions filled with loathing. Suddenly, he felt marked, and wanted to put as much distance as possible between himself and them. This was not his group. These were not his people.

Giving up on finding Kinsley in the midst of them, Grant went to the gondola station. Maybe she was there, checking to see what happened. That's what he would do, if he'd been here and heard the boom. He'd want to investigate the source, especially if he thought some of his people were involved, people who could put him in jeopardy with the authorities.

Grant jogged to the entrance for the gondola. Not surprisingly, the attendant in charge was waving people away, announcing the gondola was closed. No one was going up save for emergency personnel. Looking around, Grant saw no sign of Kinsley. He felt a tightening in his chest, a faint squeeze warning his stress level was rising. *Slow down. Back off.* It was a familiar message from his body, yet he couldn't move. He couldn't move from this scene, like he was tied to a stake in the ground. Grant pulled the cell phone from his pocket. There'd been no call, no text. His gaze drifted up the line of gondola cars, slowly moving up and down the mountain. Was she already on her way up? On her way down? Was she someplace else entirely?

Bothered by a growing sense of defeat, Grant whispered, "Kinsley, where are you?"

Chapter Sixteen

An hour later, Kinsley sat in a hard metal chair in a near-empty room, her back rigid as she stared at a police officer sitting across the table from her. There was nothing else to look at, the room empty, painted drab gray, a single lamp hanging a few feet above the table. The standard two-way mirror was embedded in the wall behind him. He was the detective assigned to her case, the case against her for the ski patrol hut bombing. Chief Davis was accusing her of the bombing—her—and not Sebastian Wu, despite her repeated attempts to convince him otherwise.

Overcome by a wave of exhaustion, Kinsley's patience was about to snap. They were getting nowhere. She was trying to be cooperative, but the man wasn't listening. "I've already told you. I had nothing to do with it."

"We have you on video for the first one. It'll be better if you confess now, while a deal is on the table. Once your lawyer gets here, it's gone." The man stood, emitting a snort of disgust. "You think about that, pretty girl. Right now you've got a chance. Once we pull it, you're going to prison." He leered and tossed out, "And you're not going to do very well in there."

Kinsley trailed the detective's figure as he exited through a metal door, the heavy clunk of deadbolt jolting her. She steeled her emotions against a swarm of nerves. Alone with her thoughts, she willed herself to remain calm. She'd been to jail, nothing serious, nothing more than a few hours in a holding cell. But this was different. This was criminal, big-time criminal carrying a big-time sentence. If she were convicted, she'd be put away for a very long time.

Kinsley crossed her arms over her chest. Her heart closed. He was right. She wouldn't do well in federal prison.

But she'd told him the truth. There was nothing more she could do.

The rapid clink of thick metal startled her. The door opened and Kinsley's eyes latched onto the well-dressed man entering the room. Serving up a fat smile, Merle Brugman dropped his sleek leather briefcase to the table with a thud, opened the buttons of his black overcoat and took a seat at the table in the chair previously occupied by the detective. The white shirt and yellow paisley tie he wore coordinated perfectly with his navy pinstripe suit. His long wavy black hair was cut just above the collar and combed back, giving Merle more of a California look than Colorado. But like many, he'd migrated east and found he enjoyed mountain living, though his attire hadn't managed to acclimate to the more casual western wear. On the heavy side, his body took up most of the chair and then some. "Hey, Kinsley."

"Hi, Merle."

Pushing aside his briefcase, he set his elbows to the table and folded his arms. "I gotta be honest with you, this one isn't good." His eyes held more than a hint of concern. "Possession of an explosive device is pretty serious and will carry some pretty stiff time if you're convicted. Right now, they only have you for the fur store bombing but are working to get you for the patrol hut bomb, too."

She tensed. "I didn't do it, Merle."

He nodded, as though the expected reply was irrelevant. "We're talking possible life sentence, if the guy dies. Add the fact that they're calling this eco-terrorism, and you've just bumped yourself into the federal court system. Right now, we have to work with the initial charge. There's no automatic bond set in federal court, so you might be in here for a while." Merle glanced about the room. "Or a federal facility in Denver. If they do set bond, it might be pretty high, considering the charges. You think your parents will help?"

Her parents. They were the reason she was on the mountain in the first place. *I hope you're not here to cause trouble.* Her father's admonition had been grave, as though he knew her intentions were not good. Then coincidentally, the ski patrol hut explodes. Would he post bail?

Not likely. Not if he thought she was responsible, he wouldn't. He'd let her rot in jail and not think twice. Her mother would want to help, but she wouldn't go against her husband to do it. "I don't know," Kinsley replied weakly. "I don't know. I have money. How much are we talking?"

"Could be a million."

Merle might as well have kicked her in the stomach. "*What*? A million? Are you serious?"

Merle nodded. "That's what they said."

"But I don't have that kind of money!"

Merle grimaced, shadows slanting across his face from the drop light above. "That's why I mentioned your parents."

Kinsley expelled her breath in a ragged sigh. Suddenly, she felt nauseous. Sick. Leaning forward, she slumped onto the table. Defeat wound through chest. "They won't pay."

"Are you sure?"

"Pretty sure," she muttered, and cupped a hand to her forehead. "What happens from here?"

"The good news is you have a friend in Chief Davis."

"I do?"

"Yeah." Merle tossed her a dry smile. "He wants you to come clean, and he'll do everything he can to get the judge to go easy on you. First offense, crime of passion—"

"But I didn't do it!" she blurted. "Sebastian did!"

"That's what he said. So what's this about Sebastian? I thought he was your number one guy."

Kinsley ground her jaw, ribbons of anger pulling tightly around her heart. "He was, until the bastard double-crossed me."

"Maybe you should start from the beginning," Merle said. He leaned back in his chair and threaded his fingers together over his midsection. "Tell me what's been going on."

Kinsley relayed the bomb-switch at the fur store. She admitted responsibility for an ink bomb, but not an explosive one. Her intent had been to destroy the furs, a crime she would gladly pay for, but she wasn't going down for a bomb that blew out the front window of the store. Someone could have gotten hurt. She would never have done something so reckless. Then there was the ski patrol hut incident. Kinsley explained to Merle her suspicions, the comments overheard, and that she was simply working off a hunch which put her on the scene at the time of the explosion. That and a fear for the safety of her parents. Merle nodded dutifully throughout, but Kinsley wasn't sure he believed her. Running through the course of events made her look guilty. Guilty as charged.

"Do you have any proof?"

"No. I don't have proof, other than firsthand knowledge I didn't do it. I assume you know about the video of me outside the fur store?" Merle nodded. "They have video, because I was there. It was me."

"Chief Davis said you denied it."

"I know, and it was stupid." Especially considering how guilty it made her look now. "But the only reason I denied it was because I didn't intentionally place an explosive in the fur store. I placed an ink spray bomb that was supposed to send a message, nothing more." Merle screwed his expression. "Sebastian *switched* the bomb on me. He rigged it so that it would blow up for real instead of blowing ink."

Cocking his head, Merle replied, "You're kinda splitting hairs there, aren't you?"

"It makes a difference in the charges, doesn't it?"

"Well, yes, depending on the amount of damage caused. But if they nail you with eco-terrorism, you're still in a twist. The real problem is the bomb in the ski patrol hut."

For the first time in the five years she'd known Merle Brugman, the look in his eyes held distrust. He didn't believe her. Panic pushed in. "You need to question Sebastian. I think I saw him on the top of the mountain just before the bomb went off. If they have video of me in town outside the fur store, there must be video cameras outside the ski patrol hut." Impatience ramped up need as she yammered on. "This town is loaded with them. There's got to be a number of them up on the mountain. One of them is bound to have captured Sebastian near the hut."

Merle pursed his lips. He tented his fingers and brought them to his lips. Peering at Kinsley, his eyes narrowed and she could almost see him combing through the evidence, her chances at beating the charges, their chances at linking Sebastian to either bombing. Merle was a shark in the courtroom. Round and easygoing on the outside, he was slice and dice on the inside. The man was relentless when it came to fact-finding. He missed nothing.

Kinsley needed that tenacity now more than ever. Even if he thought she was guilty, he'd defend her to the end.

"Let's see what we can do."

Kinsley expelled a breath. "I didn't do it, Merle. I *swear*."

Merle listened as Kinsley shared everything she could about Sebastian; how he operated, how he thought. She tried to be as thorough as possible so her attorney would find something he could work with. When she finished, he promised he'd get Sebastian in for questioning. Where she was looking for his vote of confidence, Kinsley received lukewarm encouragement. "We have something to go on. It's a start."

It was all she could ask for at the moment. With zero allies on her side, Kinsley had to hope for the best and be prepared for the worst. After Merle left, Chief Davis came in to personally escort her to the booking department. Pausing with a hand on the doorknob, he said, "I wish you hadn't lied to me about the fur store, Kinsley."

"Me, too," was all she could reply. "Me, too."

Two hours later, Kinsley collapsed onto a threadbare bed, the orange jumpsuit swallowing her body whole. Bulky, worn and tattered, the uniform was degrading for what it represented. She was a criminal. A loser. This was no longer a passionate protest arrest but a criminal offense. A federal offense. The police department considered her a terrorist. Merle had taken the time to lay it all out for her, explaining charges would be filed, bond would be set and it would be high. The consequences were serious. If they couldn't prove Sebastian was the culprit, the feds would settle for Kinsley. Dropping her head back against the cement wall, she cringed inwardly. And she had no alibi for the ski patrol hut bombing, other than a brief conversation with her father minutes before. Would he vouch for her? Would he think she did it?

God only knew when that bomb had been placed at the patrol hut. In the past, Sebastian worked off a timer or activated a device via cell phone. The fact that she had seen him moments before suggested a timer. Whichever way he chose to set it, she was going down for it. Pressing her back into the cold wall, Kinsley closed her eyes. Unable to ward off images of her mother and father, Grant, Lisa...it felt as if her life was ruined. Her future business plans, her budding romance, all ruined because of one man. Sebastian Wu.

Grant would hate her. They were supposed to meet for dinner at Adele's tonight, but it was a date she wouldn't make. She wouldn't be able to call, she wouldn't be able to explain. He would learn it from the Chief of Police after sitting alone at the bar, waiting for a no-show. Kinsley could hear it now. *We've caught the person responsible for bombing the fur store. Her name is Kinsley Fairchild.* Envisioning Grant's face, his expression...it would crush him. Whether she was wrongly convicted for the patrol hut bombing or not, her involvement in the fur store incident would be enough for him to cut her from his life—a life she'd begun looking forward to. But now, it was all gone. Ruined. And so was she.

Grant Powell escorted Giovanna into Wade's office, barely able to contain his excitement over the news. Chief Davis said he had more video evidence, conclusive video evidence regarding the bombing in the fur store, and he wanted to share it with them. Once again, Giovanna had asked Grant to join her for moral support, and he obliged. Despite the late hour, there was still plenty enough time to make his date with Kinsley.

Kinsley. Grant checked his watch, unable to shake the feeling that something was wrong. He had yet to hear from her, and he was concerned, for more reasons than he cared to admit. The protesters had been unaffected by the mountaintop explosion, as though they couldn't care less. A man had been injured, a search and rescue dog, too, yet the protesters continued their chanting, oblivious to the suffering of others. Evacuated tourists flowed from the gondola station in droves, yet the protesters continued to shout their mantras. Grant had waited for sight of Kinsley for as long as he could, but the number of people had burgeoned and he realized there was nothing for him to do but get out of the way. There was no way he'd find Kinsley in that mass of bedlam.

Instead, he had returned to his store, debated his options, mulled over the situation, his concerns, and basically twiddled his thumbs while the Silver Creek community absorbed the shock. Then Giovanna had called. She'd heard from Chief Davis. There was video evidence, clear video evidence, depicting the person responsible for the bombing of her store. Of course he would join her at the police station. He wanted to see who the culprit was as badly as Giovanna.

It would ease his mind with regard to Kinsley.

Chief Davis closed the door, his imposing presence filling in the space behind them as they took their seats. Grant could feel Giovanna's energy running high. She was about to learn the truth and it felt like her spirits were bouncing off the walls. With a name—a suspect—she could hold someone accountable. Her business had been destroyed, her life in Colorado brought to an end, but knowing who was responsible would give her closure.

Then Giovanna had told him she'd purchased her plane ticket home. *No sense in postponing the inevitable.* She had prepared an itemized list of destroyed inventory and forwarded it to the insurance company. All that remained was to pack up and head home—except to learn the identity of whom she would be pressing charges against.

Grant wished he could share in her relief, but he couldn't. His heart felt more tightly wound than a golf ball, nerves so taut he could barely breathe. He fully expected the culprit to be one of Kinsley's people—a fact that would certainly cause friction between them—but it couldn't be helped. While she'd claimed her people had nothing to do with it, Grant would have serious reservations if he learned otherwise. Did she know about it beforehand? Did she condone such acts? Had she given tacit consent?

If he found out that she had lied to him, he would have a tough time. But if she could give him some kind of rationale, some reasonable explanation—or better yet, out-and-out denial of knowledge—then he could move forward. He didn't want anything to ruin their time together, and the knowledge that one of her crew had destroyed his friend's business would definitely ruin it. Grant couldn't engage in a dishonest relationship. It went against his very core.

And Kinsley was a woman with whom he wanted to engage. He hadn't realized how deeply he felt about her until the thought of losing her hit home. Over the last few days, he and Kinsley had grown unbelievably close. They shared a chemistry that Grant hadn't experienced in years. Smart and sexy, she was gorgeous, but more important, she was his equal when it came to a passion for business. He wasn't sure what he'd expected when he tossed out the idea of a vegan clothing line, but Kinsley had snapped it up and run like a gazelle-turned-pit bull. The gazelle part he'd attributed to her age. The pit bull was pure determination.

"As I mentioned on the phone," Wade began, his demeanor one hundred percent business as he circled around them. "I located some town video that reveals the individual exiting your store."

"Yes, yes, that's what you said," Giovanna replied eagerly, leaning forward in one of twin leather wing chairs. "And the identity is clear?"

"Very."

Opting to stand, Grant slid an arm over Giovanna's chair and gave an encouraging pat to her shoulder. He was too keyed-up to sit.

Likewise, Wade remained standing. Bending over his desk, he clicked through icons on his computer. Pulling up a video, he hit the play button, then angled the screen for the two of them to watch. Leaning in for a better view, Grant noted the image was somewhat grainy, the snowfall from that evening making it appear spotty. But it was clear enough that he could see the larger words etched on Giovanna's front door. From the angle they were watching, the camera had to have been posted catty-corner across the street from his and Giovanna's stores. A couple passed at a leisurely pace, completely unaware of what was about to happen. Grant sucked in a breath. Thank God, the explosion hadn't occurred when people were passing within feet of the store. They could have been hit by flying debris.

The glow of street lights lent an air of calm to the video. The calm before the storm, he mused. As expected, a woman wearing a white jacket and hat let herself out of Giovanna's store. With a brief glance in either direction, she immediately set off across the street, slowing her stride abruptly, almost as if it were a struggle to maintain an even pace yet of the utmost importance to do so.

Grant's nerves revved up as he honed in on her face. He recalled the woman who had stepped forward the day he confronted Kinsley. She'd been wearing the same white coat and challenged Grant to accuse her of the bombing. While he doubted it would have been her, he remained anxious to see who it was.

As the woman on the video sauntered across the street, her gait graceful and lanky like a model on a catwalk runway, Grant felt his chest squeeze. Nearing the camera, the woman kept her head down, but not far enough. The tip of her nose, the shape of her lips could be seen. Streaks of pain pierced his shoulder. Just before she passed directly beneath the lens, her head tipped back slightly and she shook her head, her smile unmistakable.

Grant's heart stopped. It was Kinsley Fairchild.

"It's a beautiful woman," Giovanna cried out in surprise.

"We have her in custody for questioning," Wade said. "We also believe she's responsible for the bombing of a ski patrol hut outside the gondola station up on the mountain."

Dropping his arm from Giovanna's chair, Grant felt lightheaded. Kinsley had disappeared from view, but he could see her in his mind's eye as clearly as if she were still on the video. Over and over and over, an endless loop of video replayed in his mind—her lips, her smile, her face.

Kinsley. It had been Kinsley all along.

Giovanna gasped.

Grant couldn't think, he couldn't move. He could only feel blade after blade plunge into his chest. Pressure closed a steel band around his heart, squeezing with the power of a vise-grip. A pit formed in his stomach. For a second, Grant thought he was going to be sick.

"Are you okay?" Wade asked him.

"Yes..." Grant tried to breathe. His gaze moved to the Chief of Police. *Did Wade just say she was responsible for the bombing up on the mountaintop, too?*

Giovanna looked up at him, her thick lashes fluttering as she peered into his face. "Grant?"

Wade moved from behind his desk. "I think you should sit down."

Wasn't he? Confusion swam through his skull. He couldn't tell.

Calm. He needed calm.

"Grant!"

Everything went black.

Chapter Seventeen

Kinsley heard a key inserted into the door lock followed by the clang of a metal key ring loaded with keys. She launched up from her bed as an officer opened the door. Were they letting her go? Hope bloomed in her chest. Had Merle convinced them of her innocence and they were setting her free?

A man dressed in a khaki-gray uniform stood in the open doorway. "Come with me."

"Where?"

"You have a visitor."

Expectation popped like a balloon. A visitor. Merle? Her mother? Kinsley's breath caught. Grant?

Of course. He would have to know by now. Silver Creek was a small town. The explosion would be big news. When she didn't show up for dinner, didn't call, Grant would have put the two together and assumed she had something to do with it.

Had he called the police department? Had they told him they'd made an arrest in the case? He was a friend of Giovanna's, of Chief Davis. A knot formed in her stomach. Grant would know about it all, and he would think she was responsible. Visions of an injured patrol dog lying in the snow chopped through her mind—the naked fear shown by staff members, the subsequent anger, black smoke defiling the air as it curled upward, a man hauled to safety, his body appearing lifeless. Dead. Grant would think Kinsley had been responsible for it all.

Following the officer, Kinsley thought she would be sick, physically sick, right here, right now. Her gaze darted about the wood floors, the honey-toned walls. Suddenly, she felt trapped. After a series of doors opened and closed, Kinsley saw her visitor and nearly tripped. Dressed in a hot pink sweater and matching ski hat, Lisa Richardson stood rigid, arms crossed over her chest, her nose bright red from the cold. Brown eyes that normally held ease and affection stared at Kinsley, remote and distanced.

"Lisa," Kinsley murmured, her knees buckling beneath her. The officer ushered her toward a chair, then stood silently by the door. Shock petered through her. It wasn't Grant. It was Lisa, her best friend. "What are you doing here?"

"I could ask you the same question."

Kinsley felt the slap. Lisa was the one person who had always stood by her, defended her cause, explained to others what it meant to have passion, the power of purpose needed to effect change in the world. But as they stood face-to-face, disapproval oozed from Lisa's pores.

With a shaky hand to the back of the chair, Kinsley steadied herself. "I didn't do it," she replied, growing weary of repeating the tired line over and over. "It wasn't me."

"Chief Davis said you bombed the fur store. That you admitted to it."

The accusation stung. Looking into the angry gaze of her best friend, Kinsley felt as though her lifeboat was slipping from her grasp. She had lied. And she had been caught. Dropping to a seat, she dragged a hand through her hair, pulled long bangs from up and over her head. "I did, but not in the way that it happened."

"What? What are you talking about?" Lisa ripped the ski hat from her head and dumped her wiry body into an opposite chair, a metal table separating them. "You're not making any sense."

"Because none of this makes sense," Kinsley mumbled.

"Do you know that a dog was burned in the blast? An avalanche dog that has been with the staff for years?" Kinsley nodded. "There's a man in the hospital, Kinsley. My dad says he might die."

Kinsley nodded. Tears pricked her eyes as she digested the information. It was horrible. It was all horrible.

Lisa smacked a fist to the table, causing Kinsley to jump. "This isn't you!" she cried. "This isn't *you*. What's changed to make you do these things?"

Kinsley didn't do them. She wouldn't do them.

Lisa's lower lip trembled. Her eyes shone. "Walsh is angry that I'm even here."

The mention of Walsh snagged Kinsley's attention. Walsh had been there, been with Wade and savored Kinsley's arrest. It must have been difficult for Lisa to come. It would certainly be against his wishes and with a serious dose of resentment. But Kinsley was Lisa's friend and Lisa didn't forsake her friends—for anyone, including the man in her life. Lisa was loyal, faithful. And she was hurting.

Staring into the face of the one person in the world who understood her the best, Kinsley felt the full weight of Lisa's distress as if it were her own. Lisa was here and Kinsley was glad for it, but she didn't want her friend to jeopardize a relationship because of her. Kinsley dropped her head. She folded her hands and buried them in her lap. "You don't have to stay. I appreciate that you've come, but I'll understand if you want to leave."

"I don't want to leave—I want to *understand*. I want to know what drove you to do it."

Anger fired hot and fresh. Kinsley flipped her face up to meet Lisa directly and exclaimed, "I didn't do it! Sebastian set me up at the fur store. Yes, I intended to set an ink bomb in the fur store and send a message, but that's it. I never intended to use explosives that would blow out her front window. Sebastian switched the bomb on me. He placed the bomb at the ski patrol hut."

Lisa hovered on the edge of doubt.

It gave Kinsley a scrap of hope. "I *swear*, Lisa." Jamming her hands onto the table, Kinsley needed Lisa to hear her. "I have no problem taking credit for my actions, you know that. You know me. But I refuse to accept the blame for things I didn't do. I think Sebastian set that bomb on the mountain, but I can't prove it. Not yet, anyway. Not from a jail cell."

"What are you going to do? My dad says you could go to federal prison if they convict you."

"I have to prove my innocence."

"How are you going to do that?"

"I don't know, yet."

"Are they going to release you? Can you get out on bond?"

"I won't know until I appear before a judge tomorrow."

"Do your parents know?"

"I don't know," she murmured. Dropping her gaze to the muted gray table, Kinsley softened her focus. She'd asked Merle to call them—her mother—but she hadn't heard the first word. Lee Palmer was their friend. Silver Creek was his development. Explosives were serious business. The more she thought about it, the more Kinsley realized she'd be lucky if her mother acknowledged her on the street, let alone called her to offer support. Fighting a rising tide of defeat, Kinsley thrust, "I need to make bail. I need to get out of here and confront Sebastian."

"Do you think that's smart?" Lisa blinked, holding Kinsley secure within her gaze. "I mean, if the guy is willing to blow up a ski patrol hut, I think he might be willing to hurt you. Really hurt you."

"Maybe." Kinsley shrugged, knowing Lisa was right to be concerned. But it was a chance she'd have to take. She couldn't *not* confront him. The more she thought about what Sebastian had done to her, the more determined she was to clear her name. There were too many people who believed she was guilty. Worse—they believed her a horrible person capable of violence in the name of her cause. Kinsley Fairchild used the power of the written word to further her cause, not the detonation of a bomb. Yes, she had meant to destroy the furs, but it had been as a last-resort effort. The business owners of Silver Creek were in the back pocket of

Palmer International, and Kinsley had wanted to make a point.

Grant's face appeared in her mind, his expression after their kiss, the look in his eyes. Hot and hungry, soft and sensual, he'd enjoyed it as much as she had, wanted more—much more. They had been connected. On so many levels, she and Grant had connected and now she stood on the verge of losing it all. Sadness rolled in, cleared his image from her imagination. Grant would never forgive her. She had destroyed his friend's store, intended to ruin the furs. Despite her rationale, it was possible that one act would be enough to prevent a future with him.

Knowing that, Kinsley would own what she had done. But she would not take blame for that which she had not.

"Is there anything I can do to help?"

Thoughts and ideas fired through Kinsley's brain. Tell Grant she was sorry? Tell Giovanna, tell her parents, tell everyone that she'd messed up by trusting the wrong man? Wishes, desires—need—all battled for release, but Kinsley couldn't voice a single sentiment. She wanted to ask about Grant. She wanted Lisa to tell him that she was innocent, that she was sorry, but how could she?

Lisa didn't know about their relationship because Kinsley hadn't shared. She hadn't shared, because she wasn't quite sure how to share. *I'm seeing an older man. He's wonderful, incredible, and oh, by the way, he's a friend of your father. We're getting serious, very, even planning a trip to New York to begin my new business venture—the one I haven't had time to share with you because I've been too busy sharing with him.*

Kinsley peered into the face of her best friend and closed the lid to her heart. This was her cross to bear, not Lisa's, and she wouldn't burden her friend any more than she already had. However... A twinkle of thought erupted in Kinsley's brain as Lisa sat expectantly. The hostility had drained from her gaze, leaving only the trusting ally Kinsley had come to know and love. Maybe there was something Lisa could do.

She wanted to help. She wanted to support her friend. Could she do so without hurting her relationship with Walsh? He would be furious to know Lisa was colluding with Kinsley, a suspected criminal. Could she keep it a secret?

"I might need a favor..." Kinsley began.

Lisa perked up. "What kind of favor?"

A smile tingled behind Kinsley's lips as an idea formed in her mind. Glancing upward to a corner of the ceiling, she said, "A harmless one."

Walking into the court room the next morning, hand-cuffed and escorted by a uniformed officer, Kinsley spotted Merle Brugman at a table up front. At the table next to him, two state attorneys sat, legal eagles prepared to make their case against her. Merle had insisted this session was going to be quick. No fluff, no fancy speeches, get in and get out. Their goal was reasonable bond. While she had a slew of prior arrests, none rose to the level of criminal felony.

She filed past a bank of chairs and stumbled. *Mother?* Kinsley slowed, her attention glued to the stoic, elegant woman seated several places behind Merle. A rush of relief swept through Kinsley. *She was here*. Passing, Kinsley saw the grave disappointment etched in her dark eyes.

Kinsley faltered. Her mother was here. Unhappily, but she was here. Heartbeats pounded erratically through her chest. Victoria Fairchild's presence might be the difference in bond or no bond.

Hurriedly, Kinsley took a seat. Swallowing, she cleared her throat and straightened in her chair. Merle said nothing, his attention securely resting on the judge sitting on a raised platform at the front of the room. Dressed in the customary black robe attire, the judge was older, mid-fifties with silver hair. He appeared calm, unperturbed. Kinsley gulped, bothered by a quick scatter of nerves. The judge appeared even-tempered, fair. She flashed a glance toward Merle. Did they have a chance?

Shuffling papers on the desk before him, the judge glanced toward her lawyer. "Mr. Brugman, are you prepared to get started?"

"I am, Your Honor."

The judge glanced to the prosecutors' table where the two men sat, their postures rigid, defiant. "Are you prepared to proceed?"

"The State is ready."

"Approach the bench."

Kinsley followed Merle over and stood idle as she listened to the charges being read. Merle pleaded her case, running through a litany of reasons why Kinsley should receive reasonable bond. Stealing a peek at her mother, she felt a stab of guilt. She didn't know all the facts. She was here, most likely working under the assumption that her daughter was guilty but entitled to a legal defense. It struck Kinsley as an amazing show of support on her mother's behalf and instantly wondered, did her father know? Had he objected?

Shoving the conjecture from her mind, Kinsley decided it didn't matter. Her mother was here, and for that she was eternally grateful.

Merle continued to wrangle with the opposing attorneys until the loud smack of the gavel silenced the room. "Bail is set at one million," the judge decreed.

One million? Kinsley closed her eyes, crushed by the news. It might as well be ten million. Unless her mother stepped up and offered to pay, Kinsley had no way of pulling together that kind of money. It was ludicrous! Suddenly, she felt more scared than she'd ever been in her life. These people weren't messing around. They wanted her in jail.

Resisting the urge to look back and silently beg for her help, Kinsley walled her emotions in. She would not break down. She would not lose it here, in front of everyone. Merle leaned close and said, "Count your blessings on this one." Blessings? An unexpected knot swelled in her throat. Because it could have been higher? "Your mother has your back," he added, then pulled away.

Relief flooded in. A wave of tears pushed at Kinsley's eyes. *Her mother had come through.* Merle had called her, and she had come through for her daughter. "Thank you," she whispered through a quick trembling of her lips. Maybe now she had a chance. Maybe she could avoid a quick conviction in a rush to judgment and put the real culprit behind bars. A wave of wooziness washed through Kinsley's skull. *Thank you, Mom.*

On her way out of the courtroom, Kinsley locked onto her mother and sent an unspoken "thank you" through her gaze. Her mother was here because she believed in her daughter. She had always supported her, had always been the cushion in Kinsley's life and she would stand by her side until the end.

The end. It was an end Kinsley was determined to set straight.

After being released, Kinsley returned to Silver Creek. She knew her mother would not be waiting for her. The legal process took time and from what Merle had said, her mother had other obligations. Kinsley understood. This week was about Lee Palmer and her father, and her mother was nothing, if not a devoted wife and partner. Not like Kinsley was about to complain. Her mother had seen to her release. Kinsley inhaled deeply, grateful to be wearing her own clothes and shoes. Slugging around in a jailbird suit and handcuffs made her feel like a criminal, a thug. It also made her appreciate her freedom and the fortune of family and friends. She walked out of that jail determined never to repeat the scene again. But the only way that was going to happen was to bring the true criminal to justice. Emerging from the parking garage, she braced against the bite of wind and quickly crossed the bridge into town, perched over the town's namesake creek. She blended in with tourists and matched the flow of traffic as they trampled over heavy wooden slats, the rushing stream visible beneath. It felt good to be a part of the mainstream, the crowd of visitors flocking in for dinner and shopping, meeting friends at the slopes for a spot of après-ski.

Inhaling deeply, her senses awakened as she breathed in the icy air. Kinsley internalized the sensation, the idea of mainstream, going with the flow. It had never been in her plan to conform to the group. She was a rebel, an outlier. She fought the flow of apathy, complacency. She didn't ride with the current. The only constant in life was change. Change for the better, change for the worse. Change—because the status quo could no longer be maintained. Kinsley understood change. Now, it was time to use it to her advantage.

Walking behind a woman dressed in a long red overcoat and boots, her flaxen hair shiny and stick-straight down her back, Kinsley's focus wandered to the material of the woman's clothing. What type of synthetic fiber would best mimic wool? What would retain warmth, yet remain soft and comfortable and withstand the test of time? The elements? A man walking beside the woman wore a ski jacket, a much easier target when it came to non-animal product attire. But Kinsley wanted to design fine clothing, stylish, the kind of fabrics women craved to wear, like a favorite silk scarf or sleek leather boots. Kinsley's attention went back to the woman and her clothing. Her label would be coveted by any fashion-minded woman because her name would equate to quality, style and animal-free. A Kinsley Fairchild original.

Immersed in thought, Kinsley rounded the corner and stopped cold, stricken by the sight of the boarded fur store. Rough plywood had been nailed over the window, the wood framing scarred black, the interior dark. People sidestepped around Kinsley as she stood transfixed by the damage. Beyond the fur store was Grant's jewelry store. Heartbeats fluttered in her breast. Was he inside? Should she go to him?

Fear sliced her in two. Kinsley dug her hands into her pockets and squeezed them close to her body to ward off the chill. An ache filled her heart. Grant wouldn't understand. He would only know that she destroyed his friend's store. The more she'd thought about it, the more she'd realized the truth.

Grant was not the type of man to brush over betrayal. She had lied about the bombing. He had her dead to rights and she had lied.

Lingering in place, a strong urge to confront the situation head-on overwhelmed her, as if she was being pulled to his store by a string. A firestorm of nerves scattered through her belly. She needed to see him. She needed to set the record straight and explain herself, whether he understood or not. She needed to be honest with him. It was the least she owed him after everything he'd done for her.

Kinsley kicked into step and marched toward the store. She swung the door open and careened to a stop, bombarded by a hammer-pulse in her chest. Standing behind the jewelry case was a young man, mid-twenties. Alerted by the door chime he looked up and secured her within his gaze. Tall, good-looking, but he was not Grant. His smile was instantaneous. "May I help you?"

Involuntarily, she glanced about the store. "Uh-um," she stammered, forcing her jellified legs to walk toward him. Continually glancing about as though she expected Grant to appear any second, she asked abruptly, "Yes. Is Grant here?"

"Grant?" Shadows darkened the blue of the man's eyes as though she'd said exactly the wrong thing. "No, he isn't."

He wasn't? Where was he? Darting a glance toward the back, struck by the idea that Grant might have told this man to lie to her should she show up, Kinsley pressed against a distinct need to turn and run, "Where is he?"

A mild suspicion tensed his gaze. "Are you a friend?"

"Kinsley. Kinsley Fairchild." When he returned a quizzical expression, she added, "Yes, I'm a close friend of his. Do you know where I can find him?"

She could see him as he mentally sifted through the information. She was a friend. She was okay. The noose around her heart loosened.

With a quiet nod, he replied, "Grant is in the hospital. He had a heart attack yesterday."

Kinsley's mouth fell open as the floor gave way beneath her.

Chapter Eighteen

Fully-dressed and awaiting discharge from the hospital, Grant tossed the daily newspaper to his bed. He removed his reading glasses and rubbed the bridge of his nose, fighting a sense of urgency. He needed to leave—get out of here and get back to business. Ambivalence churned in his gut. He needed an antacid. Nearing the window, Grant gazed out over the snow-laden lawn, trees half-buried, their dark branches thick with needles and the tiny buds of new cones. Beyond was a packed parking lot, a slew of patients and visitors during the busiest time of year. A sweep of frustration overtook him. Stuck in a hospital room because he'd succumbed to the stress, the reality that the new woman in his life had betrayed him, Grant couldn't shake the need for confrontation. Kinsley Fairchild would hear about this and she'd hear about it from him.

"Knock, knock." At the sound of the familiar voice, Grant turned to see Hal Richardson stroll in. Sandy-haired and smiling, dressed in a white overcoat over green hospital scrubs, his friend greeted him with a lighthearted, "Didn't I tell you to stay away from this place?"

Grant chucked back, "You, and about four other docs."

"And you didn't listen." Hal's smile lost a trace of humor. "What happened, Grant? Wade told me you passed out in his office."

Wade Davis. Figures he'd call Hal. Must have been surprised as hell when Grant dropped to a heap on his office floor, and without a next of kin to notify, Wade had called Hal. Grant shrugged. "Snuck up on me."

"Stress will do that to a guy."

"Stress, high blood pressure, old age—it's a battlefield out there. They say what doesn't kill you makes you stronger, but I'm beginning to wonder."

"Your heart can only take so much, you know."

"Tell me about it," Grant replied, working to keep his tone nonchalant. No sense letting on the real reason he collapsed.

"You need to keep an eye on that blood pressure. Your doc told me you've been hovering near a hundred and sixty."

Grant patted the jacket lying next to him on the bed. "I've got a new script right here."

"Good."

For a moment, the two men stood staring at one another as though each expected the other to mention the huge elephant in the room. Heart attacks happened for a reason. Hal knew that better than Grant. Stress, yes. Blood pressure, yes. But there was a trigger. Hal stood waiting for Grant to reveal it.

"Heard anything new about the bomb on the mountain?" Grant asked. He lifted the edge of the newspaper and said, "There was no mention of the person responsible."

"I don't think they know who did it, yet."

Grant felt his pulse accelerate. "Hope they catch him soon. We can't have Silver Creek go up in flames because of a couple of nut jobs."

"This about Kinsley?"

Adrenaline fired through Grant's system. Pulling back, he asked, "What? Why would you ask?"

Hal dipped his head, peering at Grant as though he were a child trying to spin a silly lie. "Adele told me she saw the two of you together. Twice. If you're trying to keep it a secret, you're doing a lousy job."

Of course, Adele would have seen them together and mentioned as much to Hal. They dined at her restaurant. Adele and Hal were an item. Grant expelled a sigh and muttered, "Yes, in so many words."

Grant felt stupid. Kinsley had played him like a fool, lied to him about Giovanna's store and now everyone would know because he collapsed of a heart attack at the police station due to stress. The stress of seeing the proof—the irrefutable truth—that Kinsley was responsible for the bomb in the fur store, and who knew what else. Grant didn't want to consider the possibility that Kinsley had also been the one to plant the bomb in the ski patrol hut. He couldn't fathom her involvement, that his instincts had been so wrong about her.

Emotion whipped in Hal's hazel eyes as he took in the news. Intelligent, thoughtful, he was a man concerned for his friend, not a voyeur seeking a cheap thrill. "Want to talk about it?"

Hell no, but to say as much would be a spit in the eye of his friend. Pressing lids together, Grant forced them apart and said, "Kinsley and I have been spending time together." Uncertain exactly how to explain what they'd been doing, he wondered, were they dating? Working on a new business venture together?

Grant knew damn well what he'd been doing. He couldn't speak for Kinsley.

"Are you two dating?" Hal asked.

Grant wanted to laugh at the surprise in his expression. A forty-something man and a twenty-something woman? Is that what gave him the heart attack? He dodged the point of Hal's gaze and replied, "Kinsley and I have been spending time together. I was helping her with an idea for a new business venture and, well, we've been having dinner." Grant didn't want to make himself out to be the lovesick fool that he was, taken by a much younger woman who'd turned out to be using him—betraying him. Spewing a resigned sigh, he said, "Hell, Hal. I don't know what I've been doing."

Hal's rigid demeanor cracked, and he let out small chuckle. "None of us do." With a shake of his head, he lowered to a seat at the foot of Grant's hospital bed. Hitching his knee farther up onto the mattress, he said, "I have to say, you've caught me off guard. After your initial meeting with

Kinsley, can't say as I would have guessed it would have turned into something like this."

Grant joined him in observing the ironic turn of events. Hal had been there the day he'd confronted Kinsley. It was *his* connection to her via Lisa that had allowed Grant to approach Kinsley and make amends. Admittedly, his initial intention had been to probe her for information on the bombing. He'd been certain it was someone involved with the protests against the expansion—an instinct that had served him well. Unfortunately, turned out it was the kingpin of the organization herself, and not one of her underlings, who had taken to bombing the store.

Allowing a fresh wave of resentment to pass through him, Grant knew he'd be lying if he didn't acknowledge a part of him had wanted to spend time with her for purely personal reasons. Kinsley was a beautiful woman. A man always desired to spend time with a beautiful woman.

Grant stuck a foot onto a lower bar of the bed and placed a hand to his thigh. Sliding a sideways glance toward Hal, he said, "I thought she was different, decent. Turns out, I was wrong."

Hal held up a hand. "Sorry, but I can't go there with you. Lisa and Kinsley have been friends for a long time, and the young woman I've come to know is very decent. She has uncompromising values and incredible ethics. I've never known Kinsley to lie or cheat, or otherwise play underhandedly. She's always been straight up with her beliefs, vociferously so."

"She bombed Giovanna's fur store. I saw her on the video with my own two eyes. It's undisputable. She did it, and she lied to me about it."

Disappointment swamped Hal's gaze. "That's what Lisa told me."

"Chief Davis believes she's also responsible for the bomb up on the mountain."

Clouds gathered in Hal's gaze but he said nothing.

Grant nodded. "I'm sorry, Hal. She fell off the 'ethical bandwagon.' Trust me, no one hates to admit that more than me."

"Lisa tells me she didn't do it—exactly. That her partner was responsible."

Grant laughed, the sound harsh in the small room. "She's lying. I saw the video evidence for myself, Hal."

Hal's mouth formed a tight-lipped smile. Nodding slowly, he said, "I know. It sounds hard to believe."

Grant breathed a sigh of relief. At least his friend wasn't buying the fabrication. His daughter might, but not a smart guy like Hal.

Slapping hands to his knees, Hal rose. "I'm glad to see you're okay, Grant. You had me worried there."

"I do that to doctors."

He clamped a hand to Grant's shoulder. "Get well, buddy. You're too young to be hanging around in places like this."

At Hal's smile, Grant nodded and the two men shared the quiet sentiment only aging men could. When there were more years behind them than ahead, a man did everything in his power to slow the pace. Take more time with loved ones. Follow that dream you'd given up on as impossible. Be the man you never were but knew you were meant to be. Call it a mid-life crisis or a coming to his senses, but Grant felt an urgency when it came to Kinsley.

Hal was a good man. He understood life, loss, and death. While he might have been surprised to learn of Grant's interest in Kinsley, he understood it.

But Kinsley had been a flash in the pan. She'd been alluring in her intellect, decadent in her promise, but she had let him down. At this point in his life, Grant knew it was better to cut his losses quickly rather than fight a losing battle. He knew he was losing a part of his happiness in letting her go, but it wasn't worth his health.

Kinsley pushed out of Grant's jewelry store and took off running for her hotel. Grant had a heart attack? When? Why? Was he okay? Was he—

She couldn't allow herself to think of it. She couldn't allow herself to go there. He couldn't be dead. His employee would have said as much. Wouldn't he? He was at the hospital, which meant he was recovering.

Pelted by questions, fears, worries—a slew of what-ifs— Kinsley ran the entire way to her hotel. She had to call the hospital. She had to call and check up on him, make sure he was okay—as okay as one could be after having a heart attack. Struck by the implications, she realized at once how little she knew about heart attacks, heart conditions, other than it was something older people had, older people who ate poorly, were out of shape, smoked...

Everything Grant wasn't. *My ticker isn't what it used to be.*

His words came back to haunt her. Grant had a bad heart. A fresh onslaught of worry slammed into her like a Mack truck. A bad heart. How bad?

She had to find out how Grant was doing, but how?

Lisa. Just as quickly as the question occurred, the answer speared into her mind. Lisa would know, and if she didn't, she could ask her father. Hal Richardson was a doctor at the local hospital. He'd be able to get information. Heart racing, Kinsley leapt up the front steps of her building, swung open the heavy door and barreled through the elegant lobby, heedless to the stares she was drawing. She didn't care. She needed to get to her room and get answers.

Within minutes she was on the phone. She dialed the hospital and waited. "Hello? Yes, I need to speak with the nursing station for patient Grant Powell." After spending years around Lisa and her physician father, it all came back to her. Kinsley was familiar with how hospitals worked. She didn't need to connect with Grant's room or speak with his doctor. She could ask the nurse about his condition, though unless she claimed to be family, the nurse would likely reveal nothing. Kinsley paced her hotel room. Could she lie? Could she say she was his daughter and convince them to tell her everything?

Shooting a glance out her hotel room window, Kinsley was shocked by how easily she was prepared to lie—again— especially considering it was a lie that had landed her in this mess in the first place. If she'd only been honest with him in the first place, maybe he would be with her now.

"I'm sorry, but that patient was discharged."

"Discharged?" Kinsley glimpsed her reflection in a mirror, the jolt to her expression. "Already?"

"Yes, ma'am. That's what it says on my screen. Is there anything else I can do for you?"

"No." Stunned, Kinsley ended the call. The reflection in the mirror held as much confusion as it did shock. Discharged. *That must mean he's okay.* Relief rushed through her and gripped the back of her desk chair, feeling slightly off balance. It couldn't have been serious if the doctors had released him, though how someone could have a heart attack and not be considered serious was beyond her. Heart attacks killed people. How could they just let him go?

Overcome by a strong urge to call Lisa, Kinsley resisted. She didn't want to involve her friend anymore than necessary. It would only cause friction between her and Walsh, and that was the last thing Kinsley needed. She shook her head, cleared her mind. Grant was okay. For the time being, that knowledge had to suffice. Right now, she had a meeting to prepare for, a meeting that would set the trap for one Sebastian Wu.

Showered and changed, Kinsley fine-tuned her plan. Sebastian had agreed to meet her at Scarpetta's Italian bistro for a late lunch. She had suggested Scarpetta's because she rarely ate there, making it unlikely she'd run into anyone she knew, especially a particular someone whom she wasn't ready to see. Not yet. Not until she was ready to have the conversation she wanted to have, the one that would clear her of the patrol hut bombing.

As far as Sebastian was concerned, he knew only that she'd been arrested for the bombing of Giovanna's. He knew none of the details of her hearing, had no idea the police had her on video, and she was going to use his ignorance to her advantage. She was going to play dumb, get him to admit what he'd done, and record everything for Wade Davis to hear. She'd hidden her cell phone in her bra, concealed beneath a cable knit sweater. Hopefully it would prove close enough to record everything they were saying. After she had him for the fur store, Kinsley would then goad him into revealing what he'd done to the ski patrol hut. It was a simple plan. Almost too simple.

But sometimes simple was best. In the off-chance it didn't work, she had a backup plan. One way or another, she was going to nail Sebastian's butt to the wall.

As she walked to the restaurant, her body trembled. It was cold outside, but that was not why she was shaking. It was nerves. Her future was riding on this meeting and her ability to get the truth out of Sebastian. If she failed, her prospects for staying out of prison shrank considerably. Chief Davis had her on the fur store explosion, but there was no proof she planted the patrol hut bomb, the more serious of the two. According to Lisa, the man injured in the blast was still in critical condition and it was possible he wouldn't make it, but her father said the prognosis was good. The dog was touch and go. He belonged to a friend of Walsh's, the blond man she'd seen hovering over the dog. The same man who carried the animal off the mountain.

Nearing the restaurant, Kinsley's pulse jumped. Sebastian was waiting outside, his black-eyed gaze instantly coiling around her as she approached. Looking ever the urban sophisticate in his overcoat and fedora, he stood poised with an utterly bored air about him, as though this entire town were beneath him. Forget the fact that most of these residences cost ten times the amount of money he earned, Sebastian carried off his charade well, creating the illusion that he was one of them. One of them on the surface, but in fact was an enemy working against them.

Shaking the animosity from her mind, Kinsley worked to assume an air of her own. They were allies, friends. They worked together for the cause. It was the script she was using for this meeting, anyway, and as she neared, she summoned her best smile and directed it solely toward him. "Sebastian."

"Kinsley." Reaching out for her, he pulled her into an embrace.

Hugging, they climbed the brick steps to Scarpetta's together. Sebastian opened the door for her and commented, "You look well."

"Thanks. I'm sure you heard about the arrest," she said, certain someone from their group would have seen her carted off by Chief Davis and wanting to appear as though she were angry as hell.

"Yes, an unfortunate turn of events."

"You're telling me." Engulfed by the warm interior of the Italian restaurant, she shrugged against a hard shudder. Thick, fragrant scents wrapped around her, heavily laced with garlic and onions which she breathed in, the aroma calming as well as enticing.

Lowering his head near her ear, Sebastian whispered, "But you assured me your identity was concealed while you were in the fur store."

"It was. They've got nothing but circumstantial evidence. They had to bring someone in after the patrol hut explosion, and that someone was me."

Sebastian stepped back and the two stood in silence as they waited for the hostess to return. Scarpetta's was dark, the walls brick and covered with wrought iron bar accents. A full liquor bar ran the length of one end, people lined up three deep for après-ski drinks. Windows lined the other wall, revealing a light snowfall through enormous glass panes. Tables were black enamel and mostly occupied.

"I'm only sorry I missed today's protest," Kinsley said. "How did it go?"

"The usual. Lots of energy but few results."

She nodded. "I think it's time to ramp it up."

Sebastian's brow shot up.

"Good evening," a hostess greeted, her jet-black hair pulled back into a ponytail as black as the attire she wore from head-to-toe.

"Table for two," Kinsley said.

"Do you have reservations?"

"Yes. Fairchild."

"Right this way."

Weaving her way behind the hostess, Kinsley could feel Sebastian's curiosity crawling over her neck and shoulders. It was a magnetic pull, a hungry yearning to know exactly what she meant by her provocative comment. Gratified her ploy had hooked him so easily, Kinsley was eager to take him to the next level.

Once seated at their table, Sebastian focused in on her. He leaned forward and whispered in a conspiratorial tone laced with delight, "Talk to me."

Kinsley laughed softly, careful to keep an edge in her voice. She needed to play this right if it was going to work. Setting her menu aside, she reeled him in slowly. "I'm growing tired of the protests. I want to see change, real change, the kind that will make people listen."

"That's been our goal since day one," he said, his tone mocking.

"I'm talking about a change in tactics."

"This isn't about your clothing idea, is it?"

The derisive slant chafed her, but she revealed no such emotion. Instead, she smiled indulgently. "This goes well beyond clothes. It goes to the heart of the matter—with a spear. I think it's time we embrace your methods, and hit them with everything we have."

He chuckled. "I'm waiting," he nudged, encouraging her to elaborate.

A waiter stopped by their table, filled their glasses with water and continued on his way. Kinsley appreciated service that wasn't intrusive. It made for a better dining experience and allowed for discreet conversation. Casting a deliberate glance around the room, touching upon tables, logging in faces, potential eavesdroppers, she said, "Palmer International needs to understand that we will not be sidelined, that money cannot push us out of the way."

"Agreed." Pleasure slunk onto Sebastian's face. "It's what I've been saying for months."

"You have, haven't you," she said, and held him in her gaze. Violence wasn't the answer. Never had been and never would be.

"What do you have in mind?" he asked.

"Well," Kinsley began, following the line of dialogue she'd rehearsed back in her hotel room, "I'm assuming the bomb at the patrol hut was your handiwork, and I must admit it got their attention, but the target was too soft. It should have been directed at the Palmer meeting and not the patrol hut."

"I agree."

She nodded. With a fleeting glance to the room at large, Kinsley lowered her voice and continued below the din of conversation going on around her, "From what I understand, there is another meeting set for tomorrow. It will be a media event, which only sweetens the allure."

Sebastian eased back into his chair. With a devilish grin, he sliced a glance around them. "I see where you're going with this."

Kinsley curled her lips into a smile. "We'd not only garner the attention of investors, but the entire town, plus all of Denver. Reporters would be drawn in like a feeding frenzy and spread the word to a national audience."

"I like it."

"Of course, the other option would be to curtail operations altogether."

"How so?"

Kinsley paused. "How do you think?"

"Me? I have no idea."

"Oh, come now, Sebastian." Kinsley leaned forward, anxious to know how her phone was picking up his voice. "You're my right-hand man, my number one strategist. Don't tell me it hasn't crossed your mind?"

"You're our fearless leader," he pushed back. "I'm just a devoted minion. You know I'll do whatever you tell me to do."

Kinsley didn't like the smile on his face. It felt as though he was baiting her. "This is more your department than mine, wouldn't you say?"

Sebastian laughed. "Oh, Kinsley, you give me too much credit. You know I'm still learning my way through the organization."

"I'd say you've graduated with gold stars, wouldn't you?"

A young waiter of obvious Italian descent stopped at their table. "Good evening," he greeted, alternating his attention between the two of them. His voice was rich with accent, his brows heavy and black, and his complexion was flawless, as were his blue eyes. "Welcome to Scarpetta's. Have you dined with us before?"

"Many times," Sebastian replied.

Kinsley nodded, momentarily distracted by the man's looks but impatient to continue her conversation with Sebastian.

"Wonderful. May I start you off with something from the bar?"

"A bottle of your house Chianti," Sebastian said. "The Riserva."

"Excellent choice. Our specials are listed on the front page of your menu. May I suggest the veal this afternoon? The chef has created a masterful *osso bucco*."

Kinsley's insides recoiled. She wouldn't eat veal if it were the last food on earth.

"I think we need a moment," Sebastian pitched in.

"No problem."

As he headed for the bar to retrieve their wine, Kinsley looked to Sebastian. This dialogue of theirs was too vague, too obscure. She needed to speak in more precise terms and get Sebastian to do the same. Encircling a hand around the base of her water glass, Kinsley posed quietly, "Why did you put the bomb in the ski patrol hut and not the gondola building where they were meeting? It would have had much greater impact there than outside."

"I didn't put that bomb in the ski patrol hut."

"Did you put Norell up to it?"

Tapping a forefinger to the table, Sebastian moved it in a back and forth motion as he held Kinsley in his gaze. "Norell wouldn't be involved in something like that, Kinsley. He's a brawny front-line protester, not a behind the scenes brain type like you."

Kinsley didn't like where this was going. Sebastian was playing coy. It wasn't his style, which made it all the more unsettling. "You're telling me you didn't plant that bomb in the ski patrol hut?"

He laughed again, this time more sharply than before. "Of course, I didn't. You know very well that was your doing, not mine."

"It was not," she snapped. "It was yours, or Norell's."

Darting a glance behind her, Sebastian asked, "Why would you say something like that?"

Mindful of nearby tables, Kinsley struggled to keep her voice down. "I overheard two of the guys talking. They mentioned fireworks, explosives. They knew it was going to happen before it actually did, which tells me it had been in the works."

Raising his brow, Sebastian directed calmly, "Perhaps you should be having this conversation with them. I assure you I had nothing to do with setting that explosive."

Kinsley bristled. "Yes you did and you know it. No one else in our group would have had the nerve to carry that out, not without your okay, they wouldn't."

"My okay? Since when was I appointed leader? I believe that title clearly belongs to you."

Kinsley leaned over the table, far enough that it pinched her waist. "Stop messing with me, Sebastian. I know you were responsible."

Black eyes slanted as they coarsened. "No. You stop messing with me. We have a job to do here, and you're slacking."

"Slacking? What are you talking about? Everything I do is for the cause, to stop the expansion. You are out of line and you know it."

"Am I?"

The wine was delivered between them with swift, professional flair. After uncorking the bottle, the waiter asked for their order. Kinsley opted for a house salad, her appetite nonexistent, while Sebastian ordered a bowl of pasta and side salad. The young man thanked them and took his leave.

"What's going on, Sebastian?" Kinsley shifted gears in an attempt to regain control. "Where is this coming from? Why so hostile?"

"Hostile? After you insist on tying my hands? I'm simply trying to make an impact, same as I always have, yet you seemed determined to change focus."

"Change focus? Since when?"

"Why all this talk about clothes? One minute you say you want to stop Palmer and get his attention, and the next you're going on about some silly clothing line. In case you haven't noticed, it's creating disharmony among the ranks."

It took every ounce of self-restraint for Kinsley to remain calm and in her seat. No one among the "ranks" knew of her clothing venture. No one except for Sebastian. There was no discord unless he'd been planting seeds of dissension.

"You know the police questioned me about the bomb— an act for which you tried to deliver me on a silver platter." He cocked his head. "Why?"

With one statement, Sebastian had changed the entire trajectory of their conversation. She hadn't realized the police had interrogated him with a complete lack of finesse. Probably because they were trying to pit activist against activist. Unfortunately, it was a possibility Kinsley had overlooked when crafting her plan to capture Sebastian's confession. But then again, she wasn't a career criminal who naturally accounted for such contingencies. "Because I'm not going to jail for a crime I didn't commit."

"What are you talking about, Kinsley? You willingly snuck into that store and placed that bomb. You're on video." Sebastian pulled a deliberate sip of wine from his glass, his gaze piercing in its accusation. "It's going to be hard to deny when your fingerprints are all over it."

Chapter Nineteen

Kinsley could barely touch her lunch. Sebastian seemed to savor every bite of his, yet she couldn't shake the feeling that he was setting her up. He was too controlled, too calm. He had none of his normal fire and instead was cool and cunning, dishing out innuendos almost as if he knew her plan was to record him and he was counteracting her intentionally. It was all she could do to maintain a normal façade while they finished their meal, knowing a confrontation in public would not serve her well. Not to any end. But the second she could walk out of the restaurant and put space between herself and Sebastian, the underpinnings of their conversation became clear. Standing outside the restaurant in the frigid cold, Kinsley knew. As sure as she was breathing, she knew he was setting her up to take the fall for his explosion. She had to think. She had to plan. Something was going on. Something bad.

But what?

It's going to be hard to deny when your fingerprints are all over it. Had he been speaking in general terms? She was the leader of the organization, she would go down with the ship? Or had he been implying something more?

But anything more was impossible. She hadn't handled the explosive with bare hands. She'd worn gloves. She'd been careful.

Standing in the middle of the street, she ignored the people walking and laughing. They carried on around her, oblivious to the turmoil tumbling through her. Kinsley's cheeks stung. A shiver raced through her and she hugged arms to her body. Sebastian was orchestrating something and trying to put her smack in the center of it. He'd been vying for her position, and now it sounded like he thought he was there, that he was convinced she'd be in jail while he walked free.

She couldn't let that happen. She couldn't let him get away with it. Whatever he was planning, she had to stop him. Kinsley took off running. Mindful she was drawing attention but unable to stop herself, she ran for her hotel. Everything she had worked so hard to build was about to crumble—her reputation, her business, her life. If she didn't figure out what he was planning, she would lose everything.

Heart pounding, cheeks burning from cold, lungs cramping, Kinsley raced past Grant's storefront. Thoughts of him wrapped around her like tentacles. He'd had a heart attack, been discharged from the hospital. She wanted to talk to him, but she couldn't face him. Not yet. Maybe not ever, her heart whispered.

Standing behind a jewelry case with Beau James, Grant glimpsed a long black-haired woman dashing by. Grant's heart bucked. *Kinsley*?

Running to the window, he looked out and in the direction of the town square. Had that been Kinsley? Grant tore out the front door and yelled, "Kinsley!"

The sharp call of her name yanked her to a stop. She whirled and froze.

Grant ran toward her, his movements automatic. She didn't move, she didn't bolt, but stood rooted in place, a look of sheer horror on her face. *Kinsley*. Grant closed the distance in seconds, a swell of emotion careening into him as his heart pounded. He grabbed her by the arm and yanked her, hard. "You lied to me," he growled. Anger crashed in, and he squeezed harder through her parka. "You blew up Giovanna's store. It was you—the whole time it was *you*."

"Grant, stop!"

"You'd like that, wouldn't you? Stop and ignore the fact that you lied."

"Your heart!"

"My heart's fine," he spat, ignoring her wince beneath his grip. The only thing bad for his heart was the hurt raging inside, the hurt caused by *her*. "I hope you go to jail for what you did. I hope they put you away for a very long time." But even as he said the words, pain splintered his chest. He'd wanted her with him. He'd wanted Kinsley for himself, not rotting away in some jail cell.

"I'm sorry, Grant! I'm sorry about the fur store."

"So you admit it," he snarled, hot stabs of breath shooting between them. "You admit it was you."

Tears sprang to her eyes as she nodded.

"I can't believe you could look me in the eye and repeatedly deceive me. Over and over you lied." Eyes darting back and forth across hers, he felt the crushing weight of her admission explode inside of him. "And to think you were beginning to mean something to me."

Tears streamed free, streaking black liner down her cheeks. "Grant..."

"Save it." He ground his jaw closed. "Save it. You made a fool out of me," he hissed. "I feel like a fool for ever having the first feeling for you."

"No, Grant! You're not—you're not a fool! I placed the bomb, but it was only supposed to be ink." Kinsley's gaze leapt behind him. "I never meant it to blow her window out! It was never meant to explode!"

"You expect me to believe that?" he fired back. "You expect me to believe anything you say?"

"It's the truth! I only meant to ruin the furs, to send a message—"

"You only meant to ruin her livelihood is what you mean."

Kinsley clammed up.

Score, he mused sourly. Inoculating himself against the tears streaming down her face, Grant dropped his hand from her arm and stared. Kinsley had the audacity to think that inking Giovanna's furs was acceptable, tolerable—that he would be fine with her destruction of private property. Well, he wasn't. Vandalism was vandalism. Memories of his storefront in New York came rushing back—the thugs, the destruction, the demands—people who thought they could intimidate others by means of force.

They couldn't. Not with Grant Powell, they couldn't. He didn't care who they were.

Rage fired through his gut, a searing nausea that sank deep. He wanted to shout—hit—bury his fist into something, except it would make him no better than her or the criminals he left behind in New York. That's what Kinsley was. A criminal. With one long hard look at her, Grant turned on his heel and walked back to his store.

"Grant..."

He ignored her whimper. They were finished. Kinsley had betrayed him, lied straight to his face. She had ruined Giovanna's business in the name of her cause, ruined a woman's life because she disagreed with her choices. Kinsley was a joke. She couldn't care less about the pain and suffering of others so long as it furthered her cause. It was a means to an end—an end where she only cared about herself.

Kinsley stood shell-shocked. She hadn't planned on seeing Grant, but somehow he had seen her, confronted her and told her exactly what he thought of her. Straight from the heart, the hurt in his eyes had been clear. He hated her. He had wanted her once but no longer. He only felt hate. Kinsley wanted to run after him, explain to him how much she regretted the bombing, her deception, but he didn't have ears for her. Grant had cut her from his life, leaving a gaping hole in hers. The door to his store opened and closed. He was gone.

Strength drained from her limbs. Sadness caged her. Kinsley felt gutted. She knew she should go, knew she looked the fool standing in the street staring after him, but she couldn't move a muscle. Her cheeks felt coated in ice, her lips dry and not her own. In the midst of a village steeped in pleasure, she felt empty. She wanted to dissolve into nothing. Disappear and make it all go away.

If only she could. If only she could transport herself back through time and erase the fur store bombing, she

would, in a second. There were other ways to make a difference, better ways to evoke change. Grant understood her desire to help animals, to spare them from suffering and abuse
but he didn't understand criminal mischief. He might have
encouraged her, worked with her in a way no one else had
before, but this is where he drew the line.

Kinsley returned to her hotel in a daze. She knew she
had to make a plan but didn't feel the first inkling of desire.
She was on the verge of losing her freedom, yet she could
only think of what she'd already lost. *Grant. Grant was gone.*

Staring at her computer screen, she knew she should take
to her blog, out Sebastian in some way that would save herself, but her fingers wouldn't move, unable to type the first
word. A knock sounded at her door and she shouted, "Go
away, I don't need service!" The door hangar should have
said it loud and clear. No turn-down service. Privacy, please.

The page from her document went black and her screen
saver kicked in. A small globe bounced and spun within a
navy background. She had chosen the symbol because it represented her movement, her ambition. *Wildlife Neutral* had
global reach. While she might have lost this battle, it
shouldn't mean an end to the movement. Palmer International
would get its approval to expand the resort, displacing who
knew how many animals with its construction equipment, but
it didn't mean she couldn't prevent others from doing the
same. Unless she went to jail for crimes she didn't commit.
Then Sebastian would take over the only space in her life that
mattered anymore. Kinsley's head dropped forward. It was
catastrophic.

The knocking returned, this time louder. "Kinsley,"
came a muffled voice through the door. "It's your mother."

"Mom?" Kinsley jumped from her chair and ran to the
door. Opening it, she met her mother's gaze and asked
breathlessly, "What are you doing here?"

"I'm here to see you."

Kinsley shot her head out the doorway and glanced down the hall. "Does Dad know you're here?"

With a pained expression, Victoria Fairchild shook her head. "No, but I had to see you." Kinsley's heart pinched. Her mother was here in secrecy. The knowledge made Kinsley feel dirty. "May I come in?"

"Of course," she said, and stepped aside. The urge to hug her was strong, but shame kept her from reaching out. "I'm sorry to have put you in this position, Mom. I know it's not easy, what with you and Dad and Lee Palmer."

Reaching a hand to Kinsley's chin, her mother cupped it gently. "How are you doing?"

"Fine."

Her gaze searched Kinsley's. Releasing her chin, she brushed fallen hair from Kinsley's eyes with a look that said otherwise. "You don't look fine. You look tired. Exhausted."

Turning, Kinsley walked over to the hotel bed and dropped to the edge. She wasn't fine. She was a mess. A nervous wreck, a criminal waiting for the guillotine to fall, a lying sack of crap. Holed away in her room, Kinsley felt like she was on a listing ship with no one out searching for her, no one who cared enough to make the effort, no one who cared whether she went down with the ship or not. Kinsley flipped her gaze to her mother. Dressed in her usual elegance, she wore a slim charcoal gray wool dress and black knee-high leather boots, her legs covered in black tights, her shoulders draped by a cashmere scarf, a gorgeous pop of berry. A rush of nerves pushed into Kinsley's stomach. She had never been more grateful to see her mother than right now.

Victoria joined her on the bed. She placed a hand over one of Kinsley's, her skin warm and soft to the touch. "Talk to me, darling. What's going on? How can I help?"

Peering into dark eyes, eyes that mirrored her own, only touched by age, Kinsley felt the floodgates open. "You believe me when I say I didn't put that bomb in the patrol hut, don't you?"

"I do." Her mother smiled, the gesture more strained than Kinsley would have preferred. "You're a lot of things, sweetheart, but a murderer is not one of them."

Kinsley sucked back a gasp. Did that mean the man had died?

Victoria toyed with Kinsley's long bangs in an affectionate manner, gently combing through them with her fingers. Her mother's hands were delicate and graceful, same as everything else about her. "You're passionate, you're not violent. I know you didn't set that bomb. I only hope that we can prove it in a court of law." Worry fluttered into her gaze. "Do you know how you're going to prove your innocence?"

In that moment, Kinsley felt the full brunt of her situation. Her mother had a stake in this. More than money, Kinsley recognized her fear, the fear that her only child would be sent to prison. Kinsley had never doubted her mother's love. She had never failed her, had always been by her side, on her team.

"Do you know if the man hurt during the explosion is okay?" Kinsley asked, afraid to hear the answer but knew that she must.

"Hal told me he should pull through. His injuries are serious but not fatal.

Relief escaped Kinsley in a rush of breath. "The dog? Have you heard about the dog?"

"I haven't."

Kinsley's heart squeezed. Covering her face with her hands, she dropped her elbows to her knees and collapsed into her hands. If Sebastian killed that animal, she'd make him pay—extra.

Victoria's hand went to Kinsley's back. She rubbed it up and down, patient while her daughter collected herself. Kinsley knew from experience that her mother wouldn't push. It wasn't her style.

The familiar scent of her mother's perfume seeped in, the subtle mix of Jasmine and Ylang-Ylang easing the stress. The fragrance brought Kinsley to a happier place, a place from her youth, a place where she'd always had love and support. Her mother was that place, and she was here. She was here for answers, and Kinsley would give them. From start to finish, she would tell her everything. Kinsley massaged her temples and gathered her thoughts, then pulled up and twisted her body to face her mother. "I went up there to warn you."

"Warn me? On the mountain yesterday?"

"Yes."

"You knew the bomb was going to go off?"

"No, not exactly."

"Not exactly?" A stab of suspicion entered her mother's gaze. "I don't understand, Kinsley."

Kinsley hated the doubt staring at her. She couldn't stand for her mom to look at her that way and quickly explained, "We were holding a protest outside the gondola, at the base."

"Your father and I saw you. You were talking to Lee."

Kinsley nodded. "Yes. We had a confrontation with him before he went up the mountain. Afterward, I heard a few people talking, they mentioned fireworks." Her mother's gaze turned quizzical. "'Fireworks they won't soon forget' is what they said. It was the same terminology Sebastian used when referring to the explosion at the fur store."

At the mention of the fur store, Kinsley's mother stiffened. Guilt cut like a knife. *So she knew.* Her mother knew about the video, the bombing in the fur store. Heaving a sigh, Kinsley moved past it. There wasn't anything she could do to take it back. It was done. A scar on her record, but one she was determined to atone for. "I suspected something was going on, something outside our normal protest. Sebastian and I had been having some disagreement on how we should proceed, so after I heard them talking, I looked for Sebastian but he was nowhere to be seen, so I went to question the guys who had been talking. They didn't reveal anything, but my gut told me something bad was about to happen. Then I saw you and Dad get on the gondola and knew I had to get up there. I had to see if there was anything I could do, see if I could spot any trouble before it started." Kinsley's thoughts swerved backward through the course of events, recalling how she struggled to piece it together on the fly. "Maybe if I saw some of our people up there, I'd know what was going down. At one point, I thought I saw Sebastian but it didn't matter. It was too late." Kinsley bowed her head in shame. "The bomb exploded."

Comforting arms slid around her shoulders and pulled her close. "Oh, sweetheart," her mother murmured into her hair. "I'm sorry, so sorry."

She was sorry? She had nothing to be sorry for. This was Kinsley's problem—her burden—not her mother's. But as usual, her mom responded with compassion. It's who she was, it's what she did. She cared for others. So fortunate in her own life, she'd always felt compelled to make everyone else feel as blessed as she did. It was the main driving force behind her charity work. The more people she could help, the more satisfied she seemed to feel.

Unfortunately, it wasn't working in Kinsley's case. She had nothing to feel good about. She had done the wrong thing for the right reason, and the universe was punishing her. "I'm afraid, Mom. I think Sebastian is trying to set me up for setting the bomb, and I'm not sure if I can prove it was him."

Her mother hugged her more tightly. "I know sweetheart. This whole situation is scary. But if you tell Merle, he'll know what to do. Tell him everything, and he'll help prove your innocence. I know he will. He's the best in the business."

Merle Brugman had been helping the Fairchilds for years, which is why Kinsley had hired him, why her mother trusted him. Merle was the best of the best, but even he might not be able to protect her from federal prison. Gripped by a sudden urgency, Kinsley pulled away and blurted, "I was planning on starting a clothing line. A vegan clothing line."

Her mother drew back. "Really? A clothing line? Why is this the first I've heard of it?"

Because she'd been sharing her plans with Grant. Because she'd been relying on him for support instead of her mother. Because it was his approval and encouragement that had been filling her heart and no one else's. "It's still new. I only came up with the idea this week." *Grant came up with the idea*, she corrected silently. *The new man I've been seeing*.

Thoughts of him dunked her into a pit of gloom, but her mother's enthusiasm pulled her back to the surface. Scooting closer, she cupped a hand to Kinsley's chin and tipped her face toward her. "Tell me all about it. It sounds like something I'd *love* to be involved in."

Kinsley smiled. For the first time in what felt like an eternity, she felt a joy rise from deep within. "It's going to be amazing. I think I might have even found someone to help manufacture it for me."

Chapter Twenty

Seated comfortably at an outdoor table on the patio of The Oasis with her friend Lisa, Kinsley glanced around the terrace. Most tables were occupied by couples, friends, a group of women out for a day of shopping, if the bags lining the ground at their feet were any indication. No one blatantly stared at her but Kinsley was mindful of the fact that some of the locals working the restaurant knew who she was, knew she'd been arrested and repeatedly stole peeks in her direction.

Curiosity was a rabid thing. Undoubtedly they were speculating about the young woman rumored to have bombed the patrol hut, the one responsible for injuring a man and an animal. She wondered how many also knew about the fur store bombing, or did they automatically tie the two together, hanging them squarely around Kinsley's neck? Despite knowing she was innocent, she couldn't shake the suspicion that lurked around every corner. She realized some of it stemmed from the guilt she felt for the role that she did play, but still... It felt as though people were following her every move. Kinsley figured it was something she was going to have to live with, until she could prove that Sebastian was the guilty one.

Which brought her to the reason for the lunch date. After her mother left her hotel room last night, Kinsley fine-tuned her plan to trap Sebastian into revealing himself for the criminal he was. With her mother firmly entrenched in her camp, Kinsley felt hopeful for the first time since her arrest. She was confident she could move forward and beat the charges against her. She did not bomb the patrol hut. She did not intend to blow out the front window of Giovanna's, and she would not accept blame for the crimes.

Today she would initiate Plan B—a plan Lisa would be instrumental in accomplishing. Bundled up in a navy parka and white cable knit hat, her straight brown hair pulled forward over her coat, Lisa pulled a sip of lemon water through a straw. The knuckles on her slender fingers were pink from the cold, her blue eyes alert, moving from table to table around them. Was she also feeling the weight of prying eyes?

"Tell me the truth, Lisa. If this will jeopardize your relationship with Walsh, I can find another way to get Sebastian."

Lisa nibbled at her lower lip. Toying with her straw, she said, "Walsh understands. I make my own decisions. He respects that."

Lisa didn't have a habit of letting people tell her what to do, but Walsh was her significant other, which gave him a claim on her no one else had. Kinsley needed Lisa more than she was letting on, but she refused to ruin another relationship in the course of doing business. Her thoughts went to Grant and she felt the pinch. She'd so handily ruined her own, why take out another?

But if Lisa was game, Kinsley had to take her at her word. She was a big girl. This was her decision, not Kinsley's. Tamping back a rise of excitement, she asked, "Now are you sure you're up for it?"

Lisa nodded, setting a determined edge to her jaw. "Definitely. The man is going down. I'm only glad I can help."

"Okay." Kinsley glanced side-to-side, careful to keep her voice low. "The protest is set for eight tomorrow morning. You'll need to be in place before then."

"Gotcha. I'll run over to the Black Diamond and buy some clothes right after lunch."

"I'll reimburse you for whatever you spend."

Lisa grinned and waved her off. "You don't have to do that. It'll give me an excuse to buy some new gear!"

Pleased that Lisa was excited by the plan, Kinsley laughed. "I'm happy to be your shopping excuse. Anytime you need one, just say the word."

"Well, you know I'm not big on shopping, but this is different. It will be fun!"

Fun would be good. Successful would be better. Kinsley suppressed a surge of satisfaction as the first inkling of success wound through her. Even if her plan wasn't foolproof, it would be enough to create reasonable doubt which is all she'd need for her trial—if it went that far. During her phone call to Merle this morning, he had assured her this was a tough case for the prosecutors to prove. Without hardcore evidence, it was circumstantial, at best.

A mild tremor raced through her. Of course, circumstantial might be all some people needed to convict when it came to an eco-terrorist. Shrugging off the creep of anxiety, she straightened. But rumors and gossip she could handle. A conviction in federal court, she could not. "Okay, call me if you have any problems. I'm going to hang out in the restaurant at my hotel until I receive your text."

A thrill bumped into Lisa's eyes. "I feel like a spy!"

"Well, don't get used to it," Kinsley tossed back, distracted by the sight of an older woman crossing the patio. Kinsley's pulse accelerated. *It was the owner of the fur store*, she was sure of it. She was here with another middle-aged woman, the two following a waiter to a table in the corner. Homing in on her, Kinsley noted she was elegantly dressed, her dark brown hair pulled back into an elegant twist. Staring, she marveled at the woman's skin. Lightly tanned, it was radiant in the afternoon sun. Her makeup was artfully applied and she wore enormous black sunglasses, but there was no mistaking her identity. The large ruby ring on her finger was a dead giveaway. *Giovanna*. Grant's friend. "Excuse me for a sec, will you?" Kinsley popped up from her seat and walked over to Giovanna's table before Lisa could get out the first objection.

A column of nerves funneled down her spine as she neared. For a moment, she hesitated. This spontaneous move might backfire. "Giovanna?"

The woman looked up and her shoulders went back. Her posture became ramrod straight.

So she knew. Giovanna knew her identity the minute she saw her. Kinsley would have addressed her more formally but didn't know her last name. She only knew how Grant referred to her, same as the name scrolled across the front door of her store. "I'm sorry," Kinsley said, "and I wanted to apologize."

The woman next to Giovanna dialed into the exchange, clued in by her friend's reaction.

"My name is Kinsley Fairchild and I'm the one responsible for placing the bomb in your store." Giovanna's skin paled. Her friend drew back.

"The bomb I placed was intended to be an ink bomb. I wanted to send a message about the fur trade, nothing more. Unfortunately, one of my associates took it upon himself to switch my ink bomb with an explosive one." Kinsley's heart sank into her boots as the words spilled from her lips, "I'm sorry for the damage it caused. I never meant for that to happen."

"You have some nerve coming over here, young lady!" Giovanna's friend exclaimed.

Yes, she did. But it was something she had to do. Directing her words to Giovanna, she said, "I'm truly sorry. If I could go back and change it, I would."

Giovanna's demeanor relaxed a hair, the lines around her mouth eased.

Struggling against a storm of emotion—shame, pride, honor—Kinsley continued, "But I can't. I can only let you know that I'm truly sorry and hope you can find it in your heart to forgive me."

Forgiveness was never something Kinsley thought of before. She'd never asked for it, never wanted it. Never thought it necessary. People didn't have to agree with one another. They didn't have to like the world and the people around them. It was human nature to argue and fight. Someone had to win, someone had to lose. Why bother masking your victory with the fluff of kind words for the defeated?

But something was different now. Kinsley had changed this woman's life. She had changed the trajectory of this woman's future but not in the way she intended. Grant said she was leaving town, moving back home and giving up the life she loved here in the mountains because of the explosion in her store. It wasn't fair. It wasn't right. "Please know that I will live with the consequences for the rest of my life, something you will have to do as well, through no fault of your own."

Giovanna's expression softened. Even from behind the woman's dark glasses, Kinsley could feel a connection open between them. She had heard her. She didn't say a word, but Giovanna had heard, and she had listened. Kinsley couldn't ask for anything more. With nothing left to say, she turned and walked away.

Hal Richardson walked into Wade Davis' office, ambivalence twisting his stomach. The news wasn't good. It was bad. Very bad, and he needed to see it with his own eyes. As a friend, Wade understood, which is why he'd invited Hal to take a look. Hal didn't want the Chief of Police to break any rules, but he couldn't pretend he didn't appreciate a small break, either.

"Wade."

"Hal." Rising from his desk with concerted effort, the Chief appeared tired, as though working too much over-time. His face was drawn, his dark eyes somber, it was an expression that mirrored the emotions swirling in Hal's chest. Things were getting complicated, out of control, and Hal felt caught in the middle.

The men shook hands. "I'm sorry to see you under these circumstances," Wade said.

"Can't be helped." Hal dropped to a seat and settled in across from Wade. Between them, a wide swath of wood desktop felt like a barrier. It was unusual for Hal to feel at odds with a friend, but these were unusual circumstances. Kinsley Fairchild had crossed the line from passionate protester to criminal felon. It was a shock to the system and one that reached deep into the heart of his family. "Lisa told me about the video from the fur store, but what about the patrol hut? You have her there, too?"

"Not on video, but we're running the explosive for prints."

"Prints? You think you're going to find her prints? I mean, what is there to test? The thing blew up, right?"

"You'd be surprised," Wade replied. "At any bomb site, there's always evidence to be found, bits and scraps that can be pieced together to create a picture of the original. Walsh saw the evidence for himself. There were fingerprints on a piece one of my guys found while cleaning the scene."

Hal felt a sour pit form in his stomach. "And for some reason, you believe those prints are going to belong to Kinsley."

Wade stared. The man was used to delivering tough news, but both of them knew this went beyond tough. Kinsley Fairchild was like a daughter to Hal. She and Lisa were as close as sisters. If Kinsley was found guilty for bombing that hut, it would tear his daughter apart. Lisa was a good girl. Pure of heart, decent to her core. She'd be devastated to lose her best friend to a life in prison.

"I had a plant in the group of protesters," Wade said.

Hal flinched. "What? Why?"

"For exactly this reason. I wanted to be prepared in the event activities took a turn for the worse."

"And your plant said Kinsley did it?"

Wade shook his head. "My informant told me that there was going to be an explosion at the top of the gondola, outside the Palmer meeting. Walsh and I headed up the second we got the lead. Unfortunately, we were seconds too late."

Hal heard the words but couldn't believe them. *Bomb*? *The Palmer meeting*? But Kinsley's parents would have been there. She would have known that. There's no way she would have intentionally harmed her parents. Kinsley and Gregory had their issues, their differences, but Kinsley and Victoria were close. She would never jeopardize her mother's life in the name of protest.

"I know it's hard to believe, Hal, but she was there. Right after the explosion, Kinsley was on scene. We damn near caught her in the act."

Hal shook his head. He dropped his gaze, reeling as he tried to digest the information. "There's got to be some kind of mistake. Kinsley wouldn't have placed a bomb anywhere near that meeting." Lifting his gaze to meet Wade's, he murmured, "Her parents were there."

Wade stared, his dark eyes brooding, contemplative.

Hal was walking a tightrope, and Wade was watching, waiting for him to fall. "Have you talked to Lisa?" he asked. "She told me that she met with Kinsley and she swears she didn't do it."

"Are you serious?" Wade's voice dropped to a near whisper, and Hal didn't like the perplexed look in his eyes. It made him feel like he was some kind of crazy as he said, "She's her best friend, Hal. What do you expect her to say?"

The truth, that's what he expected. Lisa was no fool. She was smart. She knew the players. Lisa was closer to the situation than both of them. If anyone would know what was going on, it was Lisa. "You said your informant didn't say it was Kinsley. Is it possible that it could have been someone else? Her partner, for instance?"

"It's possible." Wade's mouth tightened. "But not probable."

Hal leaned forward, hanging from the edge of his seat. "I know I sound like a panicked father, but I seriously don't think Kinsley could have done this. The fur store, yes. She's a zealot when it comes to those animals, and the fur trade cuts her particularly raw. But a murderer? Someone could have been killed in that explosion, Wade. And while Kinsley is a lot of things, a murderer isn't one of them." Once again, Hal found himself jumping to Kinsley's defense with nothing more to go on than his gut—first with Grant and now with

Wade. But Hal believed what he was saying. Deep in his heart, he felt certain Kinsley couldn't be responsible.

"What can I say, Hal? People get off track. None of us want to hear it, but it happens."

Reining in a slew of objections, explanations, a dozen reasons he felt it couldn't be Kinsley, Hal asked instead, "What's the next step? You're waiting for fingerprints. If they come in positive for Kinsley, what happens?"

"She's already been arrested for the fur store bombing, but the explosion at the patrol hut is significantly more serious. The federal authorities will likely take over and prosecute her on eco-terrorism."

Hal's vision crowded with ugly images. Crazy anarchists out to make a statement, unruly crowds looking for trouble, people trying to make a name for themselves without regard for the innocents they hurt... In recent years, there'd been an uptick in violent attacks. Businesses had been bombed, resorts had been targeted. In fact, a restaurant at a sister ski resort in Colorado had been burned to the ground. Eco-terrorism was on the rise, and if found guilty, Kinsley would join the ranks of the criminally prosecuted in the quest to save the environment. So much harm done in the name of saving the planet, it didn't make sense.

Hal shoved the discouraging thoughts from his brain and channeled his energy to the issue at hand, the situation that affected him and his family directly. "When will you know?"

"Lab is working on it as we speak." Wade paused, his gaze heavy with a concern that echoed Hal's. "I called you down here, because I wanted you to hear it from me first. Once the media gets it, there's no telling how they'll spin it."

Hal nodded. Wade was giving him lead time to deal with it before it became public. More importantly, it was a personal favor from a friend. "Thanks. I'll talk to Lisa."

Wade returned a small nod, as though his job here were done.

Chapter Twenty-One

Hidden away in the center of a crowd of protesters, Lisa bottled up her nerves and focused on the task at hand. She was here to infiltrate the crowd and get close to Gabby Miller. Gabby was Sebastian's confidant and would know what was on tap for the morning before it transpired. Gabby was also the one who would know if Sebastian was involved with the patrol hut bombing, or if it had been one of his people. Lisa's job was to get close, act crazy-eager-activist and get Gabby talking. Lisa had never been one for theater acting, but found her assignment exhilarating. It was real life espionage, a plan that could secure Kinsley's freedom.

Glancing about the group, Lisa spotted her subject immediately. Stuck to Sebastian like white on rice, Gabby was easy to identify. Not because of the neon lime green wool hat she wore and long waves of blonde hair spilling down the back of her white parka, but because of the way she hung by Sebastian's side like a lovesick schoolgirl. Exactly as Kinsley had said, Gabby was totally engrossed in the guy. He looked totally indifferent to her attention and worlds more sophisticated. Dressed in fitted black jeans and red jacket, the guy's thick hair was combed without a hair out of place, his stance that of a man completely in charge and comfortable in his power. Arrogant, Lisa corrected. More than a dumbstruck young woman, Sebastian Wu had an air of arrogance clinging about him.

Lisa rubbed gloved hands together vigorously, as much to create warmth as convey excitement. Seven forty-five on a wintry morning could penetrate the most insulated gear, and this new stuff she'd bought was nowhere near the quality she normally wore. But Kinsley had been specific—no ski pants or ski jacket. Most of the protesters didn't ski and abhorred

those who did. Opting for a wool hat, gloves, jeans, and lay-
ering up beneath a non-descript coat. Lisa had done the best
she could, but longed for her thermal pants and padded jacket. Forget clothing made for skiers, her gear was so technical-
ly-advanced it could keep a hiker warm at the top of a "four-
teener" in the middle of February. Cold was fourteen-
thousand feet high on a mountain peak—that was cold. Her
present attire was sufficient for the moment, but it wasn't im-
penetrable. Unfortunately, the "spy" business was about
blending in.

Lisa began to pace. She needed to time her "fluke" encounter without raising suspicion, without drawing attention
to herself or her connection with Gabby, which meant she'd
have to wait. Once Gabby broke away from Sebastian, Lisa
could move in. Hopping lightly in place, she breathed in and
out, her exhalations a gush of steamy breath. Only a handful
of protesters were gathered around Sebastian and looked to be
exchanging items of some sort while the remainder hovered
in clusters of three and four, conversing casually, relaxed. Is
this how all protests began, Lisa wondered. As though it was
just another regular day on the mountain? Because from what
she'd seen, these people spent their days doing anything but
"regular."

Sebastian departed abruptly and Lisa stilled. It was time.
Gabby idled in place and Lisa seized the opportunity. Moving
toward Gabby, mindful of prying eyes, Lisa edged into position and posed as casually as possible, "What are we doing
today?"

Gabby looked toward the young woman who had appeared out of nowhere by her side. Mild surprise mingled
with exhilarated defiance in her heated gaze. "Hit them where
it hurts—the bank account. We plan to cost them money and
lots of it."

Lisa tapped her gaze to the container in Gabby's hands.
"Is that what the can's for?"

Gabby nodded. "The blood protest always makes a
splash." She laughed at her double-entendre. "People will

think twice about buying tickets when they have to buy them through dripping red blood."

Lisa's pulse quickened. "*Blood?*"

"Not real blood, silly. Red paint. We splash it everywhere, on our bodies, on walls and cars. In this case, we're targeting the ticket windows and gondola entrance. People will have to really want to ski today if they plan on buying a ticket."

Lisa sucked back a gasp. Seriously? That was their plan? "What if it doesn't work?" Glancing about the group, she realized a few protesters were passing around small cans similar to Gabby's. "Do we have a backup plan?"

Gabby grinned and tucked a long piece of blonde hair under her hat and behind her ear, catching her nails on a few sparkling strands of yarn from her hat. "You bet we do." Her gaze darted between Lisa and Sebastian. "This summer, when they start to bulldoze the mountain for the new runs, we're going to monkeywrench them."

"What? Monkeywrench them?" Lisa hated to sound ignorant when she was supposed to be one of them, but Gabby wasn't making any sense.

Surprise flickered in Gabby's gaze. "You know, monkeywrench—sabotage their construction equipment so they can't knock the first tree down."

"How?"

Gabby's eyes slowly widened as she made a "boom" motion with her mouth, gesturing the same with her hands.

Lisa's heart stopped. "But what if you catch the forest on fire by accident?"

"We won't." Gabby smirked over her shoulder. "We've done this before."

"But you can't predict the weather," Lisa countered, unable to stop herself, "especially in the mountains. The wind can shift at any time." She knew she shouldn't be trying to talk a fellow protester out of her plans if she expected to be accepted as one of them, but she couldn't help herself. Did Gabby hear what she was saying?

"Sebastian knows what he's doing," Gabby replied, her attention moving about the crowd.

A chill gripped Lisa as she followed Gabby's gaze which trailed Sebastian's dark-haired figure as he weaved his way in and around the group of protesters. There had to be fifty, sixty of them now, and they weren't alone. Skiers were entering the arena, the early birds who insisted on being first up the mountain. Though mostly adult men and women, Lisa noted a few families were heading down the pathway as well. Ski school would open soon and start receiving youngsters scheduled for a day of lessons.

Lisa didn't like the sound of Gabby's calculations. They were too cocky, too confident. There was no way they could control all of the variables. Not the weather, not the people involved, not even the reaction from the wildlife they vowed to protect. There was no way to predict any of it with any degree of accuracy. Peering at Gabby's profile, Lisa asked, "How can you be so sure of him?"

Turning, she stared down her nose as though suddenly annoyed. "I trust Sebastian—with my life."

Lisa could feel Gabby pulling away and forced herself to nod in agreement. "Probably because he's had a lot of experience with this kind of thing. It's why I'm here."

"Exactly. Sebastian gets results." Gabby looked away adding, "Unlike Kinsley."

"Kinsley Fairchild?" Lisa uttered the name and pounced on the opening. "But I thought she was the leader of this group."

"*Was*," Gabby corrected. "She's going to get arrested for that bombing on the mountain."

Lisa dropped her mouth open for effect. "She is?"

"Yes, and when she does, Sebastian will take over and we will become more powerful than ever before."

"So she's the one who bombed the patrol hut?" Lisa murmured, pretending she was totally convinced, and that everything Gabby said made perfect sense.

Gabby smiled devilishly and glanced back toward Sebastian. "She's going to jail for it, and then Sebastian will take her place. He's a better leader, anyway. He understands what needs to be done and isn't afraid of doing it."

"That's good," Lisa replied, summoning as much conviction as possible into her voice. "We need someone strong, who's willing to make a difference."

"Oh, Sebastian is, that's for sure."

Were they planning something beyond red paint and protest for this morning? Lisa glanced about the faces and suddenly it was as though she could see the scarcely concealed anger in the expressions of everyone around her. It was rabid, hungry. These protesters were—no question—serious about their activism. She skimmed the growing crowd of tourists and quelled the unease in her belly. "Will there be more explosives, then?" Gabby swept Lisa with a wary gaze and clarified quickly, "I mean, they seem to be working. We should do more, right?"

"We should do what works and it's Sebastian's job to tell us what."

Sebastian Wu moved among the morning crowd of protesters and ran through final preparations for the event. Stationed outside of the ticket windows, their plan was simple. Sales were set to begin at eight. The goal was to eliminate as many as possible for the day, driving the resort into the red. No tourist would want to purchase tickets from a window stained with the blood of an animal. Not real blood, of course, but symbolic blood, representing the blood these people would have on their hands by supporting a business that killed wildlife in its greed for growth.

Satisfied they were on the right course, Sebastian considered his partner and her change of heart. Kinsley was finally coming around, albeit days too late. While he wasn't entirely sure she'd ever go through with her tough talk, he liked that she voiced the sentiment he'd been championing for some time. Violence worked. It garnered attention. It shouted in no uncertain terms that the activists meant business. If people insisted on harming animals, then harm would come to them. Simple. There was beauty in simplicity.

Kinsley was only complicating matters with this new clothing venture of hers. It was inane. She was losing her focus. And if she continued to veer off course, she didn't deserve to be at the helm of the organization anymore. The cause was too important—a cause he was dedicated to, determined to win. He deserved to lead, not her. A smile crossed the shadows of his soul. With Kinsley out of the way, Sebastian Wu would take charge. He was the natural choice, the optimal person to take over where she left off. No one would question his ascension.

Pleasure erupted at the thought of Kinsley locked behind bars; a fate he'd been careful to tie up into a nice, neat package for the police. When the Chief of Police had called Sebastian in for questioning yesterday, the man's intent had been clear. Kinsley had pointed the finger at her partner and away from herself. She had told the police the fur store bombing was his idea and indicted him for the patrol hut incident as well without the first shred of proof.

Anger stained his pleasure. The patrol hut had not been the intended target, but at the last minute, he had to change plans and drop it there instead of inside the gondola building. The minute he saw Kinsley get off the gondola, he knew he'd been compromised. A public confrontation with her would have ruined everything. So like any master of revolution, Sebastian remained flexible and settled for what he could pull off—a bomb that would garner attention and send a message. The fact that a man had been caught in the crossfire didn't bother Sebastian. This was war, and unintended casualties were part of the equation.

Drawing his thoughts from Kinsley, Sebastian redirected them into a cohesive form of instruction and guidance. Surrounded by his people, he glanced from face to face. Eager, intense, his followers were ready to do whatever he asked. He was in charge. He was their leader. It was a responsibility he took seriously. Inhaling fully, he released his breath in a controlled stream. "Does everyone understand the plan?"

Heads nodded. The mood was high yet outwardly reserved. They understood this was an important day in the life of the cause. They were not to draw attention to themselves until the moment was ready. "I've distributed the paint cans. For those of you who did not receive one, find someone who did and work with them. This is a team effort. We are unified in our opposition. Our goal today is to disrupt operations on a grand scale. There will be arrests, but that is to be expected." Sebastian glanced around the crowd, landing briefly on those closest to him. Norell and Gabby manned their cans tightly, their gazes gripped by a conviction that made him proud. They understood the cause. They were committed and on the rise within the organization. They would be among the ones to watch as the action unfolded.

With Kinsley out of the picture, Sebastian could use a man like Norell. Accustomed to working the front lines, he was fearless. Dedicated and loyal, Norell would protect Sebastian to the end. Sexy and passionate, Gabby would work well with him behind the scenes where he would enjoy her company on more than one level. Thoughts of Kinsley's body surged into Sebastian's mind accompanied by the usual swell of desire. Kinsley was a beautiful woman. Smart, passionate, the two would have made the perfect team on and off the protest lines, but she had never granted him access to her bedroom despite his subtle advances. It was an insult he hadn't forgotten. Moving his gaze to Gabby, he thought about their first encounter. Submissive and willing, she had proven her devotion to him tenfold. It was a devotion he would reward.

When Sebastian gave the nod, the protesters dispersed. Gabby and Norell charged the ticket windows followed by several others while the remainder ran to the gondola entrance. Screams pierced the quiet morning air as protesters wielded their cans and chanted, "Expansion kills!"

"Leave the animals alone to roam!"

Torrents of red paint shot through the air, blasting creamy white walls and dripping down windows. Parents corralled their children from harm's way, dashing away from the protesters. Several men and women stood like frozen statues as protesters nimbly raced about, hitting the ski school, covering the walls in red. Shouts began to compete with excited shrieks, punctured by angry warnings the authorities would be called. In minutes, the bank of ticket windows had been drenched in red.

Lisa tried to dart about and keep in tune with the protesters, but her heart was torn. Staff members staggered about as though uncertain what to do. Skiers and non-skiers backed away from the scene. Careful to remain part of the group but itching to ditch them at once, Lisa hovered on the edge of chaos. Nobody stepped in to stop them and if they did, Lisa wasn't sure it would matter. The protesters seemed keyed-up and ready for confrontation. They didn't care if the police were summoned. They accepted it as part of the protest. Hadn't Kinsley said as much many times?

Jogging about aimlessly, Lisa could only think, *madness*. This was madness in the name of the movement. Getting nowhere darting about the outskirts, she stopped. Cold stung her cheeks, her nose, permeated her clothing. Kinsley would not be happy. Lisa was supposed to get evidence on Sebastian, proof that he was responsible for the bomb but Gabby hadn't admitted to guilt. Instead, she seemed to implicate Kinsley in the bombing—an accusation Lisa had also recorded.

Taking in the scene, a male protester bumped against a group of women as he ran past, shouting in their faces. Lisa hated the aggressive nature that some of these people demonstrated. This was a cause Lisa believed in, but spray-painting buildings and scaring women and children wasn't the answer. She glimpsed a couple of teenagers jog by her, the two more interested in watching the commotion, than escaping it, and they reminded Lisa of Gabby.

Instantly, Lisa sought to locate her. She had a can of paint. Had she used it?

But it was a dumb question. Gabby was totally on board with everything Sebastian wanted to do. Of course she had. Probably emptied it and was looking for a second. And what next? More bombs? More paint? Gabby had mentioned destroying the construction equipment... Lisa shuddered. It was a plan that could easily get out of hand. Fire on the mountain during summer could destroy more than a few pieces of equipment—it could destroy her toads' habitat!

Summer was mating season. Toads would be out in large numbers and so would she and her fellow researchers. If Gabby and Sebastian went through with their plans, the entire eco-system would be threatened. Edging away from the group, Lisa thought, she might not have been able to get a confession about the patrol hut bombing, but she sure as heck could prevent a summer wildfire. Chief Davis would hear about this monkeywrench plan and *today*.

Catching Gabby's eye, Lisa shook the insanity from her brain. She had to concentrate on the plan. She had to stay connected, pretend she was one of them and see if she could find another way to get someone to admit Sebastian's guilt.

Gabby ran over to her and thrust a sign into Lisa's hands. "Here, you can use this as we picket around."

"Thanks." Staring at the message, Lisa felt mixed emotions. *Give the animals their space.* It was a message with which she agreed. The existing resort was big enough. Expanding it would only jeopardize the wildlife, but marching around with a sign wasn't going to change anything. It would only antagonize. Peering at the protesters' wild-eyed zeal, Lisa tried to appear stoked and jabbed her sign in the air. "They need to hear us!"

"You bet they do," Gabby cried out gleefully, then encircled her arm through Lisa's and hauled her toward the group. "Now let's go give it to them!"

Sitting at a round table near a window of her hotel lobby, Kinsley sipped from her third cup of coffee as she awaited word from Lisa. Resort guests walked by, many lugging ski gear, others a paper cup of steaming coffee. There was no sign of protest from this vantage point, everything moving at the sedate pace of early morning. Lisa hadn't called, hadn't texted. She hadn't shown up at the hotel with the recorded evidence to prove her innocence. Nerves zipped through Kinsley's pulse. She hoped "no news" was "good news" but couldn't quite sell herself on the concept. Instead, it felt like every passing minute was another year added to her sentence.

Kinsley tapped a fingernail on the table near her saucer, her gaze trailing a small child dressed in a neon yellow ski suit. Sporting the awkward gait representative of an inability to walk properly due to an excess of clothing, the youngster seemed more pulled down the street than walked. Moving her gaze to the next family, Kinsley drew the warm mug to her lips and tried not to think about how much she had riding on her friend.

If Lisa didn't come through, if she didn't get the proof Kinsley needed to avoid prosecution, Kinsley didn't want to consider the consequences. Unfortunately, Lisa was out of her element when it came to deception and ruse. The activism angle might fit her like one of her favorite hot pink bandanas, but not the duplicity. Yet Kinsley had no one else, no one who could get close to the group. Not like Lisa. She looked the part, could act the part, and there was one person who would suck her in without question. Gabby Miller. Sebastian had been using Gabby to his benefit for some time. Now it was Kinsley's turn. Gabby saw what she wanted to see. She was vocal and passionate and one hundred percent gullible when it came to the cause. She'd take one look at Lisa and see herself—a young, passionate crusader for the animals.

Near the front entrance, Kinsley glimpsed a large man enter. Pausing briefly in the lobby, his towering figure turned and headed toward her, accompanied by two men. Butterflies swarmed her stomach. Chief Wade Davis was here. And McIntyre Walsh. Several paces behind the first two men, he caught up to them midway through the lobby. She smacked her coffee mug to the table, the thud serving to rattle her. All eyes were on her. Her.

Kinsley gulped. *What were they doing here?*

Chief Davis cut a determined path and arrived tableside within seconds. Flanked by Walsh and two of his detectives, he stared down at her. Kinsley could feel the anger emanating from Walsh. Thrashing, tangible, he was a tornado of emotion. She got it. But Chief Davis? Why did he look so angry?

"Kinsley, I need you to come with me."

"Chief Davis?" Her gaze darted between him and his men. "But I don't understand. I've been released, my mother paid the bail." The expressions hovering above her remained impassive. "Is there something else?"

"We found your fingerprints on the patrol hut bomb."

"*What?*" Alarm ripped through her midsection, leaving her a vacuum of emotion. "But that's impossible..."

"Fingerprints don't lie," Walsh clipped.

Fingerprints. Breath escaped her lungs in a rush. *There was no way...*

"Let's go," Chief Davis commanded quietly.

Kinsley looked up at him, suddenly petrified. This couldn't be happening. There was no way her fingerprints could have been on that bomb. She never touched it. Hadn't even known about it!

The Chief reached out a hand, as though prepared to drag her from her seat if necessary. Rising, shaky legs nearly gave way beneath her. Kinsley tried to avoid Walsh, but felt strangled by the pierce of his green-eyed gaze. He'd already convicted her of the crime.

Chief Davis secured a hand around her arm and escorted her out of the lobby. He waited while she put on her coat. Kinsley pulled her lapels closed, flipping her long hair from beneath the collar and buttoned the double-breasted coat. Rattling off his Miranda spiel once again, the Chief of Police handcuffed her and thrust her out the door that Walsh held open. No longer concerned with her feelings or those of his close friends, Chief Davis eyed her with naked contempt. He

was going to march her through town like a common criminal—the criminal he believed her to be—while Walsh savored her humiliation in the process.

Kinsley wanted to cry but wouldn't give them the satisfaction. She did nothing wrong. Other than destroy a few furs,
she had done nothing wrong. Justice would prevail. Biting
down on her lip as people stopped and stared, Kinsley cried
out silently, "*I'm innocent*!"

Icy cold bit into her, cutting through her jacket as though
it were a cotton sheet. Plodding the quaint cobblestone streets
in a daze, Kinsley only half-registered the people and goings-
on around her, the stares, the rabid curiosity, Kinsley lost her
thoughts in a swirl of nightmarish fantasy. She felt dirty. Un-
worthy. A fraud.

Fingerprints. There was no way. But with each step she
took, a horrible dread filled her. They rounded a corner near
the square, and the gondola came into view. People were
gathered around the base station, amassing in large numbers,
and Kinsley's heart exploded. The blood protest. She had
completely forgotten. *Lisa*. Walsh would see her!

Flinging an involuntary glance over her shoulder at him,
she realized he instantly picked up on her distress. His gaze
sharpened like a serpent on the verge of striking as he silently
responded, "*What's going on?*"

Fear peppered Kinsley's chest. She didn't want Lisa to
get in trouble with Walsh! It wasn't her fault she was being a
good friend. But with each step closer, Kinsley felt as though
she were being raked over hot coals. Lisa was taking part in
the blood protest. This type of protest was one of their more
effective tools to gain attention, because the tactic shocked
and provoked and made their point loud and clear. They were
normally used for anti-slaughter rallies to illustrate the pain
and suffering of animals as the result of choice, and that the
"blood" was on the consumer's hands. But with the paint
sprayed and the protesters on the march, Chief Davis and
Walsh would likely see Lisa.

As if on cue, the mob of onlookers separated in a wave as the Police Chief neared. Escorting another criminal on official business, he was given deference. With the opening in the crowd, Kinsley desperately searched for Lisa. Maybe she could warn her to duck and hide before they saw her. Then, Lisa could reveal her role in the protest later, on her terms. But to be caught in the act would be tough to explain.

"Expansion hurts the animals!"

"Your tickets pay for their demise!"

The usual chants ticked off across the group of protesters, each as loud and angry as the prior. Red paint was everywhere—the ticket windows, the gondola station; a few protesters had even covered their signs with it.

"Corruption kills!"

"Habitat not thrill!"

Walsh slowed at her side and instinctively Kinsley understood the cause. He had spotted Lisa. Searching the crowd for sight of her, Kinsley willed Lisa's disguise to hold strong. Maybe Walsh only thought he recognized her. Maybe she would fool him.

"Lisa?" The soft guttural displeasure erupting next to her said otherwise. Kinsley closed her eyes as the four men came to a halt, slowing her with them. "What the hell?"

There, across the open square, Lisa marched openly with her sign. Dressed in jeans and white jacket with matching hat, the hot pink of her turtleneck poked free and practically shouted her name. Her fair skin was nipped red, her hair dark beneath the white wool hat. Among this crowd of protesters, there was no disguising that face. Kinsley moaned as she stared at her friend. *No sunglasses?*

Flashing an angry glance to Kinsley, Walsh took off running toward Lisa.

Picking up on the scent of trouble, Chief Davis directed his officer to stand down, then radioed his office for backup. "Need assistance in Silver Creek Square. Protest with damage, possible riot."

Kinsley hoped not. For the sake of everyone involved, she hoped the protesters didn't escalate the situation, though knowing Sebastian, he'd probably encouraged his people to challenge the authorities, their arrests to be worn like badges of honor.

Chapter Twenty-Two

Grant looked on as Giovanna locked the door to her storefront, his cheeks chilled by the early morning air. It was with more than a pang of disappointment that he watched her lock up for the last time. Today, she was driving to Denver then flying out to Italy this evening, and he was sad to see her go. It was a trip she shouldn't be taking. She should be able to stay in Colorado, not rationalize why she should leave with excuses ranging from her mother needed her because she was getting on in years to the general "it was for the best" justification. Grant wanted to argue the fact that Giovanna had two sisters living in Tuscany who could look after their mother, but he knew better. Giovanna was quiet and demure on the outside, but she had a temper that could flare when provoked. He'd seen it only once, but once was enough. She'd made her decision, and Grant wasn't going to talk her out of it.

"Maybe I'll make it to Italy one day," he said. "You can show me around the countryside."

Thick eyelashes fluttered and she smiled like a schoolgirl, her olive skin rich and warm against the emerald green scarf bundled at her neck. Tucked inside a full-length sable brown fur coat, the scarf lent an understated elegance to the woman who had lost her livelihood yet continued to hold her head high. "You are always welcome, Grant Powell." Pleasure stretched across her face as she added with a wink, "My mother would absolutely love you. She has a soft spot for handsome young men."

Grant laughed. "I don't know that you could call me young, but I'll take the compliment any day." He leaned over and kissed her cheek, the heavy spice of her perfume lingering with him. "I'll keep you posted on what happens with the prosecution."

Shadows crossed Giovanna's gaze as she peered at him. Strange, but the anger he expected—the anger he felt deep in his bones—wasn't there. What he saw in her eyes felt more like regret. "I didn't tell you," she began, "but that woman stopped by to see me yesterday."

"What woman?"

"The one who bombed my store."

"Kinsley?" The name still cut raw as he uttered it from his lips. "She was here?"

Giovanna shook her head. "No, at the restaurant. Sylvia and I were having lunch at The Oasis and she was there with a friend. She walked over to my table and apologized for the incident. Said she didn't mean for it to happen..." Giovanna paused, as though searching for the right words. "There was a mix-up of some kind."

"There was no mix-up," Grant countered outright. "She's an animal rights nut job who wanted to send you a message. There's no mix-up in that."

Unaffected by his blunt description, Giovanna brought a finger to her lips and nodded thoughtfully. "Yes, she said as much. But there was something about her, something I couldn't put together until now."

"What's there to put together? She's a self-centered activist who thinks her way is the right way, the only way." Grant could feel his pulse skyrocket. How dare Kinsley confront Giovanna and make this situation harder for her than it already was?

Giovanna fell into a smile, suddenly indulging Grant in grandmotherly fashion. "Oh, *Grant*. This one's a crusader. A passionate young woman who is fighting for what she believes in."

Grant couldn't believe what he was hearing. Giovanna sounded like she was letting Kinsley off the hook, like she was making excuses for her, based on impetuous youth.

"I was passionate once..." Giovanna murmured, her gaze drifting to a faraway place—a place where Grant couldn't join her. "A long time ago," she said wistfully. "I fought for things, wanted to change things."

There was a difference. Kinsley was more than passionate, she was a liar. There was no room in his heart for tolerance when it came to people willing to destroy the private property of others. It was bully behavior, thug-like. Just because it was wrapped up in a pretty young package didn't excuse it.

Angling her head, Giovanna told him, "She asked for my forgiveness."

Grant gaped at her. "You didn't give it, did you?"

Giovanna's eyes moistened, glistening in the morning sun as it eased over the village behind her. She smiled, but the effort was pained. "I am a Catholic, Grant. It's in our nature to forgive."

Struck by the change in tone, Grant ejected the kindness from his mind. Only because Giovanna was a better person than him. She was a beautiful, loving person and deserved better than being put in this position but he wasn't going to insult her over it. It was her choice, her life. His was a different story. He felt guilty by association, like he was a traitor for taking up with Kinsley in the first place. She was a stain on his heart, a scar. It was a feeling he didn't care for.

In the quiet dawn, the two friends stood silent. Most stores weren't slated to open for another hour or so, but Giovanna had an early flight out of Denver. Grant had offered to drive her to the airport, but she refused. It was too much. He'd done enough already. Giovanna pulled the scarf snug around her neck and held Grant in her gaze. A thump of sound drifted over the rooftops. Muted, it was odd for this hour of the day and sounded like the explosions set off by the resort to prevent potential avalanches. Strange for them to do so at the very hour lifts were set to open.

Giovanna's eyes rounded, her gaze drifting in the direction of the gondola. "What is going on?"

It was as if the two of them registered the significance of the sounds at the same moment. Grant's chest tightened. Following her gaze, he murmured, "I don't know." But it didn't sound good.

Across town, Walsh stormed over to Lisa and pulled her from the crowd of protesters. Lisa freaked, startled by his unexpected appearance. She fought him off, glancing about the group, clearly embarrassed, but Walsh persisted, dragging her away. Several male protesters took note and surged to her aid. A man confronted Walsh and shoved him by the shoulder. Heartbeats galloped through Kinsley's chest. She couldn't hear what they were saying, but she didn't have to. Walsh took a step toward the guy. The two exchanged words. Then Norell joined in, angling his massive frame toward Walsh.

Chief Davis yanked Kinsley toward the tangle of the angry mob. That's when Lisa caught sight of her. Her mouth fell open. Her eyes became saucers. There was no mistaking the situation. Kinsley was under arrest. *Kinsley*? she mouthed.

Walsh grabbed Lisa's arm again and Norell took a swing. Walsh undercut him with a lightning strike to the stomach. Norell doubled over. As if getting a green light, two other protesters pounced on Walsh.

The police officer next to Kinsley charged forward. A wave of skiers backed up and turned to run. Chief Davis yelled, "Move back!"

Three uniformed officers ran down the main street, holding black sticks by their sides. They arrived and pummeled bodies at random, literally beating protesters out of his way as they headed into the epicenter. People bumped and shoved from every direction. Fear rose sharply in Kinsley's throat. She was going to be trampled!

Fists flew, bodies crushed in. Shouts pierced the air. The protest was turning violent. They wanted blood—real blood—not the red paint splattered across buildings, streaming down in splotchy rivulets. But this was out of control. People could be hurt. Kinsley's insides hollowed. *Lisa!*

And Sebastian. *Where was Sebastian*?

"Get down!"

"Watch out!"

Shooting her gaze over the crowd, Kinsley searched for Sebastian. Faces and heads melded into one big jumble of individuals. Several protesters held up cell phones and recorded the scene as it unfolded. Kinsley knew the photos and videos would be posted online and used to rally support. At the moment, she wished they'd all just disperse.

Norell careened into her, knocking her into Chief Davis. The Chief pushed her back roughly then lunged for Norell. Staggering, Kinsley fell to her knees. Hard brick cut into her knees as she swung her body backward to regain balance. She locked gazes with Norell. Panic curled around her heart. He looked like a crazed animal consumed by a frenzied aggression. Kinsley thought he was going to hit her, but someone pulled him back by the shirt.

Ducking, she missed who it was. Police worked to separate protesters from tourists. Between the weave of people, Kinsley glimpsed Gabby kick a police officer near a ticket window as he dragged her from the action. A gunshot fired. Women screamed. Bodies jostled around her. Kinsley froze. Oh my God—*they shot someone*?

Standing several yards from her, the Chief jerked his head in the direction of the shooting. Several police officers gathered around a man with black hair. Kinsley fought to see what happened. An officer stepped back and her heart stopped. Dreadlocks. Norell.

Slumping, he fell to the ground.

Protesters scattered.

"Stand back!" someone yelled.

"They shot him!"

"The police shot him!"

As people cleared, Kinsley could see a few male protesters on their knees, hands cuffed behind their backs. A few men struggled against the police officers, but most seemed to get the hint. *Fight and you'll get shot.*

Kinsley sucked in her breath as she watched the mob morph from agitated chaos to stunned calm. Several men collected around Norell like a fence to the crowd. They watched everything the police did, as though taking mental notes for their later statements, statements likely aimed at indicting the police force for aggressive use of force. Chief Davis thrust Kinsley to the hands of another officer and immediately took up residence between protesters and police officers. Several of his men joined him and stood like sentries on duty. The policemen stared at the men working on Norell. The Chief turned to the group and shouted, "Clear the area—NOW!"

"We have a right to protest!"

As though called by a silent megaphone, a wave of Silver Creek staff descended upon the scene in mass. Though somewhat hesitant on what to do with the protesters, they encircled them, creating a border that prevented escape. Threats ripped through remnants of hostility, the situation calmer but edgy. Resort guests were kept clear of the area and could only watch from a distance.

Kinsley worried the activists would rebel against the shooting of one of their own, but instead, they seemed held in check by an invisible leash. Once again, she scanned the vicinity, half-expecting to see Sebastian show up and accuse the police department of harassment. But he was nowhere to be found.

Suddenly, a strong hand gripped her arm abruptly and yanked her away from the scene. Tripping over her steps as she was led away, Kinsley repeatedly looked over her shoulder. Questions fired through her skull, each one more urgent than the previous. Was Norell alive? Was Lisa okay? She hadn't seen her friend since the chaos broke out, when Norell took a swing at Walsh. *Walsh.* She never saw him again, either.

Anger blew through her heart like a steam engine. Sebastian was responsible for this debacle. He was the reason they had gone forward with the blood protest, the reason Lisa had been on scene, the reason Norell had been running wild. Sebastian was the cause of it all, the instigator, but he had vacated the scene. Why?

Visions of a burning patrol hut cut sharply into her mind. Was he somewhere else executing another explosion? Kinsley stumbled and the officer squeezed her arm harder. He walked with barely controlled anger, his temper a trigger switch of release should she open her mouth. Struggling to keep pace with him, the metal handcuffs cutting into the skin at her wrists, Kinsley knew when to remain silent. She knew better than to antagonize an already inflamed temper. Other protesters mouthed off with a slur of insults but not her. Losing her cool equated to losing the battle and Kinsley refused to give anyone the satisfaction of a "win." Not over her. Not ever.

Chapter Twenty-Three

Grant told Giovanna to stay put, then ran toward the gondola, sick with a certainty that ripped him to the core. It sounded like there'd been a gunshot. Not an explosion, like a bomb, but a gunshot. His thoughts went to Kinsley. She'd bombed the fur store, bombed the ski patrol hut. Was there no end to the madness? The violence?

Jogging toward the square, Grant saw a mass of people congregating between the ticket window and the gondola entrance. Tourists stood closely packed, immobile as Silver Creek staff members created a boundary between them and whatever was going on that commanded their attention. *What the hell was going on?*

Before Grant made it to the edge of the crowd, bodies broke apart, allowing passage of a police officer and Kinsley. *Kinsley.* With a sharp intake of breath, Grant met her gaze. She was being pushed forward against her will. Was she under arrest?

Thoughts clicked quickly through his mind. Kinsley was under arrest. Something happened—a protest gone wrong, a staged attack—and now Kinsley was going to jail. As the police officer approached traveling at rocket stride, Grant couldn't tear his gaze from Kinsley's face. Her gaze was fixed on his, filled with guilt and humiliation. Shame. Staring into her dark eyes as she passed, Grant was overwhelmed by a sense of disgust. Pains cramped in his chest and he breathed, breathed as thoughts of their upcoming trip to New York City seeped into his mind, conversations about clothing lines and new directions. There had been so many things he'd wanted to do with her but none of them would come to pass. Swamped by a sudden longing, Grant tried to turn off his brain. Not now. Not ever. Grant didn't care what Giovanna thought. Kinsley wasn't a crusader. She was a thug, a violent extremist who cared nothing about others.

Gripped by a need to move, Lisa paced outside the ski school entrance. Walsh watched wordlessly. Nerves stretched taut, her thoughts rattled, Lisa blamed him for the chaotic turn of events. Because Walsh felt the need to drag her away like a child, several men felt the need to jump in and begin to fight—on *her* behalf. The irony wasn't lost on her. Instead, it aggravated the situation. Walsh should not have interfered, but neither should the men from Kinsley's group of activists have interfered. Both sides were wrong.

Walsh had been unhappy to see her among the protesters—no surprise there—but that was his fault. He had disliked Kinsley from day one and never given her a chance because he considered her to be a troublemaker. *An instigator*, were his exact words.

Well, she wasn't a troublemaker. Kinsley was an activist, a woman who voiced her support for the voiceless. Right now, Walsh was the troublemaker. She wanted to string him up by his toes, except that it would be impossible. His steely muscular body was about as movable as a rocky mountain.

Arms crossed, Walsh stood by silently, his feelings radiating in waves of displeasure. He'd been punched, kicked and nearly shot because of her, and his pale gaze was laced with disapproval. He was angry with her.

Lisa stopped suddenly, her bottled emotions slamming into her. "What were you thinking trying to drag me out of the protest line?"

"I was thinking of getting you out of there."

"Why? I wasn't doing anything wrong."

"You have no business with those people."

"Those people? They're protesters, animal rights activists. I have every business with those people—beginning with the fact that I believe in their cause."

"Since when do you believe in spray painting buildings?"

"I believe in their cause," she snapped. "Not their methods. But it's beside the point. What gives you the right to come and interfere like that?"

"You were in danger."

She stared at him incredulously. "I wasn't in danger—not until *you* showed up, anyway. A gun went off, Walsh!"

"I can only hope it belonged to a police officer."

"Are you serious?" Lisa pulled the hat from her head, the wool itchy and annoying. "Someone could be hurt." She whipped a glance toward the crowd near the gondola, the distant sound of sirens underscoring her point. "That whole scene could have been avoided if you had stayed out of it. You could have talked to me afterward if you didn't like what I was doing, and they would have left you alone."

Walsh grunted. "Doubt it."

His rejection irked her. "How can you say that? They went after you because you went after me!"

"I was there to save you."

"Save me?"

"Yes." Walsh quieted, his mood shifted. "I thought that was something you liked about me."

Lisa groaned loudly. "When I need saving, yes—great!—wonderful. But jumping into a situation because you don't like what I'm doing? That's something else entirely." Glaring at him, Lisa was besieged by images of Kinsley in handcuffs. Lisa had failed her friend. She had tried and failed, and now Kinsley was going to jail for a very long time. Walsh remained rigid and unyiclding. Uncompromising. "You need to learn when to butt out."

His gaze reflected the hit, filling with hurt. "Lisa..."

The change stopped her cold. She didn't mean that, not exactly. Not in such harsh terms. But darn it, why did he insist on bursting in like some knight in shining armor with a chip on his shoulder? She was an adult woman who could take care of herself, not some fairy tale princess who couldn't sleep on a pea! Had Walsh forgotten their time on the mountain? Had he forgotten that she could handle the rugged terrain as well as he?

Blowing out her breath in a ragged sigh, Lisa was beside herself. Kinsley was in custody, one of the protesters had been shot, and Walsh had successfully managed to blow her cover. Now, how was she going to help free Kinsley? She had nowhere near the information she needed to prove Kinsley didn't plant that bomb and there was no way to get it. Pivoting, Lisa resumed pacing. Kinsley had been arrested—again. But why? Was there something else? Did they think they had enough proof to convict?

Lisa stopped and whirled. Walsh had been with her. He had been with Wade Davis and two other officers when he spotted her in the crowd of protesters. "What's going on with Kinsley?" she demanded. "Why did Wade have her in handcuffs?"

"Because she's a criminal."

"But they already arrested and released her. Why do so again? What changed?"

Walsh set his hands to his hips and glared at her. "Why were you with the protesters? The truth this time."

"I asked you first."

Tension rose between them as he refused to answer. So used to being the man in charge, especially now that he worked with the police department, Walsh thought he could push her around and dictate the rules. Well, he couldn't. Not with her. Not after he messed up her plans. "Never mind. I'll find out myself."

Walsh grabbed her by the arm. "Stop, Lisa."

Surprised by his about-face, she said, "Why? You're not telling me anything."

"They have her fingerprints on the bomb." His voice dropped, steeped in emotion. He was the Walsh she knew and loved as he said gently, "I know you think she's innocent, but fingerprints don't lie. Kinsley put that bomb in the patrol hut. She almost killed a man, Lisa. She almost killed Canyon Laredo's dog. Both are lucky to be alive."

Lisa slumped. Fingerprints? On the bomb? *The bomb that injured a man, burned Canyon's dog.*

Staring into the eyes of a man she trusted, a man second only to her father in importance in her life, Lisa couldn't accept it. There had to be a mistake. Kinsley couldn't have done it. She swore she had nothing to do with it. She wouldn't lie to her best friend.

But as the facts sank in, Lisa couldn't fight a sense of shrinking, as though she were being sucked down a black hole. Kinsley wouldn't put her up to going through with this charade if there weren't good reason. Visions of a burned Golden Retriever flowed into Lisa's mind. Canyon's dog had been hurt. Canyon. He was a friend. A good friend. He'd been there the day she'd been shot on the mountain with Walsh.

Walsh held her in his gaze, and she could feel his heart reaching out to her. He wasn't here to hurt her. He was a decent man. He did what was right, because it was right. Lisa knew he wouldn't lie to her, but he was wrong on this one. Whatever he thought he knew had to be wrong. Lisa brushed fallen strands of hair from her eyes, her head and ears suddenly feeling the cold as her fingertips lingered near her temple. Venturing a peek toward the site of the commotion, she saw the protesters had disbanded. Police were gathered around a man on the ground, waving a team of paramedics to their victim. A man had been shot. Kinsley's fingerprints were on the bomb.

Lisa returned focus to Walsh. She began to tremble. "It can't be true. There must be some mistake."

"There's no mistake." Cradling her within his gaze, Walsh implored her to listen. "Kinsley's an extremist. She resorted to terrorist methods to get her way because the proper channels failed. I know it's not what you want to hear."

Lisa looked away. Wade Davis and his men were now involved and not in a good way. A man had been shot. Not one of theirs but a protester. Walsh placed his hands on her shoulders and gave a gentle squeeze, pulling her attention back to him.

"Lisa, please. I'm telling you this for your own good. You don't want to get messed up with the wrong person."

"You don't trust my decisions?"

"I think your heart can blind you to the truth."

"She's not guilty."

"Then she can prove it in a court of law."

Lisa's heart cracked. Exactly what she was afraid of—a court of law filled with people who didn't know Kinsley, and couldn't care less about what happened to her.

Chief Wade Davis blew into the small room, a tornado of rage swirling about him. "You and your people are going to pay for that little stunt you pulled."

Kinsley winced. Seated in the familiar interrogation room with only a table between them, she kept her mouth shut. Chief Davis was the last person she wanted to rile. He could ship her off to Denver today—and might—if she couldn't convince him otherwise.

"One of my men had to shoot one of your protesters. The man is in surgery as we speak, and you'd better hope he makes it."

Huh? Glancing around the empty room, Kinsley thought she might be dreaming. *She* better hope that Norell makes it? It was his officer that shot him! How did that put *her* on the hook for it?

"Covering the ticket windows and gondola with paint was a stupid idea," Chief Davis spat, his dark eyes flashing. "You might have succeeded in ruining a day's business, but your activists are in big trouble."

Kinsley sat stunned. Walsh was the one who started it. If he hadn't gone after Lisa like some controlling brute, none of this would have happened! Though Kinsley didn't dare voice the same. Davis and Walsh were friends, and she sitting in jail for an explosion that both believe she orchestrated, one that could send her to prison.

Smacking his large hands flat on the table, Chief Davis leaned toward her. Normally a cool player when it came to his authority, he was clearly unhinged, the skin around his starched collar flushed red. "When are you going to get it through your head that violence doesn't work? It never works. Never has and never will." He jabbed a finger in her face and said, "A man's life hangs in the balance because of you. Doesn't that bother you?"

"Of course it does!" A human being had just been shot. Someone who had been there on her behalf. Mostly Sebastian's, but Norell had been there under her banner, her cause. Of course she cared what happened to him. "But I'm not responsible for his actions or those of the police officer's. I wasn't even there—"

"Inciting others to violence makes you guilty. One of your men pulled a knife."

Staring at him, reason and question swished around her brain then swirled down into the pit of her stomach. A knife? Who? When? On Walsh?

"It's guilt by association as far as I'm concerned, and you and your organization are going down for the crime."

Guilt by association. The realization sank in. They could go after *Wildlife Neutral*, claiming it was the cause that made Norell attack. That Kinsley and the organization inspired him to violence. She pressed her lids together briefly. This couldn't be happening.

"And to think that I gave you the benefit of the doubt." Chief Davis straightened. With a tug on his suit lapel, he stated simply, "It won't happen again. You are a filthy liar who cares nothing about those you hurt."

Kinsley felt the sting. She had been interrogated before, harassed by police officers, accused of things she didn't do, but never like this. This smelled of vengeance. Swallowing back a rise of fear, she said quickly, "You said you had my fingerprints. There's no way that's possible. I never touched that bomb."

Chief Davis crossed his arms and stared down at her. "Bet you didn't buy the one-way ticket to London, either."

"What?" She gripped the edge of the metal table. "What ticket?"

"The one you purchased a week ago." A twisted smile formed on his otherwise handsome face—as though she'd done this to him personally and he resented her for it—and now he had her, cold. "Did you think we wouldn't find out? Or did you assume by the time we did, it would be too late and you'd be long gone."

He spoke as if these were statements of fact. That the evidence was in and she was guilty. Kinsley stood at once. "Chief Davis, I have no idea what you're talking about. I haven't purchased any ticket to London. And as to those fingerprints you mentioned, there has to be some mistake. I never touched the bomb that went off in the patrol hut."

As if on cue, a female officer walked into the room and handed him a sheet of paper which he slid across the desk. He stabbed a finger to the top of the page. "That's your web account. That's your company."

Kinsley stared at the sheet of paper and her insides shredded. It was a printed receipt from an online banking service she used, clearly confirming a ticket had been purchased in her name. The transaction had posted seven days ago. Almost two thousand dollars had been spent on a first class one-way ticket to Heathrow. She gaped at Wade. She never made that purchase! But even as the thoughts flowed through her system, she realized she was beginning to sound like an endless loop recording. *There must be some mistake. It wasn't me.*

She was also beginning to sound guilty.

"What, no denial?" Chief Davis smirked. "It's tough when the evidence stares you in the face, isn't it? It's tough to spin your lies to people who want to believe you when the proof is in black and white and says otherwise."

"I swear I didn't buy that ticket." But someone did. Someone bought that ticket in her name, with her money, for the sole purpose of setting her up. It had to be the same with her fingerprints. Somehow her fingerprints had been lifted and put on that bomb. Fear slithered down her spine. There was only person capable of both and with motive.

Sebastian Wu.

Chief Davis walked toward the window and motioned for someone on the other side to come in.

"Did you ever question my associate, Sebastian Wu?" Kinsley blurted. "Did you ever look into his alibi?"

Turning, the Chief's expression crusted over. "We did. Thanks to him, we were able to obtain the information about your flight plans."

"*Thanks to him*?" Kinsley's demeanor shattered. "He was the one who made the bombs!"

"And your fingerprints? Did he magically place them on the bomb, too?"

"He did. He had to have done it because I never touched the damn thing!"

When a male officer walked into the interrogation room, Chief Davis walked out. He was finished here. Kinsley gulped. As was she.

Chapter Twenty-Four

Grant stood on the rear deck of his home, a timber-framed condominium located on the edge of the village and soaked in the predawn landscape. In the muted light, trees looked darker, snow heavier. The sky had none of its usual brilliance. In a few hours, everything would change. Colors would be vibrant, white snow would glisten and sparkle. Ski lifts would be moving steadily up the mountain. Grant held a hot ceramic mug full of coffee wrapped within his hands but hadn't taken the first sip. He didn't want it, didn't need it, had only brewed it out of habit. Unable to sleep, Grant realized a cup of hot black coffee might make matters worse. All night long he'd been unable to get the image of Kinsley being hauled off to jail out of his mind. More specifically, the look in her eyes. It had been a hot iron branded to his heart, a vision he couldn't shake. There had been no arrogance, no defiance as he would have expected. Instead, her gaze had been swamped with longing. Memories of their last kiss surged, wound around his heart, commingling past conversations with the touch of her lips on his.

Kinsley had kissed him like she meant it. She had awakened something deep inside him that he feared had been lost, and then she betrayed him. A quick lump lodged in his throat. Want stirred, faint but persistent, as he recalled the soft vulnerability he'd seen in her eyes. They would have been good together. If she had been the woman he thought she was, they would have been good together. Better than good, they would have been perfect.

Maybe the surrender he'd seen in her eyes wasn't about longing but about guilt. Perhaps the look had been one of acceptance, the knowledge she had been caught and was getting her due. But Grant couldn't shake the feeling it was something more, something different. She had looked at him with sheer desperation. Her expression had been vulnerable, not defiant. Her eyes held longing and sadness, not the rebellion he would have expected. She had lied so handily about the fur store bombing. She had evaded his accusations like a nimble thief in the night. What had changed?

Staring at his priceless view of the ski mountain, the large swaths of white cut through forests of evergreen, ski lifts immobile, shadows lining the runs, Grant wracked his brain for answers. The early morning temperature was cold, biting into his skin, but he welcomed it. He needed clarity. Something was off, but he couldn't pinpoint it. He couldn't decipher that look in her eyes. It was as though Kinsley had been begging him to help her, to save her from the clutches of injustice. It was as if he could hear the words tumble from her lips.

Grant didn't want to kid himself. He knew she was a savvy woman and didn't want to get sucked into believing he saw something that wasn't there, something he only wished was there, but still... Facts were facts. Kinsley placed that bomb in Giovanna's store. The video evidence was conclusive. She admitted as much to Giovanna, apologizing for her role. She was suspected of bombing the ski patrol hut. Was she simply a skilled lover? A professional-grade con artist who could make him believe she needed him? Was she out to use him as a way to escape justice? Is that the motive behind the look?

Clenching his body against a hard shudder, Grant turned on his heel and walked indoors. The heated interior enveloped his body, melted the cold from his skin. He had three hours before his store opened. Three hours he could use to root out as much of the truth as possible and clear his mind of Kinsley once and for all. He had to settle it in his brain, force it to make sense. One way or the other, he had to determine the extent of her guilt.

A trickle of doubt eked through. *Or her innocence.* He was a fair man. He wanted truth, justice. If she was telling the truth, it would explain her desperation. *This one's a crusader. A passionate young woman who is fighting for what she believes in.* Giovanna was convinced of her passion. Could the explosion have been the work of Kinsley's partner, as she claimed?

Steeling himself against a yearning for it to be true, Grant sealed his heart. After filling his arms with her, walking away empty-handed felt unbearable but he couldn't be lied to again. He wanted the truth, and only the truth.

An hour's time only pushed Grant closer to a guilty verdict. Sitting across from the Chief of Police, he felt the dream slipping from his grasp. Kinsley was guilty. They had her fingerprints on the bomb placed at the patrol hut, they had a one-way ticket purchased from her account. A man was dead. The protester who went after Walsh had died from his gunshot wound. Controlling the torrent of emotion rolling inside him, Grant listened as Wade explained what happened next. The federal authorities were going to get involved. Eco-terrorism was a serious crime, and Kinsley would be prosecuted to the fullest extent of the law. There would be prison time. A life sentence.

Grant's hopes had been butchered, his heart crushed. He tried not to imagine Kinsley sitting behind bars with the criminal population. It was like imagining a baby chick in the middle of a dog pound. She'd be lucky if she made it a week without being accosted in some shape, manner or form. It would change her. Destroy her.

"She'll have a hearing later today," Wade continued, "and then the feds will take her into custody. My department will be called to testify, but I think we'll evade prosecution. The man charged my officer with a knife. There were witnesses. With the resort's ample video coverage, there's bound to be a camera that can corroborate the accounts on the ground."

Video surveillance. It's how Kinsley was caught for Giovanna's bombing. Wade said there wasn't video of Kinsley placing the bomb at the patrol hut, but there were finger-prints.

Fingerprints. Why would she have left her fingerprints on the bomb? There had been no fingerprints found on the device in the fur store. Why the other?

"It's been a shock to Silver Creek," Wade went on. "I have to say, no one around here will forget the name Kinsley Fairchild anytime soon."

A sudden thought struck Grant. Kinsley was too smart for such an amateur mistake. She would have worn gloves, would have known to expect video surveillance, especially after being caught on camera outside the fur store. The ticket to London was something else. "Can I see her?" The question erupted from Grant's mouth before he could calculate its impact.

Wade's brow shot up. His dark gaze honed in on Grant. "You want to see her? Why?"

"Closure," he replied. "I'd like to let her know exactly how I feel about what she's done to this town."

Wade's gaze narrowed.

Grant stood. "I know it's an unusual request, and you have every right to deny me, but for Giovanna's sake, I'd like to see Kinsley and let her know the extent of the damage she's caused. Once the feds take her, I won't have another opportunity."

Easing back in his chair, Wade regarded Grant with a thoughtful gaze. Scratching the edge of one of his thick brows, he appeared thoughtful. Contemplative. "I understand she's headed back to Italy."

"Yes, because of Kinsley."

Wade pursed his lips. He held Grant's gaze and his hesitance filled the room. It was not standard procedure. It wasn't productive. In fact, it was unnecessary. Both men knew it.

"I won't take long," Grant said, making a last ditch appeal. "Five minutes. Five minutes and I'll be gone."

With a heavy sigh, Wade pushed up from his desk. "Because you're a friend and you've been personally affected, I'll give you five minutes, but no more."

Relief swept through him. "Thank you."

Waiting fifteen minutes for them to retrieve Kinsley for her visitor felt like a lifetime to Grant. There were so many things he wanted to say, to ask—to demand—that he wasn't sure where to begin. Did she do it? Had she been careless? Did she know that one of her people had been packing a weapon at the protest? Was that unusual? Had there been attacks in the past?

But as the door to the room opened and Kinsley walked in, all questions evaporated. Even dressed in an orange jumpsuit, her face bare of makeup, brown eyes naked and vulnerable, Kinsley was beautiful. Fragile, strong...exquisite.

Kinsley's mouth dropped open. "Grant..." She glanced to the guard for explanation and stammered, "I don't understand."

Grant understood he was the last person she expected to see, this the last place she expected him to be. But driven by unseen forces, he couldn't fathom being anywhere else. Kinsley moved to the chair and sat, her gaze pinned to Grant like a laser beam. The guard took up position by the door. Folding his hands, he directed his attention to a wall. He was a statue, oblivious to their conversation unless circumstances warranted otherwise.

Seated opposite Kinsley, Grant clamped his heart closed. He couldn't allow his desire free rein, not this close to her. He was here for answers. He couldn't afford to be undercut by reckless need.

Kinsley waited. Dark eyes glistening in the stark fluorescent lighting, she appeared markedly confused.

Taking a breath, Grant plunged straight in, "Why did they find fingerprints on the bomb? Why would you leave fingerprints on the second bomb and not the first?"

"I didn't. Sebastian managed to get them somehow and put them on that bomb."

"Why would he do that? What motive does he have?"

"He's setting me up, Grant. He wants me out of the picture. He wants to take over *Wildlife Neutral*."

"What's in it for him?"

Kinsley looked at him as though he were a fool. "Money, Grant. There's a lot of money that runs through my organization and whoever controls the blog, controls the revenue."

Urgency kicked in as Wade's five minute timer ticked down in his brain. Kinsley wasn't giving him details. He needed details if he was going to get past this and help her. Instinctively, Grant knew that's why he was here. To help the woman he loved. "But that doesn't make sense. How would he get ahold of your blog? He doesn't write it, he has no way of getting the proceeds."

As though spotting her first opportunity at freedom, at support, Kinsley leaned forward and responded quickly, "There are hundreds of thousands of people who support my organization. Sebastian has been close to me for the last couple of years, he has administrative access to my website. It would be nothing for him to change the banking information and funnel the revenue dollars into his personal account, so long as I'm unable to stop him." She flicked a glance to the floor and said, "Sitting in jail would certainly do the trick. And he's the one who constructs my smoke and ink bombs—but never explosive. Sebastian builds them and delivers them to me and others. I'm telling you, I never intended for Giovanna's store to go up in flames. That was totally Sebastian."

Grant had stopped listening. He was calculating numbers. According to Hal, Kinsley's website was a lucrative one. Didn't he say she had over half a million followers? That had to equate to some serious advertising revenue. And if Sebastian had access, it was a no-brainer. Kinsley would be powerless to stop him unless she had help on the outside. Suddenly, his involvement made complete sense. "Where is Sebastian?"

"That's the thing." Kinsley slumped back into her chair. She looked Grant straight in the eye and said, "I don't know. He wasn't in the crowd of protesters when the chaos began. He was missing from the crowd right before the gondola explosion, as well."

"How would you know? I heard you were at the top of the mountain when the bomb went off."

"I was. I overheard a couple of guys talking about some fireworks and how it would get the developer's attention. Fireworks was the exact same word Sebastian had used when we were discussing the bomb in the fur store. I don't know"—Kinsley shook her head—"something in my brain clicked and I knew something was up. Palmer's meeting was at the top of the gondola. My parents were there..." Kinsley closed her eyes as though warding off ugly images, then leapt right back into her explanation, "I raced up the mountain to check for myself. I swear I saw Sebastian heading down, minutes before the explosion, but he was too far away and I couldn't be certain. Then the explosion went off and everything changed."

Grant understood patterns of behavior. It was no coincidence that Sebastian made himself scarce right before the trouble began in both instances. Gripped by an overwhelming picture forming in his mind, Grant asked, "You said he had administrative access to your blog, your accounts. He could have purchased that airline ticket in your name, couldn't he?"

"Easily," Kinsley replied, a smile taking hold. "It means exactly that."

In the space of an instant, Grant and Kinsley had joined sides. No longer at odds, it was clear she could be telling the truth. She had placed the bomb at Giovanna's. She'd admitted to as much. But destruction of property in a retail store was a helluva lot different than putting people in harm's way. A difference of life in prison.

"We need to prove it," Grant said. "We need to prove that Sebastian is behind the bombing, and not you."

"So you believe me," Kinsley uttered faintly, her excitement teeming as she leaned into the table.

"I do." The statement was out before Grant could absorb the full impact.

He believed her. He believed she was being set up and wanted to help clear her name. He wasn't sure how he would do it, only that he had to try. "I want to help, but we're running out of time."

"Tell me about it. Lisa was trying to help me during the protest yesterday. One of the protesters, Gabby Miller, is infatuated with Sebastian. She's a diehard for the cause and would do anything he asked. I told Lisa to get close to her and try to get Gabby to take credit for Sebastian on the bombing, but I don't know if she was able to do it. I was arrested and the situation blew up before we could talk. I haven't heard from her since."

"I can contact her. I'm sure she heard the same things I heard about your fingerprints and assumed the proof was rock-solid. I'll ask her if she got anything from Gabby, though if she did, I would expect she would have shared it with Wade already." Certainly during their meeting this morning, Wade had made no indication of receiving such information. It was possible he was withholding it until he could pursue its credibility, but Grant doubted it. Wade seemed pretty comfortable with Kinsley's guilt.

Settling his gaze on Kinsley, the new glow in her eyes, Grant was pleased to see the ignition of hope but he couldn't risk handing over his heart. Not yet. Not on assumption. He couldn't ignore the slim possibility that Kinsley was lying to him. Her claims sounded genuine. Sebastian was close to her. But Grant had to be sure before he risked it. "Do you have any way to keep Sebastian out of your accounts?"

Kinsley grinned. "Already done. I gave Lisa my password and she went in and changed my access information."

"Good. Are any other protests planned?"

She shook her head. "Sebastian will likely change course, now that Norell is dead."

"You know about that," Grant said, surprised by her apparent indifference.

"They told me." Kinsley shook her head, twisting her mouth as she added, "Norell was a hot-head. He was Sebastian's strong-arm man and getting physical was something that came second-nature to him. He fought first, thought second."

"I remember."

Kinsley stilled. "That's right. He was the one who stepped in when you first showed up."

Grant nodded. He'd had to tie the guy's arms in a knot to shut him down. That's when Hal showed up to intercede on Kinsley's behalf and pulled him off the scent.

Setting elbows to the table, Kinsley buried her face in her hands then dragged her hands down her chin. She rubbed the side of her neck and glanced back at the officer. "There's something else you need to know. Norell went after Walsh during the protest yesterday. Walsh was there to get Lisa, and Norell thought he was causing trouble so he went after him."

"Wade said he pulled a knife."

"Yes, I was surprised to hear about that. It's the first I've heard of him carrying a weapon but then again, Norell was Sebastian's guy. Like Gabby, Norell pinned his loyalty to Sebastian, not me."

"Which means Sebastian will be angry that they shot him."

"Very."

"Another man capable of violence."

"He is. It's one of the reasons we weren't getting along. Sebastian represents the more radical wing of thought, the members who feel no compunction in using aggressive tactics to get their way. I was trying to work the legal angles."

It was Grant's turn to smile. She was also working toward the fashion angle. "We'll get him. Whatever I have to do, I'll help you expose him."

"I don't know what to say..." Kinsley looked at him, a swell of gratitude and vulnerability swamping her gaze. Her expression had softened, her look of cunning and determination replaced by an air of innocence, a naiveté he knew she didn't possess. Kinsley Fairchild was tough, accomplished. She didn't get to where she was by being silly or stupid or naïve. But sometimes, even the strongest among us needed help.

"I do. You're not going to jail for a crime you didn't commit. I'm going to make sure of it." It was the moment his world righted. Grant couldn't explain the sudden shift, only that he felt it to his core. It made logical sense. It made emotional sense. If Grant could have gone to Kinsley and taken her in his arms, he would have. He would have held her and reassured her everything was going to be okay. As it was, he could merely promise.

"Thank you," she whispered.

It was a whisper. Beautiful, delicate, with a hint of the sexy woman he had come to know. The words breathed life back into him.

Chapter Twenty-Five

Once he secured Beau's presence to man the store on short notice, thankful yet again for his number one employee, Grant's next task had been to seek out Hal's daughter for an explanation. Kinsley mentioned Lisa had been helping her during the protest. It was time to find out what she had learned. Understandably, Lisa was surprised to hear from him and about his interest in helping her friend. According to Kinsley, Lisa didn't know about their relationship. Part of Grant couldn't help but wonder if that was because Kinsley felt odd at being seen with him. Not only decades older, he didn't imagine that he was the stereotype for an activist's boyfriend.

If that's what they were. Grant tamped down a swell of misgiving. He didn't know what they were, only that he cared about Kinsley—a lot—and wanted to help her. Who knew where the two of them went from here. As far as Lisa was concerned, she assumed Grant was here out of a loyalty to his friend, Hal. After all, Kinsley was like a sister to Lisa.

Grant had decided it was best to keep this meeting out of mainstream view and was meeting Lisa in the back of a small café located on a side street. After all, no activist in good faith would be caught dead sitting with a Silver Creek business owner, a man who stood to gain from the resort's upcoming expansion and he didn't want to jeopardize Lisa's cover on the off chance she still had an opportunity to get close to Gabby Miller. But with each word she spoke, the news got worse. Wade Davis had been consulted about the information Gabby divulged, and he wasn't buying it. He was angry. Kinsley was guilty. End of story.

Staring across the table, Lisa's almond-shaped eyes mirrored all the concern Grant felt. It seemed they were at a dead end. "Do you think this Gabby still believes that you're one of them?"

Lisa shrugged then drew a sip from her orange juice. Neither of them had touched their breakfast, and now identical bowls of oatmeal sat solidified, raisins wedged in like wrinkled stones. The café was known for its fresh-baked muffins and cakes, but the scent of baking bread floating through the dining area wasn't even close to tempting Grant's appetite. It was non-existent. His coffee was cold. The air was stuffy warm, and he and Lisa didn't seem to be feeling the optimism.

"I don't know how much Gabby saw or what she thought was happening, but Walsh was pretty intent on dragging me away from that crowd. It would be hard to imagine the group isn't suspicious at this point."

"Can you convince her that he was taking you against your will?"

"Possibly. I just don't know if she'll buy my story."

"We have to hope that she will," Grant replied, feeling none of the conviction they needed for success. As he encircled a hand around his coffee mug, the cold glass was jarring to his palm, and underscored the mood swing he felt. Word would have certainly gotten around. To hear Lisa tell it, Walsh had stormed in like the Marine he was, asked no questions and simply hauled her from the scene. That's when Norell jumped in. He had been defending Lisa. It was an irony that wasn't lost on Grant. Norell's act of goodwill resulted in his death.

"I do know they're gearing up for another protest today around lunchtime," Lisa offered. "I saw a couple of them gathering around the parking garage, talking about it."

Grant's interest perked. "Do you know when and where?"

"No. I only heard it in passing, but they usually choose pretty visible locations. I don't think we'll miss them."

Unless they were planning another secret attack.

Grant looked askance to where a mammoth Golden Retriever lay sprawled over the floor under an adjacent table, his attention locked onto his master above. An older woman preoccupied with reading a newspaper absently delivered pieces of toast to the pup beneath. One more indulgent pet owner spoiling their animal. It was the norm around Silver Creek. It was also the same type of dog injured in the blast. Pulling his gaze from the woman and her dog, Grant looked at Lisa. Palmer International had no scheduled meetings for today. He had checked. There was nothing on the agenda until tomorrow, but tomorrow would be too late. Kinsley was set to go before a judge this afternoon, and Grant needed to compile his proof before they carted her off.

"What are you thinking?"

"I don't know, yet."

After paying the tab for breakfast, Grant followed Lisa out of the restaurant where the two idled on the street. Ten-thirty. They had another hour or so before the supposed protest was set to begin. Lisa slipped on a bright pink hat then pushed the hair around her face underneath. She zipped the front of her white coat closed and waited while Grant adjusted his jacket, zipped it closed, and debated whether or not to involve Lisa any further. Clearly Walsh didn't want her anywhere near the protesters, a sentiment Grant couldn't disagree with. Hal wouldn't want her messing around with them either—a fact Grant wouldn't keep from his friend if that's how he and Lisa decided to play it. He heaved a sigh and kicked into step. Basically there were no good options.

"So you wanna go check out the protest?" Lisa asked, as she fell into step beside him.

"Why don't we see if there is a protest or not?"

"Sounds good," she replied with a grin.

At least one of them seemed upbeat, he mused. Digging hands into his front pockets, Grant walked at a fairly good clip. If there was a protest, the first thing he wanted to check for was Sebastian's presence. From what Kinsley indicated, the minute he disappeared was the minute trouble began. But after the death of his friend, would he change his tactics?

Rounding the corner to the main street that fed into the square, Grant slowed. Several blocks ahead of them a group of protesters had gathered off to the side of the fountain. There were about two dozen of them, mostly men. They stood rigid, glowering at passersby, while a few jabbed signs into the air and shouted their usual slogans. Even from this distance, Grant could see the tension weaving through them. Grant pointed and picked up his pace. Lisa followed suit.

Tourists no longer slowed to listen or engage in conversation but hurried on their way to the slopes or wherever their final destination might be. Who could blame them? Word had spread about yesterday's debacle, and people were afraid to get caught in the middle of any trouble. Grant was surprised Wade didn't have police officers posted on every corner for exactly that reason. When you have a group of activists running on anger, it was the exact wrong fuel for protest. Hanging around the perimeter, a black-haired man snagged Grant's attention. He was wearing a fire engine red jacket and white pants. Excitement surged. *Sebastian.* It had to be! Grant remembered him from that night outside Giovanna's, the night he saw Kinsley and her cohort bear witness to their handiwork.

Anger rose sharply in Grant's gut. Sebastian's handiwork. Grant noted the man's arrogant stride, his smug expression. It looked as if he'd already assumed the reins as leader.

Grant's heart thumped in his chest. The man was pompous. Ruthless. One of his men had died—didn't he care? Shouldn't he be tending to the man's family, the group's collective sense of loss and grief? And how about Kinsley? Did any of those in attendance know she was in jail because her trusted partner was working to undercut her?

Doubtful. As they neared, Grant slowed, directing Lisa to stay close to the buildings and out of sight. As they concealed themselves behind the edge of a clothing store, Grant saw no sadness in the expressions of protesters, only anger. Determination.

"Looks like they're ready to start," he said under his breath.

Lisa pointed. "There's Gabby."

Her identity was obvious, Grant thought, as she clung to Sebastian's side like a love-struck teenager. Grant agreed with Kinsley. Gabby was the weak link. Eager, young, probably not experienced enough to be suspicious... If anyone could be turned, it would be her.

Sebastian walked away and abruptly, the group followed him.

Grant's antennae shot up. Where were they going?

Following at a discreet distance, he and Lisa trailed them to an area located between the gondola and ticket windows. Already cleaned of red paint, it was ground zero in their battle. The place where their man had been shot and killed, it was the resort's epicenter of ski business. It was also one of the most visible spots in the village. And packed with skiers. Grant felt a tightening in his chest. A veritable hive of people were coming and going in various degrees of gear and across all ages. The gondola line, organized by railings and ropes, wound outside of the building and onto the snow-packed ground surrounding. Above, the skies were as blue as blue could be, the mountain already littered with skiers making their way down runs.

If the protesters wanted to make a splash, this was as good a spot as any. Several uniformed police officers approached, and Grant released his breath. Good to know that Wade was on top of things. Words were exchanged between Sebastian and the officers. Several male skiers slowed, taking note of the building tension without completely stopping. Dressed in full ski gear, goggles perched on their helmets, their expressions were keen, almost like they were expecting the need to jump in but refrained. Women veered from the growing hostility, herding their children from potential conflict as they made their way to the ticket windows and gondola station. A few protesters clustered around Sebastian. Presumably his backup, should the situation get ugly.

Grant signaled to Lisa to stay behind while he moved closer. Easing his way nearer the group, he hung in the background and out of Sebastian's line of sight. From the sound of things, neither side was backing down.

"We have every right to be here!" a woman chimed in.

"There's no law against protesting. It's called free speech!"

The police officer stiffened as he calmly replied, "This is private property. You are not allowed to loiter."

"This is public property," Sebastian corrected coolly. "Federally owned land allows for our right to publicly assemble."

"Not within ten feet of those windows. Not when you're interfering with the rights of others to enjoy the same space."

"What about the animals and their right to enjoy the space?" a man shouted, followed by a stream of profanities.

Grant clenched his jaw. Didn't the guy see there were kids around here?

Sebastian held up a hand and swirled his finger through the air. The group immediately disassembled and began to march single file up and down the sidewalk in an area equidistant between the gondola and the ticket office. They weren't in anyone's direct path, they weren't blocking ticket sales or the entrance to the gondola station. They were instead, moving about in peaceful demonstration while Sebastian stood by and watched like some kind of Grand Master of Ceremonies.

Backing away, Grant concealed himself from view behind a nearby awning and debated his next move. Sebastian didn't know him, didn't know his connection to Kinsley. Gabby would probably recognize him from his initial confrontation with Kinsley, but not Sebastian. Grant's thoughts went back to Lisa. Should he have her approach Gabby, stick close to the group where he could not?

Sebastian made Grant's decision for him as he walked away from the protesters. Gabby broke line and followed. Without thinking, Grant followed. Snaking around a building, he noticed the two had slipped behind the ski school across the plaza from him. Grant hurried over, dodging a skier and a head-on collision with the skis slung over the guy's shoulder, and stopped at the edge of the ski school building. His heart was pounding now, his senses on high alert. Darting a glance toward the line of protesters, satisfied none were paying attention to him, Grant craned his head and stole a peek around the corner.

He jerked back. Sebastian and Gabby had stopped. Hugging his back to the building, Grant eased his head far enough for one eye to see them and process the scene. The two were talking. It looked like Sebastian was annoyed by her presence yet quickly able to smooth his displeasure over with a smile. He said something, and Gabby glanced down at his pocket. Grant reached for his phone. Gabby nodded with an expression that looked like a kid on Christmas morning, one who'd secretly opened the gifts and knew exactly what she was getting. Alarm charged through Grant's system. Sebastian could be holding a bomb in his pocket!

Sebastian tapped it and leaned to within inches of her face.

Grant brought his phone face-level and snapped a photo of the two of them together. Sebastian pulled Gabby into an embrace and kissed her deeply on the lips. Grant clicked off several more photos. Sebastian pulled away, said something more, then left Gabby in place while he took off.

Every cell in Grant's body fired into action—he needed to begin the chase!—but couldn't, not without being seen. Gabby began to head his way, and Grant rolled his body away from the building, taking several steps with his back turned so Gabby couldn't see his face as she returned to the group. He pretended to make a phone call, as from the corner of his eye, he watched her return to the line of protesters and blend in seamlessly. Ducking back toward the ski school,

Grant kept one eye on Gabby while he searched for Sebastian. There was no sign of him.

Grant took off in the direction Sebastian had gone. Something was wrong. Something terrible was going to happen. When Sebastian left his group, trouble usually followed. Grant jogged down a narrow walkway between buildings, the only path Sebastian could have taken, and found it opened up onto the main passage through town. The foot traffic was light, making it easy to spot Sebastian. Two blocks down, his red jacket stood out like a flashing beacon as he walked toward the bridge over Silver Creek. His pace was hurried but controlled.

Grant pulled the collar of his jacket forward and walked quickly after him. Mindful to stay close to storefronts in case he needed to dodge inside for cover, he skirted a brick planter as he trailed Sebastian's distant figure. Where was he going? Was he leaving? That bridge over the creek led out of town. Could it be Grant had misread the body language?

Sebastian slowed before the bridge. Glancing around, he turned and went down a steep flight of stone steps. Grant knew those steps. They would take Sebastian to creek level and a sidewalk lined with a few gift shops, some clothing stores, The Oasis café and a juice bar. Park benches lined the narrow snow-covered embankment that separated buildings and water. Maybe he had a meeting with someone, Grant mused.

When he reached the top of the steps he paused, watchful for Sebastian. The rush of water was audible now, the creek flowing at a hefty clip as it tumbled over boulders beneath the bridge and along the shore as it wound its way through town. At the base of the stairs, two women idled outside a souvenir store holding cups of steaming coffee in to-go containers within their gloved hands. They seemed oblivious to anything but their conversation. Peering past them and around the corner, Grant saw no sign of Sebastian. Had he gone into one of the stores?

A dash of red caught his eye and Grant started. He ran down the stairs then stopped suddenly. *Don't draw attention.* Forcing himself to walk, he ducked behind an evergreen and locked his gaze squarely on his target. Sebastian was lingering by the creek, ostensibly a tourist enjoying the water. Grant's nerves hummed as he watched. What was he up to? A man like Sebastian didn't walk away from his protest for a view of the creek. He moved slowly toward the bridge, his demeanor relaxed, bored. Grant pulled out his cell phone and took a couple more pictures.

Slowly but surely, Sebastian made his way toward the bridge without appearing as if he were purposely moving in that direction. Grant had to hand it to him. His movements were steady and natural, as though he'd drifted there on a slow current. He was practically under the bridge before Grant realized it and heading toward the alcove where bridge met land. Sebastian crouched and pulled something from his pocket.

Grant sucked in his breath. *Was he placing a bomb under the bridge?*

Before he could think twice, Grant charged across the expanse of snow-covered ground. Sebastian looked up and froze. He slid the object back into his pocket, shock quickly giving way to suspicion as he stared at Grant.

Slowly, he rose.

"Hello." Grant spoke as casually as he could, hyper-aware of how he sounded. It was a critical moment, the possible difference between success and failure. "Did you lose something?"

"No," Sebastian replied, ushering forth a polite smile. "Thought I saw something down here and came to investigate."

Flushed with adrenaline, Grant's heart felt like it was pounding through his jacket. "I'm sorry." Grant emitted a small laugh. "I didn't mean to disturb you."

"No problem," Sebastian replied.

Grant marveled at the inane conversation. Against a rhythmic thumping of footsteps on the bridge overhead, both men were lying through their teeth. Sebastian had no way of knowing that Grant suspected him of placing a bomb—if that's indeed what he'd been doing—making him feel confident in his ruse. Grant could be John Doe for all Sebastian knew, just another curious guy out for a leisurely stroll along the riverbank.

Moving from beneath the bridge, Sebastian walked over to him, his gaze searching, as though his mind was scrolling through memory to place the stranger. "It was nothing important, I'm sure." Returning a tight-lipped smile, he added, "Probably a rabbit or something."

Grant could feel his thinly-veiled annoyance and knew it was time to take his leave. Riling Sebastian was not his goal, nor was cementing his identity in the man's brain. He'd only wanted to stop him, and stop him he had. "Well, have a great day," Grant tossed out.

"You do the same."

Grant entered the nearest gift shop and lost himself behind a rack of sweatshirts. Casually perusing the selection of garments, he moved behind a carousel of post cards, but not so far he couldn't keep a vigilant eye on Sebastian. If the man headed back for the bridge, Grant would be left with no option but to call Wade. It could mean that he was right, that Sebastian was placing a bomb and the police would have to get to it before it went off. Grant's gaze drifted upward toward the bridge. In another hour it would be noon, and foot traffic into and out of the village would steadily increase—over that particular bridge.

Tension bound Grant's gut in knots. Sliding a hand into his pocket, he thought maybe he should put a call into Wade, anyway. Certainly wouldn't hurt to have a police presence at the moment. But the call was unnecessary. Sebastian didn't head back under the bridge but walked up the stairs and over it. Moving to the front window of the store, Grant watched him all the way to the parking garage across the next plaza.

Would he try and dump his device there, in lieu of a failed attempt under the bridge?

Grant was out of the store in seconds but stopped short of the stairs. Following Sebastian at this point would only raise his suspicion. He now had a visual on a man who could identify him. Grant darted a glance to the creek then back to the bridge, the parking garage beyond. Need warred with caution. There had to be something he could do. He couldn't sit by and let the man place a bomb in the garage—or anywhere else for that matter! But what? He withdrew the phone from his pocket. He had to let someone know there was potential trouble. Pressing the number he now knew by heart, Grant called Wade Davis.

Chapter Twenty-Six

"Chief, I think we have something."

Wade looked up from his paperwork as the Sergeant walked into his office. Journalists were calling. They wanted a report on the shooting. They wanted details—who started the confrontation, was the police response justified, could they have avoided it altogether...? It was always the same. When a civilian became aggressive with a police officer and the officer responded, the response was invariably second-guessed. Was it a justified use of force? Could the officer have done anything differently?

In hindsight, someone could always have done something differently. But in the heat of the moment when a man was coming after an officer with a deadly weapon?

That was a different story. Easing forward, Wade set his papers aside and expelled a sigh. His officers were human. They shouldn't be demonized for reacting like any normal human being would under stress. Massaging the bridge of his nose, he asked, "What's up?"

The Sergeant handed him a thumb drive. "Take a look at this. It's a video taken just prior to the explosion."

Wade pushed the drive into his computer and quickly brought the video in question onto his screen. "How did we get this?"

"A visitor from Germany was running video of his kids playing in the snow. It's a little long, but watch when the kids start to throw snowballs. You'll see a guy in the distant background walking over to the patrol hut and ditching something behind it. It only takes a second but it matches Kinsley's description."

Wade watched intently as the video streamed. Sounds of a child's laughter dominated the audio, competing with a man's voice in the foreground. He was speaking German, an obviously pleased parent, though Wade had no idea what he was saying. But his words were irrelevant. Wade wasn't interested in what he had to say, only what he might have captured inadvertently.

The Sergeant leaned forward and pointed to the screen. "Watch closely in this area."

Sure enough, the kids started hurling snowballs, and Wade saw a man enter the video. He was heading straight for the patrol hut. His movements were not random but determined. The guy glanced around for onlookers, then bent over and placed something at the rear of the hut. Black hair, red jacket, the slender man matched Kinsley's description exactly. Wade checked the time stamp on the lower corner of the video. His gut tightened. Fifteen minutes prior.

Wade knew there were countless men with black hair wearing red jackets on the mountain, half of them slim. There was nothing unusual there. But the fact that this man was behind the patrol hut clearly dropping something around the time of the explosion was intriguing. More than intriguing, it was practically implicating. If Kinsley was telling the truth, this could be their man. "Get our guys on this video. I want it zoomed in. Give me as clear a close-up as you possibly can."

"Yes, sir." The Sergeant took the thumb drive from Wade.

"I want it stat."

"You got it," he replied, and exited the office.

Pushing back in his chair, Wade centered on a photograph hanging on the wall. A summer mountain range turned into wall art, it was showcased in an intricately carved wood frame. Pristine, beautiful, it was the Colorado countryside. His country.

His home state. His territory.

Wade's mind circled the possibilities before him. If Kinsley was innocent and this Sebastian fellow was their guy, this video put him at the scene. But her fingerprints were on the bomb, a rather nasty indictment to her guilt. Were they partners in crime? Were the two of them willing to do anything in the name of the environment?

Visions of the explosion billowed in his mind. There were no fingerprints on the fur store bomb. Kinsley had been caught on video at the scene, but she'd left no fingerprints. The airline ticket had been purchased from her account, in her name. Could Sebastian Wu have managed that? Thinking back to his interview with the man, Wade had to admit the guy was a cool operator. He'd seemed concerned that the police thought him guilty of a serious crime. He didn't want to go jail because of Kinsley. Sebastian said he hated to divulge the information—information that suddenly made sense to him—but thought it curious that Kinsley had purchased a one-way ticket to Europe. Then he claimed he'd seen the ticket on her desk and that he'd questioned her about it. She'd told him it was for a shopping trip, he'd said. Then Sebastian had lowered his voice and asked Wade in the blown-away tone of a duped partner, *Do you think that was her ticket out of country?*

Wade slammed a fist to his desk. *Son-of-a-bitch—*

He'd been played! So hot to arrest someone, he'd allowed himself to be had. He didn't even listen to Lisa when she came in with her recording and her story about protesters trying to disrupt summer construction. He had ignored it because he'd believed he had his suspect in jail. Believed he had the chief instigator behind bars.

Wade shoved up from his desk. Add Grant's phone message about Sebastian's suspicious behavior near the bridge and Wade felt like a fool. He had to talk to Kinsley. He had to talk to her and Lisa and Grant, and he had to do so quickly. The feds were scheduled for a pickup at two. As he glanced at the brass-framed clock on his desk, the black hands warned he was running short on time. Giving Kinsley up to the federal authorities would remove her from his jurisdiction, but at this point there wasn't a whole helluva lot he could do about it. Federal charges were their domain, not his. There was no way he could hold them off—unless he turned up something he could use before they arrived.

Grant took the steps two at a time and walked briskly back to the protest, passing skiers whose boots scraped against the brick streets as they schlepped their gear toward the slopes. He had no idea what he was going to do, which way he was going to roll, but he had to do something. He hadn't been able to convey his news directly to Wade and could only hope that he received his message. It was possible Wade might turn a deaf ear. He had to Lisa, a reaction Grant couldn't fault him for. Their information was too sketchy at this point, too random. Wade Davis couldn't act on speculation. He had to deal in facts. As it stood, the Chief believed he had the responsible party in custody.

He and Lisa had to do better. They had to get something solid against Sebastian before a man like Wade Davis would act. Avoiding eye contact with passersby, Grant focused on his last option. Gabby Miller. She was the weak link and if anyone was going to break it would be her. The problem was getting next to her. For that, he needed to find Lisa, and he needed to do so while Sebastian was out of sight.

At this point, Grant had been marked. Sebastian had seen him and was clearly suspicious. It was unfortunate, but there was no way Grant could have avoided it. He couldn't stand by and watch the man place an explosive under a well-traveled bridge. It was the main way in and out of the village! Grant wasn't even sure if Sebastian was placing a bomb, let alone how long before the thing would go off, though Kinsley said she thought she'd seen Sebastian at the gondola minutes before the bomb at the ski patrol hut exploded. Minutes. Grant couldn't risk it. He couldn't live with himself if he'd watched the thing happen knowing he could have prevented it. But it was a moot point. While Grant had photos and could place Sebastian at the bridge, it was meaningless. Nothing happened.

Reaching the ticket area where he'd left the protesters, Grant hovered behind a crowd of people standing outside a restaurant. Located across from the ticket windows, it gave him a great vantage point to search for Gabby. The bright sun reflected off a rainbow assortment of countless jackets and turned the ground into a sheet of blinding white. There were men, women and children decked out in hats, ski gear and street clothes. Beyond the gondola's disembarking area were masked and helmeted skiers moving into the gondola for another trip up the mountain.

Moving his gaze from person-to-person, Grant figured Gabby's long blonde hair and bright green hat should be easy to pick out of a crowd. Using a trio of men walking past as a block, Grant moved in, scanning the line of protesters, the surrounding throng of people. His antennae twitched. There. Gabby was walking side-by-side with another woman, the two practically identical in size and shape. Not a surprise in this town of young fit women. They were more the norm than a rarity. Everyone looked like a cover model for a sports magazine. As he narrowed in on the woman next to Gabby, Grant's heart stopped. The nip of a nose, the small mouth, straight brown hair protruding from beneath a pink hat. Lisa!

Continuing to use unsuspecting tourists as cover, Grant made his way to within ten feet of the women. Plucking a terrain map from a nearby information post, he opened it and held it near his face, prepared to conceal his identity should the need arise. He wanted to make eye contact with Lisa, and only Lisa. While Gabby didn't know him, Sebastian did, and she was Sebastian's girl.

After two passes, Lisa noticed him. Surprise lit her features and she missed a step.

"Are you okay?" Grant heard Gabby ask.

"Yes, I tripped," Lisa sputtered, clearly disconcerted by his appearance. "I need to use the restroom."

"You know where it is?"

Lisa nodded then wasted no time heading for the women's restroom where she darted inside. It was a small brick building near a snowed-over playground located adjacent to the gondola station. Grant retreated then walked over and stood near the rear of the building. Slipping a hand into his coat pocket, he leaned against a hand railing and tried to appear casual, bored. A mother and young child trudged into the restroom, the little one looking wholly uncomfortable in the massive amount of gear. Neither paid him any mind, not even a smile. None of the protesters paid him any interest either, including Gabby. She'd already struck up conversation with another one of the protesters as they marched, this one a male.

Grant waited, the ice-cold railing searing through the jean material at his hip. After several minutes, Lisa emerged cautiously. Grant whispered, "Lisa—back here!"

Spotting him immediately, she followed as he dipped back behind the building and out of sight. He whirled and said, "We've got to act quickly."

"What's happened?"

Lisa peered at him expectantly, and he felt an eagerness emanate from her. Her nose was red, her brown eyes alert. It was cold, the stakes were high, but there was no mistaking the fact that she was revved and ready to go. Taking in the faint spatter of freckles across her nose, Grant suddenly felt old and tired by comparison. But he was invested in the outcome as much as Lisa. "I followed Sebastian to the bridge. He was putting something under it when I interrupted him."

Frown lines deepened across her forehead. All enthusiasm drained from her face and her eyes widened. "A bomb...?"

Grant nodded. "I suspected it might be. There was no other reason for him to be under the bridge, an effort he abandoned when he realized he had a witness." Grant glanced around for onlookers. "I doubt it will stop him from trying again. I took some pictures, but they won't mean anything. Nothing happened."

"That's terrible. But now what are we going to do?"

"We need to get to Gabby. We need to seem like we want revenge for the shooting yesterday."

"But she knows I'm new to the group. Why would I care about getting revenge?"

"You're a radical. Don't all radicals want to act on whatever excuse they can muster?"

"Maybe." Lisa cast her gaze downward. "But do you think she'll believe me?"

I wouldn't. But Gabby might. Grant's spirits dipped. *You look as innocent as the fresh-driven snow.* He shrugged. "It's worth a try. In the meantime, I'll try and find out where Sebastian is staying. Maybe we can convince the police to put a tail on him and prevent future attacks."

"Good idea, though I think they should already be following him."

"They see no need. They think they have their criminal in jail."

Lisa crossed her arms over her chest. "Well, they're wrong."

"Agreed. I'm going to call Wade and see if I can convince him of the same."

Kinsley sat slumped against the wall. The mattress beneath her—if it could be called a mattress—was thin and worn and sagged on a weak frame of metal springs. Her throat was parched, her head ached. Silver Creek spent money on everything else, why not their jailhouse facilities? Would it kill them to make the "innocent until proven guilty" comfortable while they were incarcerated? The only good news was that she didn't have to spend another night on the flimsy thing. Because she'd be headed to the big city.

Staring at nothing, thinking about everything, Kinsley wondered what Grant was doing. His visit this morning had floored her. The fact that he had come, had tried to sort out truth from fiction had been more than she could ask for, more than she hoped. He believed her, or at least he was beginning to believe and promised he would find Lisa. Together, the two of them could work to get the evidence needed to free her.

Kinsley thought about Gabby and Sebastian. She thought about Lisa's efforts to break into the group and get information. She thought about Grant trying to confront Sebastian. Despair soaked into her bones. Heaving a sigh, she closed her eyes. While their efforts on her behalf were appreciated, they might prove useless. Sebastian was too smart. Gabby wasn't stupid. Neither one of them would give up their true intentions because neither one had any intention of going to jail. They saved that little side trip for Kinsley.

She could only imagine the messages they would post if the two of them took over *Wildlife Neutral*, the money they would spend. Merle could freeze her accounts, preventing Sebastian from siphoning her entire fortune but not before he stole a hefty hunk of change for himself. She had no way of knowing how much damage he had already done, only that Lisa had done her best to prevent him from a total and unfettered takeover. But Sebastian was cunning. He had the connections and the ability to hack into her website, redirect her followers. No doubt he would post a violent response to Norell's shooting across their social media sites, inciting supporters, maybe even encouraging them to take to the streets touting "us against them." Everything she'd worked for—her reputation, her position, her livelihood—would be lost because of him.

How could she have been so stupid? Trusting Sebastian was an error that would cost her. She was beginning to think it was stupid to have fallen for Grant, too, though she couldn't quite convince herself of the same. Recalling the look in his eyes when he came to see her this morning, his eagerness to set the record straight... She longed to see him again—on better terms, on their terms and not by the grace of the Police Chief. But did it matter? Had they ever really had a future together? Grant was a businessman. She was an activist. Crossing those lines, blending those margins... Could it be done?

Deep in her heart, the one place where total honesty reigned, Kinsley wasn't sure. It sounded great on paper. A vegan clothing line for animal lovers that created change on a person-by-person basis sounded wonderful, a seamless fit for her. But could she give up her passion for taking the fight to the abusers and become a, become merely a manufacturer of designer clothing?

Kinsley couldn't fully answer that one. Last night's dreams complicated matters, but either way, did it matter? Sebastian had cooked her carcass pretty thoroughly. On the off chance Grant and Lisa were able to manage success, it might behoove Kinsley to actually use that ticket to London and decide her future from there. She opened her eyes and looked at the locked door of her cell. If she could ever get out of here, that is.

At the sound of a key entering the lock on her door, Kinsley bolted to attention. Her heart raced, and a round of questions fired within her skull. Did she have another visitor? Had Grant and Lisa been able to gather evidence against Sebastian? Was this her escort out of here?

Chief Davis stalked in and slammed the door closed behind him, the sound blasting through her. Kinsley jumped up, her mind a jumble of thought and emotion. "Chief Davis," she said, inwardly cursing the tremor in her voice. If the hard edge in his gaze was any indication, this couldn't be good.

"I want to know everything. Everything—and don't leave a single thing out this time."

"But I don't understand...I told you everything."

"Not everything. For starters, I need to know where Sebastian gets his material for making the bombs. Where does he purchase it, who does he buy it from, who taught him how to make the things and whose money does he use to buy the stuff? And you'd better start talking and fast." Chief Davis leaned close and she could smell the acrid scent of coffee on his breath. "The feds are on their way as we speak."

Kinsley gulped.

Chapter Twenty-Seven

Wade Davis walked into his office and headed straight for a built-in cabinet near the window. Pulling a door open, he grabbed a bottle of whiskey followed by a lowball glass then pushed the door closed. He needed a drink. He needed more than one, but he didn't drink on the job. Didn't make a habit of it, anyway. But this stunt could end his career. If he miscalculated, if he had made an error in judgment, his butt was toast. Burnt toast.

Wade twisted off the black cap, poured two fingers of amber liquid into his glass, then chugged the liquor in one long swallow, biting back against the burn in his throat. He was in an untenable position. Explaining to the feds why he had released their prisoner prior to their arrival would be complicated. They would not be happy about running back and forth to Silver Creek on the whim of the Chief of Police, but he needed time. He'd be damned if he was going to let an innocent person be run through the legal grind for something they didn't do. He also knew that once the feds got hold of Kinsley, it would be sticky-business trying to extricate her from their claws. It would be out of his jurisdiction. Out of his power. Out of his hands.

Savoring the instant calm streaming through his limbs, Wade considered the next twenty-four hours. He swiped a glance out his second-story window, the sky blue, the roof-tops caked with snow glistening in the sunshine and capped his impatience. It was a dicey plan. There were too many variables, too many holes. Wade didn't like leaving things up to chance, but he had no choice—except to call Walsh. Walsh would be his ringer. Walsh would be his secret weapon to ensure nothing went wrong. The fact that his main man wasn't on board with the plan didn't sit well with Wade, but sometimes a man had to run on instinct and instinct alone.

Unfortunately, Walsh was running on emotion. He'd only agreed because Wade asked him. That was it. Walsh put it on the record. He wasn't a fan, he wasn't convinced, but he'd give it a try. Because his Commander-in-Chief asked him to do it—a Commander-in-Chief he respected.

Wade dropped his gaze to the bottle. He hung his hand from the rounded glass neck and the desire for another drink swam through him. He was asking a lot of Walsh. He was putting him in the direct line of fire for a cause he didn't believe. McIntyre Walsh was ex-Marine, a Marine who refused reenlistment because he'd lost faith in his superiors. He'd left the service angry and disgruntled because people had placed him in harm's way without a care to the personal outcome of the soldiers they commanded. Walsh was only here in Silver Creek because he'd met Lisa and fallen in love. And now that love was costing him. Wade snorted. Love really could untie a guy, drag him to the highest mountain peak and sink him in the deepest river. Love took hold like nothing else.

Overtaken by a heavy sadness, Wade slackened his hold of the bottle. He braced against the onslaught of memories, the painful, the joyous. Wade understood what love could do to a man. His wife had been the greatest thing that ever happened to him. The day she left had been the worst. After dedicating almost twenty years of his life to the security detail for Air Force One and decorated for his outstanding service on numerous occasions, Wade lost the one person who meant the most to him. She'd moved on, finally getting around to telling him after she had found someone new, someone who would put her first. Twenty-five years, four sons, decades of memories—shattered because someone lost faith.

Allowing old wounds to ache and fade, Wade tightened his grip on the bottle. It was possible Walsh was right on this one. It was possible Wade was wrong and Walsh was right. It was possible. Anything was possible. Kinsley could be lying. She and Sebastian could be in on the scheme together using the dichotomy of evidence to create reasonable doubt—for him, for her, for the both of them. Wade could be playing right into her hands. Kinsley was a smart one, no doubt. He'd seen her intellect in action. He'd read her blog, knew the sizeable force she'd created at her fingertips. He'd also seen her fervor. Kinsley was a true believer. Hard-core to the bone, she believed people were the source of animal suffering and she was their voice, that she and she alone could save them.

Wade yanked the bottle and poured himself another drink. Tossing it back, he returned the bottle to the cabinet, left the glass on the counter then walked out of his office. Only time would tell who was right.

Grant pushed in through the front door of his jewelry store, plagued by a sense of defeat. He pulled the jacket from his shoulders and tossed it to a hook on the wall. Lisa had made no headway with Gabby. Sebastian Wu wasn't registered anywhere. Grant called and asked for his room at every hotel he could think of, beginning with Kinsley's. Every time the reply was the same. *I'm sorry, sir, but we don't have a guest registered by that name.* Grant had hoped to find him in one of the Silver Creek hotels. A search of every condo and villa in the surrounding area would prove insurmountable. There was no way he could call them all.

It was futile.

"Good afternoon."

Grant broke from his thought and replied, "Hey, Beau."

"How was your day off?"

"What?"

Beau looked at him queerly. "Your day off? The time you needed away from the store? Did you have a chance to hit the mountain?" Beau beamed, and despite his professional attire of suit and tie, appeared every bit college freshman on the lookout for a good time. "Some of the guys were out shredding this morning and hit nothing but powder."

"No," Grant replied, recalling that had been his excuse to leave the store on short notice this morning. He'd blamed the stress of Giovanna's departure and the recent bombings for his need to cut loose for a day. "I had some errands to run."

"Too bad," Beau replied. "Sales were good. We did almost two thousand dollars today."

"Really?" Grant asked, struck by the number. Seems the protesters weren't making as big a dent in business as they'd hoped. People were still shopping, still skiing. Though if Sebastian had managed to set off a bomb beneath the bridge, there was no doubt in Grant's mind the sales number would have been zero. "Good. And thanks for coming in on short notice. I really appreciate it."

Beau's smile returned full force. "No problem. The extra money will go a long way towards my down payment."

Grant grinned, despite himself. Beau was saving up for a house. No wife, no kids, but he insisted his future was about stability, long-term investments. He was building a future for himself first, his prospective family second. Currently he lived with four other guys in a condo ten miles outside of town with no serious girlfriend, but that didn't stop him from thinking like a sensible businessman. It was one of the reasons Grant valued him. And paid him a generous commission on everything he sold. "Thanks again."

"Do you need me to stay on?"

"No. I've got it covered from here."

"Okay. I'll catch you in the a.m."

"Sounds great," Grant replied. As he watched Beau head out the front door, Grant reached for his phone. He had to try Wade again. He had to talk to him and get him to understand Kinsley was being set up. As he dialed Wade's number, his cell phone rang. Caller ID indicated the Chief of Police was calling *him*. Grant jabbed the answer key. "Wade."

"Grant."

"Did you get my message?"

"I did."

"I don't have any proof to back up my suspicions," Grant rolled quickly into his explanation, "but I swear Sebastian was in the process of placing a bomb under the bridge. There was no other reason for him to be there."

"I believe you."

Shock and disbelief exploded in Grant's brain. "You do?"

"I do."

Relief flooded his system. *He believed in her innocence.* It was all Grant needed. "She didn't do it, Wade. I'd bet my life on it. Sebastian is setting her up."

"I agree." Wade paused. "We received a video from a tourist that places Sebastian at the scene of the patrol hut minutes prior to the explosion. However, our lack of tangible proof remains a problem."

Panic clutched his stomach. The feds were supposed to come for her today. Isn't that what Kinsley said? Grant tightened his grip on the phone. Had they already taken her away? Grant clamped his mind closed, refusing to succumb. "We need to get her out of there, Wade. We need to get her out of there before the feds come."

"She's already gone."

Grant's legs gave way beneath him. Already gone. He grabbed the glass counter to steady himself. The federal authorities had already come for her. He felt a swell of nausea. He was too late.

Kinsley placed a hand on the phone but didn't pick up the receiver. Thoughts of Grant swirled in her brain. She needed to tell him. She needed to tell him what was going on. After squeezing the plastic receiver until her knuckles turned white, she abruptly released it.

She couldn't. She couldn't call him. It wasn't fair to get his hopes up. Hell, it was hard enough getting her own hopes up without thinking about the potential for disaster. Kinsley stared at the phone. Tension clenched the muscles of her shoulders, rippled down the length of her back. Warmth built under her thermal undershirt. She couldn't move. She couldn't think. She could only feel. Ambivalence stewed in her heart. She knew what she was doing was risky and she needed Grant to know her heart. He had touched her life. Being with him had been unexpected. Marvelous, crazy, memorable. Whatever happened, she would never forget him. But she needed him to hear the words from her and not from someone who thought they knew the inside scoop. Grant deserved that much. After he came and offered his help, he deserved honesty from her. From her own lips.

Kinsley slipped her hand back onto the phone and picked up the receiver. Placing it to her ear, she listened to the dial tone. A flurry of nerves skipped through her pulse. She was baiting a man she believed she knew well enough to manipulate. It was a calculated risk. She understood the consequences, accepted them. It was a dangerous game she was playing, but her freedom was on the line, and that made it worth every second of doubt. The dial tone drummed loudly at her ear. In her chest, her heart beat erratically. She was playing with fire, fire that could burn.

"Grant," she whispered.

The tone at her ear beeped then turned busy. Sliding the phone down her neck, she began to shake. Tears pricked her eyes. Kinsley curled her fingers around the handle of the phone and set it back to its cradle. "I love you, Grant. If there's one thing you need to know, it's that I love you."

Tears dripped from her eyes. This was anguish she had never known. It felt as though her heart was being ripped from her chest. She might never see him again. The one man that was coming to mean everything. But there was no other way. All avenues had failed. It had only been by chance that she had this last opportunity—and the consent of one reluctant Police Chief. Kinsley wasn't going to blow it because of selfish need. She was going to make it right.

Unfortunately, the less people who knew, the better.

Dropping into a metal chair outside a popular take-out café, Kinsley ripped open a brown paper packet of sugar and emptied it into her coffee. The air chilled her skin but she felt so alive on the inside, it could have been twenty degrees colder for all she cared. She was out of jail, breathing the fresh mountain air and it couldn't taste sweeter. Using a plastic straw, she stirred, careless that hot liquid spilled over the edge of her cup. Sebastian sat across from her, his posture guarded. Surprising, but after everything that had happened, their partnership remained solid. Intact. Enough to plan their next step, anyway. "They're going to pay for shooting Norell," Kinsley said. "If they think they can get away with killing one of our people, they are dead wrong." Slicing a wary glance around them, she noted that no one was close enough to overhear their conversation. An elderly couple lingered by the order window, but they were thoroughly engaged in their own conversation. Satisfied their chat was sufficiently private, Kinsley flipped her attention back to Sebastian and reiterated, "I'm done playing by the rules. We're hitting back, all barrels blazing."

Sebastian arched an elegant brow. The black turtleneck and overcoat he wore punctuated his black hair and eyes, giving him a sharp, no-nonsense appeal. "Nice to see you've finally seen the light."

"I've seen more than the light, I assure you."

"Was it the time sitting in jail that brought you around?"

She speared Sebastian with a glare, mildly astounded by his gall. He was the reason she'd been sitting in jail. Did he think he was teaching her a lesson? That he was puppeteer to her mindless actions? "Jail time was only the beginning," she replied evenly. "Once that police officer fired on Norell, it was game over."

"So how did you get out?"

"Damn good lawyer. One I'm tired of paying."

Sebastian chuckled. "Luckily you have deep pockets."

Pockets Sebastian was trying to shove his greedy hands into. "Pockets with *my* money," she replied bluntly. "Money I don't intend to waste defending frivolous arrests."

"So where do we begin?"

"What, no ideas of your own?" Kinsley slid her tongue over her teeth and slowly pulled in a sip of steaming coffee. Biting back the sting of scalding liquid, she said, "Please, Sebastian. I expect more from you."

"You give me too much credit."

"Do I?"

Sebastian slid into a smile. "You are the supreme leader of this organization, not me. I merely do your bidding."

Kinsley held him in her gaze and nailed him with a pointed glare. "Let's not play coy, Sebastian. I couldn't do half of what I do without you."

His mouth tipped up into a practiced smile. "Your compliments are appreciated, but I am not worthy of such high esteem. I'm simply a crusader for the cause."

Sebastian spoke as though he expected a recording to be in process, carefully choosing his words so that his comments could only be construed as acknowledging her initiative in the bombing, not his. Fine. Kinsley wasn't recording him. She had bigger plans. "I'm taking out the gondola station."

Surprise flickered in his black eyes. "Are you serious?"

"You're damn right I am. I'm taking out the gondola, and I'm doing it tomorrow, first thing."

"You have the means?"

"I'll get them."

"How?"

Kinsley smiled. Arrogant. The man was as arrogant as they came. Explosives were his department, and he was surprised she didn't need his expertise? Tough. "I have my ways."

Concern shot holes through his conceit. "Is someone helping you?"

"Why would I need help? One search of the internet provided all the information I needed to know. Didn't take you much effort to turn my ink bomb into a fiery one. I think I can manage a small explosion on my own, don't you?"

Sebastian didn't respond.

"I'm not looking to make a huge blast. All I need to do is to disable operations. If people can't board the gondola and ride it up, half the mountain will be unserviceable. Besides, I don't want to risk your involvement, not with the police breathing down our backs."

She could see the exclusion lodge deep in his gaze. Sebastian didn't take kindly to being left out of core decisions. In his mind, it should be him making them, not her. Circling his hand around his untouched cup of coffee, he said, "I'm more than willing to do my share for the cause, Kinsley."

"I know you are. You've never wavered and I appreciate that, but you're too valuable." Kinsley took another sip, this one longer, allowing the intense Brazilian roast to tantalize her taste buds now that it was cooling. Swallowing purposefully, she said, "We can't lose you to an arrest. Not now, not when we're making an impact."

Sebastian nodded. "Yes, Gabby told me she saw you in handcuffs yesterday."

Kinsley nodded. "Where were you, by the way? I didn't see you in the crowd."

"I was there."

She screwed her expression. "Why didn't you step in? Why did you let Norell get caught up in that mess? He was your man, Sebastian. He would have listened to you and pulled back."

The insult hit its mark. Sebastian bristled, his tone assuming an edge as he lobbed back, "Norell was driven. He would have done anything for the cause."

Kinsley paused, fine-tuning the point of her thoughts. She wanted Sebastian to hear her, loud and clear. "I don't think Norell intended to give his life to the cause, Sebastian. I think he was provoked, and his temper got the best of him."

Unaffected by her appraisal, he retorted, "When do you plan on carrying out this plan of yours?"

"Six a.m."

"Early," he replied, nodding as though he approved.

"Earlier the better. Less people, less eyes."

"Agreed." Pausing, he wrapped his full attention around her and asked, "What then? How do you expect to get away with it?"

Kinsley smiled, holding back the emotion raging inside her. *I'll use a one-way ticket, similar to the one you purchased for me.* "I have it all planned out," she said offhandedly, as though the details were above his pay grade and he need not worry. Then Kinsley lifted her coffee and held it before her. "But are you sure you want to be involved in this? You don't need to be there. It will only cause trouble for you."

"I'll be there."

Of course he would. Kinsley's smile broadened. Sucking a slew of nervous energy from her gut, she softened her tone and spewed it free as she replied, "Thank you, Sebastian. Your support is appreciated, more than you know."

Clearly pleased with himself, Sebastian returned a slight nod. He was the Master of Chaos. This was his department, the area of activism in which he excelled.

Truthfully, Kinsley was grateful for his support. Sebastian had been instrumental in growing the organization, feeding the frenzy of confrontation when necessary, stoking the flames of discontent, but he didn't know where to draw the line. He didn't know when to quit, when to pull back and regroup. Sebastian knew one speed and one speed only. Full throttle. It was a weakness that cost Norell his life. Ultimately, it would cost Sebastian, too.

Kinsley pulled a twenty dollar bill from her wallet, slapped it on the table and stood. She was finished here. At Sebastian's surprise, she savored a private smile and winked. "See you in the morning."

Kinsley strode out of the restaurant without a glance back to see his reaction. She didn't have to. She could feel the wheels spinning in his pompous brain. Sebastian would be there. Not a speck of doubt in her mind.

Chapter Twenty-Eight

A milky-white flat light bathed Sebastian's face as he stood next to Kinsley in the frigid shadows of evergreens, fat with snow. A few aspen stood in the distance like dotted-black twigs in a cascade down the mountain amongst a tangle of vacant ski runs. Kinsley clasped the handles of her shopping bag tightly. Her bomb was inside. Gazing across the expanse of snow-covered ground, unspoiled after a front had moved through overnight, Kinsley thought the gondola building was eerily quiet. A string of cars hung motionless, up and out of sight over the first mountain ridge. Beneath, the lower ski hill was bordered by a line of upscale condominiums.

The place looked like a ghost town, which surprised her. She would have expected at least a few brave souls to be strolling around at this hour, maybe a jogger out for an early morning run or a shop owner getting ahead of the day's business. But there was no one. Kinsley shivered. Cold air coated her down jacket like a case of ice. Her cheeks stung in the near zero temperature, her toes numb, though her head was passably warm, covered by the thick wool hat. She might be uncomfortable, but this was her center stage. This is where it would all go down.

Kinsley turned her attention back to Sebastian. His red jacket was zipped completely closed, allowing only the collar of a black and white fleece turtleneck to poke free. Like her, he wore black pants and snow boots. The village remained empty. Storefronts appeared frozen into the streetscape, cobblestone streets were stained a deep red. The only thing moving were the exhalations pillowing between them. Sebastian had been pleased with her bomb. It was real. And it was deadly. "I'm going to place it beneath the overhang," she informed him, "where the first car is positioned as it leaves the station. It will eliminate any need to break in to the building, yet wreak enough havoc to cease operations by disabling the main engine just inside." Standing like a sentinel, Sebastian gave no response, offered no direction. He was a silent partner, a willing accomplice. "Keep watch," she instructed. "If you see anything, whistle."

He nodded, his complexion sallow.

Kinsley took a deep breath, held her bag close to her body and slunk along the tree line. She looked in both directions, then darted across open snow to the gondola station. A distinct trail of footprints revealed her travels quite clearly in the fluff of snow. But leaving a trail was of no concern to her as she slipped around the corner of the building and went straight for the center post. The support beam for the gondola cars was massive and made from thick steel. It could probably handle an explosion, but the glass wall separating the beams from the engine room and office could not. Pulling the cylindrical device from her bag, she lowered to a squat and wedged it into place. Instinctively, she looked for onlookers. Witnesses.

There was no one. Folding her empty bag, she stood and assessed the position, the angle, the imagined impact her device would have. The quick pound of her heart felt like it was coming out of her chest. With a deep breath, she worked to calm the hammer of pulse. Satisfied her placement was sufficient, she hurried back to Sebastian.

His nose was nipped red, his eyes flat, opaque. Emotionless.

Gesturing for him to follow, Kinsley sprinted behind the ticket sales building and pulled out her cell phone. "We need to stay clear. The debris will go everywhere."

Sebastian joined her, his silence unnatural, almost as if he was in some kind of trance—not the reaction she would have expected. She thought he'd be more ravenous, excited. Perhaps this detached disposition of his was how he coped with the violence. He mentally removed himself while in the act of destruction.

Kinsley dialed the number she had memorized last night and called the phone attached to the device. There was no response. She looked toward the gondola building. Pulse pounding in her ears, she muttered, "Damn it."

"What?"

"The damn thing isn't communicating with my phone."

With a quick scan of the vicinity, Kinsley jogged back to the gondola building. Snow caked the outside of her black snow boots, a few chunks tumbled inside, chilling her socks instantly. Kinsley took several minutes to finagle with the device then ran back, ignoring the icy wet forming against her thermal leggings. Out of breath, she looked to Sebastian. "I think my circuit is faulty."

"Are you sure it's not your fuse?"

"I don't know."

"How did you configure it to respond?"

"It's supposed to go off when the phone receives the call and vibrates."

"Are you sure it was programmed correctly?"

"I told you—I had help. If you recall, this isn't my area of expertise," she replied hotly.

"Did you call the right number?"

"Are you calling me an idiot?" she snapped, irritated by his condescending tone. "Of course I called the right number!"

Sebastian scowled. Glancing toward the gondola building, he flashed back to her. "I'll go take a look."

Kinsley's pulse thwacked as she watched him run and duck behind the building. She scanned the perimeter and her anxiety ticked up several degrees. Seeing no one, she felt the pressure in her chest begin to build. This was a dangerous game they were playing. She had no way of knowing what he was doing. Nerves crawled up her skin. He wasn't familiar with the device. It was possible the thing could explode in his hands!

But Chief Davis assured her this was the only way. With Walsh on hand and a dozen police officers, there would be nothing to worry about. She checked her watch. This was taking too long. Something was wrong. She searched the building for sight of Sebastian but saw nothing. In fact, she saw no one. She hated to second guess, but couldn't quell the instinct.

Seconds passed, and Sebastian suddenly re-appeared and hurried back to her. Chest heaving, he smiled thinly. "Impatience breeds error. You knocked the connecting wires out of place."

"Oh," Kinsley murmured. Leaning close to the ticket sales building, she craned her head around the corner and called the number again. Waiting, she watched the tan and brown gondola building with bated breath. As the phone continued to ring, she clenched against a mild shake to her hand. Still nothing.

Sebastian yanked the phone from her. He examined it and cursed. "You have no service."

"What? I had service a second ago."

"You don't anymore," he growled, then thrust the phone back. Suspicion filled his gaze. "What the hell is going on?"

"I'm trying to blow up a friggin' building, that's what, and the damn device isn't working!" Kinsley groaned loudly and ran toward the gondola.

"Where are you going?" Sebastian called out to her.

"To fix it," she called back, then tripped. Kinsley shrieked in pain.

Sebastian started. "What's the matter?"

"My ankle!" she exclaimed in a hushed tone. Kinsley reached for her boot, clumps of snow gathering at her wrists, icing her skin. "I think I twisted my ankle!"

Sebastian rushed over and knelt beside her. His nostrils flared in disgust, disdain coursing through his features. "Can you walk?"

Rising to her knees, she tried to stand but fell limp, clutching him for support. "I don't think so. I need you to help me get to the gondola."

"Kinsley," he hissed, "we'll make a spectacle if I have to carry you over there."

She pulled at him. "No one's around. We'll be fine."

Sebastian whipped his head around and searched to see if they'd been spotted. Thankfully, there was no one. No sound, no movement. Nothing.

Everything was still as death.

Looking down at her, he commanded, "Get up."

When she didn't respond, Sebastian grabbed her.

Kinsley reeled as he started to drag her away from the gondola. "Hey—what are you doing?"

"I'm getting you out of here."

"Sebastian, we can't leave it there!" Kinsley dug her hands into his arms. "I need to check the bomb!"

"The bomb isn't working," he returned, then half-carried, half-dragged her back to the ticket office. Shoving her roughly behind the corner of the building, he yanked the phone from her hands. "Sebastian, *stop*. I need to fix it. I'm not walking away from this."

"There's nothing to fix. I checked it myself." Reading the number displayed on her screen, Sebastian redialed it with his own phone.

Kinsley pulled him from open view. "Get down! That thing's going to blow!"

Sebastian turned and dropped behind the building with her. After several seconds, he ended the call. "Something isn't working."

"Tell me something I don't know." Cupping her gloved hands, she blew into them. Her fingers were freezing from her fall. The exposed skin at her wrists was beginning to burn from the cold.

"Who the hell made this for you anyway? Some idiot off the street?"

"A source," she blurted. "One of my sources, and he's not an idiot." She glanced askance. "We're missing something. We must be."

"I'm not missing anything," Sebastian replied coolly. "Either you're calling the wrong number or the construction is flawed."

She clutched his arm. "Well, we have to *do* something. We can't leave a live bomb sitting beneath the gondola, not without knowing when it's going to detonate."

Sebastian stared at her, his expression heated. The tops of his ears were beginning to redden. His gaze was as icy as her skin. She could feel the failure biting into his ego. He was pissed.

And she was to blame. "How could you be so inept?" he asked, not bothering to conceal his displeasure. "How could you fail so miserably?"

"What? *Me*? I'm not the one who made it. This isn't my fault."

"Yes, *you*. You're the one who insisted you didn't want me involved, that you could handle this by yourself."

Kinsley straightened and stilled. "I was trying to *protect* you, Sebastian."

"And look where that got you."

The steely annoyance staring back at her was almost more than she could bear, but she bit back her reply. No sense in warring with him out here. There would be plenty enough time later on to hash out their problems.

"You should have trusted me, Kinsley. But that's been your problem of late. You don't trust me."

Disgust rolled through her. "Considering the fur store, I'd say I have cause, wouldn't you?"

Sebastian leaned forward and spat, "The bomb worked, didn't it?"

"And this one isn't," she kicked back angrily. "Now what are we going to do about it?"

Sebastian hurled a nasty glare at her, then turned on his heel and stalked over to the gondola building.

Kinsley honed in on his location and counted the seconds after he disappeared behind the building. It would take him at least a minute to retrieve the unit, another to mess with it and another to make a decision. Reaching into her pocket, she dialed the cell number programmed into her phone. Timing was everything. Without precision, coordination, it would all be for naught.

Kinsley's breathing grew shallow. Tension clamped hard at her neck, her shoulders. At the two minute mark, her gaze leapt from tree line to gondola, to restaurants and nearby condos.

"What the—?" Kinsley's heart hammered. *"What the hell is he doing?"*

Running across a snowbank on the opposite side of the gondola building, a black-attired figure sprinted toward Sebastian. Kinsley dashed out from hiding. Was that Walsh? About to yell out in warning, she glimpsed the red of Sebastian's jacket as he bolted from the gondola building. He was headed for the area behind the playground.

Kinsley gasped. Along that sidewalk there were numerous alleys where Sebastian could lose himself. Suddenly, a pack of police officers raced across the snow behind Walsh and stormed the gondola building. Shouts punctured the silence, followed by angry commands. Alarm bells sounded in her skull. *Sebastian was getting away.* Did the officers not see where he'd run? They should be in pursuit!

Fear skated up her spine. Her plan was falling apart. Seconds mattered. If Sebastian got away, she was *history*. On impulse, Kinsley whirled and ran through the narrow passageway that led behind the ticket office. From there, she could cut between some businesses and end up on the path Sebastian would likely travel. She could map this town with her eyes closed. She had to cut him off. She couldn't let him escape. Kinsley ran as fast as she could, the cushioned pound of her boots competed with the panting of her breath.

In seconds, the alleyway dumped out onto a main street through town. In the distance, she caught sight of Grant. He was running. "Grant!" she called out, shocked to see him.

He didn't turn but instead raced across the street. He dodged between buildings as though hot on the trail of something. Or someone. *Had he seen Sebastian?*

Hope exploded in her chest. Had Grant seen Sebastian and instinctively known to chase him? It was a longshot, but it was all she had.

Chapter Twenty-Nine

Kinsley tore after Grant, running as fast as her snow-booted feet would take her. Side-stepping an embedded planter outside a restaurant, she took a hard right, knowing it would take her in the direction Sebastian had gone. The police would likely follow Sebastian past the playground and through the trees. And lose valuable time. Dodging tree branches, she found the walking trail and slowed, unable to maintain her speed. This area was littered with condo buildings and townhomes. Sebastian could easily lose himself between any one of them or enter an open lobby and race upstairs. It would take the entire police force to search for him then, and by that time, Sebastian could be long gone.

Winded, Kinsley forced herself to jog. Sebastian had a head start. He could easily have made it this far. Searching between condos and trees, she saw nothing. Not Sebastian, not Grant. *Grant.* How did he know? she wondered. Was his presence a coincidence? Had he come to work early?

Questions bombarded her, but she continued to search, combing the landscape for any sign of Sebastian. Rooftops were heavy with snow, a meringue-like covering that appeared capable of crushing the structures beneath. Evergreen trees were more white than green, snowdrifts locked around their bases, same as the buildings. Automatically Kinsley glanced at the ground and checked for footprints. Cold pinched her ears, smacked her cheeks. Distant shouts pierced the air. She whirled. The sounds were coming from somewhere down the line of condos. Without warning, a thudding pound of footsteps startled her and she cried out.

"Did you see him?" a police officer asked as he ran past, flanked by three others.

"I think he's down there!" One hand against her chest, she pointed with the other. "I just heard shouts!"

The men didn't stop, and Kinsley chased after them. The police had to find Sebastian. They had to get him before he got away or this whole charade will have been a waste.

Kinsley tried to maintain her optimism. She tried to count the fact that the police were in hot pursuit as a good thing, but as she ran, panic unraveled her. Wade had given her one chance, one chance to help prove her innocence, and it was slipping away.

The policemen were pulling away ahead of her. Trying to close the distance, Kinsley pumped her arms harder, faster, and pushed herself to keep up. She scanned the area as she ran, in case they missed him, but saw nothing. Up ahead, black-uniformed figures cut left. Mentally marking the spot, Kinsley followed. When she turned, she saw Sebastian on the ground. Grant was rolling off him, his arms entangled with Sebastian's as McIntyre Walsh rolled on, shoving Sebastian to the pavement. The police officers quickly crowded around them.

Relief flooded through her. *They caught him.* They caught Sebastian!

"Kinsley!" Grant called out to her.

Grant. Grant! Kinsley rushed toward him, her gaze darting between him and Sebastian.

Walsh violently thrust Sebastian's hands to the ground and pinned him by locking his body over top. Sebastian fought, but he was no match for Walsh. The man was solid steel to the bone.

Grant ran to her and scooped her into his arms. Squeezing her, he breathed her name, "Kinsley...you're okay."

Clinging to him like a life-buoy, she closed her eyes and buried her face into his shoulder. Joy washed through her as she murmured, "I'm fine." *Now that you're here, I'm fine.*

"It's over," he whispered. "You *did* it."

Kinsley wanted to believe him. She wanted to believe that Grant was right and everything would be okay without even questioning how he knew but couldn't. She wouldn't be convinced until Chief Davis set her free. For good.

"Sebastian's going to jail," Grant said.

The words jolted Kinsley back into the moment. Pulling away from Grant, she looked over at Sebastian in time to see Walsh jerk him up from the ground and hand him over to the police. One man yanked Sebastian's arms behind him while another cuffed him. Sebastian spit, and stared at her with a knowing gaze. He understood.

He'd been set up.

A quiver raced through her. If looks could kill, she'd be lying in a pool of blood. Kinsley turned from him abruptly, a mix of fear and euphoria streaming through her veins.

Chief Davis walked up behind her. "I see we got our man." She pulled away from Grant in what suddenly felt awkward as one of the officers began to read Sebastian his rights. Dressed casually in a black ski jacket and wool slacks, a black turtleneck snug at his neck, the Chief offered a small smile. "You played him well."

"Thanks," she spluttered, not sure who knew what when it came to her and Grant. Kinsley cleared her voice and asked, "Do you think it will be enough?"

He delivered a quick smile and replied, "Should be enough to create reasonable doubt on your behalf. The hard part will be tying Sebastian to the bomb at the patrol hut."

Acutely aware that Grant remained close by her side, she pushed back, "But it's possible, right? You have ways?"

"Depends." Chief Davis slid a hand into his front pocket and said, "My guys are working on it as we speak." Flicking a glance toward Sebastian, he added, "Though it might come down to your word against his."

"Does that mean she's still going to jail?" Grant asked.

"Depends."

Yes is what Kinsley heard. Pitting partner against partner would not keep her from going back to jail, to trial, and possibly taking the fall for something she didn't do. Panic pushed into her stomach. She could still serve time for something she didn't do.

"We still have a case to prove," Chief Davis stated matter-of-factly. "This is by no means an open and shut case."

Walsh walked over and took up residence next to Chief Davis. Decked out in a black jacket and pants, his expression was somber, placid, giving no indication that he'd just run a half mile at top speed and tackled a man to the ground. He was the quintessential Marine—hard, edgy, and in outstanding physical shape. Walsh looked at Kinsley then to Grant, then back to Kinsley, as though putting their relationship together for the first time. An odd surprise glinted from his green-eyed gaze then disappeared, softening to what felt like acceptance.

Or disinterest. "Lisa had an idea," he said.

When he didn't elaborate, Chief Davis looked to his side and asked, "Care to share?"

"The ticket to London. It's possible you might have an alibi for your whereabouts when the ticket was purchased, proving you couldn't have done it."

Grant perked up. "Like maybe a time-stamped receipt from a restaurant or business somewhere?" Excitement lit up his eyes as he said, "That's a good idea."

"Except that I could have bought the ticket using my phone."

Walsh grunted. "It was a thought. I told her I'd pass it along."

"It's a good one," Chief Davis said. "With electronic purchases there are electronic receipts. I'll have one of my detectives call you with the date and time for the ticket purchase and you can retrace your whereabouts to see if anything fits."

"What about the feds?" Walsh asked. "You can't hold them off forever."

Kinsley thought the edge in his tone suggested he didn't think the Chief should, either.

"I'm working on that. I have a friend in D.C. who might be able to work some magic on my behalf. In the meantime, we'll do everything we can to build a case against your friend, Sebastian."

"He's not my friend," Kinsley spit back. Shaking off a quick chill, she stabbed her hands into her jacket pockets and squeezed arms in against her body. With the adrenaline wearing off, the cold was setting in.

Chief Davis smiled, his dimples on full display. "Figure of speech. Grant, would you like to escort Kinsley back to her hotel?"

"Consider it done." Eyes dancing, he grinned. "How long should I keep her there?"

Chief Davis chuckled. "Until I call you. We should know something in the next few hours."

Grant took Kinsley by the hand. "Shall we?" She hesitated and he prodded, "I think we've been outed."

Involuntarily, she glanced at Walsh. The gleam in his deadpan gaze confirmed it. "Sure." Allowing him to place an arm around her shoulders, she cast a last glance over her shoulder and noted that Sebastian was gone, probably halfway to the police station by now. Kinsley paused. "Thanks again, Chief Davis. I owe this opportunity to you."

"You're welcome. Do me a favor and make sure we don't repeat it, okay?"

Relief escaped her in a small grin. "Done." She had no intention of getting herself anywhere near jail ever again. Not when she had so much to look forward to in the future. She looked to Grant and a flurry of desire scurried through her pulse. *Outed.* Did that mean everyone knew? Exactly what did they know?

Grant hugged Kinsley close to him and walked her the few blocks to her hotel. Energy drained from her limbs and the cold crept in, seeping in around the edges of her coat, her gloves, the socks on her feet. A light flicked on in a second-story condo as they passed. Snuggling into the warmth of

Grant's body, she had so many unanswered questions that needed response. "How did you know where to find us?"

"I spoke with Wade. I called him about my suspicions regarding Sebastian planting a bomb beneath the bridge."

Kinsley gasped. "Sebastian planted a bomb beneath the bridge?"

"I'm not sure," Grant replied, cocking his head, "but that's what I think he was doing. Lisa and I were spying on them, trying to gather evidence against them when I saw Sebastian break away from the group. Your words came back to me about how the minute Sebastian disappears from the group, the trouble begins. So I took that as my cue."

Kinsley grinned and visions of Lisa and Grant conspiring on her behalf bloomed in her mind's eye. They had gone after Gabby, after Sebastian. When Kinsley thought about everything they tried to do on her behalf, affection and gratitude swarmed her heart.

"I called Wade to tell him what I knew and that's when he told me you'd been released. That *he* released you. He wouldn't go into detail, but he told me that he had a plan underway and to sit tight.

Inches from his face, she peered into his dark eyes. "I wanted to call you but I couldn't. I had strict instructions not to call anyone and reveal the plan." As hard as it had been, she'd held back. She had honored Chief Davis' request.

Grant nodded. "I understand. He indicated as much. No surprise, I couldn't sleep last night, and decided to head to the store early this morning. When I saw Sebastian running behind a row of condos, my gut knew it was connected to Wade's plan and something had gone wrong." He shrugged. "I took off after him."

Recalling the image of Grant chasing Sebastian then wrestling him to the ground filled Kinsley with pleasure. "I don't know what to say..."

"There's nothing to say."

"Sebastian could have hurt you."

Grant drew back. "Why? Because I'm an old man?"

His skin flushed and Kinsley pulled him to her, pecking his cheek. "No. You're a sophisticated, smart, good-looking man. There's nothing 'old' about you."

"Well, I wish that were true, but..." Grant slowed and gave a pat to his heart. "I'm not as young as I once was."

"Quit. You're as strong and virile as any man I've ever known."

Grant smiled. The two stood outside her hotel. The lights were on inside but there was no sign of life. In the distance, a lone jogger ran at a pretty stiff pace, his red thermal skintight pants outlining every curve in his muscular legs as his breath steamed out in spurts.

Grant turned her chin so that she faced him. Gazing down into her eyes, he confessed, "I love you, Kinsley Fairchild."

Her breath caught. It was the first time he had said the words. Directly, unmistakably, Grant was making it official. "Grant..."

"I hope you feel the same."

The gleam in his gaze suggested that he already knew the answer to that one. "I do. I would have told you last night, if I could have."

"Last night?"

She nodded. Lowering her gaze, she thought about the longing she had felt, the fear, the desire... As the evening tumbled through her heart, there had been nothing more that she'd wanted to do than to call him and tell him exactly how she felt. But Chief Davis had been clear. Don't utter a word to anyone but Sebastian. Out of desperation, she had obliged. But now... Kinsley lifted her head and faced Grant. She had no such restrictions. "I love you, Grant. If I could express how deeply I feel inside, how consuming my feelings for you are, I would. But I only have words."

Grant winked. "Maybe an old man can show you a few other ways to express yourself."

Kinsley giggled. Like a foolish girl, she realized at once what he was referring to and suddenly found herself unable to contain a spurt of laughter. "Grant!"

"You're kind of on house arrest, aren't you?"

"But you're not."

"No, but I have Beau."

"Beau?"

"Only the best employee this side of New York City."

Without waiting for a reply, Grant grabbed Kinsley's hand and led her up the steps to her hotel. Boots pummeling the half dozen steps, she breezed into the door he held open, swamped by a tidal wave of heat. New feelings and emotions overcame her—exhilaration, anticipation, trepidation. A hungry ache wound deep and low in her belly. Striding across the lobby, Kinsley followed Grant's lead. This was right. This was perfect. This was where she wanted to be, with whom she wanted to be with. A thousand loose ends remained, dozens of phone calls, a myriad legal strategies and meetings, but there was only one perfect moment and that moment was now. With Grant.

The elevator tone beeped and lit up the circle of light numbered 1. The doors slid open. As Kinsley stepped inside, all caution and worry slipped free. For a brief space in time, all was right with the world, and she was going to seize her moment.

Chapter Thirty

Cradled in the arms of her lover, Kinsley propped herself up next to him and peered into his lazy gaze. Through the closed curtains, a slant of sunlight cut through, marking a white line across the deep brown carpeting of her hotel room. Every cell in her body felt full, complete, from her heart to her mind and everywhere in between. Being with Grant, holding him close gave her a sense of wholeness she'd never experienced before. She'd had boyfriends, relationships, but none as all-encompassing as he. It was as though Grant were her second half, the perfect fit.

"Penny for your thoughts?" he asked.

Pleasure surged as she revealed, "I was just thinking how wonderful I feel."

"So the old man still has some tricks in his bag, huh?"

Kinsley swatted his bare chest. "I was referring to my feelings."

Grant waggled his brow. "So was I."

She paused and asked pointedly, "Is this how it's going to be all the time?"

"This, how?" he asked, a hint of concern crowding out his ease.

"You reminding me how old you are."

Grant stilled, and something changed. His eyes were no longer easy and free but guarded. "I don't want to kid myself, Kinsley. I'm not a young man. You could have your pick of the ski mountain, but you're here with me."

The skin beneath her palm warmed as she pressed into his solid build. "Because I love you."

"For how long?"

"Forever," she declared simply and knew in her heart that truer words had never been spoken.

"Easy for you to say." Grant tried to shrug it off but seemed unable. "I've been around the block a few more times than you have. I know how these things play out."

"So. Your point is?"

A sadness swamped his gaze. "I don't want you to regret throwing your youth away on me and moving on when I need you most."

Kinsley laughed. She hated the way it must feel to him, but she couldn't believe what she was hearing. "Are you serious? I've never been looking more forward to my future than right now, and that's because of you. Besides," she said, the words drifting between them, "I'm the one who should be worried. I bombed your friend's fur store. How will you ever be able to forgive me for that?"

Grant stared at her, and she instantly regretted bringing up the subject. It was a problem. She could see it in his eyes. "I think it was wrong," he said. "I think what you did was wrong." Kinsley felt him pulling away from her and cast a quick glance toward the window and the world outside, a world that suddenly seemed meaningless if she couldn't have Grant by her side. "The same type of thing happened to me back in New York," he told her. "I was driven out of my store by thugs, by people who thought intimidation was the answer. They believed they could force me into paying them money to protect me against them so they wouldn't vandalize my business, but they were wrong. What you did to Giovanna isn't much different."

Kinsley's heart sank. Despite the warm connection of their skin-to-skin contact, she felt a sudden chill enter the room. "I'm sorry, Grant. I never knew."

"You don't know a lot of things about me." A smile grazed his mouth but it had no luster, no joy. "There hasn't been the time to tell you a lot of things." He grew more somber, his voice fiercely quiet as he reached a hand to her face. "You're better than people like them. You have the power to make a real difference but not like that, not by destroying private property."

Tangles of want and need wrapped around her heart as she struggled with her feelings, old passions warring with new desires. She didn't think the two incidents were similar at all. She'd done what she'd done because she was trying to better the world. Those men in New York did what they did for money. Power. There was a difference. "I'm sorry for what happened to you, Grant, but I'm not a thug. I believe animals have the right to live a life free from pain and suffering. I believe they have inherent worth and should not be valued only on the basis of how they can benefit us. Can you understand that?"

"I do understand your heart is in the right place, fighting for the right thing."

"Do you mean that?" Kinsley asked, needing it to be true.

Grant leaned close and slid a hand behind her neck. Curling his fingers, he pulled her close. Butterflies ripped through her belly as she stared, waiting for his next words. She could hear him breathe, feel warm wisps against her skin. This little rendezvous of theirs boiled down to what he said next. His gaze moved back and forth over hers, contemplative, measured. "I do," he murmured, pleasure slipping in to untie the knot in her chest. "It's who you are, your passion. And it makes you the woman I want."

The hunger staring back at her peeled away Kinsley's last defense. Grant understood. He accepted and he understood. When he slid his mouth across hers, the touch erupted deep inside her. Spasms of desire exploded as she surrendered. Closing her eyes, she breathed in the scent of him. Masculine, sexy, his expensive fragrance worked into her mind, filled her senses with want as his warm tongue slipped inside her mouth. Hot stabs of desire punctured as she melted into him. Since the first time Grant had kissed her, she had wanted him, wanted this, the two of them together. She wanted to be in his arms, next to him. She wanted to be with him in every way.

Grant pulled back and said, "We will put Sebastian behind bars."

"I know. We have to. We have to," she repeated, unable to fathom anything less.

"But tell me something...that was a pretty gutsy move on your part this morning. How did you know Sebastian would fall for your ploy?"

Gratification ripped through her. "Because I know Sebastian."

"I'm surprised Wade allowed the thing to play out in the first place. The last time I talked to him, he was pretty convinced he already had his suspect in custody."

"He did until someone showed him proof to the contrary. Apparently a German tourist captured Sebastian on video dropping something behind the patrol hut. I guess Chief Davis realized that I could be telling the truth and decided to hash it out with me."

"But where did you get a bomb so quickly?"

Kinsley laughed at the jab of suspicion cutting through Grant's gaze. "Don't worry. I didn't make it. That was Walsh's handiwork."

"McIntyre Walsh? Lisa's boyfriend?"

"One and the same. The two of us aren't exactly the best of friends, but when Chief Davis asked him to get involved, he couldn't say no. The man has issues with duty."

Grant cocked a brow. "Lucky for you."

Blowing out a sigh, she nodded. "Lucky for me. In practically no time at all he was able to produce a crude-looking cylindrical bomb with a cell phone attached to it. Lisa said he made it from materials like peroxides, fertilizers, and other stuff that when combined, became explosive. The cell phone allowed me to remotely detonate it—if I were actually so inclined. It's kinda scary to think that something so deadly could be so easy to make."

"When you know what you're doing it is," Grant corrected. "I doubt I could handle such a feat."

"Maybe. Anyway, he sent a sheet of instructions with it and I was good to go."

"It wasn't actually a live bomb, was it?"

"I think so. It had to pass Sebastian's inspection so it must have been real."

Grant ran a hand through his hair and glanced about the hotel suite. "Now I'm really surprised Wade went along with it."

"Me, too. But I think with a dozen officers and Walsh on hand, he felt confident they could intervene before anything bad happened. Besides, I didn't give Sebastian the real cell phone number to activate the bomb."

"Well, I'm only glad everything worked out."

"Thanks to you. How did you catch Sebastian before Walsh?"

"Good timing."

"I'd say... Without you, Sebastian could have gotten away and my butt would be back in jail. But what about your heart? You could have had another heart attack!"

"Another?" He peered at her with a questioning gaze.

Realizing he didn't know that she knew, Kinsley confessed, "I went to see you at the jewelry store. After my mother put up bail for me, I went to see you and your employee told me that you were in the hospital. I called, but you'd already been discharged."

Nodding, Grant replied, "It wasn't anything but a mild stress event."

"Because of me?" she ventured.

"Because I'm old and have an old heart," he said.

Kinsley didn't believe him. She wasn't a doctor, but she knew enough to know that stressful events could cause a heart attack in someone already prone to the disease. And finding out that your new girlfriend had betrayed you would probably count as a stressful event.

"I'm fine," he told her. "It wasn't a big deal."

Kinsley eyed him warily but realized arguing the point would get her nowhere. She'd have to remember it, was all, and make sure he avoided as much stress as possible in the future. Images of him lying on the ground, clutching his chest were more than she could handle. "Well," she said, shaking the visions from her brain, "you shouldn't have chased him like that, but I'm thankful you did. If we had lost Sebastian, I don't know what I would have done."

"You're welcome." He leaned over and kissed her. Soft, supple, his lips pulled a powerful longing from within her. Reaching a hand to his cheek, Kinsley gently stroked his face, his freshly-shaven skin. She ran her fingertips through his short sideburns, and want filled her. Their morning had been amazing. Was he up for another go 'round?

Kinsley jerked at the sound of her cell phone ring. She vaulted over Grant's body to grab it from her nightstand.

"Can I help you with that?" he asked, amusement dancing in his eyes.

Ignoring his lustful gaze, she answered, "Hello?" Kinsley pushed up to a sitting position and pulled the sheets up over her chest. Warmth flushed her skin. "Lisa."

"Hey," her friend's chipper voice sang through the phone, "I heard everything worked out this morning!"

"Well, maybe not *everything* but hopefully enough to get me off the hook."

"So tell me what happened. Did your plan go as expected?"

Grant waved her off and rolled out of bed. Kinsley watched his backside as he entered the bathroom, a tiny thrill zipping through her. "Yes," she replied. "Everything went almost like clockwork." Thanks to Grant. Thanks to Walsh. "You need to tell Walsh I owe him one."

"Oh, you don't owe him anything. He was more than willing to help."

Kinsley tightened her grip on the phone and said, "I know he and I have had our differences, but he needs to understand that I really am one of the good guys."

"He knows that."

Kinsley smirked and Lisa laughed. "He does! Seriously, somewhere beneath that metal armor of his, he knows. He just doesn't understand your style of expression, that's all."

Deep in Kinsley's heart, gratitude diluted the resentment she'd always felt when it came to Walsh. "I get that. We're definitely of different mindsets."

"Actually, I think he enjoyed making it for you."

"What?"

"I meant in a mental challenge sort of way. I think it was stimulating. You know, interesting."

"Working with the police force isn't doing it for him?" Kinsley asked, and swung her legs over the edge of the bed. Clothes were strewn about the floor, a haphazard display of rapture in motion. Kinsley chuckled under her breath. If only Lisa could see her now!

"The police force is fine," Lisa went on, "but there aren't enough bad guys in Silver Creek to keep him busy."

Dialing back into the conversation, Kinsley asked, "Does he want to move?"

"I don't think so. He hasn't mentioned it, anyway."

"Have you asked him?"

"No." Lisa paused. "That makes me a bad person, doesn't it?"

"No. It makes you a single-minded scientist type." Kinsley grinned. "The way research consumes your brain, it's a wonder anything else gets in."

Lisa replied flatly, "That's not good."

"It's not good, it's not bad, it just is. It's you, and probably one of the things Walsh likes most about you."

"Hm. Maybe. But still, I should probably ask him what he wants, huh?"

Kinsley laughed. "If for no other reason than it might provide for some stimulating conversation. Personally, I'd like to see him try and talk you into leaving your toads!"

"Definitely not a good conversation. But enough about Walsh. What are you doing? Wanna go out for breakfast?"

"Um," Kinsley glanced toward the bathroom, then pursed her lips.

"What? Are you busy?"

The complete surprise in Lisa's voice made Kinsley smile. "Kinda." She brushed a clump of hair behind her ear and pressed her bare feet into the plush carpet. "Grant's here."

"Where—in your room?"

"Yes." A heavy pause followed, and Kinsley allowed the significance to sink in. Grant was here, in her room. The two of them were alone together. Kinsley could visualize the look on Lisa's face—a combination of surprise, curiosity and delight. She'd want to know everything.

"Oh... I get it. I figured he was helping you for more reasons than a favor to my dad."

"Is that what he said?" Kinsley asked, suddenly curious how the two of them managed their arrangement without raising any questions.

"In so many words. I told my dad you were innocent, and Grant said that he agreed with me. I didn't really give it too much thought after that. So, you guys are together?"

"Together." Kinsley mulled over the word. Together meant a lot of things, but yes, they were together. "Yes. I'm in love with him, Lisa," she said, amazed how easily the words rolled off her tongue. "We're together."

"Wow."

"Wow?" Kinsley laughed. "Wow as in good, or wow as in weird?"

"I don't know... Just wow." It was Lisa's turn to laugh. "I would never have expected it! I wouldn't have pegged him for your type."

A litany of past lovers breezed through Kinsley's mind. Sculptor, writer, biology grad student, musician—she had always gravitated toward free spirits, not businessmen. She was drawn to creative minds, free thinkers and passionate revolutionaries. Stodgy old businessmen weren't her thing. Images from earlier shot through her mind and she laughed.

Grant wasn't stodgy or old. In fact, he was in fantastic shape and as promised, carried a lifetime of experience. Truthfully, she was still sort of amazed herself. Suppressing the rise of pleasure rippling through her, Kinsley chuckled. "Tell me about it. I'm dating a meat-eating Silver Creek business owner. If word gets out, I'll lose half my followers!" Kinsley was only half-joking. It was possible people would not see in Grant what she saw in him. But did it matter?

No, she thought swiftly. It did not.

"Okay, and listen, that dog that was burned in the bombing?"

Kinsley sucked in her breath. "Yes?"

"I just wanted you to know that he's doing fine."

Kinsley released her breath in a ragged stream. *Fine.* Thank God!

"Walsh called me this morning and told me that his friend Canyon is taking the dog with him when he goes to a rodeo in Texas next week."

"He's well enough to travel?"

"That's what Walsh said. And I know Canyon. He wouldn't do anything to jeopardize his dog's health. Trust me, he loves that animal like he was his own flesh and blood. If he didn't think he was ready, he wouldn't take him on a road trip."

An animal that had been nearly killed because of Sebastian.

Kinsley took a moment to digest the news. The dog was going to be fine. He had an owner that loved him like a person and he was going to be fine. Chief Davis had said the man injured in the blast had been discharged from the hospital and was on the road to recovery.

Kinsley couldn't ask for anything more. "Thanks for telling me, Lisa."

"I knew you'd want to know." Changing subjects swiftly, she asked, "So how about a double date? You up for it?"

With Walsh? Kinsley's mouth fell open. The four of them at one table? She shook her head. This really was a brave new world she was entering!

Chapter Thirty-One

Chief Wade Davis closed the door to his office then resumed a seat behind his desk. He'd called the four of them here for an update, a meeting to apprise them of where the case against Sebastian stood. Kinsley and Lisa were seated, while Grant and Walsh stood behind their respective partners. Grant massaged Kinsley's shoulders, his touch deep and reassuring. He'd been amazing. After a few stumbles, Grant had come to her aid and never looked back. Lisa was still getting used to the idea of her father's friend together with her best friend. Something about it felt strange, but they were working through it. Walsh was Walsh, and nothing seemed to surprise or bother him.

Chief Davis leaned back in his chair, neat and elegant in his navy suit and red paisley tie. Taking the group of them in, he bore no sign of tension or animosity. He was a man doing his job. A job for which Kinsley was grateful.

"Sebastian is facing three felony counts of eco-terrorism for the fur store bombing, the patrol hut and the attempted bomb at the gondola. He's pleading not guilty, but the feds think they have a pretty solid case. The video from the tourist capturing him near the patrol hut places him at the scene. A scan of his computer proves he knew how to construct a bomb based on his recent searches. Add the fact that a live bomb was found in his hotel room, and they have probable cause."

"That must be the one he was trying to place beneath the bridge," Grant said.

"Likely," the Chief agreed.

"Odd that he didn't try to place it a second time," Walsh said, his gravelly voice quiet and reserved.

"Didn't have to," the Chief replied. "Not with Kinsley dangling her own bomb in front of him a few hours later."

She nodded. "He was practically salivating over the thought that I'd finally come around to seeing things his way."

"It worked, except for some sixth sense of his. Your plan to stage an explosion was a good one, until at some point he must have realized he was being set up and took off." A shadow of a smile entered the Chief's gaze. "I have to admit, my heart stopped when I saw him run for it." He looked up at Walsh, "Good thing you were there."

Kinsley hid a knowing grin at what Chief Davis *didn't* say. There was no way any of his men could have run like Walsh. None were in near as good a shape as him.

"Thank this guy," Walsh said, and Kinsley glanced up in time to see him hitch his chin toward Grant. "He's the one that caught him."

Grant laughed, the sound hollow in his embarrassment. "I wouldn't go that far. I got lucky based on my position. You were the one who wrestled him to the ground."

Walsh grunted and in the very next moment, Kinsley and Lisa shared a chuckle.

"Something funny?" Walsh asked.

"You," Lisa said. "You grunt like a toad!"

Humor tickled the Chief's gaze but he didn't laugh. "Anyway," he continued, "after a little checking, it turns out that Kinsley was on a flight home to Colorado at 30,000 feet in the air when the plane ticket to London was purchased. I think that blows Sebastian's credibility out of the water. Further forensics also proved those were not your fingerprints on that bomb, but a fake."

"I don't get how he was able to do that," Kinsley said, stunned by the revelation that Sebastian had been plotting against her for quite some time.

"Lifting fingerprints is child's play," Walsh put in. "Sebastian could have taken them from you at any time. All you had to do was touch a glass or a doorknob and then the minute you're out of sight, he pulls out a tube of Super Glue and your prints are copied. Done."

"There was no trace of latent fat or DNA in those fingerprints we found," the Chief explained. "They were copies. Good ones, but copies upon further inspection."

"Glue," Grant muttered.

Chief Davis smiled. "Glue."

It bothered Kinsley to think how easy it was for Sebastian to betray her. She'd trusted him. And because of that trust, it never occurred to her to doubt him. Sure, they had differences in opinion on how to proceed with certain actions, but all partners had differences. Yet while she was trying to work out a compromise, he was crafting a plan to get her out of the way.

"So what now?" Lisa asked. "Is Kinsley free to live her life without worry?"

The million dollar question, Kinsley mused. She felt Grant's hands tense at her shoulders. Seems he felt it, too. She could still face charges for the fur store bombing, charges that could carry jail time which would ruin their future together. Things would likely change after spending a year in jail.

"In light of the fact that Kinsley has made full restitution to Giovanna for the destruction of her property, the State has agreed to accept her lawyer's plea deal and reduce the charges to criminal mischief with no jail time."

Relief coursed through her. *Merle was a magician.* In addition to the money Kinsley had paid for the furs, he had told her she'd likely pay a hefty fine for the crime, but it was possible to eliminate jail time. Seems, he did it. He did it!

Grant slid a hand from her shoulder to her arm and squeezed. Cupping a hand over his, her palm warming instantly, Kinsley felt a push of tears behind her eyes. They weren't strolling down the jetway yet, but this meant they were one step closer. "What if Sebastian claims entrapment?"

"He can't. You made a plan the day before. It was the only reason he was there. He knew that calling that cell number would set off an explosion. Sebastian had no way of knowing the material Walsh used was inert."

"It was?"

"You don't think I'd give you a live bomb, do you?" Walsh asked.

She had, but didn't want to reveal as much and only shrugged.

"So you're free!" Lisa exclaimed.

"I think it's a safe bet," Chief Davis said. "Sebastian called the number for the cell phone attached to the bomb, which goes to intent. We have his phone. We have the call log. And we have a witness to his bomb-building expertise."

Kinsley blinked. "A witness?"

"Gabby Miller," Chief Davis revealed, "a woman I believe you know well."

"Gabby." The name escaped her lips before she fully registered the significance.

"When we questioned her and threatened prosecution as an accomplice, she started talking and quick."

Kinsley swiped a glance toward Lisa. "Did you tell them?"

Lisa nodded, her eyes lighting up. "You were right. That girl was totally into Sebastian. I think she'd do anything the guy asked!" Lisa shifted in her seat to fully face Kinsley. "When I was prying her for information, she told me about their plans to monkeywrench the summer expansion. That means to sabotage the construction equipment."

Monkeywrench. Kinsley groaned inwardly. She knew exactly what it meant.

"When Lisa first told me about the conversation in an effort to save you," the Chief interjected, "it didn't occur to me that I'd be using the girl as a wedge against Sebastian in the case of the bombing. But it worked. She rolled like a ball of tumbleweed."

Kinsley laughed softly, entertained by his analogy but slightly saddened by Gabby's predicament. The girl was young and impressionable. It was a shame she'd been caught up in Sebastian's lust for power. "Will she go to jail?" Kinsley asked.

"No. Feds gave her immunity."

"Good," Kinsley murmured, more to herself than anyone in the room. Gabby didn't deserve to go to jail due to naiveté. She was a crusader, not a criminal.

"So where do we go from here, Wade?" Grant asked. "Is Kinsley free to do as she pleases?"

Wade Davis leaned forward and shot them a brilliant smile. "She's all yours."

Grant laughed. "I like the sound of that!"

Kinsley felt energized. No longer awkward in her role as girlfriend to Grant, she felt good. It was all good news. She was free to go, free to get on with the rest of her life. Grant circled her chair and offered a hand. "Shall we?"

Placing her hand in his, she replied, "We shall."

"Stay out of trouble, will you?" the Chief teased and stood. "I can only wield my influence so often."

Kinsley stopped abruptly. Chief Davis had done exactly that—wielded his influence on her behalf, allowing her the chance to prove her innocence. His department had come under fire over the shooting, but since there were enough witnesses who saw Norell pull a knife on one of the officers, no charges had been filed. Kinsley had been saddened to hear about Norell because, like Gabby, he'd been a true believer. Only a misguided one.

Staring up at the Chief, she realized she owed him a huge debt of gratitude. Things could have turned out much differently. "Thank you, Chief. For everything you did for me, thank you."

The lines around his eyes relaxed as his mouth opened into a paternal smile. "You're welcome, Kinsley. And for the record, I don't see why they need so many ski runs either. I kinda like small-town living."

A sense of victory swept through her, one she felt clear through her toes. "Me, too."

"You take care. I'm sure I'll see you around soon."

"You will. But it won't be for professional reasons."

Kinsley linked her arm with Grant's and walked out of the police department, accompanied by Lisa and Walsh.

Moving ahead of them, Walsh got the door and held it until all four had exited the building, then joined them outside in the sunshine. The air was brisk, the sky super-sunny. In the distance, the ski mountain boasted a blanket of crisp green evergreen laced by a pattern of snow-covered runs dotted by skiers. It was another busy day at Silver Creek Resort, a place people flocked to from all over the world.

The place her parents loved. Once charges against Kinsley had been dropped, her mother had insisted father and daughter clear the air between them. It had been an invitation Kinsley welcomed. She owed her mother a debt of gratitude. Not only for working with Merle to get her out of jail, but for everything. Victoria Fairchild supported her daughter, for better or worse. Kinsley's father was a different story. There were limitations to his acceptance, boundaries which he wouldn't cross. It wasn't that he didn't love her. He simply failed to understand her.

It was a reality Kinsley would have to accept. But when her father heard of her clothing line venture, he surprised her with an immediate offer to set up a meeting with Lee Palmer. The man wasn't an animal-hater. He was a businessman.

Another reality she would have to accept. But more than a businessman, he was a borderline conservationist. Thanks to a phone call from her father, Mr. Palmer had given Kinsley a personal tour of the facilities and introduced her to the inner workings of his company where he'd boasted a phenomenal record for recycling. Not only did the man walk the walk, but his organization was responsible for numerous grants and research funding in the area of green technology, as well as education. If ever there was a business that could claim responsible growth, it was his. However, the question of displaced animals remained. Silver Creek Resort was here to stay. Palmer might be willing to go a long way to safeguard the planet as he developed his properties, but he wouldn't fold up his tent and go home.

It was an area of contention where Kinsey would have to accept compromise.

Clinging close to Grant, the warmth of his body blending into hers, Kinsley breathed in, the frigid air icing her nostrils. There'd been a lot of compromise of late, on her part as well as the part of others. Looking up at Grant, she thought about his compromise. He'd offered to go vegan. He knew how she felt about the subject, and he said he would try. Said it would be good for his health. Kinsley couldn't suppress a smile as she recalled the gesture. It had been sweet. Noble. Loving. And if Grant could give up meat, she could surely give up her "all or nothing" approach to activism.

"Anyone up for some skiing?" Lisa asked.

Grant looked to Kinsley and said, "I think I'll take a pass."

Kinsley smiled. "I guess I will, too."

"Aw, you two are no fun." Lisa turned to Walsh and wrapped her arms around his waist. "Guess that leaves you and me." She wriggled her brow in excitement. "Wanna race?"

Walsh looked down at her. "No, I don't want to race. I only just learned how to ski this season!"

"And you're already so good at it!"

Walsh dipped his head and purposefully grunted in her face. "Good, huh. You just want to race past me to get back at me for running circles around you on our last marathon."

"I'm not a runner, I'm a skier."

"I'm not a skier, I'm a runner," he volleyed back.

Kinsley laughed. "I think you two have this competition thing nailed!"

Lisa smirked. "Walsh doesn't like losing."

"And you do?" Kinsley tossed the hair from her eyes. "I think someone needs to look in the mirror."

Lisa grunted in reply and everyone burst into laughter, including Walsh.

Surrounded by her friends, Kinsley felt good, fortunate. The last few weeks had proved life-changing in more ways than one. More than her freedom, she had a new life to look forward to. She was pursuing the clothing line, pouring all of her energy and resources into the venture. Even she and Walsh had begun to tear down the walls between them, he accepting her, she accepting him as they looked for aspects they shared in common. Kinsley had learned there was good to be found inside everyone, no matter how different they appeared on the outside.

And Grant. In the beginning, there had been no two people further apart. From his salt and pepper temples and receding hairline to his resort-based livelihood that stood to profit considerably from the habitat-destroying Silver Creek expansion, Grant represented her opposite. He was the essence of everything she had been fighting. Money over wildlife. Greed over green. But that wasn't the total of who he was. Grant Powell was a man who cared deeply—for his friends, for his family, for his freedom. He didn't want to be pushed around or told what to do. He didn't want to hurt animals, and instead felt compromise was the right way to go.

Funny, but now she felt as though she stood on the same side. Shoulder-to-shoulder, eye-to-eye, they were equals. Nobody pushed Kinsley Fairchild around. And nobody forced her to quit. Compromise didn't mean she had to forfeit her values or position. It simply meant she had to alter her tactics, change course but stay on target.

Grant leaned in for a kiss. "Want to go to my place?"

She laughed. Roll her around, *yes*. Push her around, *no*. Kinsley squeezed him to her and said, "You bet I would."

# # #

The End

Zucchini Tomato Sauce

1 large zucchini, diced (ends removed)
1 TBSP olive oil
1 TBSP butter (optional)
3 cloves garlic, minced
1 cup fresh diced tomatoes (or 8 oz. canned)
1 TBSP fresh Italian flat leaf parsley, finely chopped
1 TBSP fresh basil, finely chopped
Salt & pepper to taste
Grated Parmesan (optional)

Sauté zucchini in olive oil and butter. I use both because I enjoy the flavor of butter and like the way it browns but it's wholly unnecessary. This step takes about 5-10 minutes, turning the zucchini cubes every few minutes to evenly brown. Once browned and soft, add garlic and sauté another minute, careful not to burn garlic. Turn heat to low and add tomatoes, parsley, basil, salt and pepper. Serve over pasta.

For variations, try sautéed onions, sun-dried tomatoes, for a more intense flavor—even mushrooms. It's all good!

About the Author:

Dianne Venetta lives in Central Florida with her husband, two children and part-time Yellow Lab Cody-boy! An avid gardener, she spends her spare time growing organic vegetables, surprised by what she finds there every day. Who knew there were so many amazing similarities between men and plants? Women, life and love and her discoveries along the way provide for never-ending fun on her garden blog: BloominThyme.com. When she's not knee-deep in dirt or writing, Dianne also contributes garden advice to various websites.

You can also find her on twitter @DianneVenetta and facebook.com/DianneVenetta. Plus, learn how you can become a member of her street team, Bloomin' Warriors, where you'll be eligible for special discounts, advance excerpts, author swag and unique gift items throughout the year. For full details, be sure to check out her website, DianneVenetta.com.

Other novels by Dianne Venetta:
Mystery/Romantic Adventure Fiction
Silver Creek Series:
NOT WITHOUT YOU #1
BECAUSE OF YOU #2
ALL ABOUT YOU #3
ONLY WITH YOU #4

Mystery/Romance Fiction
Ladd Springs Series:
LADD SPRINGS #1
LADD FORTUNE #2
HOTEL LADD #3
LADD HAVEN #4
LOSING LADD #5
LADD CHRISTMAS #6

BECAUSE OF YOU

Romantic Women's Fiction
The Gables Trilogy:
JENNIFER'S GARDEN
LUST ON THE ROCKS
WHISPER PRIVILEGES

Women's Fiction
CONDEMN ME NOT

BECAUSE OF YOU

www.ingramcontent.com/pod-product-compliance
Lightning Source LLC
Chambersburg PA
CBHW020226180626
46810CB00006B/2066